STEVEN BLACKMORE

THE HOLE IN THE WALL

ISBN: 9798773276135

Because of Kez and that black dress...

PRELUDE

3 February...

Amy blames her boyfriend of three years and his cheating ways for the death of their relationship.

James Howard Ruck.

She had, for a time, blamed herself. A part of the healing process, sure, but in reflection, and rightly so, Amy saw it for what it is; a torture of his making, and for that, she hates him, absolutely and to his core.

Lilly, her sister, who had been suspicious of him from the very start, sold him short when she labelled him a silver-tongued devil. A mirror-whore, soulless, and vain, James and men like him, the talkers and bullshitters, the experienced type, can manipulate and convince, and James, a photographer, being both handsome and successful, had for a time anyway, perfected the art.

'What can I do?' James asks from the passenger seat.

'Fuck off and die,' Amy spits.

'Amy, please, I'm sorry, I really am.'

Guys like James are always sorry. Why is that?

She considers this.

Because he got caught, that's why.

He said it had been her detachment, their lack of intimacy, and like a good girl, she accepted his reasoning. Again, for a time. With the assault two years prior, Amy recognised how her mind had darkened, shadowed with heavy sorrow, a bleak veil corrupting every aspect of her life, consuming her, leaving her empty and unable to love. Her doctor said it would take time for her to accept her new reality, one where she will forever be a victim of a violent crime, but in trusting James, needing and weighing on him, being so exposed, only to be deceived in such a way, did she acknowledge the depth of her despair.

So, Amy accepted him back into her life, believing James when he chalked it off as a mistake. 'Chalked,' a word of his, a turn of phrase, another one of his minimisers. He was good at that, making the big seem small. Making her feel small.

Again, for a time anyway.

He loves her, he had cried, but it had been in cheating, did he recognise by just how much. Trusting every word, every excuse, blinded by the pain, she had even sat with him when James cried and pleaded, right up until she finally got clarity. Only when she was free of the guilt, the malaise so eager to fog her mind, her twisted, confused conscience, did she finally see James for what he really is.

Weak.

A chameleon.

A fraud.

Not even a man.

Where Amy had snapped between emotions- loathing to need, hate and love, back and forth, round and round, she finally and correctly so settled upon despising him.

She, too, hates Erika.

The model.

The slut.

Beautiful and sexy, young and intelligent, modern and witty, Erika was all-encompassing.

Is, Amy reminds herself.

Erika is missing. People are still looking for her.

Amy diverts her focus away from the younger woman, who, like her, is mere collateral, a victim of James and his alter ego. Having seen the messages and emails, Amy read it as him who had led and lied, who pushed and pestered, slowly breaking the woman down over time. To her credit, Erika had been resolute, putting James off with excuses, for a time anyway, until finally agreeing to meet him. A drink, the two of them, under the pretence of friends, and the rest, as they say, is history. Another sordid tale of lovers, cheats, the breaking of hearts, and the breeding of jealousy hate.

Amy believed, even sympathised with the younger woman, coming to her apartment like she did, in tears, apologising, saying how she hated herself for her part in the affair. Nonetheless, no matter what she said, how innocent she had seemed, whether she was, in fact, a vegan, or the charity work she did, thoughts of her with James, her smell, her hands and perfect nails, her slender back and neck, were like daggers, each an attack, slicing into Amy with a level of savagery like nothing felt before. Even with Erika being missing and awash with shame, Amy can only feel bitterness, an utter and total resentment, the darkest kind, and not for the hatred fueling her dark heart, it would scare even herself.

'Amy, please, can we talk?' James whines beside her.

Headache inducing, his words, his pitiful pleads, bring a tremble to her hands, a familiar throb to her head, a tightness to her throat. No longer able to stand the sight of his face, with it bringing fresh waves of nausea, Amy keeps her eyes forward on the road. His forced doe-like-eyes, his protruding bottom lip, the sheepish, pathetic expression plastered across his face, mixed with the image of him and Erika together, all of it repulsing her, turning her stomach, removing her appetite and joy, stripping her of all desire and hope. She hates him for that too, for damaging her, for changing her, forever. Her enmity and revulsion run deeper than she thought possible and are now the all-consuming and irreversible type. In fact, if not for his deception, for the damage it has caused, her loathing would terrify her.

Eyes front and centre, peering through broad swipes of the wipers, Amy drives on, vaguely aware of the brooding storm lashing against the car. Her gaze follows the rain-sleeked two-lane as it snakes a path through the forest, resisting the urge to look at him. Thankfully, James again has gone quiet in the seat beside her. Without the sound of his voice, she can think.

It's short-lived.

'Why are you acting this way? Please, we talked, and you forgave me, remember?'

His words, cadence, and parent-like tone have Amy gripping down on the wheel, numbing her fingers. It takes every inch of her to remain facing forward, to stay still, firm in her resolve.

Again, it's short-lived.

'It was just sex, nothing more, not love....'

Amy, stomping down hard on the brake pedal, drags the wheel to the left, pulling the car from the road, across the white line and into a muddy layby. Beneath her, the tires struggle for traction. They hiss and slip, slicing through the rain, spraying up dirt and gravel, before shuddering to a stop.

'Talk, you want to talk? I despise you. You make my skin crawl. Is that what you want to hear?'

'So why agree to spend the weekend with me if you....'

'Why, because you begged me, remember, on your fucking hands and knees?

'Yes, but...'

'Don't you get it, I hate you, for the years I've wasted, for the promises and the time I'll never get back. You speak, and I want to rip out your tongue, but you going quiet just leaves me wanting to scream in your face.'

'Amy, please, you'll feel different in time. You'll see, it was a mistake....'

'Last night, when you were asleep, I thought of taking a knife and...' she spits but stops short. 'I thought you decent, a dedicated partner who understood me, who had been patient, even with the assault, but it's just a lie. You're a shade, James, a forgery, and I don't love you, not anymore, and I never will again.'

Sitting in the car, him in the passenger seat beside her, sniffling, she finally feels nothing for the man, as if her words have somehow exorcised him from her soul. Everything they had, all she had given up, her heart, her life, melts away, and he, James Ruck, is nothing more than a blotch, an ugly stain on her past.

His eyes, glassy and red, grow wide, and for the first time, he looks as if words have abandoned him. Swallowing, blinking rapidly, James turns from her, directing his gaze out the passenger window, through the rain, to the wall of trees surrounding them on both sides. As he starts to cry, Amy, sitting still, doesn't feel a thing. Not pity, sadness, remorse or resentment.

Nothing.

And it feels wonderful.

Cleansing.

Liberating.

Letting out a deep breath, emptying her lungs, a breath seeming held since the discovery of the affair, Amy's eyes too well with tears, not for him, but in release; a result of venting her inner torment. With it, her cloud-clogged mind begins to melt away, and the weight upon her chest, though slight, is eased.

Turning back to Amy, his face now pale and flat, James opens his mouth to speak, but his words catch at his throat, dying upon his lips before they can form. Looking past her, James peers out through her side window. With a contraction at his brow, creasing a vertical strip between them, his eyes narrow as they blink in confusion before snapping open and wide.

Agape, he mouths the words, 'What the....'

Now mute, pushing open his door, James climbs from the car, his eyes fixed on a portion of the tree line across the road. Turning, Amy looks out but sees nothing. The rain-streaked glass distorts her view with silver rivets, making a mystery of the tree line and the dark space within.

Turning her eyes back to James, while being pelted by rain, he steps backwards, out from the open door. Trance-like, rounding it, moving around the side, James stops at the front of the vehicle. Looking in at Amy, his face pale and sleek with rain, something in his eyes unsettle her. A type of frantic worry, an absolute fear unnatural for his features, leaves his face foreign.

Watching him, his distorted form moving again, Amy tracks him between the glistening streams of rain. His lips moving, ghoulish with the distortion, he mouths a series of inaudible words swallowed whole by the storm. As he steps out into the road, Amy opens her mouth to scream. The thundering rain and the sound of steel rip the words from her throat. Her second attempt, a high-pitched cry, is met by the storm and the scream of tires and asphalt. In a blur of movement and passing, James, in one moment, edges out from the car, eyes fixed on the trees ahead of him. The next, he is gone, ripped from view by an eighteen-wheeler, showering the windscreen with blood and surface water.

PART ONE

THE DISAPPEARANCE OF AMY PORTER

1

2 March...

Unable to afford a taxi, Thomas is forced to take the bus, along with the dregs and the desuetude.

Thomas William.

The great writer.

How far you have fallen.

The trip across town, with its numerous stops, should take a little over fifteen minutes, but with the bus being an old rickety thing from centuries back, with great distress, it struggles against the timetable. Labouring on its wheels, rocking from side to side, its used springs cannot mask a road riddled with divots and potholes. It is as if the bus now exists for the sole purpose of mocking Thomas. Worse still are the fellow occupants now swarming between the cluttered seats. Where the bus had been sparsely filled at first, it is now flooded with school children. Fourteen, to be precise. All loud and crass, energised by the end of the school day. Matching in their uniforms, it's in their rucksacks, lunchboxes, and wireless headphones, where they express their individuality. Where most appear aged between eleven and fourteen, a small number of older, more assured teenagers litter the pack, bringing an air of confidence and a freeness afforded solely to the young.

A tall boy stacked with muscle and natural height takes the vacant seat beside Thomas. Towering high, the teenager looks down at him, grinning through a mouthful of braces. Managing a nod, Thomas quickly turns his attention back to the bleak view through the window and the darkening and rain-swept streets beyond. Having already closed in, a brooding sky drops its black veil over the world, cloaking it behind the window's reflection. Still, it cannot shield him from the evenly spaced detached homes, each afforded the privacy of long driveways. With manicured lawns, high walls, and lavish gates, each one is a slap across the face, and him having to watch from the bus is nothing short of a devilish piece of theatre- a harsh reminder of a life once lived.

Beckley Green, a market town of moderate size, minutes from High Wycombe, sits within the unitary authority of Buckinghamshire and some twenty-two miles from London. With its numerous tube and train links, schools, and rising property prices, it has become a magnet for the up and coming, those with money, young families with parents with daily commutes to the city. A mix of modern self-builds, Victorian and Edwardian period, identifiable by their sash and deep bay windows, elaborately carved porches, Dutch gables, steep-pitched roofs, and in mock-Tudor fashion, an exterior half-clad in timber. In some, where dormer windows hint at loft conversions, the homes remain loyal to the era, pristine with their historic features, and do so almost arrogantly.

A familiar lump appears at his throat, arriving like a piece of gristle might before swallowing. Like a contracting coil, before dropping deep inside, where it settles, rooting within his stomach, his soul, or what's left of it anyway.

You were never interested before: you want custody to hurt me.

Mary's words return to haunt him.

You love your solitude, your writing. Not me, not Robin.

Her words, her headmaster tone, had been enough to force him up from his chair and out the door, cutting short their meeting. Now, left short-changed and embarrassed, Thomas can only sit and watch the world as it passes him by, a now common occurrence, a poetic reflection in more ways than one.

Is she right?

Awash with shame, it rushes through him, condemning him for even considering it.

'We have Lewis now, Robin and I, and we don't need you, not anymore,' she had told him with her usual ice-cold conviction.

As the bus slows to make the next of what seems like an endless set of stops, in protest, the tyres hiss out against the wet tarmac. Even so, Thomas is grateful for this, for the distraction, even it if means watching those younger than him leave the bus for large homes lit by glowing lights and welcoming warmth.

Moving again, the bus pulls away from the curb, and with it, the thoughts of the meeting return to taunt him, as does the image of Mary, torturing him with her outfit, her perfume and long flowing hair. Mary was always an attractive woman, perfect in fact, and too good for Thomas from the very start. This he knows with painful reflection, but since their divorce, it would seem, she has only grown more beautiful and equally so, determined never to let him forget it.

Out of the shadow of our marriage, the flower was free to blossom.

How very poetic.

Peering through the window, attempting to avert his thoughts, Thomas focuses on the street, the large, spacious homes making way for far smaller properties. Detached, semi-detached, are no less affluent. Expensive cars and perfect landscaping continue here, linking the period buildings to newly build, characterless semi-detached homes. Disjointed and disconnected, the view from the bus only reaffirms how dysfunctional the city and its surrounding boroughs are. An amalgamation of designs, periods, and exhaustingly never-ending attempts to modernise and alter.

After a series of turns, the road ahead narrows and does so at an incline. Trees and shrubs close in on both sides, banking up to squeeze in on the bus, darkening the interior. Branches, wild, rangy like outreached fingers, loop up over the top, both sides closing it like an unfinished roof. The bus climbs but struggles atop labouring wheels, squealing against the wet asphalt, desperate to bite with traction.

As if demanding a response, Mary's words return, berating Thomas and shrinking him in his seat.

'You love your solitude, your writing. Not me, not Robin.'

With pain now flooding his mouth, finding he's grinding down on his teeth, Thomas slackens his jaw, but still, her words remain, stinging him, leaving a fever in his chest.

I love my daughter, I do, and she, mother of the year, can't tell me any different.

Finally, civilisation returns as the bus breaks cover, and his heart returns to a beat somewhere close to normality. The houses here are staggered with the continuation of the hill's incline with a zig-zag ladder effect. While not a sharp slope, it is such the bus is forced to slow as it climbs. Large Victorian homes line the street, and though far from dilapidated, they require a fresh coat of paint for the most part. They sit together in the darkening evening like sorrowful, old souls. In fact, a layer of disquiet hangs between the houses like they shared some deep, dark secret.

Reaching up and pressing the call button, Thomas pulls himself up out of the seat. Signalling for the teen beside him to move, waiting for him to jump out into the aisle, he does so with spiritly energy. Thomas is left in equal measure, both envious and frustrated.

Standing back, giving Thomas room, the young man offers a nod and a smile, a gesture Thomas takes for sympathy.

Stepping down from the bus, missing the last step for good measure, Thomas's right foot thumps the curb. The impact, electrocution-like, sends a jolt of pain up through his knee, his spine, where it settles at the base of his skull.

Collecting himself, muttering, breathing hard, with the bus wheezing away from the curb, Thomas is greeted eagerly by the rain. Engulfing him in seconds, sleeking his hair down, his beard, Thomas is forced to wipe his fringe from his eyes. Huffing, puffing against the cold air, shuffling his collar, turning it out, Thomas stuffs his hands in his pockets and starts up the hill.

Across the street, his attention is drawn to a dog walker and her huge Great Dane. Pulling its owner- a woman sporting a pink tracksuit, headband and bright white pumps, her dog all but dragging her down the hill. Offering Thomas a wave, he finds he can only glare at her, unable to respond to such banality, that gleeful smile of hers. The weather, the scene, his mood all conspire, leaving him at odds with such a gesture.

Climbing, having to fight the incline in fast becoming, wet clothes, spotting *Pinegrove* some ways up the hill, Thomas pushes on through gritted teeth. Ahead of him, he tracks a car turning into the driveway two houses up. Parked, the suited driver darts to the front door using his briefcase as an umbrella. Opening and then closing in the space of a few seconds, it is enough time, however, for Thomas to see the wife waiting for the man inside.

In unison, warm buttery lights all around Thomas bring life to the different homes. While deciding to maintain a forward gaze, as if pulled, he finds himself drawn to the windows as they flick from black to yellow. In seconds, they each ooze with comfort and family, a further test of Thomas and his resolve, his fraying mood.

Climbing the last few meters, Thomas finally leaves the street, turning right into *Pinegrove*. Slipping in between the row of fir trees lining the property's front, Thomas breaks cover through the walled boundary. Moving along the cobbled garden path, *Pinegrove* is revealed before him like an old painting might, one of faded colour, deterioration, and heartbreak. In fact, the house is dripping with it, of age and a history of misery. It seeps out from every line, every shadow. Ornate and decorative for the period, the detached three-story brick monstrosity, shadowed by wild vine growth, stands almost apologetically in the fading light. One's attention is first drawn to the building's height, the grand tower and copula, the numerous dormers at roof level and cast-iron guttering, and finally, the rugged, leaf-covered lawn. As with the rest of the garden, and while not precisely wild, it appears pitiful and in need of attention. Worse still is the fused stench of damp foliage, wild mint and lavender, a product of the dead leaves, unkempt bushes, and near-death bramble.

If it stood a mile down the hill, the ageing house would be highly desirable, but sitting on the edge of town, it instead forms part of a small community slowly being edged to the fringes, to the shadows, just waiting for developers to arrive with money and aggressive intent.

The cracked path leads Thomas to a set of tiled front steps. Climbing them to the small porch, Thomas is met at the door by a stocky woman with a crown of white hair.

'Mr William?' She scoffs.

'Yes, Mrs Turner?'

'Leslie, please,' she smiles, offering two rows of lipstick-stained teeth.

'Ok,' Thomas says, all too aware his voice is absent of both life and energy.

Following her inside, she smiles at him through thick-rimmed spectacles and a pancaked face of makeup. While relieved to be out of the rain, he is struck by the scent of the woman's overly sweet perfume. Equally unpleasant is the feeling of cold from his wet clothes. His coat, shirt and trousers cling to his skin like clingfilm and pulling at them only adds to the discomfort.

'I hope your journey here was painless?' She asks.

While she offers a smile, a jovial nod of the head, Thomas sees it for what it really is. An act, an illusion, the forced demeanour of someone else hiding beneath the shell of a seasoned salesperson.

Standing, dripping, Thomas can only glare at the woman, already regretting his decision to view the one-bedroom apartment on the edge of town.

'I see,' she says, the mask slipping for a moment. 'Well, if you would like to follow me. Built in 1888, Victorian era, the year of the Ripper,' Mrs Tuner starts. 'Complete with original period features, a half mahogany panelled interior with wood dating back to the turn of the century. Renovated in the late nineties, maintained, and well looked after. Four apartments set out over the first and second floors, with this floor belonging solely to the landlord,' she reels off, pointing to a door labelled 1a.

Thomas traipses in after her, dripping water over the worn mosaic style tiles. Dimly lit, he eyes the stairs to his left, tracing them up as they ascend into shadow.

'And that?' Thomas asks, pointing to a second door, all but hidden beneath the stairs.

'Basement, I believe, though I'm sure you'll have no use for it,' she says.

Impressed with the Victorian period, the coving, wood-panelled walls, be it a little faded and in need of fresh lacquer, Thomas notes the property appears to be well maintained, on the surface anyway. With the leaded stained-glass front door letting in enough of the afternoon gloom, the entrance hall is afforded a sense of mystery, be it one bordering on despair.

Tailing her and her heavy, awkward gait, Thomas follows her up to the first floor. All the way, as if glued, like passing a wreck on the motorway, his eyes are plastered to her colossal rump, unable to look away.

Far darker than the ground floor, the light here recedes to a point where wall lamps dotted along the landing are needed to maintain illumination. Panting beneath a tightly drawn scarf, obviously struggling with her weight and odd, almost hunched form, Ms Turner waits for Thomas before proceeding higher. Her enthusiastic gesturing not only agitates Thomas but, in doing so, sends wild shadows scurrying across the walls, back and forth, stopping briefly to congregate before again scattering.

Joining her, Thomas takes the smile she offers as both forced and uncomfortable. Thomas notes that the woman's makeup has been applied with seemingly two coats, with all distinctive features firmly hidden beneath. Her round cheeks are bloated and hamster-like, while her eyes, shrunken behind circular lenses, appear distant and non-descript. In truth, Mrs Turner could be thirty-five or sixty-five, or any age in between, though her slow and laboured movement would suggest the latter. Nevertheless, her appearance and makeup, its heavy application are enough to have Thomas look away.

'The property has a garden, small, which is to be expected, but it is shared, with its upkeep being factored into the rent,' she rattles off.

Rounding the spindles, Thomas stops briefly to eye the two closed doors, 1a and 1b, before trudging in behind her to the stairs.

The top floor sees a return of natural light, be it slight. The dying afternoon sky slants in through the small circular window at the front, but with the tower's overhang, the light penetrates part away across the landing, leaving most of the floor in deep shadow. Awaiting further inspection, 1d and 1e, two doors sit closed.

Following her to the former, Thomas waits, agitated, while she thumbs through a set of keys.

Smiling, she says, 'from our previous call, I remember you saying you're a writer, am I right?'

Well, that didn't take long.

Exhaling deeply, without an ounce of conviction, Thomas answers, 'I am yes.'

The door opens into a narrow hallway, where, after a couple of meters, it disappears with a sharp turn to the left. Gloomy and cold, the apartment sits in shadow, silent but for the rain above them. Following the woman inside, along the hallway and around the corner. Again, and while he fights it, his eyes return to her backside, watching it wobble, it mere inches on either side, fearing it might get wedged in.

'The apartment shares the floor with 1e, which like this one, is currently unoccupied. Parquet flooring throughout, one bathroom, one bedroom,' she says, throwing the words over her shoulder.

Poking his head inside the first of the two rooms, if only to be courteous, Thomas fully intends to accept the apartment, having no other choice. With his budget having been stretched as far as it can, this one-bedroom, north of the city, will have to do. As if on cue, pipes beneath their feet moan out, mocking Thomas as a cruel reminder.

Quick to interrupt the groan of the old building, Mrs Turner turns and smiles. 'Plumbing, I can assure you, has been maintained.'

Two doors, one on either side of the hallway, sit open. The left leads to a bathroom—small, standard, fitted with a bath/shower, toilet, but not much else. At the second door, Thomas stops and swings a glance inside the small, unfurnished bedroom. Letting in a narrow strip of dim light, the small window at the far wall cannot mask how cramped the room is, but Thomas, sizing up the room, is confident a double bed will fit, be it as a push.

'Built-in wardrobe and cupboard space,' she announces before leading Thomas through to the open-plan area at the end of the hallway. 'Small, yes, but charming, wouldn't you agree?'

My god, is this what it's come to?

Attempting to ignore the raindrops irritating the back of his neck, the cold sinking into his bones, Thomas looks to the woman for distraction. Yet, her continued animation, her waving arms, only add to his discomfort. Worse still, her perfume, disbursed by her actions, fills the tight space with musky, heavy scents, reeking of ageing and mothballed clothing.

Swallowing his indifference, stepping forward, Thomas levels his eyes and tries and see what positives, if any, the apartment has to offer. Small and while far from dingy, it is nonetheless a million miles from being airy. Light creeps into the room through two small skylights and a medium-sized window at the east-facing wall, be it framing an overcast and dull sky.

'Fitted kitchen, spacious, a perfect place for a writer,' she smiles, waving her arms again like some stage performer.

Thomas attempts to return the gesture but instead feels a grimace pull at his features. Turning from the woman's grinning face, he surveys the small kitchen area and breakfast bar on one side of the room. The remaining floor space is stingy but adequate. Unfortunately, it sits below a sloping attic room which adds to the oppressive squeeze of the area.

Closing his eyes, attempting to breathe, the afternoon rain, monsoon-like, thuds the roof and windows in rhythmic waves. It may be his state of mind, his current situation and the fucked state of his finances, but the sound of the rain on the roof might just be the saddest sound Thomas has ever heard.

How can I live here?

He considers this and does so glumly.

You have no choice, remember?

Betraying him, Thomas's mind traces back to his old home, the plum trees at the bottom of the garden, his study, and the view of the woods beyond.

And Robin's bedroom.

The tealights above her bed, her books, the fish tank, and her collection of guppies: Wanda, Tony, Steve, Natasha, Bruce, and Peter, the smallest of the group.

Opening his eyes, Thomas finds Mrs Turner glaring, her smile slightly lopsided, her eyes unable to hide her annoyance at the weather and its poor timing.

Thomas breaks the uncomfortable silence by crossing the floor to the window, her watching him all the way. He attempts to steel himself and focus on the positives and possibilities. A life alone, a place to write, was what he had wanted all along. Wasn't it?

Looking out, rain meeting him at the glass, lashing the window, the view is grossly distorted with shimmering snake-like streams. Still, the window's position at the side of the building allows for an almost uninterrupted view of the sloping hill and the tightly knit community of slate-roofed structures. Many built with brick or stone quarried locally form part of an amalgamation of old Yellowstone, buff, red-brick, and fading exterior rendering. Where some appear rundown, others are decorated lavishly, leaving the community a contradiction that, in some small measure, adds to the illusion of individuality among the homes.

'If you don't mind me asking, what are you working on; currently, I mean?' She asks.

'Nothing, currently,' he snaps.

'Oh, I see,' eyes growing wide, her attempt at a warm smile is falsely apparent. 'Well, I imagine these views, this space could inspire you. Would I have heard of anything you've written? I'm sure I would....'

'Probably not,' he tells her, cutting her off, now bored.

Moving to the middle of the room, stopping and surveying, Thomas focuses on the long far wall. Opposite the hallway, three old fashionably framed paintings hang at evenly spaced intervals. The theme is consistent- late 18th, early 19th century, Napoleonic War era, all depicting the same battle. The outer two paintings are standard-hotel-room fare. In one, a rickety Spanish frigate, and the other, a French Navy Corvette. Each suspended in time, battling waves and taking fire, faded and dull behind cracked canvases. The centre painting, slightly larger than its siblings, demands further attention. Instantly recognisable as the HMS Victory, framed in bronze and wood, frozen forever at the battle of Trafalgar.

High and pitched, the woman's voice startles Thomas. 'Mr William?'

Confused, turning to face her, Thomas stands mere feet from the centre painting.

'Sorry,' he tells her, his eyes pained from staring.

'As you can see, the apartment comes as seen, unfurnished. Still, a further deposit is required,' Mrs Turner says, joining Thomas to gaze at the paintings.

'In case I decide to steal the priceless antiques?' He mocks, rubbing his tired face.

'In case you spill your red wine and stain the floor. In truth, I wasn't aware these were here. I can have them removed if you like?' She asks, forcing a smile.

Attempting but struggling to collect his thoughts, Thomas reviews the apartment one last time, feeling somewhat off-kilter. Taking a moment to listen to the sounds of the building, the rain as it clatters the window, he traces its shadow as it streaks across, staining the wooden flooring.

Turning back to the paintings, the Victory and the team of sailors upon its deck, animated, wrestling to keep the ship level, a growing shadow, hollow and dull, fixes in his stomach. Not typically taken in by such art, Thomas does, however, recognise the level of detail, the interpretation and foreboding, and something, though elusive, has taken a firm hold of him.

'It's fine. They can stay,' Thomas says, surprising himself.

The colours used, its palette, the browns and deep greys, the poetry of its shades and highlights somehow make the scene come alive, dragging his eyes back to the wall, the pull now stronger. Letting his eyes roam over the broad-brush strokes, the contours, the cracks left by age, greedy to take it all in, Thomas fears missing even the smallest of detail. His eyes seek out and find each sailor, six in total, and the three further uniformed officers but stop when they settle upon he who stands at the stern. Admiral Lord Nelson, proud and unmistakably British, standing tall, his sword held aloft in defiance. Though his features are nothing more than small smears, somehow, Thomas can feel the weight of the moment, the emotion, Nelson's guile, his steeliness against such adversity.

Thomas considers, briefly, whether others would see him in such light, a great man burdened by his own destiny, but quickly decides without debate what he already knows to be true- Thomas William, the once bestselling author of *'Dead Right,'* is now merely a shade, and this apartment, this small corner of the world, is where he belongs.

'So, Mr William, what do you....' Mrs Turner starts.

'I'll take it. When can I move in?'

'Oh, great, um, immediately, the landlord is eager to collect rent.'

'Good, sooner the better,' he tells her.

Leaving, trotting out behind her, a dull ache takes up root within him. It blossoms, expanding, flooding his insides with a coldness new to him, a feeling he recognises as a warning though he doesn't know.

2

5 days later...

Thomas sits staring at his four-year-old Mac, purchased back when he still had money. With the screen dimming due to inactivity, he runs a finger across the trackpad, bringing it back to life. The cursor blinks back at him and does so tauntingly at both him and his lack of activity.

Just need to fire up my imagination, and it will come.

Leaning forward in the chair, he stretches out with his fingers, allowing them to hover above the keys, ready to type.

Start writing, and it will come.

Thomas tries to focus, yet his fingers remain unmoved.

That easy, huh?

Thomas considers if he'll ever be able to write again? Whether, if by some minor miracle, he'll find that one idea, the spark, that nugget that forms and grows into a story.

It will come, it will come, he tells himself.

Yeah, right, sure it will.

Instead of typing, Thomas reaches across the desk and pours himself another glass of wine. To avoid any unwanted spillages, he fills it three-quarters full. Setting the bottle back down, taking a drink, a tart mouthful sends a jarring shudder through his jaw.

With Thomas struggling to identify the grape, he returns to the bottle. Dragging it across the desk, he reads the muddy, scantly detailed label and the blurb spouting phrases like *a blend of red grapes* and *soft, mellow and fruity.*

An Opus One, it is not.

Forcing his eyes back to the screen, to the cursor, it blinking against a blank page, his mind searches for the words, ideas, anything.

The Curse of the Cursor.

A smile tugs at his face, be it a faint one.

That's one idea, at least.

Seeing it in his mind, a down on his luck writer, haunted by his talent, cursed by his own writing, never again able to recapture the success of his first book. Recognising this to be reminiscent of his own story, a clone, his smile quickly disappears. Thankfully he is not left to lament this for too long as his eyes are dragged back to the screen to the instant messenger pinging with excitement. Opening the message, Thomas takes another sip of wine before responding:

Captain-O: *Drawn another blank?*
Thomas: *Yup.*
Captain-O: *What are you going to do?*
Thomas: *Get drunk!*
Captain-O: *Well, I've got one if you're still interested?*

Pausing to consider this, Thomas pulls back to check the two large cork boards fixed to the wall above him. With his only contribution being a collection of different coloured pins, he recognises the need for help. Likewise, knowing all too well the complications when using the ideas and suggestions of others, let alone a fan. Along with the obvious concerns over royalties and recognition and the million other reasons entering such a relationship could be disastrous, there is none more than self-respect.

Thomas: *Sure, why not.*
Captain-O: *Search the name William Telfer, Clydebank.*
Thomas: *What am I searching for exactly?*
Captain-O: *You'll know it when you see it, and I think you might like it. Trust me.*

Opening the internet, searching the name as instructed- *William Telfer of Clydebank.* With the laptop struggling with the request, labouring as it hunts, Thomas takes the opportunity to have another sip of wine. Again, it sends a tingle of sweetness and God knows what through his teeth, setting them on edge.

Finally, with the screen displaying the search results, Thomas sits forward in his seat and begins scanning, be it loosely. Not knowing what he should be looking for or whether he, in fact, cares, his eyes roam the page before coming to settle upon the headline:

TRIPLE MURDER - *Madness, Murder and Mannequins.*

Great start.

Thomas clicks on the link. Displayed is an article from a small newspaper local to Clydebank, Scotland. The report reads:

William Telfer, 21, upon responding to an advert selling a used laptop, escaped the clutches of a killer or killers. After what can only be described as a series of irregular conversations via SMS texts, Mr Telfer agreed to drive and collect the item from a house in the neighbouring town of Ryinne. Arriving at the address at 9pm, a time set by the seller, Mr Telfer found the home to be dark and seemingly empty.

After knocking for over five minutes, the confused young man received an additional SMS from the seller, claiming to be disabled. The door was unlocked, and for Mr Telfer to come inside. Against his better judgement, Mr Telfer entered the property before being beckoned upstairs, from where he could hear the voice of an elderly lady. Mr Telfer followed the voice upstairs, along a hallway into the darkened master bedroom. On the bed, inked in shadow, lay a person. When Mr Telfer called out to them, he received no answer. Moving to the bed, Mr Telfer was alarmed to find the body was not a person at all but a mannequin. Stepping backwards, fearful, turning to leave, the familiar voice of the elderly woman stopped Mr Telfer at the door. Turning again to face the bed, Mr Telfer quickly recognised the danger he was in. In fact, the thing on the bed was not a mannequin but merely someone pretending to be one. Seeing the figure start to rise, its head moving to face Mr Telfer, it screamed, which would later be described as, 'like a banshee, something out of a nightmare.'

Fleeing, Mr Telfer managed to promptly alert the Police. However, upon attending the scene, neither an old lady nor the mannequin was found. Instead, shockingly, in the woods behind the house, murdered and left on display, laid out in a line, the authorities discovered the grisly remains of the Lyne family, dad (43), mum (37), and twins (6).

The Police have confirmed several items have been removed from the scene and will be tested for trace evidence and their forensic potential. Det Supt Liam Crowe, who is leading the inquiry, said detectives had received separate strands of information. However, after a lengthy search of the home and the surrounding area, nothing of obvious significance was found. At this time, the case remains open, and enquiries are ongoing. Anyone with information that could assist the investigation should contact North Yorkshire Argyll and West Dunbartonshire police on 101.

Sitting back, Thomas considers the news article. Running a hand through his beard, stroking it down his face, he moans with discomfort. It's long, itchy and unkempt, and like his hair, it needs a trim. A tidy-up. A fresh look. A change of style.

I need a makeover, more like.

A full MOT.

Captain-O: *So... You like?*

Thomas: *Well, it's a little dramatic. A little drive-in horror, don't you think?*

Captain-O: *Yeah, it is that... how about the murders of Della Kuhn and Robert Alman?*

While already familiar with the double murder of the two university students shot dead on a lover's lane, Thomas takes a moment to consider it. Taking another drink of wine, running the facts over in his mind, he concludes the circumstances of the crime: missing their clothes, removed and stolen, the bodies had been left on display, posed as if making love out in front of the young man's car, illuminated in the headlights. With their bodies exposed to freezing temperatures, the pair had to be defrosted before being separated. Romantic? Some saw it as such, while others saw it as another grotesque element to the horrific crime, just one of a fledgling serial killer. In fact, though still unsolved, the crime itself was isolated to the one incident. If the unknown killer had struck again, the Modus Operandi, the particular way the killer works, had changed. And while the circumstances are indeed strange, Thomas is quick to conclude it offers nothing in the way of mystery or complexity to carry the narrative of a complete story.

Heavy eyed, with the effects of the wine tugging at them, Thomas wipes them with his forefinger and thumb, but he cannot remove the grogginess from his mind. Stretching in the lamp's dim light, turning in his swivel chair, he casts his eyes across the room, the clutter, the mess of boxes still yet to be unpacked. With the kitchen taking up one side of the room, the other, transformed into a makeshift office, consists of a desk, filing cabinet and corkboards. A sofa and TV complete this side of the room, be it crudely pressed into one corner, leaving him exhausted and uninspired.

About ready to call it for the night, Thomas finds his gaze pulled to the set of three paintings on the long wall, notably the HMS Victory and her crew. Staring at it in the defused light, with the wall in shadow, the ship seems, though impossible, to be in motion. It's not, of course, but still, Thomas straightens up in his chair to confirm this is, in fact, the case.

A ping from the laptop pulls Thomas's eyes back to the screen. The effort required surprises him, and his confusion with the painting adds to an ever-growing weariness.

Captain-O: *Thomas?*
Thomas: *Sorry. Maybe... how familiar are you with the 19th century, with Napoleonic wars, Lord Nelson, stuff like that?*
Captain-O: *I've seen Pirates of the Caribbean. Does that count?*

The comment is enough to drag a stunted laugh from Thomas's throat.

Thomas: *Not quite.*
Captain-O: *Why the interest?*
Thomas: *Not sure. It's probably nothing.*
Captain-O: *Well, that's vague, thanks.*

Smiling, almost against his will, Thomas drags himself out of the chair. His muscles, taut and cold, threaten to snap with the strain. Rounding the desk, Thomas shuffles to the paintings. The single floor lamp and the shadow it leaves illuminate the wall and illustrations with a hazy bloom, softening them, almost highlighting them. Focusing on the one in the centre, his eyes roam leisurely over the cracked canvas. From the bow to the stern, lingering on the crew, the Admiral, Thomas's eyes rest upon the port side cannons protruding from their portholes. With Smoke billowing about them, eager to fire, the scene captures the moment between volleys. The dark tones, the streaks of colour and depth, lurid in their flashes, act like a black hole, eager to suck in and absorb all light about it. Still, the composition has an overall softness, a burnish, not like a photograph, but better. A window into the past. Stepping closer, Thomas looks for an artist's mark, signature, a dedication but finds none.

Leaving the wall, recognising the pain in his chest, Thomas realises he's been holding his breath the entire time with painful effect. Shaking his head, Thomas decides it's time for bed. Having done its nasty work, the wine has left his teeth with an ugly sweet film. Craving water and lots of it, he turns to the kitchen but stops short. Almost invisible, a glint of light catches his eye, dragging Thomas back to the wall. Something from the painting, within it, flutters with the lamp's light.

Moving back to the wall, Thomas searches the painting for a source but finds nothing of note. Stepping to the right, adjusting his angle, dipping his head in and out, but still, nothing. Stood in thought, tired and weary, Thomas removes his mobile phone from his pocket. Activating the torch feature, sweeping the beam across the canvas and back the other way, finally exposing it as a small hole. Half the size of a five pence piece, all but hidden within the sail, it twinkles against the light, hinting at a living world beyond.

Jabbing his head forward, pressing it to the painting, the hole, growing large, fills his eye with light and colour. Blinking with confusion, the sudden glare subsides but is replaced with an image, forcing him to snap his head back from the wall with jarring violence.

I thought I was alone on this floor. Unless someone since moved in?

Unconvinced, Thomas returns to the painting and the hole. Peering through it into the neighbouring apartment, confused, Thomas finds it lit, furnished, and most definitely, occupied. Thomas can only assume Mrs Turner had been mistaken. There is no other way to explain it. Regardless, the moment's confusion is yet to leave him satisfied with this reasoning. Thomas tries to recall ever seeing or hearing anyone coming or going but struggles to remember even one occurrence.

Unlike his own, the neighbouring apartment appears well-lived, showing no signs of someone having recently moved in. There are no boxes, cluttering, or indication of the tell-tell disorder that almost always accompanies a move.

Turning from the painting briefly, glancing an eye over his own apartment, Thomas scrutinises the collection of boxes yet to be unpacked, taking up space, labelled by his own untidy hand.

I'll get to it, sure, but not tonight.

In his hand, his mobile phone twitches- a subtle nudge, the third of the evening. Reading the message, Thomas quickly understands why the device is acting so sheepishly.

> **Mary:** *Ignoring me, really? So, you've moved in. Are you ever thinking of having your daughter visit? Oh, wait, you only have ONE bedroom. Well done, Tom, you've managed to surprise me yet again.*

Now chewing the inside of his lower lip, all but gnawing on it, Thomas considers his response.

Is she right?

Instead of waiting for an answer, Thomas returns to the painting, the neighbouring apartment, and the woman occupying it. Short and slim, the brunette is attractive, in an effortless, natural way; the type of pretty where makeup isn't needed to change the face but instead used to elevate it. Taken aback, the woman's appearance is like a thud against his chest, leaving a dull ache at his core. Hair up, her ponytail bobs and sways as she organises a bookcase. Serious and sombre, she goes to the activity with a thoughtful, deliberate approach. While estimating her to be in her early thirties, Thomas observes her appearance to be far younger when at home, makeup-less and dressed down in casual clothes. A loose-fitting shirt and faded blue jeans are underlined by bare, olive-skinned feet.

Again, holding his breath, air bursts from his lips. Hearing himself say, 'my God,' he shakes his head in confusion and well, amazement.

With her apartment mirroring his, the hole allows Thomas a relatively comprehensive view of her open plan living space, with a direct shot down the hallway towards the bedroom and bathroom, be it one in shadow. Where Thomas has boxes taking up space, her apartment sports potted plants and an ornament looking side table. Where he has a desk and corkboards, her apartment instead boasts a bookcase running the entire length of the wall, flanked by more plants. Chest height, potted in deep ceramic bowls, a Kentia Palm and a Yucca have taken up residence, lending the room an organic, fresh appearance.

An overly large and obscenely coloured rug sits at the room's centre- oranges, yellows, greens, all woven with no particular pattern. Beside it, an old, tanned leather sofa sits, though a little worn, appears invitingly comfortable. The small television neatly positioned in the far corner complements the room rather than smothering it. On it, a news report plays out in silent dispatches. Thomas's attention is drawn to the screen as it makes way for the evening weather report. At the bottom right-hand corner of the screen, Thomas notes the date - *24 January*. Confused, he checks his phone for today's date.

7 March.

Strange, it must be a recording.

Still, this reasoning and the discovery of a neighbour hidden from him until now leave Thomas a little off-kilter.

Turning his attention back to the woman, with half of the books stacked in neat columns on the rug, Thomas tracks her as she moves from them to the bookcase and back. Transferring books to their new set location, she occasionally stops to read a portion of a book or sip white wine. Where his fingerprinted, fishbowl wine glass serves the simple function of getting wine down his throat, her tall, stemmed glass, slightly frosted, chilled with perpetration, screams *sip and savour.*

Holding an A4 sized, heavy-looking red hardback, the woman takes a break from the back and forth. Sitting facing Thomas, legs crossed on the rug, she plops the open book in her lap and leisurely moves through the pages. Where her expression had been fixed, serious and muted, now reading the text, a smile creeps into her features, spreading, softening them. And like that, whatever it was which had been troubling her is seemingly forgotten. Looking at her, Thomas joins her in smiling, though he doesn't know why. And though he cannot be sure, Thomas pictures the book as a scrapbook of sorts, a collection of memories, of times better spent, an idea supported by the woman's sudden warmth.

Unable to look away, his eyes glued, he follows the contours of her face, her slender neck and her hands as they reach up to adjust her ponytail. As she dips her head forward, with her loose shirt pulling open, in seeing her bare chest, like a sledgehammer, Thomas recognises how wholly inappropriate his behaviour is.

Stepping back from the wall, a dull ache washes over him. Though strange given his limited time with the woman, a cold blanket of loss has firmly taken hold, and it's a sickening feeling.

Ashamed for watching her, or sad because I can't continue?

Either way, Thomas feels cheated.

One last look?

Not waiting for an answer, Thomas returns to the hole.

Oh shit.

Amy stands, staring back at him. While not directly, her eyes roam the wall on her side as if searching for something. Watching her close in, a streak of heat flares up Thomas's back, his neck, settling in and warming him through his clothes, before moving up to his face, where it heats his cheeks with a fiery intensity, leaving the skin uncomfortable and on-edge. A meter or so from the wall, the woman slows her approach, narrowing her eyes and ever so slightly tilting her head to one side. Though it's not a time to stop and stare, as if against his will, better judgement, Thomas finds he cannot look away. Though concern now contaminates her features, stripping her face of its smile, her eyes are such they manage to retain a level of warmth and the enthusiastic interest of an optimist.

Drawing in closer, her face opens further—a sprinkle of light freckles flare at her nose and cheeks, the type hidden by makeup, but all the better without it. Soft, babylike hairs inch at her hairline, softening her high cheekbones, elevating her deep, brown eyes.

Holding his breath, unable to move, Thomas prepares for her arrival, for her eye to fill the hole from her side. Closing his eyes, slamming them shut, he waits in darkness.

Ok, now what? Count to three?

One... two... three...

Opening them again, expecting to see her glaring back at him, his vision is first a blur of shapes and colour. With her apartment coming into focus, squinting, Thomas finds she is now gone. Feeling relieved but strangely, again cheated, he searches for her- over at the kitchen, back at the bookcase, the darkened hallway.

Nothing.

She could be on her way here right now?

Springing back from the wall, turning, waiting for the doorbell to chime, for the thunder of fists. Waiting, Thomas considers what she might say:

'Fucking pervert, get out here,' or, 'the Police are on their way,' or *'stop looking at me, come in, and I'll pour you a glass of wine.'*

Get real.

Still, he waits.

But for the throbbing between his ears, he hears nothing else. No angry screams, no sound of pounding fists, just silence, which somehow only unsettle his nerves further.

Gingerly, Thomas returns to the wall, his hands shaking a wild dance. Again, his vision is marred from the transition, but as it clears, he spots the woman as she appears from her hallway, from the shadows, but now, she is no longer alone. Behind her, out from the dimness, a man joins her. Tall, dark, and yes, handsome, he strides into the room with the bluster of someone who knows it–the type of guy yet to find a mirror he doesn't like.

Turning to face her guest, the woman stands, hands on her hips. Her demeanour is now different, evident by her arched back and her chest's rise and fall. Pensive, standoff-ish, agitated, Thomas recognises the change in her, and the man, whomever he might be, is the cause.

Arms wide, the man's tight shirt sits open at the navel, tight across his chest and arms. Stepping towards her, he smiles, but he is rebuffed by her taking a step back, away from him. Approaching her a second time, mouthing inaudible words, she again moves back. In noting the shaking of her hands and the rise and fall of her chest, her desire to keep space between the two of them is painfully evident.

Seeing this himself, the man stops, runs a hand over his perfectly neat stubble, through his wavy medium-length hair. Dropping them down to his sides, looking at her, he levels her a look with soft eyes, a doughy mix of playfulness and fake sadness. As he again begins to talk, his words carry no sound. Observing this, perplexed, Thomas attempts to recall hearing anything from the neighbouring apartment.

No bangs or crashes, no loud tv or radio, no music or talking.

The walls must be well insulated, I guess.

Focusing again on the woman standing with her back to her guest, solemnly, her head low. Folded arms, fresh tears stain her face, leaving silvery streams at her cheeks. The man steps forward, opens his mouth and speaks soundless words. Eager to listen, needing to hear, Thomas presses his head to the wall, his eye peering through the hole, his eyelashes flicking against the painting in erratic spasms.

Wiping her face, the woman turns back to face her visitor, who now stands, eyes on his phone. Sheepishly, eyes growing wide, he looks up from his device and mouths what appears like a plea of some kind before taking a step toward her. Meeting him halfway, pulling her arm back, the woman slaps the arrogant look from his face.

Eyes wider still, stunned, his cheek turning pink, the man stands, his mouth a gaping hole. Watching his eyes darken with fever and cruelty, exposing the man who hides beneath the pretty shell, Thomas's blood runs cold. Watching on, breathing heavily against the canvas, his heart now a bouncing mess, his pulse elevates to being painful.

Darting forward, the man closes the gap between him and the woman in one step. His outstretched hands grip her arms, pinning them at her side, shaking her wildly, as a child would a piggy bank.

Snapping back from the wall, Thomas moves to the kitchen. Scoping up his keys from the countertop, he hurries for the hallway. Outside his front door, his mind now hazy and at odds with his actions, his feet pound the floor. Ill-equipped to handle such a situation, Thomas arrives at his neighbour's apartment, all giddy and jelly-legged and utterly unprepared for what may come next.

3

It's not bravery that has Thomas leaping into action. In truth, he can't explain precisely why he is acting in such a rash manner. Maybe it was the way the man looked, cocky and cock-sure, or how he had mistreated the woman. Or perhaps, it's because the man had interrupted a moment between Thomas and her, where their paths would have crossed for some strange, fateful reason. Or maybe it is how he had clearly hurt the woman, long before today, not physically but in ways far more damaging. The staining, long-lasting kind. The type of hurt you can't wash off or pave over with gifts and promises of change.

At her door, panting, Thomas stops short before knocking. Placing his ear to the cold wood, he recalls in shock from its cool touch, it jangling with his nerves.

Listening, Thomas hears nothing but the blood in his ears.

He could be hurting her right now.

So, knock, what are you waiting for?

Still, Thomas stands rooted outside the door, motionless, listening but hearing only the whine of a bus from the street below, struggling, grinding as it works the hill. With the invisible force that dragged him from his apartment now all but abandoning him, the sudden rush of adrenaline dissipating from his system has Thomas shivering and edgy.

Who the hell do you think you are?

Mocking himself, a common theme, has him again chopping down on his lower lip.

You can turn around and forget all about it. Who is she to you anyway?

Stepping back, recognising his own limitations, Thomas can only stand, nauseous and shamed. Wanting to leave, ready to go, his heart already departing, somehow his feet remain stoic and defiant.

A coward dies a thousand times before his death, but the valiant taste of death but once.

Recalling the words, Thomas shakes his head.

Damn Shakespeare.

Seeing the woman's face in his mind, her tears and sadness, Thomas recognises the pain. Thomas takes the man hurting her long before today for absolute certainty. It's all the same, big things, little things, though he probably doesn't see it the same way. It's in those dark eyes of his, clear as day, though he and his type will try to hide it. His good looks cannot mask it entirely; like the wind changing, a shadow in passing, the chameleon is revealed for what he really is. Wicked, cruel, an actor and imposter. Thomas could see it flash across the man's face, and like magic, it was gone. It was just a slip, nothing more, but Thomas saw it, and it is enough to have him return to the door.

Knocking with closed knuckles, a timid attempt full of apprehension, he stands and waits.

Nothing.

Pounding on it with a closed fist, rattling it against its frame, a sound like thunder is sent crashing through the apartment.

Nothing.

He could be keeping her from coming to the door.

Rapping on the door for the third time, this time harder, another set of boom's cascades through the hallway beyond.

Funny, I can hear that, but I can't hear voices?

Again, an impulse has Thomas moving, leaving the door, dashing to and down the stairs. Rounding the first-floor landing, down the second set of steps, he darts across the ground floor to his landlord's front door. Ringing the doorbell, a soft chime from inside echoes out to meet him.

Again, He is forced to wait. Now sweating through his clothes, ringing the doorbell a second time, his finger jabbing at it, once, twice, three times.

'Who there?' Asks a low voice from behind the door.

'Mr Chen, it's Thomas William, apartment 1d,'

'Yes, what you need?'

Are you kidding me, through the door, really?

'Um, my neighbour, I mean, there's a disturbance... could you come to the door, please?'

'Hold on ... give me minute to get trouser on.'

Take as long as you like. It's only an emergency.

The sounds of muffled movement and rattling are followed by a series of low bumps and grunts, but the door remains closed.

'One minute...'

More bangs and groans, and silence...

'Is everything ok?' Thomas asks, his head pushed forward towards the door.

Silence is finally filled with a loud crack from somewhere deeper in the apartment. A distant thud follows it, then, unmistakably, the sound of the chain guard clattering against the wood as it's dragged through the rail.

The door opens, pulling inwards slowly. From the darkness beyond, a short and hunched, elderly, East Asian man shuffles forward. Dressed in a lavish white dressing gown, an oversized shower cap crowns his head. Confused, his shrunken eyes squint at Thomas behind overly large, slightly tinted spectacles.

'Yeah, I help you with something?

'Yes, please.'

'Your apartment, it good, yes?'

'Yes, I mean, I'm here about my neighbour....'

Mr Chen looks at Thomas, his eyes tiny behind those thick lenses, which have narrowed to thin slits. 'What you talk about?'

'My neighbour, I think, well, she needs help. Have you got a key?'

'Neighbour?'

'Yes, neighbour, 1e, do you understand me?'

'Understand you, me Chinese, not stupid.'

Give me a break.

'Yes, sorry, but....'

'You have no neighbour. I don't understand what you saying.'

'No, neighbour?'

'No neighbour, apartment vacant. You have bad dream, ok, you go back bed.'

'What, no, listen, please, she's in danger, so I'm asking you to look, ok, please?'

The old man looks at him, his large spectacles covering a large portion of his face. With a shake of his head, he moans, 'ok, give me minute.'

Muttering, heading back inside, he quickly closes the door on Thomas's face. Other bumps and groans of movement come from inside, and again, silence.

Take your time, please.

The door springs open. Now wearing a heavy coat and a dark coloured, buffalo leather Stetson, Mr Chen removes a ring of keys from a wall hook beside the door and shuffles out to meet Thomas. With the man's huffing and puffing, breathless and fully consternated, Thomas can only glare at the man. Moving as if his ankles are in chains, Mr Chen moves to the stairs and slowly, very slowly, starts to climb, while Thomas is forced to crawl in behind him, one step at a time.

Slow, his gait is one of a rugby ball; with every step, he looks as if he might fall but somehow manages to stay upright.

'You'll see, no neighbour,' Mr Chen moans upon arriving on the second floor. 'You hear them, hear shouting?'

'No, I, um....' Thomas stumbles, reluctant to confess his spying on his neighbour. 'Yes, sorry, I heard, um, shouting, shouting coming through the wall.'

Shaking his head, Mr Chen moves to the door and fishes for the correct key. Finding it, he slips it into the lock, turns it, and pushes the door inwards. Together, they peer into the gloom.

Nothing but darkness and silence.

Mr Chen moves inside, flicking on the hallway light. Following him, numb and a little bewildered by it all, Thomas rubs his hands together to stop them from shaking. His stomach, tightly wound, threatens his throat with fresh bile. Thomas follows him around the corner at the end of the hallway, past the bed and bathrooms into the dark open living area. Pushing past the man, finding the light switch, he flicks it on but stands stunned at what he sees.

No bookcase. No books. No rug. No glass of white wine. No, him. No, her. The apartment is empty and vacant, which is impossible.

Spinning on his heels, Thomas scans the room, all four corners—the wall where the bookcase should be, the potted plants, the rug and sofa, all now gone, leaving the place cold and void of life.

'I, I don't understand,' Thomas's voice a whisper, no more.

'See, you have bad dream. You go back bed,' Mr Chen tells Thomas.

With Mr Chen heading for the hallway, Thomas turns to follow him out but stops short. On the long wall adjacent to his apartment hang three framed paintings. And not just any old paintings, but three doppelgängers - duplicates of the ones from his apartment, which again leads to the impossible. Thomas eyes the French Corvette, the Spanish frigate flanking the exact, enigmatic retelling of the HMS Victory's most famous battle.

'The woman, the woman who lived here, where is she?' Thomas asks, his eyes fixed on the painting, on the Admiral.

'The woman, Amy, she gone.'

'Gone where?'

'Just gone, disappeared, left.'

Turning to Mr Chen, his vision now cloudy, Thomas struggles to think, to process it all. Confusion with the strangeness of this reality and sadness and loss twist his mind.

'How long has she been gone?'

'No one seen her in month. They say she gone, just gone, runaway.'

Tears fill Thomas's eyes, welling, and he lets them, unable to stop them.

'But she was here, I don't understand,' Thomas says, a whisper no more.

'You worry me, Mr William, you not some crazy person, you not like Ned Bundy?' Mr Chen asks, his voice now raised.

It's Ted, Ted Bundy.

Mr Chen peers at him, out through his lens. Though he cannot get a full read on the man, Thomas recognises the nervous energy he is giving off.

A change of tack is needed, Thomas.

'I'm sorry, I, you're right, I had a dream. I think I'll go back to bed now,' Thomas lies.

Following Mr Chen from the room, down the hallway, around the bend, Thomas waits until they reach the front door before acting.

'Damn, I must have dropped my keys, sorry,' Thomas tells him, turning back. 'I'll just be a second.'

In his most leisurely fashion, Thomas returns to the living area. Now safely out of sight, he darts across the room. One step, two steps, three, and he reaches the window. Turning the handle, pushing it open, a burst of cold air slaps him in the face, followed by a sheet of rain spraying in on the angle.

Poking his head out through the opening, firstly looking to the right to locate the mirroring window of his own apartment, he looks down, his eyes straining against the darkness. It's high, vertigo inducingly high, and while it might be the cutting wind, his breath is pulled from his lungs.

Don't think about it, that's later.

'Mr William, you ok?' Comes a voice from behind him.

Shit!

Turning, Thomas hustles back to the hallway. Mr Chen stands, halfway down the hallway, yet unable to see the now open window. With his face shadowed by his hat, his eyes peer out from beneath its brim, all narrow and suspicious.

Time to leave.

Having removed them from his pocket, Thomas smiles and shows him his keys, 'found them, ready when you are.'

Thomas returns to his apartment with a question repeating, bouncing around inside his head like some crazed rubber ball.

How is this possible?

Blinking, attempting to rub his eyes clear of fatigue, but failing, Thomas goes back to the hole but pauses before looking through. With shaking hands, hesitating, he moves his gaze to the hole, treating it as if it is toxic. Light fills his retina, a blurred image of colours and shapes. Slowly, the man from before comes into view. Whoever he is, he stands over at the kitchen, alone, his back to the countertop. Drinking from a beer leisurely, his attention sits squarely on his mobile phone. Feverishly typing away, his fingers a blur, a half-smile corrupting his handsome features. Having rolled up his shirt sleeves, his exposed, muscular and tanned forearms twinge with every letter typed into the phone.

Where is she?

Her lack of activity adds a new level of anxiety to proceedings, bringing with it heat, uncomfortable, seeping in beneath his clothes.

Awaiting her return, Thomas considers what he'd observed. Apart from the impossible, what sparked the confrontation between the couple?

It was him using his mobile phone, right?

Considering this further, doubting the use of a phone would warrant such an extreme reaction; Thomas suspects this alone is not the issue, but something else, historic maybe.

A more pressing question, one Thomas is yet to pose, but one he must if he is to understand this- what exactly does he see when he looks through the hole? It's the same apartment, but his mind struggles as the cogs turn. Though semi-drunk and not exclusively the reason for his groggy mindset, the cheap wine isn't helping matters, leaving his mind a haze, lightheaded and fuzzy. Nevertheless, he attempts to focus on the hole itself, the view through it, and how the world beyond appears unfiltered, nor is it distorted. A scene seemingly from another time and place, yet the hole itself gives no indications of it being anything but simply that.

Another time and place...

Another time?

His mind, now heavy with questions, presses down hard on his eyelids. Pulling away from the wall, he rubs his wrung face, a simple action that requires considerable effort.

His eyes, too, require attention. Dry and sore, rubbing them leaves them raw and watery. Thomas, of course, recognises the need for sleep and considers turning in.

Yeah, right, there's no way you're sleeping.

Returning to the hole, to his surprise, he spots the woman as she exits the bathroom. Slowly and from the shadows, she appears from the hallway.

Amy is what Mr Chen called her, wasn't it?

As if hearing her approach, the man quickly moves his phone to his pocket before standing straight, meeting her gaze as she enters the room. It's evident, though having freshened up, Amy has been crying, the type of sobbing resulting in the eyes turning red and puffy, like Thomas's when he's been around cats. The man moves toward her, his outstretched arms, wide but empty, an obvious observation, even with

Thomas's limited view. Hesitating, Amy stutters before sliding into them, allowing her head to rest upon his broad chest. Placing his chin on her head, James smiles with achievement.

Asshole.

Lifting her head with a forefinger, gently placing it beneath her chin, he kisses her. The kiss, a little lopsided and forced on his end, is met by her nevertheless.

His hands drop to her waist.

She flinches at his touch.

Squirming uncomfortably within his arms, Amy appears trapped. His big arms, wrapped around her, hug her like a straitjacket. Still, she doesn't seem to be fighting him. Awkward, sure, but far from being held against her will, as such, Thomas sees her new demeanour as one of submission.

As the man leads Amy away, along the darkened hallway, into the bedroom, all Thomas can do is stand and watch on, his eyes left to linger on the empty space outside the bedroom door. Knowing what happens next, his gaze relents, and Thomas is released; as if setting him free, he is allowed to leave the hole.

Moving to the desk, his feet manage a shuffle but nothing more. Plopping down in front of the laptop, accessing Google, Thomas searches for the address: *1e Pinegrove.*

No matches.

While broadening the search with the full address, except for the usual property sites, those offering to buy your property for a low, low cost, and Google, providing a map and street view of his exact location, Thomas finds nothing further of note.

Moving to the messenger, Thomas opens the app and starts typing.

Thomas: *You awake?*

Captain-O: *Always! What's up?*

Thomas: *I've got one for you. Another errand?*

Captain-O: *Sure, what is it?*

Thomas: *Apartment 1e, Pinegrove, Beckley Green. Female, early to mid-thirties.*

Captain-O: *Sounds intriguing. What else can you give me?*

Thomas: *Only a name, Amy.*

Captain-O: *Who is she? You got a surname?*

Thomas: *No surname, only Amy. She's my new neighbour.*
Captain-O: *Ok, searching...*

If anyone could find anything, it would be Captain-O. While yet to meet them in person, Thomas pictures them as someone in law enforcement. Their wealth of knowledge, investigative skills, and deduction says as much, and with their availability, like it is, always online, hint at retired but active.

Having to wait, Thomas's attention returns to the painting, to the hole in the wall.

It's the past. I can see the past.

Sitting forward, he takes another slug of wine, its sharpness setting his tongue alight, tingling it.

But how?

How the fuck should I know.

Taking another drink, Thomas considers this.

Lewis might?

Thinking of your ex-wife's new husband is never an enjoyable trip, but tonight, with everything the evening has thrown at him, plus with the effects of the shitty wine, Thomas recognises the need to distance himself from such thoughts.

He is a professor, science, PhD.

A headache, razor-sharp and intrusive, racks at his skull.

Bachelor's degree.

The pain deepens, intensifying with whip-like throbs.

Yeah, yeah, you name it, the asshole has it. His successes make mine as a published author trivial in comparison.

Well, that's how Mary sees it, anyway.

Is she right?

Captain-O: *Did you say she's your new neighbour?*
Thomas: *Yes, why, what have you found?*
Captain-O: *I don't have an address match, but I found results for an Amy Porter, Beckley Green, but it says she's missing.*
Thomas: *That's her.*
Captain-O: *Your new neighbour is missing?*
Thomas: *Yes, it's hard to explain.*
Captain-O: *Well, you'd better start!!!!!*

Thomas: *I will, I promise, but first, let me have what you found.*
Captain-O: *I'm going to hold you to that! Click on this link and let me know - http//brightnews. Amy-Porter-disappearance.*

Clicking on the link, Thomas pitches forward in his seat, eager but sluggish from the alcohol. As the screen loads, the laptop twirling and crunching, his impatience has him biting down on his thumbnail. Revealing itself small section by small section, the screen finally displays a local online news article. The headline, leaping off the screen, reads:

Pretty Local Woman reported missing.

The Metropolitan Police are appealing for fresh leads in searching for a local healthcare worker, Amy Porter, who was last seen returning home on 11 February, where she lives alone. With her last known communication being with her sister, Lilly Porter, the Police are still trying to piece together a timeline of events leading to her disappearance that same evening.

Miss Porter is not a stranger to tragedy, having witnessed the death of her long-term boyfriend weeks earlier, James Ruck, making her disappearance all the more heart-breaking. It is believed Amy was suffering from depression before her disappearance, while unofficial reports claim Amy is medicated and in regular contact with a mental health practitioner. Though unsubstantiated, the Police have yet to rule out suicide.

The Metropolitan Police, though being fully committed and determined to solve the case, and after a comprehensive review of leads and information, are at a loss as to what happened to this attractive young woman. At present, Detective Chief Superintendent Lisa Ritter and her team have confirmed new lines of enquiry will be explored, with fresh public appeals to be renewed within the coming weeks. DCS Ritter has gone on record as stating: "the decision at this time is to focus and prioritise our efforts by undertaking a comprehensive review of all case information."

Sitting back with his wine glass, sipping through gritted teeth, Thomas ponders the article's content.

Suicide?

She does seem upset but suicidal?

Rereading the news article, several points gnaw at him.

1) *Attractive*, in the headline, is infantile, redundant, and completely irrelevant.

2) *Death of her long-term boyfriend, James Ruck*- could this be the guy with her? It might be related and will need investigating.

So, I am investigating this?

Well, you need an idea for your next book, right?

3) *The decision at this time is to focus and prioritise our efforts by undertaking a comprehensive review of all case information* – Thomas takes for the Police being clueless.

> **Captain-O:** *That her?*
> **Thomas:** *Yup.*
> **Captain-O:** *So, she's missing?*
> **Thomas:** *It's hard to explain. Fancy digging into it for me?*
> **Captain-O:** *Sure, I love to dig.*
> **Thomas:** *Truffle pig!*
> **Captain-O:** *Wretch!*

Smiling, Thomas leaves the chat and returns his thoughts to Amy.

24 January was the date on the weather report.

On his laptop, Thomas opens the calendar and traces back through the dates. He concludes, unbelievably - when looking through the hole, he sees precisely 43 days into the past, meaning, almost blowing his mind in the process, with Amy last seen on the 11 February, she will disappear 18 days from now, in his timeline. Considering his options, whether to investigate the case or write about it, Thomas recognises the need to know more.

So, I guess I'll go and see Lewis. He knows his science; he has a PHD, remember.

Before that, through gritted teeth, Thomas quickly recognises his next step.

I need to break into her apartment.

4

17 days before Amy goes missing...

It's 2:33am, and after opening a second bottle of cheap wine, after draining half of it, Thomas stands ready to commit inevitable suicide. Heavy on his tongue, fogging his mind, the wine leaves him with a clouded sense of immortality.

It had been a stupid idea the moment it was conceived- to break into the woman's apartment, from the outside, nonetheless. Thomas knows this, but still, be it the alcohol or stupidity, the task appears easy, straightforward, and exciting in some moronic way. With the window he deliberately left open being his way in, now feeling two sheets to the wind drunk, the idea now somehow seems logical.

'No guts, no glory,' Thomas says aloud, looking at the window.

Maybe they'll write that on your tombstone.

Snorting a drunk filled laugh, Thomas finishes his wine and gets up from the desk, swaying through a jagged, almost uncontrolled movement. Stuffing his phone into the pocket of his jogging bottoms, he zips it close.

Shuffling, his knot-like stomach leaves him with jittery butterflies, a little discombobulated, Thomas moves to the window.

Great, it's still raining.

The smell of dead, damp leaves, pine needles, and earthy electricity wafts in. Outside, lightning flashes, a zig-zagging bolt unzips the night, illuminating a sky of black, turning a billion raindrops into diamonds, if only for a second. Opening the window, pushing it wide, Thomas pokes his head out and peers to his left. Thankfully, Amy's window sits four meters away and has remained open.

Just how I left it.

With hair already wet, he looks down and winces at the height. A forty-foot drop disappears into mostly darkness, illuminated sporadically by flairs of lightning. A line of bins sits against the building, their faint outline made possible by a strip of light from a window on the ground floor.

Ok, so how do I do this?

Pulling his head back inside, he studies the window- a meter square, two panels, with only one that opens. Where the open window at Amy's apartment gives Thomas a sizable space to aim at, he will first need to navigate his way around his window just to get outside.

Ok, here we go.

Using the television unit as a step, the glossy, shallow two-tier unit creeks beneath his weight. Climbing, lifting his knees, hooking them onto the windowsill, he pushes upwards. Now perched, he plants both feet on the inner ledge, inches from the opening. Taking hold of the open window with his right hand, he leans out tentatively, rain slashing at his face as he pulls his left arm through the opening.

Reaching up, his fingers stretching, searching, rain slapping them, impeding them, soak his arm. From a crouched position, using his knees, pushing up through the narrow space, shuffling his feet outwards, from the safety of the inner wooden sill to its outer concrete sibling. Stretching still body outside the building, his fingers claw at the wet brickwork until finally, they reach cold iron.

Now standing, his feet balancing on the wet concrete sill, a mere inch from total disaster, he traces the guttering's curve upwards with the fingers of his left hand. Clamping around its rim, tightening his grip, his fingers dip into a cold, deep stream of water. Pulling on it, the gutter rattles but holds. A second, harder pull, and the entire length of the gutter shudders, but like before, shows no signs of failure. And while not the heaviest, Thomas is far from being the lightest five-eleven.

It's cast iron; it will hold.

Another tug on the gutter brings a pained groan, one of age and wear.

Not waiting for another warning, reaching up with his right, grabbing a firm hold with both hands, he stands between the frame and open windowpane. Exposed, the night rain attacks him ferociously, soaking and pulling at his clothes, weighing them down in seconds.

Feet planted with the front two thirds on the concrete sill, the rest hangs precariously over the edge. Transferring his total weight to his hands, the gutter creaks and pops, the fascia board squeals as if in pain, but importantly, it holds firm.

Pulling upwards, his clothes, now sodden and twice the weight when dry, tug at him, and his iron shackle-like ankles. Still, he manages to lift his head to meet the gutter, to finally, his chin is level with it.

Lifting his legs, the right one first, now the left, he loops them over the open windowpane. Now sitting on the window, Thomas stretches out with his right hand along the gutter. Pulling his left hand across to meet it, gripping hold of the drain, he shuffles his bum off the window. Transferring his entire load to his arms, pulling them tight and strained with the effort, his body tangles below him. With fingers now numb from the cold water, they slip, dropping him an inch.

SHIT!

Thomas moves in haste, one hand after the other, moving mere inches with each exchange, shunting them along the gutter in a stuttering movement, until a loud crack halts his progress.

He studies the gutter through impaired vision as rainwater lashes at his eyes, streaking his face, matting his hair, blinding him. This time, a second rumble far higher than the one before snaps his head back. A flash of lightning makes the night luminous through the rain's heavy stream.

It's just thunder. Keep moving.

In response, the guttering pops above him. A loose screw rattles against iron before plopping inside the drain.

Now firmly between his ears, his heartbeat rattles like the gutter, creaking, bending, beginning to fail. And just like that, like a slap to the face, as if he has been sleepwalking the whole time, caught up in the moment, half-drunk on shitty wine, it hits him- where he is and what he's doing, and the inevitable death waiting for him below.

Looking down, the height, as if seeing it for the first time, is quick to squirm at his insides.

Move idiot, move.

Fighting the urge to urinate, he shuffles his hands to the right. With his legs dangling beneath him like dead weights, he edges closer, feeling a sudden burning sensation in his fingers. Gritting his teeth, he pushes on. He must; there's no way around it. If he stops, he's dead. It is that simple.

Another clap of thunder rattles through him, loosening his grip and bowels in equal measure. Somehow managing to hang on to both, his wet trainers and jogging bottoms join the party, pulling at his waist like neglected children. Now looking for an escape, he turns back to his apartment.

It's too far.

Shit!

Attempting to breathe, to steady himself, he drops his head and closes his eyes. Shaking hands all but failing him, he feels himself slipping. The wet gutter, his lack of energy, the rain, and the alcohol's cloudiness, seemingly all now have conspired against him. In the gloom of the moment, darkness drops over him, a cynical, devilish accusation – was this your plan all along?

Suicide?

At full stretch, dangling, and though he wants to cry, he doesn't. Instead, in the darkness, to his surprise, he sees her.

His daughter.

Robin.

Looking up at him with doughy eyes.

Having finished a bottle feed, instead of falling asleep as planned, Thomas's then three-month-old daughter looks up at him, smiling, completely unaware of the obscene time.

He misses everything taken from him in the divorce: his wife, home and security, but he misses those moments with his daughter the most.

And I love her, goddamn it.

Thomas finds himself moving again with a new sense of purpose, an inner strength seemingly hidden from him for his entire life. He pulls through gritted teeth upwards with everything he's got, slowly dragging his head towards the gutter. Again, lifting his right leg and ramming his knee into the narrow space, he plants his right foot on the concrete sill, stomping it down.

Pushing further still towards the open window, and though sluggishly, his body follows. Breathing hard, panting through an aching chest, Thomas reaches out and takes hold of the open window with an outstretched right hand. Bending at the knee, he pulls himself into the empty space. Dropping through, the darkness of the apartment is quick to swallow him whole.

Breathless, panting and somewhat surprised he made it inside, Thomas finds himself sitting on the floor of the darkened apartment. Chased in through the open window by the slashing rain and the rumble of thunder, the hum of a fridge, the flashing clock at the oven, is the only light or noise in this space.

Pulling himself to his feet, hands on knees, he attempts to collect himself.

That was stupid. Um, you think.

Unlike him to do such a thing, Thomas attributes the alcohol to such a rash venture and quickly goes for his phone. Removing it from his pocket, flicking on the torch feature, a bright spot of light appears at his feet. Sweeping the beam across the room, from left to right, shadows lurk and leap with the movement, each sending a jangle through his nerves.

Calm down. The apartment is empty.

Yet still, apprehension continues to grip him. Along with the rain's heavy patter on the roof and skylight, his wet clothes have left him with a shiver of deep cold running up through his core. It's funny how the night, the darkness, can alter something so mundane. The apartment before, a shell of plaster, now appears malign and deceptive, as if hiding its true self.

In the dark, Thomas scurries for the light switch in, moving through the room, leading with the torch beam. Moving to the wall, the stream of light shaking in his hand, it takes two hands for him to steady it. Finding the button and flicking it on, the overhead light first blinks before springing to life.

The apartment is how he left it. Cold and empty, yet now, haunted somehow. In Amy's shadow, walking in her footsteps casts an uneasiness over the room, like walking through a graveyard late at night. Like before, Thomas searches for furniture, her belongings, anything, but finds nothing. Wondering what had happened to them, Thomas makes a mental note to find out later.

Returning to his phone, dousing the beam, he moves to the hallway, traipsing water in behind him.

Ok, bathroom first.

Flicking on the light, the sudden glare is blinding. As it subsides, it does so over a plain, small bathroom identical to his own, but for the walls painted in a pastel yellow. Moving on to the bedroom, like the bathroom, except for being empty and a single wall painted lilac, the room mirrors Thomas's.

With his thoughts shifting to Amy, he sees her in his mind, asleep, at peace, a side lamp on, and a book, open mid-chapter, stretched out across her chest. Smiling, he wonders what it is she would be reading. Though a mere fantasy, his writers-mind working, a dull ache runs over him.

I'll never know for sure. I'll never know her.

Again, referring to her in the past tense, Thomas corrects himself.

Disappeared doesn't mean dead.

Still, given the circumstances, it seems likely. With no leads and the only information coming from the Police being speculative at best, Thomas's experience tells him this story ends one way. Crimes like this, women vanishing, usually end with the discovery of a body in some ditch somewhere or in woodland partly covered by leaves. Worse still, the ones never found, their bodies never recovered and returned to their families, are forever left with the torture of hope.

It's just a matter of time until someone, perhaps a dog walker, stumbles upon the body, and the case will again become front-page news, for a while anyway. The thought of Amy being found in such a way, naked and dumped, violated and decomposing, brings with it a fresh wave of nausea. Still, nothing concrete supports this theory, so he quickly reminds himself of this fact. Adults disappear all the time. It's their right. Some want to get away, turning up months down the road, anew and energised.

But, if you want to know for sure, you'll need to dig deeper. You'll need to make that commitment.

Lightning flashes in through the window, saving Thomas from making any form of rash commitment. The morbid thoughts follow Thomas back to the living area, where he is greeted by a second strobe of brilliant white light. In its wake, as a low, almost guttural roll of thunder bleeds into a third flash, his eyes are dragged to the far wall, where they settle upon the paintings - the three doppelgängers. Two sets of three pictures, identical in every way, hung back-to-back. Usually, he wouldn't focus on such a fact; Mr Chen could have bought matching ones, maybe they are the same in all the apartments, but the hole and the ability to see the past, them acting as almost a gateway – Thomas concludes this can't be a coincidence.

Moving towards the pictures, inspecting them, one by one, he takes his time.

They sure look the same.

Rather than another set of prints, it's evident by the broad-brush strokes, the striking delineation through broody whirls and slashes, like the ones in his apartment, these too are originals- not a print or copy, meaning they each had been painted twice.

With his phone, Thomas takes a series of photographs. Moving from left to right, taking three shots per painting. Happy he has enough for a comparison, he decides it's time to leave.

Turning, heading to the window, not needing to return the way he came, Thomas pulls it shut, hushing the heavy rain to muted thumps against the glass.

Heading towards the hallway, his progress is halted by a fork of lightning. Turning the room white, the flash draws his eyes back to the paintings. As a further bolt sends a concussion of light across the wall, it reveals itself to him.

The hole.

Surprised he hadn't thought of it sooner, Thomas moves back to the wall and considers what he might see from this side. Inches from the centre painting, Admiral Nelson and his battered ship, agitated with questions, Thomas fixes his right eye forward and moves it to the hole. Struggling to understand what he's looking at, blurred light and shapes separate before coming into focus.

No one's home.

Thomas's apartment appears as it is now—night-time, with the lamplight casting shadows across the floor and walls. With a half-full wine glass, the laptop screen open, and the dark night sky brooding over the scene- Thomas cannot help but feel disappointed.

Ready to leave, his eye stops to focus on the glass.

I finished it, didn't I?

Yet it sits on the table as if just poured.

It's a different time.

As if on cue, a figure cloaked in shadow shuffles into the room from the hallway. Disbelieving yet unable to look away, Thomas watches on to find himself stepping into the light. Zipping up his fly, getting it stuck, yanking on it, he rips it from his jeans. As if recognising this moment, as preposterous and surreal as it sounds, his doppelgänger looks up from his zipper.

It's me, I'm looking at... me, but I haven't broken a zipper.

Thomas attempts to recall the occasion; sure, he would remember it. Stopping, his eyes grow wide in revelation.

It hasn't happened yet.

Thomas considers what he does know.

Ok, so from one side, you see the past, and the other... the future?

Ok, but how?

How the fuck should I know.

Whatever this is and however it came to exist, the hole in the wall is beyond his understanding. Everything he knows of life, the universal laws we all follow, is now forever changed, and it sends a wave of sickness through him leaving him on the brink of vomiting up his guts. Presented with such a thing, the impossibility of it all leaves Thomas feeling small, like a child again, insignificant, and inadequate.

The how's and why's can wait, Thomas tells himself. But, for now, as a responsible writer, he recognises the opportunity. Now is the time to act, investigate, and research the story. If he's diligent, prudent, proactive, and lucky, he might solve this thing.

Still waiting himself, Thomas watches his future-self lift one finger as he moves to the desk. Returning with a pen and pad, the other Thomas writes a message. Holding it up, it reads:

She's at the front door
If you leave now, you'll catch her
Don't let her get away

She, who's she?

Jumping back from the wall, numb, Thomas turns and heads for the exit. Turning off the light as he goes, disappearing down the dim hallway, he rounds the corner but stops abruptly. The front door is framed by a thin line of light seeping in from the landing outside.

She's at the front door.

Yeah, but who?

While temperamental and a little inconsistent, the landing light on each floor is energy-saving and motion-activated. Knowing this fact, Thomas's heart responds accordingly with wild gallops of pain-inflicting panic. Warmth soars up through him, pooling sweat beneath his arms, masking the closeness of his rain-soaked clothes.

Just have a look through the peephole, one step at a time.

A knock on the door, almost deafening in the hallway, sends a sickening thud through him, forcing him back on his heels. Gingerly, sliding his feet to the door, at the peephole, Thomas peers out.

Amy?

Facing the door, though somehow different, Amy stands waiting for someone to answer. Numb, wanting to open the door to greet her, Thomas reaches out to the lock but stops short, snatching back his outstretched hand.

You're in her apartment, remember?

Swallowing hard, Thomas returns to the peephole and studies her further. Her eyes shine like glassy spheres behind a dense fringe of matted damp hair.

Fringe?

Though the view offered by the peephole is warped and elongated, confused, Thomas tries to recall her appearance from before. He places her ponytail, brown and straight and long, and how her hair was scooped back from her face. Now, somehow it appears shorter, curly. He cannot say precisely how, due to the limited view allowed by the peephole, but this Amy is different somehow.

Lifting her hand, she stops before knocking a second time, her hand hovering between her and the door. Finally, in dropping her head, she turns and leaves, shrinking from view.

If you leave now, you'll catch her.

Thomas waits, eye-tracking her path back to the staircase, where she disappears from view.

One... two... three... four... five...

Unlocking the door and pulling it open, he edges out into the landing, closing the door behind him. Without keys, he cannot lock the door, which is to his advantage, meaning he can return at any time.

Moving to the stairs, he peers around the knoll post.

Empty.

Starting down after her, his eyes search the space before him. While the first floor is empty, moving to the final flight of steps down to the ground floor, he finally sees her. As she nears the front entrance, his mind races with things to say. Thomas considers calling out but doesn't, thankfully. Instead, stopping two thirds from the top, he spies Mr Chen standing outside his door through the spindles. His tiny form, all but hidden behind his cowboy hat and overly large bathrobe, lingers within the shadow of his doorway.

'You good?' Chen asks her.

'Yes, thank you, and sorry for the hour. Like you said, no one's home. I just wanted to check, so thanks for letting me,' she tells him and leaves through the front door.

Watching Chen disappear back inside his apartment, Thomas races down the stairs to the front door. While watching his landlord's door, Thomas heads outside through the front entrance. Stepping out onto the porch, his mouth running away from him, he calls after her, 'excuse me, hello.'

At the bottom of the porch steps, stood beneath a recently erected umbrella, Amy snaps round on her heels to face him.

'Yes?' She asks, her face half in shadow.

'My name is Thomas, um, I heard you knocking. I mean, I live at 1d.'

'Ok?' Her tone, a cocktail of confusion and annoyance, is icy.

'I wanted to see if you are, ok?'

'I'm fine, thank you.'

A beat between them.

'Come in from the rain, for a minute, please?' he says, his voice a higher pitch than he would typically like.

Stood there, shaded by the umbrella, it is unclear whether she is looking at him or not. Squinting, the porch light impeding him, Thomas stands and waits, vulnerable and giddy.

Finally, she responds with, 'alright.'

Stepping forward, she climbs the steps back into the light of the porch. Thomas steps back, smiling, a little light-headed and feeling the need to give her space. Closing the umbrella, shaking her hair free of rainwater, when she fixes her eyes on Thomas, he recognises the reason for the inconsistencies in her appearance.

'You're Amy's sister?' He asks, assuming.

'Yes, Lilly. Are you new? I haven't seen you here before?'

'Yes, I am. I, um, I heard about your sister, Amy, I'm sorry,' he stutters.

They lock eyes.

Lilly's face, stoic, offers coldness, and with it, a sick feeling rolls over him, weakening his knees.

Unlike Amy's dark hair, in the light, Thomas sees Lilly is, in fact, a redhead. Shoulder-length with loose curls that complement her freckles and her cheeks' pinkish hue. Like Amy, Lilly is devastatingly attractive in an almost effortless way. Jeans, t-shirt, cardigan, and burgundy running trainers, someone he imagines prefers a girls-night-in rather than a girls-night-out. Her eyes, red and sore looking, shift him an impatient look.

'I'm a writer,' he tells her like it's some badge of honour.

'A journalist?'

'No, fiction.'

Another beat between them.

'Are you writing about Amy?' She asks, her eyes returning to his.

'I wasn't planning on it, but since moving in I....'

Her eyes grow wide, staring at him, glaring, she snaps back with, 'and?'

'Well, yes, I am thinking about it.'

So, you've decided to write about Amy, that's news to me.

'Why?' She asks, her eyes narrow.

'Why, what?'

She steps forward, her eyes darkening. 'Why write about my sister now? No one else is. She just up and left, isn't that what everyone thinks?'

'Well, I'm not sure....' He starts.

'I fear you're a little late to the party. I mean, the bones have been picked well and truly clean; people have moved on to the next story. So maybe you should too?'

'Well, it's a fascinating story, her disappearance....'

'Fascinating?'

'I didn't mean for it to sound like....'

'Sound like your another bloodsucking vampire? Well, I guess you're an overachiever. How many books have you written?'

The truth or a lie?

Thomas considers it for the time it takes to complete one breath. ‘Four,’ he says, deciding on the truth.

Her eyes narrow further. ‘How many published?’

He hesitates before answering, but he is committed now. ‘Two.’

Whistling, she smiles, ‘So, not an overachiever after all.’

‘You sound like my ex-wife.’

‘Ex-wife, so you’re an underachiever,’ Her icy words are followed by a sly smile. It flickers there for a moment, warming her face before her expression again turns cantankerous.

‘Maybe yes,’ Thomas smiles. ‘But with your help, maybe not.’

‘My help?’

‘If I’m going to investigate your sister's disappearance, your council would be...’

‘Not interested,’ she snaps.

Flipping open her umbrella, Lilly struts to the steps but stops before leaving the shade of the porch. Turning over her shoulder, she looks back at him, her eyes dark. ‘I don’t know you, but please, don’t dirty her name. I hope you are a man of principle....’

‘I am,’ he tells her.

Thomas tries to find reason in his voice, to speak with a light, friendly tone, but instead his voice comes across as unconvincing.

‘So, I hope your work reflects this fact. If not, and so you understand, you turn my sister into some depressed, sad woman who went and killed herself, I’ll come back here and cut out your heart. Understand?’

He looks at her, holding her gaze. 'I understand.’

Her eyes linger on him for a moment longer than expected. They flicker, water, and waiver. He goes to open his mouth to say something, anything but, in a blur, Lilly turns and leaves, disappearing into the night, the rain, and its almighty cacophony.

5

16 days before Amy goes missing...

Lewis has Thomas waiting out in the corridor, leaving him to loiter among the remaining student body. The science building, a jumble of old and new, is brightly lit with downlights and shiny surfaces but shadowed in places by worn brickwork and Edwardian architecture. The atmosphere, the energy of youth, is enough to have him pacing back and forth. Worse still is the low squeals of the wet rubber soles of his shoes. Pacing, haunting his footsteps, his own follow him, turning his stomach with every whine.

The old red brick building, located at the northwest corner of the campus, sits partly hidden among a tall family of mature oak trees, well-kept lawns, and smaller, far more modern satellite structures. The amalgamation of young and old is further evidenced by a pair of ancient major-oak trees, matched with younger species- the type elegantly pruned into streamlined, stylized works of art, and as such, Thomas's walk through the grounds had been made in haste, his head down, cast with an envious shadow.

Checking his watch; 4:57 pm.

55 minutes and counting.

Thomas scans the corridor, eying Lewis's office, the closed door.

Asshole.

Thankfully, except for a few kids shuffling about with books pulled tight to their chests, the place is mostly deserted. Still pacing, attempting to divert his attention and his boiling frustration, Thomas makes do with inspecting the hallway. The red brickwork continuing inside allows the hallway a rustic feel, be it one slowly consumed by modern times.

Well-maintained and controlled vines grow in places, lace the walls, leave the interior more pretentious than ornate. Rows of lockers are staggered along the corridor, broken in places by potted plants, notice boards pinned with messages and updates, and blackboards scribbled with riddles and challenges for students to puzzle over. They read: Why do we dream? Is there life on other planets? What is the purpose of life? How are rainbows made? Are sharks mammals?

Oh brother.

Thomas peers into the nearest classroom through a narrow slither of glass at the door. With backs panelled in glossy birch, five long benches are equipped with expensive-looking apparatus that appear new and unused. Tidy and modern, almost clinical, a million miles away from the chaotic shithole school of his youth. Thomas, allowing himself a moment of self-indulgence, travels back to Cromwell High School. Part Sunday school, part military boot camp. A school where disgruntled students punch their teachers when receiving low grades, and likewise, where the teachers hit back and did so harder. It was rough, but to Thomas, it was fair, with bullies and geniuses in equal measure.

'Mr. William, Thomas William?'

Thomas turns to find a young, pretty, be it a simple-looking teenager smiling up at him.

'Yes?'

She proudly produces a book from her rucksack and holds it out to him like a medal.

'Dead Right, it's a great book. I mean, would you mind signing my copy?' She asks.

Long gone are the days when Thomas would be pestered for signed copies of his books. In truth, his relatively short time in the spotlight, a fleeting moment and nothing more, was over in the blink of an eye. If Thomas is honest, he couldn't say if he missed it or not. At first, Thomas simply wanted to tell stories and share them with the world, but with success came the endless demands of marketing. His agent, an advocate for an excellent social media presence, had attempted to make it her mission to educate Thomas on how modern authors should interact with their fans.

Then there were the promotional tours. Through television, radio and podcasters, the long and arduous interviews all felt like bragging to him, and he hated it, all of it.

'Glad you liked it,' he tells her, offering his best smile.

Taking the book but waiting for her to fish a pen from her bag, she hands him an overly long, pink thing with a smirking troll at its tip.

'Who should I make it out to?' He asks.

Blushing, she says, 'Lacy, please.'

Hearing a door open to his left, his eyes are diverted for a moment from the teenager. Dressed in a well-turned-out green tweed, three-piece suit, minus the jacket, Lewis ignores Thomas and instead heads over and removes a small blackboard from the wall across from his classroom. Stopping before disappearing back inside, he throws an agitated glance along the corridor. Now waiting on Thomas, his eyes glaring, Thomas decides to let him stew.

'Will you ever write a follow-up? People say you're retired?' Lacy asks.

Thomas looks at her, his eyes snappy, a reaction to her words. However, seeing the genuine concern in her eyes, his response is receptive rather than resentful.

'People?' He asks.

'Well, the internet, forums. You haven't updated your blog in....'

'Two years, I know... god, retired, really?' He asks, shaking his head.

'I'm afraid so,' she smiles.

Finished scribbling his note, Thomas hands her back the book. Opening the front page, she smiles when reading his words. Shifting a look towards the waiting Lewis, her smile grows as she whispers, 'he's not that bad.'

'I know,' Thomas tells her. 'Just don't tell anyone, ok?'

As she heads off the other way, Thomas turns to the waiting Lewis.

'Please,' Lewis says, holding the door open.

Moving to the door and through it, Thomas tells him, 'thank you for seeing me.'

'I don't have much time, so if you don't mind,' Lewis shoots, strutting to his desk.

Laying the mini blackboard out on his desk, he pauses over it, chalk in hand.

'Need a hand?' Thomas asks.

Over his glasses, Lewis shifts him a look. 'What can I do for you, Thomas?'

Handsome and tall, slender rather than lanky, Lewis is well-read and financially sound. The son of not only an Oxford professor but the genius designer of space telescopes. A family from good stock, well-off but serial givers. Regardless, unable not to, Thomas views Lewis, his replacement, like Amy's late boyfriend, James Ruck, as both vain and petulant, even if he knows deep down Lewis is none of these things.

'Time travel,' Thomas tells him.

'Time travel?' Lewis asks, a smile pulling at the corners of his mouth.

'Yeah, that's a science thing, right?'

'Science fiction, Thomas. Why the interest, looking to go back and re-write your past?'

Ignoring the jab, Thomas perches himself against the front bench. 'It's a new project I'm working on.'

'Have you read Einstein?'

'Of course. Relativity, the fourth dimension, space being a three-dimensional arena, the traveller and coordinates – length, width and height,' he says.

'Well, it sounds like you know what you're talking about. Looks like you're all set,' Lewis says, the chalk still pending in his hand above the blackboard.

Looking at him, Thomas says nothing and instead waits.

He will answer me. Considering what he's taken from me, he owes me that much.

Having spent the morning digging, trawling the internet, researching time travel, speed of light, and space, Thomas ultimately came away none the wiser. Usually, this would be fine, but considering his current situation, simply not knowing is no longer good enough.

Finally, as if recognising he can't see Thomas off with some half-baked response, Lewis looks up and removes his glasses to rub his eyes. 'Look, when you talk about time travel, you need to be more specific. I mean, when we look up at the moon, us seeing it is a form of time travel, the time it takes for the light reflecting from the moon to reach us is 1.3 seconds, meaning you see it in the past....'

'Like with sound, when hearing, yeah, I get it, but I mean actually being able to move through time?'

Returning his spectacles, sighing, he fixes Thomas with a look that boards on exhaustion. Hands on his hips, with Lewis's sleeves rolled up, Thomas takes note of the gold and black Breitling sitting boastfully at his wrist.

That's five to eight grand, right there.

'It's been researched, sure, from Hawkins to internet nuts, but all we have are just theories. Time travel, the kind you're talking about, would require a time machine, a device of some kind able to bend space-time far enough the timeline turns back on itself to form a loop. I believe they call it a *closed time-like curve.'*

Considering this, Thomas asks, 'how about seeing it, viewing *time* I mean, the future, the past, I mean beyond the speed of light?'

'What, like watching a television?'

'Yeah, whatever?'

'Time travel involves going at a speed and distance where time is bent, but....'

'But what?'

'There are other theories,' he says, sighing again. 'Like black holes, wormholes, voids in space-time.'

'Voids?'

'Yes, like breaches, fractures in our reality.'

'Interesting,' Thomas says.

'No, it's not; you've considered it already, I can tell,' Lewis quips. Going back to his blackboard, chalk in hand, he starts writing. 'I am surprised why you'd come here. Believe it or not, Mary does see you as... while not particularly resourceful, as an intelligent man.'

'Does she? That's big of her. A waste of good potential, that it?'

'When she speaks of you, it's not all bad.'

'Mostly, though, right?'

Lewis responds with, 'mostly, yes,' and while he smiles, it's neither one of sarcasm nor belittlement, but one born in soft reflection.

'Has there been any studies, attempts, experiments?' Thomas asks, eager to get back to the point at hand.

Returning to his blackboard, now scribbling away, seeming to look to conclude the conversation, Lewis says, 'time travel, no, but I don't work for NASA. So, what you're talking about is, well, fantasy.'

'Ok, ok, I get it, but....'

'Thomas, why are you here? You could have found this stuff out just as easily online.'

'I could, I agree....'

'Coming here, seeing me, won't change Mary's mind. She believes you to be unfit as a parent. I'm sorry, but there it is.'

Is that why I'm here?

Looking at him, Thomas's jaw tightens. 'And you, what do you think?'

Lewis looks up at him, his eyes meeting Thomas's. Confident and assured, his eyes study Thomas for a moment without the need for arrogance.

'I agree with her,' Lewis finally says. 'I'm sorry, but your daughter has always come second to your writing.'

Chewing his lower lip, Thomas musters a solemn nod and heads for the exit. Passing Lewis's desk, glancing down at the blackboard, Thomas reads, *F = H*((m sub 1*m sub 2)/r^2) – what am I?*

'Anything else you want to discuss, warp speed, the Mothman, spontaneous human combustion, bases on the Moon?' Lewis asks.

At the door, before leaving, Thomas looks over his shoulder and says, 'Mary's wrong about me; I am a good dad.'

'Sure, you are, Thomas, sure you are.'

'And so are you,' Thomas says, waiting for him to look up from the blackboard.

'Me, wrong, how?' He asks, irritated but also slightly amused by the challenge.

'Your formula. Gravity, its *F = G, not H.* I thought you'd know that, but I guess we all have flaws,' Thomas informs him, leaving, letting the closing door slap the smile from Lewis's handsome face.

* * *

Watching Amy with pained eyes, Thomas finds, and not for the first, how hard it is to look away. Late afternoon has quickly darkened with the arrival of night, and fatigue now gnaws at Thomas, who has taken to leaning against the wall for support.

Amy, appearing to have had a day off work, lays stretched out on the sofa, reading a book. Her face, a smear of pale green, sits behind a facemask of some kind. Though Thomas attempts to follow her eyes as they move over the words, from his viewpoint, they sit like small black olives, sunken within the facemask and out of focus.

As her attention again slips from the book, Thomas notes this as being a constant feature. Her gaze, an indifferent stare, is angled towards the window. Confident the view requires no such scrutiny, Thomas concludes that something else is to blame for stealing Amy's attention.

Putting the book down, Amy sits up and collects the television remote from the side table. With a flick of a button, the display pops on. Snapping through the channels from the news, a reality cooking show, then with shaking hands, Amy lingers for a moment on the face of a prison inmate. Her expression drops, and her eyes widen. And though impossible due to the face mask, it is as if all light and colour fade from her face, leaving it a pale semblance of discontentment and discomfort.

Dressed in the unmistakably all-orange jumpsuit of a convicted felon serving time on America's death row, the greying man is seen in court, wearing a mask of holier-than-thou, one of a god-like mentality. With a shock of wavy grey curls, the man in his sixties stands with stoic eyes. *Robert Joseph Long* labels the bottom of the screen, underlined by the man's numerous crimes – *Serial killer of ten victims & serial rapist of at least fifty.*

With it being unclear how the image of the already executed murderer could affect Amy, Thomas considers whether the man's crimes, not the man himself, are to blame for upsetting her in such a way.

The news article about Amy's disappearance had referred to a previous attack. It could be linked. It could be a lead?

Shutting off the television, Amy stands up, but her movement is slow and jaded. Taking a moment to collect herself, she leaves the room, leaving an empty shadow in her wake.

A ping from Thomas's laptop peels him from the wall. He is hesitant to leave the post, as if in fear of missing even a second of activity, so darting, he moves to the desk, to the screen, he finds the instant messenger flashing, waiting for a response.

Captain-O: *I have something for you, and it's quite the mystery, I can tell you.*
Thomas: *Tell me.*
Captain-O: *Well, like the news reports, after speaking to her sister, Amy, disappeared on the evening of 11 February. When she failed to report to work on the 12th and 13th, her sister called the Police. Attending the scene, they found no signs of forced entry, no signs of a struggle. It appears she simply up and vanished, with no leads whatsoever.*
Thomas: *How is that possible?*
Captain-O: *It Beats me, and the Police, it would seem, from what I can gather, are at a complete loss. First, someone accessed her computer the evening of her disappearance, then all computer and phone usage stopped. Plus, and though not necessarily connected, Amy was raped at knifepoint four years ago.*

I guess that explains her reaction to Bobby Joe Long.

The serial killer from the television who terrorised the Tampa Bay area in Florida for eight months in 1984, it seems, continues to haunt women even now. Thinking of Amy in such a way, used, abused, or worse, a lump is quick to form in Thomas's throat, making it hard to swallow, stinging his eyes.

Thomas: *How did you come by this information?*
Captain-O: *A friend, a fellow arm-chair-dic, but he won't give me anything else over the wire. He wants to meet.*
Thomas: *How much more can he give?*
Captain-O: *A lot, I'd say. He's probably law enforcement or knows someone on the inside.*

Thomas considers this and the fact this step would also mean meeting Captain-O. A big step, but one he knows needs to happen if he wants to progress the case.

Thomas: *Ok, but before you set it up, I want to meet you. There's something I need to show you.*
Captain-O: *You want to meet me?*
Thomas: *Yes, it's essential.*

Captain-O: *Send a photo?*
Thomas: *Won't work; you'll understand when you get here. Can you make it tonight?*
Captain-O: *Tonight?*
Thomas: *Yes. Unless you've got anything better on.*
...
Captain-O: *Tomorrow, 5pm?*
Thomas: *Ok, tomorrow at 5pm. Do you have my address?*
...
Captain-O: *I do, yes.*
Thomas: *Good, see you tomorrow.*

Getting up, as if pulled, Thomas returns to the hole. Having removed her face mask, Amy is now joined by someone new. With Amy sitting at one end of the sofa, at the other sits a woman Thomas doesn't recognise. Younger than Amy and taller, the woman, whoever she is, appears to be in some distress. Where Amy sits aloof, her expression cold and unmoved, the woman with her head down, sobbing, knees together, sits perched on the edge of the cushion. Thomas notes the stranger's choice of clothing- conservative, with a long skirt, blouse and jacket, though it clearly doesn't suit her. With a body shape and look more accustomed to summer dresses, skinny jeans, and bikinis even, and while not a deception, Thomas labels her outfit as inconsistent and obviously false when paired with her looks. Still, even with ruined makeup, puffy, raw eyes, and cheeks stained with rivers of black mascara, the woman remains strikingly attractive, be it artificially so. Thomas takes her for a models-model with her high cheekbones, her natural height, and the tightness of her waist. Like a million others, Thomas recognises her as one of those social media models, the type offering videos with titles such as *try on haul, summer swimwear collection,* and *date night outfits.* Attractive but non-descript. Alluring but forgettable.

Seemingly unmoved by the woman's show of emotion, Amy watches her with cold eyes, the type of glare reserved for those people we truly despise. The woman, while taller than Amy, is far less imposing. Her eyes dare not meet her hosts. Instead, the woman fixes her eyes on the floor like a sheepish child.

Standing up and in doing so, Amy startles the woman. Taking a moment to look down at her visitor, Amy turns and heads for the kitchen. Pulling open a drawer, Amy, as if frozen, looks down into the open space. Like the woman, Thomas waits nervously for Amy's next move. Expecting the worse, as she finally turns to face the weeping woman, his eye strains with the limited view, the distance, with what she now grips in her hand.

Leaving the kitchen area and heading back to the sofa, slowly, the item she holds comes into view.

A thong.

Pink, skimpy; the *blink, and you'll miss it* type. Standing before her with an outstretched hand, Amy offers the lacy garment to the woman.

Reluctantly, while not making eye contact, the woman looks up at Amy. Climbing to her feet, taking the sordid item from Amy's hand, the woman steps back. Watching the woman, Amy gestures to the hallway. Nodding, the woman moves past her but stops before leaving. Turning to face Amy, the woman's drained face, a tangle of emotion, ravaged by tears, mouths the words before leaving, 'I'm sorry, I really am.'

I'm sorry, sorry for what?

From what Thomas can see, Amy says nothing in response. Instead, her face, a vacant, expressionless mask, says it all, as do her hands, balled into fists at her side, twitching with adrenaline and what Thomas takes as hatred.

Recognising this herself, the woman relents. The visitor turns and shuffles down the hallway, away from Amy, all but cowering.

Watching Amy follow the woman from the room, Thomas finds her apartment is cold and colourless without her presence, even with her harsh demeanour. Fidgeting, shifting his weight from one foot to the other, Thomas chews down on his lower lip and considers what exactly he's just witnessed.

Pink underwear, another woman crying, saying she's sorry... an affair?

Thomas ponders this further, believing an affair would explain how Amy had interacted with the unknown woman and the man from before. James Ruck. If the news article is to be believed, who is now dead.

Having researched the man online, the picture and news article from over a month ago matched the man he saw through the hole, right down to his chiselled chin and wavy brushed back hair. Dead now, killed in a motor collision. Another event and time yet to materialise through the hole. Sure, another limb to the same tree, but strands lost to one another but with no real connection to the next.

His attention returns to Amy's apartment, the hallway and the dark pocket of space at its end. His nerves begin to jangle as he is forced to wait, be it impatiently with growing agitation.

Come on, where are you?

Finally, Amy reappears from the shadows, shuffling into the room. Her expression is one of detachment, of someone who is genuinely lost. Looking around as if attempting to gain her bearings, she does so despondently. She closes her eyes, her breathing irregular; she shakes her head in what Thomas takes for frustration. Stamping her foot, once, twice, she mouths the words, 'no more. Forward, time to move forward.'

6

15 days before Amy goes missing...

Though he's expecting it, the buzz of the intercom startles Thomas, dragging him from the wall, away from Amy. Wiping his blurred, sore eyes, checking his watch, a yawn breaks out, straining his jaw and neck.

5:00pm.

Right on time.

Against his best efforts, Thomas's movements are that of the damned, moving to the intercom, dragging his heels as if chained and shackled. Pressing his fingers to the talk button, he says, 'hello?'

'Hi, it's me.'

'Me?'

'Captain-O.'

Really?

While male, Thomas is surprised by the sound of his voice. High and lacking an expected authoritative timbre, Thomas buzzes him in with trepidation. 'It's open, top floor.'

Heading to the front door, a second yawn, stifled into a fisted hand, pulls at his neck muscles. Rotating his head anticlockwise, the tip of his spine pops and groans, leaving his head fuzzy and disconnected. Putting his eye on the peephole, Thomas waits for Captain-O to arrive.

Thomas came across him a year earlier when trolling the website, *ArmChairDics*. Having recognised Thomas's username, RoyDawn88, a reference to his first published book, the pair have been speaking ever since. Who started out as a faithful fan, Captain-O has become invaluable both as a researcher and a companion.

Likewise, ArmChairDics.com has been an excellent resource for Thomas over the years. An online community of members and wannabe detectives, a place where users can discuss, trade and post information relating to all types of crimes while mostly centring on those still unsolved. Being a member, Thomas has used the site as a reference resource for many of his budding story ideas. It offers access to documents, links, photographs, and experts who spend their spare time attempting to solve the unsolvable. But unfortunately, while a lot of it amounts to nothing more than conjecture and wild theories with no basis in reality, others, as with the world we live in, use the site to spread lies through unsubstantiated claims, verbal diarrhoea and cryptic posts.

Still, some good has come from the endeavour. Genuine enthusiasts, those seeking the truth, are happy to drop hours of their free time to investigate leads, request documents, and traipse through files of lost people. Night after night, people worldwide spend their free time digging, reviewing, comparing, and theorising. Case in point, back in 2016, a user by the name of LynnWright39, a retired teacher living in Looe, Cornwall, identified a match between the image of Hayley Eves, a long-missing teen from the South Shields area, to that of a forensic portrait of a murdered young unidentified Jane Doe. As a result, the police not only made a DNA match between Miss Eves via her mother, but the information led to the arrest and conviction of her half-brother for her murder.

Through the peephole, a contorted form appears from the stairs. Short, petite, they approach the door with an almost irregularly fast gait. Canter-like, he moves with both speed and decisiveness.

He's a goddamn school kid.

Not the burly six-footer Thomas had been expecting, but instead, upon opening the door, Thomas finds himself looking down at a young man, sixteen, maybe seventeen years of age. 5.5ft at a push, slim and lean. Dressed in a fitted navy suit, both tailored and sharp, is set off with a crisp white shirt, red tie and handkerchief. A matching cherry red scarf and a closed umbrella harkening back to the one owned by Mary Poppins act as a complete contradiction with his youthful looks. Handsome with intelligent eyes, his young, boyish face is a collection of puerile features he'll never be able to outgrow, further evidenced by the sporadic growth of his facial hair.

'You've got to be kidding?' Thomas snorts, unable to hide the surprise in his voice.

Eyebrows raised, he smiles, 'please, call me Peter.'

Confident and assured, the young man stands before Thomas, toe to toe.

'Ok, Peter. How old are you?'

'Seventeen days shy of my twenty-sixth birthday. Would you like to see identification?' Peter asks.

Narrowing his eyes, studying him, Thomas considers it. His voice, while young, is undoubtedly well-read, laced with an air of chivalry. If and when his voice breaks, Thomas pictures it turning deep with a rich depth, the type perfectly suited for the narration of audiobooks.

'Allow me to explain, when I was twelve, it was believed I was suffering from Fabry disease, a genetic disorder whereby the sufferer has a defective protein-encoding gene known as the GLA gene, but after tests, well, the reality is far less exotic,' Peter pauses. 'A *late bloomer*, they call it, nothing more. I am well-schooled, graduating early in all forms of education, with a PhD in Criminal justice.'

'I see, so you want to work in law?'

'No, surveillance.'

'How's that?'

'As a private detective.'

'So, you see yourself as a Sherlock type?'

'Not quite. I'd like to say more like Philip Marlowe, and you'll do well to remember it.'

Smiling, holding the door open for him, Thomas says, 'ok, Bogart, I guess you'd better come in.'

Peter follows Thomas inside, along the hallway, and into the living area.

'Find it, alright?' Thomas asks.

'Fine, you should know this area is becoming quite the hotspot.'

Turning, Thomas looks at him blanketly.

'Amy's disappearance being one, but it would appear there are several deaths which remain unsolved.'

'Deaths?'

'Yes, it seems you have taken up residence in the murder capital of the world; for cats and dogs, it is reported an alleged assailant is partial to both species.'

'Alleged?'

'Well, the Police and press can't quite agree. The Met has attributed the grisly remains to that of starved-crazed foxes, while the media appear to be following a more *serial-nutcase* theme; a serial killer preying on the local population.'

Thomas offers a thin smile, uninterested, unable to hide it, but observes Peter is merely making conversation.

'Drink?' Thomas offers.

'Earl Grey?'

'I have tap water, coffee, cheap wine... or aged Cognac.'

'Thank you, I'll pass,' His eyes fix on the kitchen counter and the collection of wine empties. 'But don't let me stop you.'

Rolling his eyes, Thomas steps across the room towards the wall, to the hole.

'Ok, now what I'm about to show you stays between us. To be honest, I'm still struggling to understand it myself, but until I do, it needs to remain a secret,' Thomas tells him, his eyes seeking out Peter's.

'Ok,' Peter says, his eyes weary.

'Keeping it secret gives us the edge in finding out what happened to Amy. If it gets out....'

'Your next novel will be ruined?' Peter asks, his eyes narrowing.

'Yes,' Thomas pauses. 'Do you have a problem with that?'

'No, I'm a fan, remember, so I guess, in doing this, I get the opportunity to help.'

Watching him further, the young man, though direct, is eager. Thomas tells him, 'ok, follow me.'

Leading him to the wall, to the centre painting and Admiral Nelson, Thomas gestures towards the hole.

'Is this why you asked me about the Napoleonic Wars?'

'Yes. Now tell me, what do you see?'

Peter steps closer and studies the painting with a tightening of his jaw.

'I can tell you the painting depicts the Battle of Trafalgar, 1805,' he says. As if drawn in by it, his head moves closer. 'They look old, Edwardian, possibly Victorian eras.'

'Now, look carefully at the sail.'

Peter, with one eyebrow raised, looks at Thomas.

'Please,' Thomas adds, smiling. 'You'll be fine, I promise, though I am willing to hold your hand if it helps?'

Still looking at him, unimpressed, Peter removes his spectacles from his inner suit jacket pocket. A neat, expensive-looking pair with a brushed metal, copper-coloured finish. Putting them on, sliding them to the bridge of his nose, he turns his attention back to the painting. 'Ok, the sail, and what am I looking....'

His mouth drops open.

'See it, the hole, look through it, please.'

'Why?' Peter asks, clearly concerned.

'You'll see, please.'

Considering this, slowly, he does as instructed but pauses in thought before moving his eye to the hole. With Peter being considerably shorter than Thomas, he must climb up onto his tiptoes to meet the spot. Slowly, climbing to the hole, his eyes grow wide in surprise.

'Do you see her?' Thomas asks.

Still at the hole, Peter's words are muffled, 'Who is she?'

'Amy Porter.'

Turning from the painting, his eyes blink rapidly. 'I, I don't understand.'

'Follow me,' Thomas says, leading him to the hallway.

Thomas stops to wait for Peter, who joins him with a blank expression. The cogs working, clearly, as are the warning signs flashing before Peter's eyes.

'Come on, Bogart, don't go shitting yourself. It's fine, I promise,' Thomas smiles.

Thomas leads him to the neighbouring apartment. Pausing at the door, he looks at Peter. While hugging the wall, his eyes have turned wild with questions and concern.

'Trust me,' Thomas tells him before turning the handle, opening the door, and disappearing inside Amy's apartment.

'Thomas?' Peter asks, his voice quivering along the hallway.

Stood at the hallway's junction, Thomas stops and waits.

Slowly, Peter appears in the doorway, peering around the opening. 'Oh my,' he whispers but continues to follow Thomas.

Moving through the living area, turning on the light, Thomas again waits for Peter's arrival. Appearing, Peter does so at a crawl, his mouth widening into a black pit.

'Confused?' Thomas asks.

'Where is she, this room....' Peter's words are quick to abandon him.

Spinning, Peter checks the room, all four corners. While not frantic exactly, the level of confusion stretched through his features as it bordered on it.

'Is this the correct apartment? I mean, I don't get it?' Peter asks.

'It's the same apartment, alright, there are only two on this floor. Now I need you to listen to me, ok, I mean really listen. I don't understand it myself, none of this, the how's and the whys, like you, I saw this all for the first time a few days ago,' Thomas says, collecting himself. 'It would seem, when looking through the hole into this apartment, you see the past.'

Peter stands, mouth agape, his eyes wild with questions. Finally, looking at Thomas, he says bluntly, 'bullshit.'

A laugh bursts from Thomas's lips, and in doing so, he drags one, kicking and screaming from Peter.

'What I do know is this- it allows us to see exactly forty-three days into the past, meaning in fifteen days, our time, Amy will disappear from this apartment, and I've, we've got a front-row seat to it.'

'Why fifteen days?' Peter asks sceptically.

'Well, I confirmed it to be forty-three days by the news via her television, so the Amy we see today through the hole is the Amy of the 27th of January.'

'Which is forty-three days ago?'

'Yes, and with her last sighting on the 11th of February....'

'Jesus Christ,' Peter says, shaking his head. 'So, in fifteen days from now, it will be, what the 25th of March for us? but the world we see through the hole will be the 11th of February?'

'Yes, exactly forty-three days in the past and therefore, and presumably, her disappearance?' Thomas tells him.

'Incredible...' Peter stops short when seeing the line of duplicate paintings on the wall ahead of him.

'Take a look,' Thomas offers.

'Not sure I want to.'

'Sure, you do.'

Nodding softly, looking at Thomas, Peter moves across the floor, approaching the wall as if it's radioactive. So, as to not crowd him,

Thomas hangs back. Hesitating, Peter lifts to his tiptoes, leans in and places his eye to the hole.

After a couple of seconds, he laughs, 'it's you.'

'I think it's the future,' Thomas tells him.

'Future?' Peter asks, turning from the hole. 'How is this possible?'

'Bogart, I have no idea. Want to help me find out?'

'Yes, yes, I do, and look for Amy?'

'Yes, to both, but I need to be able to trust you, can I?'

'Yes, absolutely, and for anything,' Peter says, his face deathly serious.

The look on his face and the tone of his words is enough to convince Thomas.

'Very well,' Thomas says.

Smiling, Peter returns to the hole. 'Wait, someone is with you.'

'What?' Thomas asks, interested.

Thomas moves to join Peter at the wall.

'Wait, where did he go?'

'Let me look,' Thomas orders, gently moving Peter to the side.

At first, looking through the hole, a blurred blob morphs into a view of Thomas sitting at the desk. Strangely, the desk is no longer in its current position across from the hole, but instead, below it and slightly to his left as Thomas looks through it. Speaking into his mobile phone, his future-self appears oblivious to what Peter saw.

'You took a call, and he, well, someone disappeared,' Peter adds.

Thomas searches the hallway, straining against its dark length.

Nothing.

'How sure are you someone else was there, on a scale of zero to ten, ten being absolutely sure?' Thomas asks, his eye pressed to the hole.

Taking Thomas by the arm, turning him, Peter says, 'eleven. Someone else is in there with you, and I think they're hiding.'

* * *

They sit in silence, Thomas and Peter at different ends of the sofa. Thomas gulping at a glass of red wine, Peter merely nursing his.

'And you didn't see a face?' Thomas asks.

'No, only an outline, the shape of a person, nothing more. One minute they were there watching you, and the next, they turned and disappeared.'

'It doesn't make sense,' Thomas moans, taking another drink. 'Could it have been you?'

'Been, is in the past tense. Was the person I saw, me, it's possible. Look, whoever it is, we have forty-three days until the event happens.'

'Forty-three, how can you be sure?' Thomas asks.

'You said when looking back and seeing Amy, it's forty-three days in the past, so I think it's fair to say it is the same the other way.'

I hadn't thought of that.

'Have you done any leg work, research?' Peter asks.

'The hole, time travel? Yeah, but...' Thomas shakes his head; it is now fuzzy and full. 'Look, it could be a window in time, some fracture in this reality, but the truth is I don't know, and I don't think anyone else could claim to either. I mean, Forty-three days, why forty-three?'

Shaking his head, Peter's eyes are awash with possibilities. 'There may be no reason whatsoever, not one we might make sense of. Or it could be the answer to a million questions, questions we will never know or are qualified to pose.'

Thomas looks at him and nods, but the weariness of it all, the impossible situation, and the rapid intake of the wine leave him slow, his movements, even his breathing, jaded.

'I remember reading about this man, Dienach was his name, or something, anyway,' Peter starts. 'It was back in the early 1900s, and he had some illness, or stroke, I can't remember, but he was in a coma for a year. When he came out, he claimed to have spent the time asleep over two thousand years in the future, sighting the coming of World War Two, the dropping of the nuclear bomb, future technology, well, you get the picture.'

'And your point?' Thomas asks, growing frustrated with fatigue.

'My point is there are stories like this littered through history, people dreaming of the future, déjà vu, Nostradamus... I mean, there are literally hundreds of reported sightings of time travel. For example, take the Charlie Chaplin film, *The Circus* from the 1920s, where an elderly woman is seen walking on the street, holding what looks like a mobile phone to her ear.'

'Yeah, and the present-day hipster photographed in 1941, captured wearing what looks like clothing and sunglasses not of that time.' Thomas tells him, rubbing his exhausted face.

With his head now hurting, pained with fatigued, the hours of trawling the internet, dismissing story after story, time travel and travellers, twisted stories intertwined with fiction, reading everything from Hawkins to Star Trek, Thomas levels Peter with his eyes, desperately trying to keep them steady.

'Ok, set up the meeting with your contact from ArmChairDics, and investigate Amy's boyfriend, James Ruck. Unfortunately, he's dead, but still, dig.'

Nodding, Peter stands and fastens his jacket with a single button. Walking him to the hallway, Thomas stops to place his wine glass down on the kitchen counter. Feeling lost without it, following Peter to the front door in silence, Thomas's mind cannot let go of what Peter had seen.

Unless he's mistaken?

Caution, Thomas reminds himself. *Finding out you can see the past and future, my future no less, the unknown rippling effect on anyone it encounters, distorting what we see or what we think we've seen...*

Thomas rubs his tired, wrung face. His plump skin and the weight of his weary eyes leave it painful to touch.

At the door, collecting his umbrella, Peter looks at Thomas.

'Keep your head on a swivel, ok?' Thomas tells him. 'This whole thing is... well, just keep your wits about you.'

The light drains from Peter's face, turning it an ashy colour. Opening the door for him, Peter gives Thomas a nod before stepping out onto the landing. Moving to the stairs, he makes way for someone before descending. Passing him as he leaves, the shadow replacing him on the landing comes into view.

Mary.

For fuck's sake.

'New friend?' She asks, gesturing towards the stairs, the departing Peter.

'Research assistance.'

'Really, so you are working again?'

'Never stopped.'

Her eyebrows lift in unison. 'That's debatable.'

'Just because it's not published doesn't mean I haven't been working. A book is still a book; it still counts.'

'Sure, it does,' she says, stopping before him.

'Nice dress, you almost pass for a woman,' Thomas tells her.

In fact, her dress, a soft flowery number, is perfectly complemented by her brown knee-high boots and long beige parka. And like always, at her mere presence, his stomach buckles, and his shaky knees, look to fail him. To stop himself from collapsing, Thomas uses the doorframe for support. Turning and heading back inside, Thomas calls over his shoulder, 'I see you're still pregnant.'

'Not like you'd remember, but it does take nine months,' she sends back, following him inside.

So here we go again- another dressing down, another reminder of how inadequate I am as a writer, a father, a man.

Joining Thomas in the lounge, her eyes roam over the small space. 'I love what you've done with the place.'

'Well, you took everything else so....'

'Oh well now, fighting talk. Are you sure you want to go there?' She asks, strutting over and stopping to view the corkboards.

Thomas says nothing. Instead, he mashes down on his teeth. Watching her, tracking her eyes as they roam over the pinned notes, the map, stopping on the picture of Amy sitting proudly at the centre. Linked to other key people, facts, and places by a network of red string, Thomas's accumulation of information is nothing more than a vague mess. Still, Mary fails to notice. Biting her lower lip, her eyes are fixed on Amy's photograph instead.

'Who is she?' Mary asks, her words flat and cold.

'None of your business.'

Turning back to face him, the lifting of one eyebrow goes to underline her icy words, 'Thomas, really?'

'That's how it works, Mar; you don't get to ask me those questions anymore or walk in here and throw shit over my life. Those privileges become void the moment you took my daughter from me.'

Her response is nothing more than a loud cackle of laughter, and it's enough to bring a fiery redness to his cheeks.

'Is there something I can help you with? I'm a little busy, so if you don't mind,' Thomas says, ready for her to leave.

'I can see that,' she shoots back.

Thomas again traces her line of sight to the collection of empty wine bottles on the kitchen counter. Thirteen, to be exact. All red, mainly Rioja or Syrah, all strong, cheap, and in taste, one step up from paint stripper. A smile, one almost triumphant, passes across her eyes. And just like that, like always, in Mary's mere presence, Thomas feels, in equal measure, intimately scrutinised and masculinely downsized.

A striking woman, along with the success of her recruitment business, her remarrying and moving on, now with her ex-husband having fallen on hard times, on cheap rent and cheap booze, it would seem Mary has now only grown all the more powerful. As visible as Thomas's failures are, her energy and magnetism now follow her like a shadow, a cape, the type of vigour and luminance he will never possess.

'And where does Robin sleep?'

That didn't take long.

'My bed, until I get a bigger place, I'm happy on the sofa.'

'Aw, the sofa, your best friend, you'd know how it feels, I suppose....'

'Look, I know how you enjoy running me into the mud, you always have, but I love my daughter, and believe it or not, I'm writing, I'm trying, but right now, I don't have time for you. So, if you don't mind,' Thomas snaps, gesturing for her to leave.

Looking at him, her response is caught on her lips. Pain pulls at her features, followed by a hand dropping to her protruding belly.

'Jesus, Mar, is it... time?' Thomas asks, moving to her.

'Of course not, you moron, he's a little kicker, that's all...' she spits back, her eyes snapping wide when reading his reaction to her words.

'He?' Thomas asks, the question pained, leaving his voice fragile.

'Yes,' she starts, standing straight. 'We're having a little boy,' her eyes, struggling to meet his, glaze over when they finally do.

A Lewis-sized lump forms in his throat, blinding him, squirming his insides, twisting like a knife, bleeding Thomas nice and slow.

'I'm, I'm happy for you, Mar,' turning from her, Thomas runs his shaking fingers down his beard.

Mary opens her mouth to respond but again stops short. Instead, she heads for the hallway.

'You were always a beautiful mother,' Thomas calls over his shoulder. Turning, looking at her. 'You carry it well, is what I mean to say.'

Looking at him, her eyes like shiny spheres, her words are fragile as they finally reach her lips. 'Robin's recital, remember when it is?'

'Jesus Mar, of course, I do,' he snorts, lying.

'Well, she's playing her first solo, and if you like, you can come?'

'Really, yes, I would love to,' unable to hide the surprise in his voice.

'Ok, I'll email you the details, and after, we'll be going for pizza. Don't let me down. If I tell Robin you're coming, and you don't show, I swear to god I'll....'

'Mar, please.'

'Remember, if you want custody, you have to make an effort, and this one-bedroom apartment, won't cut it.'

'I'll be there,' Thomas says, forcing a smile.

'Promise?' Her eyes wide, hopeful.

'Cross my heart and hope to die,' he tells her, his words, when leaving his lips, hang between them like a dark omen.

His mind traces back to what Peter had seen. The person loitering, watching him from the hallway. A darkness falls over him, a shadow, one of pending doom, leaving Thomas to consider if he's next.

7

13 days before Amy goes missing...

Slipping on his coat, finding Peter's car waiting for him at the curb, Thomas stops before bounding down the porch steps. Still raining, the afternoon sky is a ceiling of grey melancholy, sitting low and oppressive. They weigh heavy, the clouds, alive and moody with the sounds of a distant storm, pinning him to the spot. The uneasiness of his new reality, this new piece of dark cinema he finds himself in, clings to him even now. Sleep, it would seem, is not the great rejuvenator.

Rubbing his shaky hands together, he cannot rid himself of the feeling of deep foreboding. Having followed him so aggressively to bed the night before, poisoning his dreams, darkening his morning, and now, the coming evening. A crack of thunder overhead jolts Thomas forwards and off the porch, down the steps, leaving him scurrying to Peter's car, a vintage Ford Capri.

'Excuse me,' a voice calls from his left.

Soft but husky, the rain all but masks its sound.

Stepping back, letting the woman glide past him, her Great Dane out in front, Thomas quickly recognises her from before. Once again decked out in a tracksuit, this time wearing a suede, pale blue all-in-one number, finished off by a matching baseball cap and bright white running shoes. She swishes past Thomas effortlessly, her butt swaying in her wake. To his surprise, she flips Thomas with a smile of bright white teeth before following the hill's slope down and away from him.

Ducking down to meet the low coupe, climbing in from the rain, his back creaks with the stress. Thomas joins Peter, and rather than filing in beside him, with the lack of support, his rump all but slams the ground. Grunting, trying in vain, Thomas goes to the task of straightening out his jacket in the cramped space. Though short, Thomas's journey from the porch to the car allowed the rain enough time to matt his hair, leaving the shoulders of his jacket sodden and turgid.

'Rough night?' Peter asks from behind his sharp rimmed spectacles.

'That bad?' Thomas asks.

Checking his appearance in the visor's mirror, Thomas grimaces back at himself through a pale mask and eyes punctuated by dark rings.

'The alcohol is positively sploshing behind your eyes,' Peter smiles.

On the other hand, Peter looks like he's fresh off the front page of GQ. Tight, not skinny, jeans, black rollneck, tanned brogue boots, finished off by a long grey, tightly woven trench coat.

'Who was she, last night, the woman I passed when leaving?' Peter asks.

'My ex.'

Closing the sun-visor, unable to no longer stand his own reflection, Thomas adjusts his butt in the small, black leather seats.

'Ouch,' Peter signals before pulling the car from the curb. 'Pretty lady.'

Changing the subject, Thomas asks, '1971 GT?'

'Indeed, a gift from my parents. Do you like it?'

'I do. I grew up watching *The Professionals*.'

Peter looks at him blankly.

'A bit before your time,' he says.

'A bit? Or do you mean decades,' he smiles, eyes on the road.

Rolling his eyes, Thomas turns his attention back to the car. An excellent representation of the era, the Capri appears to have been maintained rather than restored. Its original solid yellow mustard paintwork, being spotless, is trimmed with white stripes streaking both sides of the exterior. Having received the same loving attention as the exterior, the interior sparkles. The black leather sports seats, trim and unsupportive by today's standards, are minimally creased. The dash, a combination of walnut panels and black plastic, is furnished with what possibly looks like the original steering wheel, gear stick, and ageing radio-only unit.

'James Howard Ruck, Amy's boyfriend,' Peter starts, navigating the ford along the street lined with parked cars. 'Travelling back from a weekend away, having just left, he was hit and killed by a passing lorry. Having pulled over at the side of the road for unknown reasons, he climbed out of the car and stepped into the road.'

'Dead at the scene?' Thomas asks.

'Yes. He was hit by an articulated lorry travelling at 60mph, so there wasn't much left of him, and Amy, well, she saw it all, stood there in the rain while the emergency services boxed up his remains.'

'Jesus,' Thomas says.

Thinking, looking out of the window at the passing world, a blur of concrete and brick, metal and glass, amalgamated and disjointed by the rain laced window, Thomas considers James's actions.

'Why get out of the car?' Peter asks.

'To relieve himself?'

'They had only been on the road for five minutes. How about a disagreement, an argument, from what you've told me, they weren't the happiest of couples? Still, it was raining, heavy too, like today, so getting out of the car is a little strange.'

'It's stupid, that's what it is, but maybe he had a reason. The lorry driver, any connection?' Thomas asks.

'None. Male, Spanish, transporting a shipment of fruit. Travelling at the speed limit, with all the correct papers and licences, he's been cleared of all wrongdoing.'

Turning his attention back to the passenger window, the passing world beyond, Thomas sees Amy in his mind, in her apartment, drinking wine and filing her books. He, too, sees James grabbing and shaking her. Though the connection still alludes him, Thomas knows, somehow with certainty, James's death and Amy's disappearance must be, in some way, connected. How, well, it seems impossible, but Thomas knows there's no getting past this possible connection, not until he knows more anyway.

As if to match his thoughts, the sky above them darkens. As the streetlights pop on in succession, Peter's ford chases them until the world of concrete and brick is replaced with a green wall lining the road on both sides. The road, now far narrower, allows barely enough room for two small cars to pass safely. With the trees closing in as a canopy of sorts, the road becomes tunnel-like. With the rain now receding, its roar absent against the roof and hood, they are left with a hollow void, which is somehow far worse than the thundering of rain on metal.

Leaving Beckley Green, away from the affluence, expensive cars, and perfect landscaping, the road has turned cluttered with far smaller homes on both sides. Close-knit, single-storey properties, stunted by small convenience stores, narrow parking lots, phone shops, takeaway joints, and nail bars, are wrapped with a film of misery. A mile from Beckley Green, yet this small community could just as well be on the moon. With the disparity with its neighbours, the contrast is absurd. Like much of London, the rich and the poor live side-by-side as a cruel ironic mirror to one another. Soon, the detached, disconnected homes and commercially rundown businesses fade into a derelict industrial park of beige concrete and exposed structures. Storage depots, old warehouses for delivery firms, sheet metal fabricators, meatpacking, all now hollowed-out and long out of business, the bus labours mockingly as it crawls past.

'Your ex, would you like to talk about it?' Peter asks.

'With you? Been married, have you?'

'No, but I have virtually,'

'Virtually?'

'Video games, role-playing games. Believe me, there have been many a-wife.'

Staring at Peter in the dim light, his mouth, a gaping hole, softens as a smile creeps across his face. Shaking his head, Thomas meets him with one of his own and a laugh.

Outside, fields and the odd home are a welcome return while being a little on the dejected side. In fact, the drab land, the cropless kind, stretches out for miles, dead or dying, waiting for the development of new homes to come rushing in to give it purpose.

Ahead, as if peering out from the glooming sky, the dark brickwork of the westbound viaduct reveals itself slowly, like a monster from the dark. The closer they get, the viaduct grows, and in seconds, it looms high in the sky. Built back in the late 1890s, measuring a height of thirty meters, and constructed from reddish-grey brick fired from clay quarried on-site, it appears almost black in the fading light.

The gates of Hell?

Passing beneath it, gloom drops over Thomas and lingers, gnawing its way inside his mind. He diverts his gaze, his attention, tries to anyway, but he cannot shake the feeling, the darkness. Before them, the road narrows to a single lane. Peter slows the Ford to give way to a lime-coloured, two-seat Smart car. Finally, after a succession of vehicles, a bus, and a white van, Peter gets the Capri moving through the viaduct.

After another thirty meters, Peter swings the car off the road to the right before accelerating down a narrow lane. With it running parallel to the viaduct on their right, and with it being so close, the car travels within its overhang. Its dark stone melding with the coming night sky drops over the car like a black shroud, darkening the interior.

Thomas eyes the darkened homes sitting back amongst wilting spruce trees, patchy grass areas, and inconsistent shrubbery on both sides. Detached, disconnected, most of which are single-story bungalows, each faceless, lacking any real character. There is a general lack of colour; dead or dying, the ground is mottled with dry brown grass.

'Here we are,' Peter announces.

Ahead of them, a house sits alone, deep within the shadow of the viaduct. If not for a light being on in an upstairs window, there would be no indication anyone lives there. The house is flanked by two small barns and an old caravan minus its wheels. A chain-link fence segregates the land from its neighbours. A large plot crowded with dark, dying trees, boggy ground, and long stretching shadows cast by the viaduct.

A home for a serial killer if ever I've seen one.

Pulling the car to the right along a short driveway, Peter skids the Capri to a stop atop wet gravel and loose mud.

'How is it again you came across this guy?' Thomas asks, his eyes nervously moving over the house.

'ArmChairDics, he's posted several theories about Amy's case online.'

'Theories?'

'Yeah, well, he seems to have information which isn't in the press.'

'Information only someone involved would know?' Thomas points out.

'I guess, but wait, you don't think....' Peter says, looking at Thomas in the dim light.

'Tell me you've met this guy before?'

'Not in person, but he seems like a straight-up gent, I mean....'

A lone, dim figure appears at the front door. A hulking shape silhouetted by the hall light, they stand watching, leaving their face a mask of black.

Climbing from the passenger seat, rain lashing in at him in waves, Thomas meets Peter at the car's hood. Exchanging a look, Thomas whispers, 'you have seen the film, The Texas Chainsaw Massacre, right?'

Grimacing, Peter leads Thomas to the house. Stepping out from the shadows, they are met by a balding man with a potbelly and a pungent smell, and while not overly offensive, it is laced with cheap aftershave.

'Captain-O, I presume?' He asks, his voice reminiscent of a squeaky wheel.

'Yes, StarKiller-Base-01?' Peter asks, his words surprisingly assured.

'Yes, it's great to finally meet you. And your companion?'

'StarKiller?' Thomas asks.

'Yes, with a capital S and capital K.'

Stepping forward, Thomas thrusts a hand towards the tubby man. 'Thomas William.'

'A fellow Arm-Chair-Dic?'

'Yes, well, I'm a writer.'

'I see. Well, it's nice to meet you, Gentlemen. Please come in from the rain,' Starkiller offers, heading back to the house.

Stepping into the house, Starkiller makes way for them before closing and locking the door with a key.

'You never can be too sure. Now, if you would like to follow me,' Starkiller smiles, Turning from the door.

Again, Thomas and Peter share a look.

This could be him. How would I know?

Him who? You don't even know what happened to Amy yet.

Confused at his own readiness to attribute Amy's disappearance to something far more exotic, Thomas is forced to remind himself that until he witnesses it, it could be simply of her own doing.

Following him along a wood-panelled hallway, the smell of dried and ageing wax clings to the air. While a staircase on the left leads upstairs, StarKiller directs them towards the back of the house, past an open lounge and dining room, to a surprisingly small but tidy, almost spotless kitchen.

'You have a... lovely home,' Peter says, his words choking slightly upon his lips.

'It's old, but we like to keep it neat. Mother likes it that way,' StarKiller says.

Mother? Great, just another Norman Bates.

Fully expecting *mother* to pop out at any moment, her dressed skeleton dropping down before them from some stuffy hiding place, Thomas follows their host to a small wooden door. No more than five feet in height, with StarKiller opening it, the door creaks with age, acting with a heavy sense of foreshadowing.

StarKiller reaches inside and flicks a light switch. Though faint, light flashes on from somewhere below.

'Step into my office,' StarKiller beams.

'A basement?' Thomas asks.

With the words having left his lips before he could stop them, grinning, StarKiller recognises his discomfort.

'My torture chamber, please be careful to avoid the bodies on your way down,' he says, still smiling.

Peter, stuttering, takes the lead, disappearing through the doorway, bending slightly before entering. Watching his descent, Thomas moves to the door. Hesitating, looking over his shoulder, StarKiller stands, a broad smile pulling at his chubby cheeks.

No longer can Thomas stand to look at the man's grinning face; quickly, he follows Peter through the door. Ducking down, leading with his low head, he pauses at the top of the rickety old staircase. Wooden and frail, the thin steps moan out as Peter descends to the lower level.

'Mind your footing; wet feet on waxed wood are as slippery as baby poop.' StarKiller calls over Thomas's shoulder.

As he starts down, the light is quick to recede around him, as does the stuffy, damp air. It pinches in at Thomas's nose like musty, cotton-balled clothes, watering his eyes.

With Peter waiting for him beneath a bare bulb, as Thomas reaches the bottom, they turn in unison, looking up as the steps above creak and whine with the weight of their host. Joining them, StarKiller jostles past, humming softly, leading them along a narrow hallway supported by massive timber struts. One on either side of the passage, two doors sit open, with light spilling into the hall from both sides. Musky, a little damp, quick to fill Thomas's lungs, mould and dust taint the air.

Passing the door on the right and peering inside, Thomas notes the room as an unorganised storeroom of boxes, storage, and old bookshelves. Boxed vintage toys, Star Wars and Transformers mainly, and Corgi trains, hundreds of them, stacked and labelled, probably worth a fortune, but never to be played with.

Thomas eyes another plastic container stuffed with loose toys, actions figures, spaceships in pieces, and others, bulging, stuffed with worn vintage-looking comics.

Turning, following the others to the door on the left, Thomas steps into a small room full of monitors, computer equipment, and movie memorabilia. An ununiform network of shelving plays home to a collection of painted models: sci-fi stylist spacecraft, colourful transforming robots, superheroes, scantily clad Japanese girls with oversized breasts. The dimly lit room, a boys-den of sorts, is encased in plaster over brickwork, with two large threadbare rugs interlaced to form a floor covering.

Taking a seat in what can only be described as an overly elaborate swivel chair, designed presumably for gamers, StarKiller offers, 'please sit.'

Thomas watches him as his broad form settles in between the two padded armrests, his fatty prodigious gut wobbling as he wrestles for the perfect position. Following Peter to a leather sofa, sitting down, Thomas's butt all but falls through the cushion, sinking in deep, leaving his eyes struggling, peering over his knees.

'Thank you for seeing us,' Peter offers, his eyes fixed on the collection of models, specifically, one teenage girl/cyborg with exaggerated breasts the size of giant watermelons.

Spotting this, eager, Starkiller asks, 'are you a collector?'

'No, but...' Peter tails off.

Thomas traces his eyes, which have moved and now sit firmly frozen on a young female samurai model with powerful legs and breasts doubling as machine guns.

Thomas sits forward, eager to get to it, fighting the urge to return his gaze to their host's exposed gut. 'Amy Porter, Peter tells me you have information on her disappearance?'

'You the Police?'

'No.'

Looking at Thomas with still, fleshy eyes, undecided, he says, 'you look like the Police.'

Thomas's attention again returns to the man's stomach. The visible pale strip of skin between his loose joggers and t-shirt glistens like links of raw sausage and is enough to pull Thomas up out of the sofa.

'I told you, I'm a novelist,' Thomas says.

'You said you're a writer,' StarKiller corrects him, be it with a smile. After studying Thomas for a moment longer, StarKiller turns his gaze to Peter. 'And you, I know, and trust, but....' His eyes slide back to Thomas. 'If you are writing about this, I expect to be credited for the help I give you. Fairs, fair, am I right?'

'Of course,' Thomas lies.

'Well, ok, great,' he nods in surprise and places his hands in his lap. 'So, Amy Porter, thirty-two, a healthcare worker with a residency at Edgware Community Hospital. She was last seen returning home on February 11th by a witness at the local COOP, who remembers serving her at 8:37pm. Stop me if you know this already?' When Thomas and Peter shake their heads, he continues. 'She bought wine, free-range chicken breasts, vegetables, sourdough bread, low-fat butter, and a five-pack of Curly Wurlys. Well, her last known movements and communications are still a bit of a mystery.'

'How so?' Thomas asks.

'Well, it is believed Amy called her sister when she got home, then followed it up with an SMS text message at 10:14pm. Later, at 10:43pm, she makes a call to the Police. It rings a couple of times, but when the operator gets no one on the line, the call is terminated, and it wasn't followed up. At 01:03am, a further message was sent from Amy's phone to her sister before the phone was turned off. The content of the two messages is unknown. Later, at 01:10am, Amy or someone else accessed her laptop, which remained in operation for over an hour. Like the phone, it was then shut down for good. After that, Amy is neither heard from nor seen again.'

'Accessed, why?' Thomas asks.

'That I don't know,' StarKiller grimaces.

'And the laptop and phone?' Peter asks.

'Missing,' StarKiller nods. 'From what I understand, the Police are clueless, like pissing in the breeze. Still, the consensus is that after the death of her boyfriend, she up and left, possibly to commit suicide somewhere. I admit I didn't know much about planned suicide, so I dug a little deeper. Apart from the old Kodak building in town, a past magnet for those looking to end their lives, which is now all but inaccessible, I checked for any other known suicide spots locally but found nothing.'

'So, are you saying we can rule out suicide?' Peter asks.

'Well, I wouldn't say that, but I don't like loose ends. So, I took the liberty of checking with all hospitals within a thirty-mile radius for suicide victims, for Jane Doe's matching Amy's appearance, but again, nothing. So, if Amy took her own life, her body has yet to be found.'

Leaning against the wall, feeling the gentle patter of loose plaster against his neck, Thomas asks, 'and there were no signs of a struggle?'

'Nope, nor were there signs of forced entry. The door was locked, and her keys are missing,' StarKiller says. 'The Police did find several items gone: a small overnight bag, clothes, a pair of shoes, toiletries.'

'Movement on the bank accounts, credit cards?' Thomas asks.

'Nope,' StarKiller says.

Peter, looking at Thomas, cannot hide his confusion. 'Could she have just left? I mean, nothing screams abduction?'

'It's possible,' StarKiller says.

'Then why call the Police?' Thomas asks, more to himself than Peter and StarKiller.

'There is that,' StarKiller says. 'And Erika Sobo, of course.'

'Erika?' Thomas asks, his eyes snapping back to their host.

'Amy's ex-boyfriend, before his death, was poking this Swedish model, Erika, you know, on the side. For a while anyway, he was seeing both women.'

Remembering the dejected woman who had visited Amy, pulling himself away from the wall, Thomas asks, 'have you got a picture of her?'

Smiling, StarKiller swivels in his chair and says, 'sure.'

His PC, an alien-looking contraption, comes to life with a wiggle of the wireless mouse. Like the PC tower, the keyboard is illuminated, inked with neon orange. Fans kick in, and the computer roars to life like a diesel engine. In seconds, navigating the desktop, he locates the desired file, clicking through sub-files until the centre of the three widescreen monitors is filled with the image of a woman.

The same woman from Amy's apartment.

Erika Sobo.

'You might not know that, like Amy, Erika is also missing,' StarKiller declares proudly, his smile wide with achievement.

Thomas and Peter exchange a look, the news enough to pull Peter from the sofa, asking, 'Missing?'

'I thought that would tickle you,' Starkiller beams. 'From what I've gathered, Erika and James have this big fight, right, a major blowout, and shortly after, no one hears or sees her again.' StarKiller says.

'When did this happen?' Thomas asks.

'A few weeks before James's death, but get this, speaking with her friends before her disappearance, she firmly believed James was planning something.'

'How so?' Thomas presses.

'Well, for starters, her mobile phone had gone missing, and the keys to her apartment had been cut. Along with the copied set of keys, after pings from a local tower, the Police found both items at James's place.'

Thomas pauses to look at StarKiller. 'How did you come by this information?'

Smiling, he says, 'the internet, it's everywhere. You just need to look on social media forums to piece it together. It's all about patience. It really is surprising what you can find out about someone when you go looking. You just need time, patience, and the means.'

Thomas watches the young man, undecided by his reasoning.

'Was James ever arrested, charged?' Peter asks.

'Nope, they spoke to him, but nothing came of it,' StarKiller says, his eyes finally leaving Thomas.

Peter shifts Thomas a look, his face almost stricken with questions. Turning back to StarKiller, Peter asks, 'is there a way we can confirm the content of the messages Amy sent her sister the night of her disappearance?'

'I wish the Police have the case locked up tighter than a nuns....'

'Amy's sister, Lilly,' Thomas interrupts. 'Got an address?'

'No, but I can get it, her number, where she works, but what makes you think she'll speak to you?' Starkiller asks, his eager fingers returning to the keyboard.

Assured, Thomas tells him, 'Don't worry, she will. We've met.'

8

12 days before Amy goes missing...

Burnham Street, a jumble of small shops, a bank, hairdressers and overpriced eateries, serves as Beckley Green's high street. Off-cutting roads branch away, leading to independent boutiques, a baker, two more coffee shops, and the lone charity shop – as if thrown in as an afterthought.

As a reference point, Burnham Street does an excellent job summarising Beckley Green – a civil parish with the average property price exceeding a million pounds. The perfect suburban commute to London, 22.2 miles to be exact, for those with a family and the young and up and coming. You'll find no single teenage mums here nor crying babes. Instead, they laugh within their prams as if knowing the luxury and privilege they've been born into. It's sarcastic and bitter, but towns like this detest people like Thomas; it's inked in its DNA.

Like plague sufferers back in the 1600s, ostracised, their homes marked with a large painted cross, Thomas can feel the eyes of the community. Watching, judging, loathing his presence.

With it being Mary's preferred location, she fell in love with it when they first arrived to visit the schools. Mary was welcomed in with open arms, and Thomas, not so much, leaving him judged and inadequate. The house they bought, the BMW, the line of credit, the endless furnishings all felt like a lie to Thomas, but Mary, well, she just took to it, easing in among the picket fences, the smiling faces. But then, when the sales dried up for *Dead Right*, the spending spree stopped, as did the dinners out, the fineries, and while it was never said, Thomas always felt Mary held it against him.

There are no signs of high street chains except for a bank and supermarket- a discreetly placed Waitrose. The businesses here speak of start-up, youthful enterprise and pretentious arrogance, and it offends Thomas to his core.

Leaving the bus, Thomas is greeted by the rain and an army of eyes from one of the many cafes. Sat below the extended canopy, families, couples, pairs of guys and girls, and loners, enjoying their lunches, look on in disgust as if his arrival is illegal and immoral.

Ignoring the onlookers, Thomas hurries past them, moving north on Burnham Street, passing a lady's hairdresser, a designer clothes shop and a bank. *Lil Things*, a small shop at the far end of the row, a mismatch of items, Nik-Naks, is lit with warm tea lights at the front. The display is made up of a wooden chair, and a small table is wrapped and warmed by a string of small, tangerine coloured fairy lights. Casting a pleasant hue over the other items on display: a picnic basket, a rolled-up rug, a wooden trainset, the collection drags Thomas to the door.

Before entering, at the door, looking back at him is Amy. A poster reads, *Missing, Amy Porter, Daughter, Sister, last seen on 11th February.* The photograph, her standing in her NHS greens, smiling, happy and content - gone is the worried, haunted expression Thomas has grown accustomed to seeing.

'Beautiful,' the word leaks from his lips, followed by a dull ache at his core.

Readying himself, puffing out his chest, pushing through the door, he enters the shop. A bell pings above his head, setting his teeth chattering together. Stopping, breathing heavy, his heart labouring beneath his wet coat, Thomas scans the small shop. He spots Lilly standing at the far end, behind a counter, her back to him as she straightens a display shelf full of candles.

'Be with you in a minute,' she whistles over her shoulder.

'Right you are,' he shoots back, moving further into the store.

Jittery and nervous, his eyes roam across the items on sale. Vases, clocks, indoor plants, tea lights, mugs, wine glasses blown into unconventional shapes, ornaments and candleholders in the form of cats, dogs and llamas, all wrapped with the cosy glow from a scattering of lamps positioned perfectly throughout the shop.

'You,' she calls almost accusatorily.

Thomas finds Lilly looking at him. Approaching her, her glare is enough to unsettle him, leaving him stuttering, his gait awkward.

'How are you?' He asks, attempting to slither his way into a conversation about her sister.

'Fine. What the fuck do you want?'

Her sharp tone brings Thomas to an abrupt stop. Looking at her, offering his best warm smile, which only aggravates her further, he says, 'I only want to ask a few questions, ok?'

'No, it's not. I've told the police everything I know, you know, people who are looking for my sister. Not bloodhound, journalists, wannabe mystery writers, you. Please do let the door smack you on your way out.'

Mouth agape, Thomas stands and stares. Lilly's look in return is one of disgust and is enough to have him recalling back on his heels. Turning, making his way back to the door, Thomas stops before leaving. His head pitches forward, low, his eyes find their reflection in the glass. Looking back at him is a hollowed-out version of himself. A pale mask, dull, dark eyes, a soulless shell, nothing more - a true reflection of the man he's now become.

Something, possibly anger, has him turning back to Lilly. Staying at the door, he takes a moment before saying, 'I know Amy's boyfriend, James, was having an affair. I know she, Erika, is also missing. I know James is too dead and that you and Amy spoke on the evening of her disappearance. I know that she sent you a message at 10:14pm and a second at 01:03am before her phone was turned off.'

A beat, her eyes working, looking at him.

'And?' She asks, with hope creeping into her tone.

'And at 01:10am, someone accessed her laptop, which remained in operation for over an hour, and then, like the phone, was shut down for good.'

Finally, he has her attention.

'Who, who accessed it, Amy?' Her words probing.

'I don't know, but I have someone working on it.'

'Who?'

'A colleague,' he tells her and slowly approaches the counter.

'What else have you found out, or is that it?' She presses.

'I know James was a cheating asshole, and his behaviour around Erika's disappearance was suspicious at best.'

Tears appear in her eyes, the reluctant kind. Blinking them away, she turns from Thomas, so he is quick to seize the opportunity to further close the gap between them.

'The Police don't have a clue, do they?' She asks.

'I'm sorry, but no, it would seem they have run out of leads.'

'How can she just disappear from her apartment, in the middle of a busy neighbourhood, near the city?' She asks, turning to face him.

'I don't know....'

'You don't know?' She spits. 'So why am I wasting my time speaking to....'

'Yet, I don't know yet,' he interrupts as gently as he can, stepping up to the counter. 'I *will* find out what happened to your sister.'

'How can you possibly say that when the Police can't? What makes you so special?'

Remembering the hole, Thomas considers telling her but quickly decides against it. Knowing she would surely call the Police, or label him as crazy, or both, not wanting to lose the traction he's made, be it slim, he decides to hide it from her, for the time being anyway. So instead, Thomas decides to use a different approach.

'To the Police, Amy's disappearance is just another case, another missing woman. One hundred and seventy-thousand people are reported missing every year in the UK, one every ninety seconds. One in every two hundred children, one in every five hundred adults. Sure, I'm using your sister's disappearance as a source for my next book; I'll admit it right here and now. To save my career, repair my fragile reputation, and yes, I know how it makes me sound, but this is what I'm good at. Once I investigated crimes and wrote about them, I wasn't always a novelist.'

Good, Thomas considers if that is still the case.

'A journalist?' She asks.

'An investigative journalist, but yes,' he says. 'So, you can believe me when I say that getting to the bottom of this means everything.'

Looking at him, eyes narrow, Lilly considers his words, his openness.

Shifting his weight, uncomfortable with her glare, buying time to think, Thomas looks around the shop. His eyes are desperate to find an outlet, growing more painful. Finally, with them coming to rest upon a cat-shaped vase, he asks, 'have you got something, um, I mean it's my daughter's birthday, she has a thing for elephants.'

Standing, her chest heaving, her eyes staring, piercing.

A beat between them.

'I have a lamp, I think. Give me a minute,' she says, finally.

Watching her disappear through a darkened doorway at the rear, Thomas lets out a deep gut full of air. His armpits and back have grown wet, and a quick sniff confirms his level of discomfort.

Lilly returns with an elephant sculpted in clay, painted pastel pink, dotted with small holes. Sitting it down on the counter, Lilly bends over and plugs in the lamp. An orange centre, warm and autumn-like, illuminates the elephant from within, the light poking out through the numerous holes. Thomas recognises it to be kish but cute, and Robin, without hesitation, would love it.

'Thank you, it's lovely. How much?' Thomas asks, aware of how sickly sweet his words are becoming.

Looking at him, pausing for a moment, she says, 'take it for what you're doing for Amy.'

'At least let me buy you a coffee?'

The look on her face is a contest of both surprise and disgust. Unsure which emotion will prevail, Thomas awaits her reply.

* * *

Silently, Lilly watches Thomas intently from across the table. With the elephant lamp sitting off to one side, with its wide, overexaggerated eyes, it cowers in the shadow of the pair's discomfort.

Sipping his coffee, growing uncomfortable, shifting his eyes to the selection of pastries ordered, sitting untouched between them, Thomas shuffles in his seat.

Placing his phone down on the table between them, he waits before activating the voice dictation function, 'is this ok?'

'Sure, why not,' she snaps.

Tapping the screen, pressing the red record button, Thomas sits back. Nodding to his right, through the window of the café, across the street, he asks, 'your shop?'

'Mine and Amy's, she helped me get it started and off the ground.'

'I understand. Were you close?'

'You mean, *are* we close?'

Stupid.

'Sorry, yes,' Thomas takes another sip of his overpriced coffee.

'She's my sister, so yes.'

Staying silent, Thomas lets her reflect on her answer.

'You mean, are we close-close?' She asks.

'Yes.'

She takes a drink of coffee and looks down. 'Very. She's my better half, a mirror to what I strive to be.'

'Tell me about her?' Thomas asks.

'Tell you about her?'

With her mirroring his words, Thomas lets her response hang between them. Her eyes, darkening, flicker with a repugnant appraisal.

'What do you want to hear? She's the best person I know; her every thought is about being good, honest and fair. Isn't that what everyone says when asked, grieving family members describing their loved ones; full of life, good and decent, not an enemy in the world... she wouldn't run off and leave her sister alone...'

Her words catch in her throat, choking tears at her radish-like eyes. Turning from him, wiping her face, Thomas decides to allow her a minute.

'And James, what did you make of him?' He asks.

Lilly's eyes fall dark; a shadow, a brooding hatred, turns them cruel.

'He was self-serving, arrogant and vain, and Amy was far too good for him. Of course, I told her as much, but she did love him for a time anyway. I think she would see that as a lie now; it was the idea of what he could be, what she wanted him to be, she had fallen in love with. It was a dream, and eventually, we all have to wake up.'

'And you?' Thomas asks. The words leap from his lips before he can stop them. 'Are you married, boyfriend?' Thomas asks.

The question surprises Thomas as it does her. He tries to hold a stoic gaze as if the question is unimportant.

'Why?' The word snaps with the turn of her face.

'For support, I mean, having to go through this alone, I can imagine is....'

'I have friends, I have work, I manage,' she tells him, jaw twitching, her brow drawn tight. 'And you, Thomas William, you have a daughter?'

'I do, Robin, she's five, almost six.'

'Robin, I like that,' she smiles faintly. 'Your choice or your ex-wife's?'

'Mine, it was the one thing Mary, my ex, liked.'

Her smile grows, unable to stop it.

It's short-lived.

'So, what's your story, Mr Thomas William, one-time published author?' She asks, condemnation returning.

With her remembering such detail, Thomas is equally flattered and annoyed.

'Not much to tell, my first published novel, *Dead Right,* was well-received, but my second, not so much. Where *Dead Right* was a bestseller, the legacy it laid out for me has, well, been littered with obstacles.'

'Your divorce?'

'No,' he says, shaking his head. 'That I managed to fuck up all myself.'

The look on Lilly's face is one of dissatisfaction. Thomas recognises this as – *you want me to open up, well it goes both ways.* Taking a deep breath, readjusting his bum in his seat, Thomas steadies himself.

'Things were good between us for a while. That's what I used to think,' Thomas starts. 'But I don't know anymore. I think we were happy, that's how I choose to remember it, but the mind can be a funny thing,' his eyes drift off in remembrance. 'I can still remember the moment I met her, Mary. The scene, the music playing, the drink in my hand. A friend's birthday, an Italian restaurant in Shoreditch. She sat across from me, we started talking, and that was it. I was terrified, constantly watching the clock, wanting, needing to ask for her number, but running out of time. So, and I guess as a precursor, Mary asked me for mine. A sign, I guess, that it would be Mary who would control our destiny. I remember the risotto, wine, and laughter when my gift, a Japanese peace lily, was received with amusement and surprise. I remember her summer dress, skin, hair up... and how she looked at me that first time. But it's a lie, and the memory now mocks me.'

Lilly offers a smile- gone is the malice replaced with sympathy, or is it empathy? Thomas takes the look in her eyes as appreciation, as if his words have her conceding an inch, giving him a break, a small one.

Finding himself shaken, his palms sweaty, he is forced to drink his coffee in fear he might cry. But, instead, the words, dredging them up from the depths of his soul, now sit between them, permeating the air thickly.

'Your next book, what you're doing for Amy, will it be another dramatisation, blood and betrayal, romance and murder?' She asks, cynicism returning to her eyes, her words turning icy.

'To tell you the truth, I don't know yet; I'm still gathering the information,' he lies, fully intending to turn it into such.

Continuing to watch him, her eyes narrow.

She's sizing me up.

Again, Thomas is forced to divert his eyes. As if taking in his surroundings, he surveys the café. Having all but emptied after the rush of lunch, a small team of three waitresses scurry about, cleaning, straightening chairs, chatting in low, inaudible tones. It might be a nice place if not for the outrageous prices and the incredibly pretentious menu. Littered with words like *artisanal, natural,* and *hand-selected,* the menu reads like a misleading, unsubstantiated piece of propaganda. For example, bacon-wrapped, mozzarella stuffed, grass-fed beef, finished in a slightly glazed brioche bun = cheeseburger.

Turning back to Lilly, her still looking at him, their eyes lock firmly. Finally, resting back in her chair, as if she had been on edge until now, she nods, 'ok, what is it you want to know?'

Finally.

'The evening of her disappearance, you spoke to Amy when she arrived home. What time was that?'

'9:15pm.'

'What did you talk about?'

'James, mainly, and Erika. It was still stinging her, you know, she blamed herself for his death, for Erika's disappearance. Working for the NHS, she worries about everyone, you know, she cares, even for assholes like James,' she says. Her eyes glaze over and drift away in remembrance. 'But that night, she was different.'

'Different how?'

'She had something on her mind; I know she wanted to leave her apartment. She had been looking for a place closer to me.'

'And the messages she sent?'

'Well, that's where things turn a little strange. The first message said she loved me, and... she didn't feel safe in her apartment.'

'Really, how so?'

'Not sure, I mean, she was feeling funny in general, like someone was watching her.'

Thomas's heart stops.

Could she mean me?

But how?

'She was receiving letters, love letters, not sure who from, plus she had gotten it into her head things were out of place, like small items; perfume, hair clips... underwear,' again, her eyes drift away from his. 'I didn't pay much attention to it. She had a lot going on, with James, with work.'

Ok, thank God, not me then.

'And you informed the Police of this?'

'Of course,' her eyes quickly fix on his. 'Do you think it's linked?'

'I don't know, maybe,' he takes a moment before continuing, recognising the shaky ground he's about to venture into. 'Is it possible Amy just left? It's reported an overnight bag and some belongings are missing from her apartment?'

'No,' she says.

'Maybe she was stressed....'

'She didn't fucking leave, ok?'

Her tone and icy conviction are enough to end this line of questioning.

'Ok,' he says, meeting her eyes. 'What about the last message sent at 01:03am?'

Looking at him, her eyes, their shade, darken. Turning, she looks out through the window, back across the street, back to her shop. Wiping her eyes, she sniffles and turns back to her coffee. Seeing her hurt in such a way, the not knowing, the fire in her eyes and words, has Thomas wanting to reach across the table.

Don't you dare; sit right where you are.

Brushing the fringe from her face, her eyes find Thomas's, and for the first time, she looks lost. With her strength, her armour, being stripped away, she sits exposed—a beautiful young woman lost in the jumble of her own life and the disappearance of her sister. Though impossible, Thomas's heart swells with feeling, so much so that when he thinks it might break, words rush to his lips, saving him the pain. 'I'm sorry, I truly am.'

'I don't need your sympathy, Thomas; I don't know you, understand?' She tells him, her eyes darkening once again.

Dropping his head, frustrated by her guard, Thomas says, 'I understand.'

'Amy's last message, I know for a fact, wasn't from her.'

Looking up, Thomas asks, 'why?'

Collecting her handbag from the floor, placing it down on the table, a flowery Ted Baker-type, she pulls her phone from the cluttered contents. Unlocking it, she begins scrolling.

'Lilly, I'm sorry,' she reads. 'And you'll hate me, but I must leave,' Lilly reads. 'James, Erika, too much has happened, and I see now there's no getting around this. I love you, mum and dad, but this is something I must do. I hope to see you again, love Amy.'

Growing cold, Thomas can only look across the table at her. Lilly's eyes, laced with tiny red veins, stare back at him. They share a moment, acknowledging the weight and the heavy insinuation staining Amy's words.

'How do you know it wasn't sent by Amy? I mean, it was from her phone?' Thomas asks with words as soft as he can make them.

'Two reasons. One, my sister never calls me Lilly. It's Lil, always. And two, she never referred to Erika by name, only as of *the model*.'

Nodding his head and noting her answer, Thomas asks, 'it's reported that Amy was suffering from depression before her disappearance?'

'Amy was taking medication, yes, but not because of what James did, or because of his death, but because of the assault years ago - James cheating on her upset her, but she's seen rock bottom, the darkest of times, trust me.'

'So, if she didn't send it and someone else did, they would have to know all about her, James, Erika, the affair,' Thomas says. 'I'm sorry, but I have to ask... the attack on Amy, was she raped?'

'Yes, two years ago. A cretin named Joe Briggs. He worked with her at the hospital, wouldn't leave her alone, always pestering her,' her eyes again flutter from him to the street, the rain and the darkening sky. 'It happened right there on hospital grounds, fucking laundry room, can you believe it? He choked her, tried to kill her, he thought he had to, with her passing out.'

'Sounds to me like Amy's a survivor.'

Looking at him, her eyes wide, for a moment, all her doubt, her strength, her reserve, is gone, stripped, again leaving her exposed.

'She is,' she agrees, nodding in thanks.

'Could he, this Joe Briggs, be involved in her disappearance?'

'I doubt it,' she says, snorting a laugh. 'He killed himself in prison, set himself alight in the mess hall, a match and lighter fuel, a perfect end to the man, wouldn't you agree?'

9

6 days before Amy goes missing...

Having spent the morning writing, plotting, and sketching out the book, Thomas again feels the pull of the hole, of Amy. Resisting the urge at first, he rearranged his corkboard, pinning pertinent topics and questions, attempting to find some order in all the chaos.

The letters/notes, what do they say?

Where were Amy and James heading back from the day he was killed?

Are there other similar disappearances matching Amy's and Erika's?

Having finally started to write, loosely and sporadically, Thomas is yet to fall into a comfortable rhythm or for how he wants to book to read. The voice, for now, remains unknown to him, hidden.

'Amy was a victim long before her disappearance. She was attacked years before, but later, mistreated by her partner, Amy now lingers, occupying space, unable to fill it. A flower continually clipped. A bird caged by her own heart. A slow killing of something so beautiful. A crime, long before her disappearance.'

Staring at his words, Thomas feels nothing. Now that he knows her, attributing such words to Amy doesn't just feel wrong, but instead improper and impersonal. Once, his work was described as *personal and beautifully written* and *a call to arms, a support blanket for voiceless victims.* Now, they couldn't feel more different. Looking at how he is skirting around the facts, Thomas considers whether he has it in him for another go-around. Writing a book, dedicating his time and life, he wonders whether he has the drive required for such a sacrifice.

Six days and she'll be gone.

Now at the wall, Thomas watches Amy uncomfortably take a seat beside a suited man while a second loiters ominously over by the bookcase. Obviously, both police officers, with one being tall and athletic, the other, as if contractually so, is a short ball of a man with a neatly trimmed moustache. Young and old, fresh and tired, the two men appear to have just walked off the set of an early evening television crime show.

While Thomas cannot hear what is being said, he can occasionally make out the odd word or phrases such as *Erika, disappearance*, and *your whereabouts.*

The taller of the two men leisurely works the room. His eyes scan, catalogue each item, mentally noting. He moves with a swagger, an assured weight to his shoulders, lending him an almost unfettered freedom as he walks around the room. Still, it's his eyes that give him away. Thomas can see his tell, his bluff, and the discrepancy in them. Investigating people, interviewing them like Thomas once did, you soon learn to spot the real from the fake, the proficient from the pretender. This is evidenced perfectly by the subtle way he steals glimpses of Amy's chest. With her sitting forward, perched on the end of the cushion, the slope of her right breast is visible through the narrow opening of her loose shirt.

Likewise, his older partner appears more interested in Amy's physical appearance than real police work. His view of her chest, while limited, is enough to have him foaming from his lips. Pitched together like pink stripes of fleshy lard, a flappy, swollen tongue licks at them with nervous excitement.

What it would be to be a woman.

Grace Kelly said it best, a women's hardest job is juggling wolves.

As if noticing this herself, Amy quickly adjusts her cardigan, pulling it tight across her chest.

Having earlier moved the desk to the wall with the paintings, matching it to its new position taken up by his future-self, Thomas can now access his laptop without leaving the hole. Diverting his eyes from the hole to the instant messenger, he finds it flashing with activity. Bending over, he reads before providing a response:

Peter: *I've got the number you wanted, for James's father, Ricky. I've sent it to your mobile.*

Thomas: *Thank you.*
Peter: *I'm still working on his mother and friends.*
Thomas: *Ok, keep me posted.*

Going back to the hole, finding James Ruck to have joined the group, Thomas sighs with a mixture of disappointment and annoyance. Stood just inside the living area, hands-on-hips, his eyes unable to contain an inner worry, a frantic fear jerks at his eyes, his neck muscles, heaving his chest through his neatly pressed Ralph Lauren shirt. His eyes move between the two officers, to Amy, and back as if following some invisible repeating circuit.

The two officers and James exchange what looks like unpleasantries. Following James, the two officers disappear down the hallway and out of sight. In their absence, Thomas's attention turns to Amy. Still sitting, her hands in her lap, her face low and dire- Thomas is left wanting to reach through the wall, to sit beside her, talk to her.

But I'll never get the chance.

A dullness falls over him. The woman before him, beautiful and hurt, is lost to him, and soon, when he watches her disappear, he knows with certainty he'll never see her again.

You don't know that.

Yet he does because women who disappear under mysterious circumstances almost always never return home.

Returning to the room, James stands, his eyes trained on Amy. Appearing like nothing more than a pair of dark cherries, they nonetheless speak of inner torment. With Amy failing to look at him, James crosses to the sofa, taking her seat.

Jumping up, Amy moves to the kitchen, away from James and his eager hands. Their conversation now appears heated. James's posturing, Amy animated, and though Thomas cannot make out what is being said, it is clear they are both unloading on one other. Reading her lips, with a 'fuck you,' Amy stomps from the room, with James, his confident stride now wavering, is quick to trail out behind her.

Left alone, Thomas takes the opportunity to collect his phone from the table. Reading the number provided by Peter, typing it into the keypad, Thomas calls James's father. A nervous beat, with it connecting, ringing and answered, his heart lurches with hesitation.

'Hello?' He says into the phone.

'Yes?' Comes a voice creeping in from the speaker.

'Mr Ruck?'

'Yes, and you are?'

'My name's Thomas William,' he says, scrambling for a pen and pad, moving around the table. 'I'm doing a piece on your son, James. I'm sorry for your loss. I know this must be a difficult time.'

Thomas cringes at the sound of his own voice, his impersonal words and obviously false tone.

The line goes quiet.

Listening, Thomas hears nothing except the pop and crackle of static.

'Hello, Mr Ruck?'

A long silence is replaced with breathing, low and distant.

'Yes, sorry. What is it you want to know?' Ricky asks, his voice a pained whisper.

'Well, I'm hoping to paint a clear and accurate picture of James, not focusing on his death or the disappearance of Erika Sobo, but to report on his life,' Thomas lies.

'Ok, well, he was a photographer, a great one too, mainly fashion stuff, but he also shot cars, events, glossy stuff.'

'I've seen his work, very striking,' Thomas says, lying still. 'And I understand Erika was one of his models?'

Another beat of silence.

'Yes, that's how they met. They worked alone, became friends, you know how it is. But, James, he was a good-looking guy, like me, and like me, he has a wandering eye, I mean, Erika wasn't the first.'

Frozen to the spot, Thomas's ear twitching. 'First?'

'Yeah, girls, I mean he loved Amy, he did, but when he got attention from those models, he couldn't help himself, guilty as charged, but I'm telling you, what people are saying about him, him killing Erika is utter bull, he had a temper, sure, he could get heated, but I taught him to never hurt women.'

Yeah, he's a saint. Like cheating somehow doesn't count.

Thomas pauses to breathe before asking, 'I understand. Did the Police ever interview him?'

Silence.

An uncomfortable beat between them. Strange, but Thomas can feel it through the line- the tension the question has generated.

'They did, yes, but like I said, he had nothing to do with it. But, I mean, sure he was angry with her, I mean Erika had got herself pregnant....'

Wait, what... did I hear him, right?

'Pregnant, Erika was pregnant?' Thomas stutters.

'Look, I've said too much already, have a good day,' Ricky ends the call.

Numb, Thomas stands, frozen.

Pregnant, well now...

Is that enough of a motive to want her out of the way?

Needing no time to consider it, knowing James, the type of man he is, vain and self-important, Thomas takes it as an absolute certainty.

His phone, ringing a second time, almost knocks him on his rump. Like electricity, it jolts him upright, leaving him on edge and stark.

'Hello, Ricky?' He says into the phone.

'Mr William?' Comes a strange voice.

Pulling the phone from his ear, checking the number on the screen, Thomas finds it listed as *withheld.*

'Yes, sorry, Thomas speaking.'

'I know what happened to Erika Sobo. Are you listening, Mr William? I know who killed her.'

Clambering over the table, returning to his pen and pad, panting, he asks, 'who, who is this?'

'A friend,' the voice crackles in from the darkness.

Male or female? The voice sounds more alien than human.

'How did you get my number?'

'Your post, ArmChairDics, this is the same Thomas William I'm speaking to?'

Shit.

Heat floods his face as embarrassment takes over. Having forgotten his post days earlier, up late, drunk, in need of a lead and in a moody stupor, Thomas uploaded the post online advertising his investigation into Amy and Erika's disappearance, leaving his mobile telephone number and full name. Having included a paragraph about being a published author and investigator of true crime, he only now realises how stupid this was.

'I am, yes, sorry. What can you tell me?'

A pause.

The line crackles with interference.

'You need to speak to a guy called Khaliq. Erika's ex-boyfriend.'

If Thomas had to guess, the voice, while reaching them faintly, possibly deliberately so, belongs to a female of European descent.

'Why?' Thomas asks.

'Before she went missing, he had his boys looking for her.'

'Ok, ok, and you are?'

'I've already told you, a friend.'

Another pop, static.

'What do I call you?' He presses.

'Road Runner, you can call me Road Runner, ok?'

'Thank you. This Khaliq, you think he killed Erika?'

'She owed him money so.'

A bit thin but money is always a good motive.

'Ok. How can I reach this Khaliq?'

'He runs things out of his shop, *Moonlight Toys*. You'll find the address online.'

'Ok, but...'

'That's enough to get you started, but understand Mr William, this Khaliq, men like him, the world they occupy... well, he's extremely dangerous.'

'Ok, why do you say that?'

Another beat.

'He's killed before,' she says in a whisper.

The line, full of static, darkness and unanswered questions, is vacated, leaving Thomas stranded, listening to a dead tone.

Closing the call, feeling indifferent, Thomas slowly returns to the wall and the hole. Amy and James now sit on the sofa, his arm around her, they watch television. They wear an expression of detachment, with a level of distress hiding below the surface. It is as if they know the truth, but both lack the strength to say what needs to be said.

After a while, Amy's expression changes, emotion pulling to the surface. Discomfort makes way for frustration, a red face, and anger. A boiling pot ready to...

Jumping up from the sofa as if electrocuted, Amy moves to the kitchen. With her back to James, head down, presumably speaking. James, peeling himself off the couch, rolling his eyes in frustration, trudges to the hallway. The two exchange words, what exactly, Thomas cannot make out, but James's demeanour appears flippant. His eyes, bored rather than tired, look at her as a parent might a child when acting out.

Finally, he leaves her alone. Disappearing, down the hall and around the corner, the sight of the man going breathes life back through Thomas's chest.

The man's dead, Thomas, jeez.

For a fleeting moment, surprising himself, Thomas feels a little compassion for the man and his father, who would outlive his son. Yet, a shadow crosses over him, a sickening thought, of himself, like Ricky having to live on without his child.

Don't think about it.

Thomas turns his attention back to Amy. Resting against the kitchen counter, her head down over the sink, her back heaving, rising and falling, panicked and shuddering. Though he wants to step away from the wall, to let her cry alone, Thomas instead lingers, like a ghost at her side.

Turning at the hip, Amy snaps her head round to face the hallway. A startled expression having chased the tears from her eyes, she stands pensive, anxious, frightened even.

Had she heard something?

Expecting to see James's return, she is instead greeted by shadows as she moves to the dark strip of space. Her shoulders having pulled back, her hands shaking at her sides, she approaches the area as you might a haunted house. Like James, Amy leaves the room following his steps, her form shrinking into the shadows until the darkness takes her in whole.

She'll be fine; she doesn't disappear today.

Unless they got it wrong?

The question brings with it a thudding to Thomas's chest.

She's gone, and I'll never see her again.

Quit it.

A ping from his pocket, though a welcome diversion, rattles at his nerves. Removing his phone and studying the screen, he grimaces.

> **Mum:** *Hi Tom, I hope the move went all ok. I only ask because I haven't heard from you. I'll pop over as soon as the invite arrives! Maybe if you could ask Mary, I would love to see Robin? I could*

bring lunch? Anyway, I hope the job hunting is going well. I'll leave it with you. Love Mum.

Thomas sighs a long, painful, soul exorcising sigh, leaving him all but collapsing back in his chair. Thomas considers responding, but the comment regarding job hunting irritates him. Not just because he's a writer but because his mother knows as well as anyone his plan for this apartment, his solitude, and a forthcoming next book. Plus, since she took him in after Mary and he sold their house, and subsequently him moving back out, it was as if something sat between them, like some unresolved matter. What exactly, Thomas isn't sure- fear in what she might say, shame in his lack of progress, or guilt from the fact he still owes her rent.

All the above?

Deciding to leave it for now, unable to deal with it, getting up, Thomas steps to the wall. Before the painting, closing his eyes, he shakes his head, smiling in recognition at how stupid he is acting.

Thomas returns his attention to Amy. Just inside the living area, Amy stands holding an envelope. Staring down at it, she regards it as someone might a dog turd.

Pulling a neatly folded sheet of paper clear of the envelope, Amy swallows hard as she opens it. A pressed violet drops free from the page, swirling, before landing at her feet. Reading whatever is written, her face whitens, her eyes cloud over. A series of shudders ripple through her, dropping the letter.

Amy rushes to the sink and vomits.

I need to know what that letter says.

A noise, faint, distant, has Thomas spin on her heels. Recalling Peter's words, *'wait, someone else is with you,'* Thomas eyes the shadowed hallway suspiciously. Moving to it gingerly, he stops before passing the threshold. Narrow, short and shadowed, it awaits his arrival with seemingly sinister intent. Flipping on the light, a single bare bulb hanging at the end of the hallway blinks on. Watching the hallway, Thomas stands back, unable to proceed any further. Instead, he listens intently, though he is unsure why and what he expects to hear.

'Fucking stupid,' he mutters.

Shaking his head, he turns and clicks off the light. This gesture is met by a noise, faint, almost masked by the rain as it creeps along the hallway to meet him. Taking it for movement, not of a person, but of the building, a second thud rips the breath from his lips. This time, possibly a displacement of something, closing or opening.

Turning back, attempting to trace the sound, his unblinking eyes sting and water. Swallowing hard, Thomas stares into the waiting space. The darkness there is all but absolute. Thomas hesitates as the hair on the back of his neck, and his forearms stand up in unison.

The front doors locked, dipshit, there's no one getting in here.

In his mind, he sees a lurking figure, watching him, ready to leap from the shadows, a butcher's knife in hand, stalking him, prepared to kill.

Don't be absurd.

Yet still, he stands rooted to the spot, unable to move.

'Hello?' He calls out.

He shudders as his voice echoes uncomfortably through the apartment. It takes incredible effort to again reach out and flick on the light, so much so that he surprises himself when he does just that.

With the bulb popping on, flooding the space with bright vanilla tinted light, he takes one shaky step forward. While his feet follow his command, they do so with what feels like lead plates in his socks.

Coming to the bathroom, Thomas stares into the blackened room. Pressing the light switch, the shadows gathered in the cramped space dissolve like butter in the haze of bright light. The room is how he left it, the towels flung over the bath, the small collection of items cluttered around the sink.

He checks the bedroom before leaving, beneath the bed, the wardrobe.

Nothing.

No crazed axe-wielding madman.

No masked lunatic.

No spectres, no demons.

Of course not.

Yet still, a lingering shadow occupies his attention, his mind squeezing in on him. A cold sweat sneaks in beneath his clothes, leaving his hands shaking, dragging a nervous laugh through his lips.

I'm haunted by goddamn shadows.

And so very alone.

10

3 days before Amy goes missing...

It's 10:37pm, James is dead, and Amy stands alone in the kitchen with a look of utter dejection. Or is it detachment? Not just sad, but distant, like she's lost something, or more to the point, as if something has been stolen.

Amy returns to the dirty mugs from earlier coffee but again stops to stare off into space. A victim of a long line of hardship, Amy has suffered far more than anyone should. From her rape and attempted murder at the hands of Joe Briggs, James's affair, and then his accidental death, right up to her disappearance and murder...

You don't know she's dead; there's still time.

Thomas considers the unfairness of life and how some people get lucky, and others don't. How some get to see out every day of a privileged life, while the rest, like Amy, are continually forced to overcome turmoil and loss. Then, only after overcoming the odds are they cruelly snatched from the world, like survivors of cancer or the businessman who missed his flight before 9/11, only to die two months later when crossing the street. Either way, fate, penance, rules of nature, or plain old dumb luck, life can be so unfair, well, for some anyway. Others, the lucky ones, get to see out their days with not just luxury but with freedom and options. Of late, such thoughts have begun to plague Thomas. Destiny, karma, foreordination nonsense, hell, even religion. Now, seeing both the future and past, with the impossible being possible, he is left to wonder if this was the plan all along. As in, guided by some higher power. The failure of his second, third, and fourth book, Mary divorcing him, somehow led him to this one-bed shithole, a hole in a wall, and Amy.

Of course, he realises this is a mere fantasy, a way to avoid responsibility for his failures. He is an observer, a man sitting on the periphery of life.

Returning his gaze back to Amy, now done with the washing up, loss, guilt, and separation all tug at her face, competing, darkening her features. The long day, its weight now sits heavy on her shoulders.

The morning started with Amy waking early. She attempted to eat breakfast but instead drank two cups of coffee. Then, after disappearing to shower and dress, she reappeared wearing a conservative black dress, matching tights and flat shoes. Sombre and trance-like, Thomas watched her drink another mug of coffee before removing a photograph from a frame. She studied it for what seemed like the longest time. Finally, she cried, alone, her and the picture, then returned to the bathroom, where presumably she went about re-applying her makeup. Taking it with her, securing the photograph in her purse, Amy left the apartment just before 11am.

And Thomas was left alone once again.

With her attending James's funeral, Thomas left the hole alone, and for a time anyway, he had attempted to write. When it didn't stick, he tried to research aspects of the case, from Khaliq to James Ruck and his photography work. His website, while still live, has gone quiet since his death. Glossy, well put together, the site appears far better, more professional than Ruck's work portfolio. James's work followed a familiar theme of female models in bikinis, driving sports cars, sunbathing, exploring foreign locations. And while splashed with colour, sun and pomp, MTV-video-like, his work presents as obviously deliberate, lacking natural creativity or flair, and utterly void of all human warmth. Like statues, unable to capture the life and soul within, the images are nothing more than toned bodies, moody stares and a general lack of inspiration.

In fact, it was enough to leave Thomas hunched, looming over the keys, dejected, wallowing in a passive stupor. He skulked about the apartment, pacing the floor in heavy stomps. He called Peter, StarKiller, and Mary, and like always, Robin couldn't come to the phone- homework with Lewis yet again. Unlike him, everyone, the entire world it would seem, was busy, all with someplace to be.

When Amy returned to the apartment, she did so with Lilly and their parents. Where their dad, Nigel Porter, a tall 6.2 retired lorry driver, mainly stood with his hands in his pockets, a look of 'how do I comfort my daughter?' slapped across his awkward face, their mother, Lynn, a beautiful seamstress with an ageing face fully embracing her twilight years, had been busy- hoovering, dusting, flipping the sofa cushions.

Thomas stood and watched the four of them together, drinking coffee, chatting. Good people, well-rounded, ready as a family to leave the shadow of James Ruck behind, unaware of the darkness still awaiting them on the horizon.

When their parents left a little after 9pm, Lilly, for a time, stayed with Amy. Sat on the sofa, they finished their coffee, spoke in what looked like low tones, and embraced, both unaware of the envelope sitting over at the kitchen counter.

Thomas is unsure of its significance, but he is confident it wasn't there when Amy left this morning. Instead, someone with access to her apartment had placed it there, and in watching the apartment sporadically, Thomas had missed that someone who'd delivered it.

But who, who has keys?

Mr Chen?

Her landlord could have dropped it off, Thomas considers, it is possible, but it does seem unlikely. A breach of privacy, an invasion of space, yet if they were friends, he might feel comfortable doing so. While Thomas makes a mental note to check with Lilly, the envelope has a striking resemblance to the one Amy received days earlier.

Now alone, done with the washing up, standing disconnected and indifferent, no longer crying, Amy wipes her puffy cheeks. Drained, hollow, her eyes stare off across the living area. If not for her chest's slight rise and fall, Thomas would take the image as a freeze-frame.

Watching her, Thomas's gaze flips to the envelope propped up against the wine rack and back, waiting for her to notice it.

Moving again, leaving the room, Thomas follows Amy as she disappears into the bedroom. Pulling his face back from the wall, he rubs a hand over his tired, turgid skin. Stroking down his beard, closing his eyes, he sighs with fatigue. Upon opening them, he finds them unresponsive and heavy.

A buzz and a ping from the table have Thomas turning with the weariness of someone far older. Collecting up his phone, needing the wall for support, he opens the phone to a message from Mary:

> **Mary:** *Robin's recital, Thursday, don't forget. She's excited to play for you, so please don't mess this up.*

A warmth of anger rises within him, superheating his skin. He considers how to respond. Kind and thankful, or with profanity. Closing his eyes, breathing, he instead decides on:

> **Thomas:** *Thank you. I'll be there, I promise.*

Back at the hole, Thomas finds Amy standing, her back rigid, stark, her eyes transfixed on the envelope. With her stricken expression, Thomas finally understands the gravity of what it means. Thomas had been right; it hadn't been there before. Her sick-filled eyes act as a visual confirmation.

Looking over her shoulder, spinning, Amy studies the room, her head and eyes checking all four corners. Her puffy face, makeup-less, now flush and pale, twitches as her eyes blink wildly. Snatching a knife from the block on the counter, Amy turns, dashes for the hallway, down it, clicking on the light as she goes, before disappearing around the hallway's juncture.

She's leaving?

Sweating, Thomas waits for her return with bated breaths, each one kicking out from his chest like some inner creature dying to get out.

Reappearing holding the knife, moving with purpose, she disappears into the bedroom.

She checked, possibly locked the front door?

Emerging again, peering into the bathroom, she returns to the living area, her feet a blur of motion. Over at the kitchen counter, her face now red and constrained, placing the knife down, Amy snatches up the envelope and tears it open with such utter disdain Thomas can feel it through the wall, in his chest. As she reads, her grip on the paper clenches into fists, creasing the page, turning her knuckles white.

Even from his limited view, Thomas recognises the letter as being in the same style as the one she received days earlier. As she unfolds the single sheet of paper, with another pressed violet dropping free, Thomas takes it as a certainty.

How many did she get?

Now read, she slams the note down, and in the same action, Amy moves along the counter and scoops up her phone. Punching in the numbers; boom... boom... boom.

999?

Speaking into the phone, she does so in an energised, animated fashion - left hand to her ear, her right, busy posturing, gesturing.

So, she reported it to the Police, yet it appears it wasn't followed up.

Thomas continues to watch her, her red face darkening with frustration, her gestures becoming laboured with disappointment.

Thomas concludes that she was being stalked before her disappearance, receiving yet another letter days before her last sighting.

A coincidence?

But you don't believe in coincidences, remember?

Finally done with the call, Amy removes the phone from her ear and falls back on her heels. Concerned she might collapse; Thomas is relieved when she takes support from the kitchen counter. Panting, her demeanour is one of release, the dissipation of adrenaline.

Or from fear?

It is now she cries.

With angry tears, fists slamming the countertop, and though impossible, Thomas is sure he can feel the concussions, one after another, until she collapses to the floor, utterly dejected, appalled, leaving her retching.

11

1 day before Amy goes missing...

Thomas is running out of time. He knows this, yet he is left floundering. His fading mind and body, his resolve, as with every other challenge in his life, now falters, flirting him with utter failure. Worse still are the persistent headaches, the type beyond sleep and medication. The stress-filled kind, twisting behind his eyes like barbwire, that of a man with a catalogue of disappointments, false starts, and wasted time. Not to be outdone by an upset stomach and an irritable bowel, like an electrified current, the pain bounces around his skull with jubilant enthusiasm.

Spending at least ten hours each day spread between the hole, writing, drinking wine, little has been left for himself, for sleep. Then, when he does sleep, his dreams are nightmare filled. He sees Amy and, Lilly, Mary, all at the mercy of some faceless monster. Tall and hulking, his face obscured behind black tights, he stomps through the nightmare, wielding all manner of horrific tools and implements.

Rape.

Torture.

Murder.

And not always in that order.

Why?

Thomas cannot say, but it's clear that in watching the past, the present has now become haunted. Shadows now gnaw at the fringes of this new reality, darkening it. The nightmares cling to Thomas, more than a burden; they shackle him, bleeding him slow like some insidious wound.

Earlier, when Thomas managed to shower, he had failed to shave.

He was too tired.

He's always tired.

Washing his hair and body was taxing enough for one day. Then, he put a wash on and hoovered, but got bored partway through, so he abandoned the project.

He then spent time with the paintings, removing them from the wall, from his apartment and Amy's, inspecting them under lamp light for over an hour. Side by side comparison, internet research, he found nothing of note, except the names written on the back, scribbled on the paper backing—*Grace* on the ones in his apartment, *Marlene* on Amy's.

Grace and Marlene.

Thomas wonders who they might be.

The artist(s)?

Their inspiration?

A dedication?

Hell, they could merely be the people who had the paintings framed.

Either way, given the painting's age and the lack of any disenable markings, and while doubting he'll ever know for sure, Thomas continued his investigation regardless. Loosening the frames backing paper, he found nothing hidden, nothing of note whatsoever. Thomas was hoping, naively, for an explanation for all this. He pictured himself finding some secret message, a letter explaining the paintings, the hole and why it offers a view into the past and future.

But of course, this was not the case.

After the lengthy inspection, after scrutinising every inch of the paintings, all six of them, Thomas was left just as clueless as to when he started. Before returning the frames, he examined the adjoining wall for what must be the tenth time. The size of a five-pence piece bored out through the outer plaster, the brickwork, the hole is a perfect cylinder. It is smooth, almost impossibly so, like the inside of a gun barrel but cleaner somehow. Approximately 50cm in length, Thomas considered running a pencil through it. But, with no way of knowing what good it might do or what earth-shaking cataclysm it might lead to, he decided against it.

The butterfly effect had come to mind—the phenomenon whereby a minute localized change in a complex system can have large effects elsewhere. Meaning, small things can have non-linear impacts on a complex system, as in, one small incident in the past can have a big impact on the future.

His future.

Cause and effect but magnified.

Like the concept imagined with a butterfly flapping its wings but causing a typhoon, the unknown had scared Thomas enough to leave the hole alone. Like *Fichte* once wrote, *"you could not remove a single grain of sand from its place without thereby ... changing something throughout all parts of the immeasurable whole,"* the words echoed in Thomas long after returning the painting to their hooks.

A bottle of wine and a microwaved Lasagne later, Thomas is back at the wall, watching Amy and her sister. He wants to leave them alone, allow them some privacy in these last few days, but any detail could be crucial, no matter how small or insignificant it might seem.

Last few days, you make it sound like she's dead.

Thomas considers this again, the circumstances of her disappearance, and its inconsistencies. *Disappeared doesn't mean dead,* he tells himself and tries his damndest to believe it.

The two sisters sit crossed legged on the rug, a selection of Chinese takeout cartons between them. Drinking from brown, stubby-beer bottles, Thomas laughs along with them, watching Lilly struggle with chopsticks. With every scoop of chow-mein, the noodles slither from her sticks, leaving her the tiniest morsel.

They chuckle, eat, drink, and for a moment, like Amy, Thomas is spared the truth, shielded from the reality of what's to come.

It doesn't last.

Sadness falls over Amy like a veil, darkening her features. Spotting this, Lilly drags over an open laptop. Wrapping an arm across her sister's shoulders, waiting as she wipes her cheeks, they focus on the screen together.

Squinting, straining with the distance, Thomas does recognise the property website they sit viewing.

Huddled over the screen, scrolling through new homes, apartments, different buildings and interiors, they stop on one to discuss it but then move on.

Thomas casts his mind back to what Lilly had told him: *She didn't feel safe in her apartment,'* and *'I mean, she was feeling funny in general, like someone was watching her.'*

Thomas concludes with certainty – before her disappearance, Amy was being stalked. Because of this, she was preparing to leave Pinegrove for new pastures. This leaves two theories that hold weight. The first, Amy was about to move out, and someone acted before she could. And two, Amy just up and left.

From what he's witnessed so far and from what Lilly has told him, it is clear that Amy wanted to leave; plus, with her belongings being missing, it is plausible that Amy decided to get away and start afresh somewhere new. But, of course, this explanation would go against Lilly's belief. It's cold and straightforward, but her leaving does fit. Sexually assaulted and almost murdered, only later to be deceived by the boyfriend, before watching horrifically killed. Not forgetting the letters were unwanted and appeared to cause her great distress. With that in mind, Thomas concludes that it is wholly possible that Amy did up and left, or worse, went somewhere to end her own life. It's not uncommon to hear of people packing up their things before disappearing, only to be found later dead in a forest somewhere.

Still, Thomas remains unconvinced.

In watching Amy, her daily struggles, her desire to fix her life, to Thomas, her then deciding to run away or kill herself seems like an utter contradiction.

Watching on, with Thomas's mood darkening with the situation's absolute weight, he quickly recognises that watching Amy is like watching her ghost, like the damned, wandering among the living. Like CCTV footage, the type released by the Police, showing people now missing, those presumed dead, them going about their lives, utterly unaware of their fate, lurking, waiting to snatch them from the world. It is something that's always unsettled Thomas, the last known footage of missing people. Like that of Brian Shaffer, the second-year medical student at Ohio State who disappeared during a night out with friends. While CCTV captured the twenty-year-old entering the Ugly Tuna bar, he was never seen leaving for unknown reasons. Instead, the footage showed Brian drinking, chatting with friends, completely unaware of the dark mystery awaiting him. Brian Shaffer was never seen or heard from again, disappearing in plain sight, as if erased from existence.

'Fate, chasing it, tied to it, forever burdened by it.'

Recalling his father's words, them tugging at his heart, Thomas again struggles with their meaning. The words, so bleak, almost hopeless, he takes for *control,* or lack of it- as in, what will be will be, no matter the path we follow.

You can't change what happens to her.

You do understand, right?

Thomas reminds himself, fate is already determined, but he can't shake the feeling there might be a way, somehow, if he...

Forget it.

Shaking the stupidity from his head, he again focuses on the two sisters. Seeing them laugh, them zeroing in on a new place to live, while not happy, now out from the shadow of James Ruck, they appear at least hopeful for the future. But, knowing the truth makes it all the more painful, the bleak future laid out for both Amy and her sister. Thomas finds he can no longer watch. It's a cruel joke, a dark irony, a piece of evil theatre, a cross to bear, one Thomas takes as what fate has chosen for him.

A chance at redemption?

While he considers this, Thomas is quick to dismiss it.

More like punishment.

Chest heavy, his mind gloomy and depressed, Thomas leaves Amy and Lilly alone. Heading to bed, intent on sleep, he fears what waits for him there, what evil creature lurking in his subconscious, ready to pull him down into the darkness.

12

The day of Amy's disappearance...

Queasy, bend over the toilet, Thomas vomits—no half measures. While thin due to a lack of food, it is eye-stingingly potent due to toxic levels of wine seeping through his veins. It smashes the bowl in the form of a pale imitation of cheap merlot, staining the water a cloudy ruby-pink colour.

Having laced a glass of water with salt, hunched over, Thomas fully intends to retch until his stomach is empty. To function, to process everything about to unfold, he recognises the need to be on an even keel.

Finally done, he flushes the toilet and moves to the sink. Splashing his face with water from the cold tap, he spends a moment washing the sick from his beard. Stopping, he finds himself in the mirror. Looking back at him is a dull, colourless mask of a man he once knew. Once youthful and handsome, this new Thomas is nothing more than a cruel imitation.

'You can't save her,' Thomas tells himself.

Nausea is now replaced with a hollow hole at his core.

'All you can do is watch, learn, and record what happened, nothing more,' he adds.

Thomas checks his watch after leaving the bathroom, flicking off the light, moving along the hallway to the living area.

8:35pm.

In a minute or two, Amy leaves the COOP and heads for home.

He checks his phone; the battery sits at 93% charge.

Ok, good.

Crossing the room to the wall, the desk is prepared, it sits ready with a fresh pad and pen. Stopping before it, Thomas turns back and considers pouring himself a glass of wine. Over at the kitchen, a two-thirds full bottle sits open, a clean glass beside it. Moving to the waiting bottle, as if pulled by an invisible force, the force only alcohol has, he stops before it.

Not tonight. I need a clear mind.

Yet still, looking down at the bottle, the pull of it, the alcohol, is sickeningly overwhelming. Picking it up, looking at the label; a cheap cabernet. Turning to the sink, Thomas drops the bottle's contents down the plughole.

Glug... glug... glug...

Breathing deeply, he attempts to collect himself.

Another check of the watch.

8:40pm.

She'll be home soon.

Soon it will be over.

And she'll be gone.

Forever.

Moving back to the wall, the hole, his legs a little giddy beneath his weight, he checks Amy's apartment. Dark except for light slanting through the window blinds in blades of streetlight orange. Searching the space, his eyes work the darkness.

Nothing.

No movement.

No one lurking, no one waiting in the shadows.

With the COOP being two hundred meters up the hill, minutes away by foot, Thomas decides to wait at the hole. But, with the waiting, nausea returns, along with the feeling of utter helplessness.

After tonight, I'll never see her again.

This realisation is like a sledgehammer, knocking him back from the wall, leaving his eyes welling and blurred, his hands shaking.

How can I live, knowing I'll never see her again?

With the appearance of spilling tears in his eyes, a series of convulsions are sent down through his body. Something shifts inside him. A deep clogging at his chest, his tummy, his core as he struggles to maintain even a shred of dignity. Like a conveyor belt of memories and feelings, they hit him with the force of a hurricane—Mary, Amy, his career… and Robin.

Funny how Robin came last on the list.

Loss, bitterness and anger rise up and compete before exploding through his wet eyes. Finally, in release, sobbing uncontrollably, unable to stop them anyway, Thomas lets the tears fall.

Falling to his knees, lightheaded, as the surge drains away, shame and regret leave him as if expelled through his tears.

In his mind, he sees Robin smiling, playing with LEGO out in the garden.

His little girl.

His only child.

I love her, I do, and I'll be different.

The intercom buzzes, and with it comes a terrible truth. One he's forgotten.

Robin's recital.

Wiping his face with his shirt sleeve, dragging himself up to his feet, Thomas moves across the room. Hesitating, the receiver buzzes again, and though impossible, the sound is now somehow far more urgent. Lifting it from the cradle, Thomas whispers, as if all energy has left him, 'hello.'

'Thomas, let me up, please.'

Mary.

Buzzing her in, swallowing hard, Thomas checks his watch for the one-hundredth time.

8:52pm.

His eyes move to the wall, the hole, and Amy, who is soon to arrive home.

'Fuck,' Thomas hisses.

The sound of a thumping fist at the front door, whilst expected, startles him. Leaving the room for the hallway, turning on the light, Thomas chases the bare bulb as it flicks on. At the entrance, pausing, he braces himself for the wrath surely waiting for him beyond the door.

Oh boy.

Opening the door, Mary stands, hands down at her sides, her face, her eyes, both vacant.

'Mar, I'm sor….' He starts, but his words are slapped from his lips.

'You're an asshole,' she spits.

Heat sears across his left cheek. Running a hand across it adds to the intensity, leaving it sizzling.

Leading her inside, Thomas says, 'I guess you better come in.'

Following him into the living area, her eyes burning holes into his back, expecting to receive another slap, Thomas turns to face her, expecting the worse.

Chest heaving, eyes billowy, she works on her lower lip, chewing with angry energy.

'Why?' She asks. 'What's your excuse this time?'

Licking his lips, he considers the words to use. But, out of excuses, finding words to have deserted him, he cannot look at her.

'Nothing?' She presses.

Taking a deep breath, Thomas shifts his eyes from the floor to her, but Mary's glare, her fierce stare, has him again returning his gaze to the floor.

'I'm working on something, a book, it's been intense, and....' His words tail off as his eyes are again drawn back to the hole.

I'm going to miss it.

'And what, that it?' She snaps. 'Do you know how your daughter is this evening, do you, crying, crying in my fucking arms?'

'Ok, Mar, look....'

'Will you stop with the Mar? It's Mary, and you don't get to call me that anymore, understand?'

'Yes, I'm sorry, I'll call her, I'll make it right, I promise.'

'No, you won't. You owe me an explanation, Thomas, you can't treat us this way,' her words catch in her throat.

'Us?' He asks.

'Fuck you, Thomas,' her face now enraged.

'Why are you here, Mary? We could have done this over the phone?'

'Don't turn this on me. You don't get to do...'

'I'm sorry, I....'

'You're sorry, what is our daughter supposed to think? It's not fair, breaking her heart like this, it's cruel, just so cruel.'

Seeing tears in her eyes, her strength abandoning her, her pregnant belly, Thomas drops his head. 'I'm sorry, truly I am, and I'll make it up to her.'

'That's the thing, what I don't think you truly get – you'll make it up to her, and I'm sure you will, but missing her recital, it doesn't affect you, sure you feel sad for upsetting her, but it's the fact it wasn't important enough for you to be there. You fight for custody because you think it's what you should do, not what you want to do.'

Looking at him, her eyes glassy and dark, Thomas can no longer read her expression. Sure, she wants to say more, but Thomas can only watch her leave, her long coat billowing behind her. The slamming of the door leaves Thomas with a new sickness in his stomach. A hollow, deep cold, and silence, as if the world around him has all gone quiet.

Shamed, his gaze returns to the hole, to Amy.

You must look, don't let missing Robin's recital be for nothing.

Returning to the wall, he is relieved to see light poking through from the other side, but to his horror, Amy is nowhere to be seen.

13

9:35pm...

Amy's apartment is lit by three lamps, warmly but indirectly, leaving most of the room and the hallway beyond draped in shadow. Having been at the hole for fifteen minutes and having not seen Amy, concern has now firmly turned to fear.

I've missed it.

Checking his watch: 9:36pm.

Lilly said Amy called her at 9:15pm when she got home.

Yeah, and where is she?

Thomas scans the hallway, looking for movement, but finds nothing. Staring, straining against the clotted shadows, towards the bedroom, its doorway all but cloaked by the gloom, he can make out a thin strip of light but not much else.

Someone's in there.

Come on, Amy, where are you?

Thomas waits and waits and waits. Forced to, he cannot do anything else but stand like a fool.

Still, she is yet to reappear.

Leaving the wall, Thomas rushes from the room to use the toilet. He splashes his face with cold water. Before leaving, he relieves himself a second time.

Returning to the hole, whispering, 'please be there, please be there,' his breath catches when he sees her. With Amy's bedroom door pulled open, spilling yellow light into the hall, Amy appears from the doorway. Just the sight of her, all wet haired and showered, in shorts and an overly baggy t-shirt, a wave of electricity rifles through him, energising his muscles, bringing him back to life.

With eager eyes, Thomas tracks Amy all the way. Along the hallway, out of the shadows, into the light of the living area. With a mobile phone to her ear, her expression is pensive, her deposition- urgent. There is a stutter to her movement, a kind of affliction to it. Looking over her shoulder, with wide eyes, she checks the room, all four corners. After what seems like the longest time, her stark, upright posture slackens, her tight shoulders slowly ease.

Ok, so that's the call she made to Lilly.

Done with the phone, Amy moves to the kitchen to a half-finished bottle of wine waiting at the counter. Dragging a glass across the counter to meet it, she pauses before filling it. Pushing the glass back to its original position, she carries the bottle to the sink, where she pours the contents away.

My god.

Looking over his shoulder at the sink, to the empty bottle of wine he too expelled earlier, and that call of fate, destiny from before, returns. Still pondering this, he returns to the hole. Now preparing soup at the hob, Amy empties a can into a pan. The gloppy orange contents hint at tomato or minestrone. Head down, she stirs the soup with a wooden spoon in slow rhythmic swirls. He watches on, such a benign action, yet still, his heart makes a wreck of his nerves.

Thomas checks his watch

9:50pm.

24 minutes until she sends the first of the two messages.

Before he can get back to Amy, his phone buzzes at the desk as if feeling left out. Shuddering across the surface, the rattle fills the room with bone-jarring energy. Snatching it up from the table. A new message reads:

Lilly: *Can we meet? Tomorrow?*

Staring at the phone, dumbfounded, he shakes his head. Both excited by her message and terrified in equal measure, he responds:

Thomas: *Hi. Sure, where?*
Lilly: *Mine, 8pm? I'll send you my address.*

Thomas: *Ok, see you then.*

Warmth surges through him, from his chest, his arms, down through his legs.

Why does she want to see me?

She's found something, a new clue?

Or, he considers, maybe she just wants to see *him.*

Can't resist my charms?

In his mind, he sees himself entering her apartment, a warmly lit, sensual place of fantasy, and her, Lilly, fixing him a drink.

Get real.

Thomas returns to the wall.

9:55pm.

Nineteen minutes till Amy sends the first text.

Amy, now moved, with her back to Thomas, stands looking down the hallway. Her position, two meters from him, blocks his view of what she is looking at. Noting her stance - her right foot slightly ahead of the left, the rise and fall of her shoulders, her fisted hands at her side.

Someone's in there with her.

But how?

If you'd been watching, you'd know.

Feeling heat swarm his cheeks, he kicks himself for being distracted by the laptop, his phone, for letting Mary up to unsettle, scramble his mind.

He asks himself, 'What was I supposed to do, not answer?'

Yes, asshole, you stay focused when presented with a gift like this.

And Robin, she simply needs to suck it up, is that right?

Ignoring himself, running a hand over his face, stroking down his beard, he shakes his head with utter frustration. Returning to the hole- Amy, moving forward, leaves the room, stopping at the end of the hallway. Facing the front door, seemingly happy, she turns and disappears into her bedroom.

Returning to the hallway, being gone for no more than a few seconds, she checks the bathroom before hustling back to the living area. As if in competition, both confusion and worry wrung her features, leaving her with a look of utter despondency. Twitching, her head darts about as if tormented by some invisible intruder.

Like the Invisible Man?

Whatever.

Well, that's how it appears to him, nonetheless. He recalls the movies, the different iterations, from Claude Raines's 1933 portrayal of the title character to the most recent version with Elisabeth Moss. Amy moves in the same jittery way, haunted or insane, but hopeless all the same.

Leaving the room again, Amy disappears, either to exit the apartment or to check the front door and locks. Reappearing again, peering into the bathroom, Amy takes her time before turning and heading into the bedroom.

Again, Thomas is forced to await her return.

Something could be happening right now, and I'm unable to see it.

So, again, Thomas waits.

His helpless form twitches against the wall.

His eye fixed, fighting the need to blink, the strain from the stare starting to sting, blurs his vision with swirls of fog. He wants to cry, sob, and run his fist through the wall—anything to put an end to the agonising wait.

At the bedroom door, shadows shift. Amy reappears but looks confused. She again checks the bathroom, her head snapping inside the door frame, searching. Thomas notes her expression as being unsatisfied and agitated. Watching her move into the living area, tracking her all the way, Amy collects her phone from the kitchen counter and begins typing.

Thomas again checks his watch: 10:14pm.

First text sent.

So, if Amy locked the door, no one was getting in there.

Yeah, and what about the letters she was getting?

Someone delivered them, someone with access to her apartment.

Moving back to the wall, to the hole, shock-like ice runs through him, turning his blood cold. Amy stands a foot from the wall, staring at him with wide, almost feral eyes.

Oh Shit.

14

10:25pm...

Thomas stands frozen to the spot. His eye to the hole, and Amy, inches from the adjoining wall, pushes her head forward to meet him.

She's going to see me.

Snapping his head backwards, but not before her eye fills the space, Thomas turns to his laptop and proceeds to fiddle with the keys.

Smooth, like she won't think you're spying on her.

He waits and ponders this, all the while drowning in the moment. Slowly, turning his head back to the hole, he considers his next move.

How does this alter things, her seeing me?

Regardless, she disappears tonight, and I need to watch her no matter how uncomfortable it is.

Unless, by her seeing me, I can change it?

This possibility brings fresh tears to his eyes. Warm, salty tears sting as they form, distorting his vision. Swallowing hard, he returns to the hole with a new kick of adrenaline. At first, confused by darkness from the other side, with a flicker, Thomas quickly recognises it as an eye.

Amy's eye.

In shock, Amy jerks her head back. She mouths something unreadable before thrusting her eye back to the hole. As if now playing some type of invisible tug of war with their heads, he mirrors her action by pulling back.

Breathing hard, panting, Thomas stops.

Think damn it, think.

Lifting his hands is all he can think to do. Palms showing as if in peace, mouths the words, 'I mean you no harm.'

Slowly, stepping back to the wall, taking a deep breath, he looks through the hole with bated breath. Amy again pulls back, but this time slowly, her eyes aflutter with confusion and thought. With narrowing eyes, anger builds on her face, reddening it. Turning, Amy bolts for the hallway, on the way, collecting up her keys from the kitchen counter.

She's coming here.

Stepping back from the wall, Thomas turns to face the hallway, waiting for the sound of angry fists pounding on wood.

Now sweating, he waits, confused... and it clicks. It will never come.

Because it's the past.

Back at the wall, he awaits her return.

Thomas pictures her at his door, a fist sending a thunder of concussions through the wood. Her then waiting, furious and desperate, her face in pain. He quickly recognises the hole, and his actions have only added to her list of ordeals.

Stomping, she appears from the hallway. Out of breath, she heads to the kitchen and begins rooting through a drawer. Returning to the wall, holding a marker pen and a pad. Taking a moment to write a message, Amy thrusts the paper at the hole:

PERVERT, ANSWER THE FUCKING DOOR

Ok, so how the hell am I supposed to explain this?

Lifting a finger, indicating the need for a moment of pause, he turns and bends over the table. Gathering up a pen and pad of his own, breathing hard, he puffs out his chest and attempts, in vain, to settle himself.

Ok, you can do this. You can save her.

So, no pressure.

In writing, the words are a blur upon the page. Holding up the pad to the hole, Thomas attempts to steady his jittery hands.

My name is Thomas William. And I know you have no reason to trust me, but you must, please

Turning over the page, he continues with his message.

You don't have a neighbour, you know this. This will sound crazy, but you must listen to me

He pauses, not for dramatic effect, but because he knows now, what he writes next, could possibly change her fate.

Someone is watching you. You know this. Tonight, you'll go missing

He gives her a moment to digest his cryptic message. He offers a smile, friendly-like, and approaches the wall slowly. As his eye finds the hole, having been watching him the entire time, Amy pulls back.

Ok, well, she's not running away; that's a start.

Amy instead stands rooted to the spot, but the look on her face leaves Thomas cold. Confusion and fear have taken hold. As it tears through her features, the confliction leaves her blinking wildly. Slowly, she returns to her notepad and writes:

Ok, so I don't have a neighbour. So, who are you, and how did you get in there?

Gasping, his chest heaving, he tries to think, to find the words, but his mind is a hazy ball of candyfloss. So finally, going back to the pen and pad, writing his following message, he holds it up for her to see:

You have no reason to, I understand that and what I'm about to say will sound insane, but you have to trust me. I'm begging you. We're neighbours, we are, just at different times, and I know how it sounds, but it's the truth

Returning to the hole, Amy again pulls back and writes her own note.

I want you to leave me alone, understand?

Again, Thomas attempts to buy himself a few more seconds by raising one finger. But, thinking hard, the words needed again appear elusive.

I guess now is the time to tell her what awaits her.

> **I can't do that. Please listen to me. Tonight, you disappear. That's all I know. Either by your own volition or someone takes you**

Holding up the pad and allowing her time to understand the weight of his words, counting 1... 2... 3... 4... 5... 6... 7... 8... 9... 10... he returns to the holes. Wiping his eyes, he focuses on Amy. Shifting her weight, her mouth twitching, her eyes wide with questions. Yet still, she remains, her gaze fixed on the hole- leading Thomas to assume she is at least considering his words.

Turning sharply, snapping a three-sixty on her heels, Amy leaves the room, again disappearing down the hallway.

We don't have time for this.

A moment later, reappearing, she returns to the hole. Hunched, she stands, scribbling another message:

> **The front door is locked, bolted and chained. No one is getting in. I'll call the Police, understand? Now leave me alone**

Amy follows her words by returning to the hole.

Thank God, yes.

Stepping back, nodding emphatically, Thomas goes about writing a follow-up message.

> **Yes, do it, please. Call the Police or leave now. Don't stop, don't hide, you run**

Returning to the hole, continuing their game of silent-hole-tennis, Amy pulls back her head, this time at a crawl. While nodding in agreement, confusion and torment pull at her features, darkening her wild eyes.

Finally.

Moving to the kitchen, slamming down the pen and pad onto the counter, Amy goes for her phone.

At 10:43pm, she calls the Police, it rings a couple of times, and the operator gets no one on the line.

Remembering what StarKiller has told them, Thomas's heart, the world around him, stops dead.

I haven't changed a thing.

A new terror rises in him, stiffening his spine, bringing the threat of urination and chest collapsing panic attacks.

Instead, my actions from the future have altered the past, shaping it forever.

Hyperventilating, sweating through his eyes, his clothes, trying to comprehend this, the weight of it, he finds his eyes are drawn to Amy's hallway. Struggling with an impaired vision of pulsating light, nonetheless, he sees it– something lingering back behind the veil of the darkness, on the edge of shadow. A shifting form, cloaked, makes the dark space swell with presence.

Icy fingers quickly creep in beneath his clothes, gripping his core and shrinking his penis. The hole around Thomas's eye waivers, leaving the boundaries of his reality-bending and swaying. He wants to vomit, and while he keeps it down, it burns his throat in fiery protest.

Helpless, Thomas can only watch as a dark figure slips in from the shadows, edging closer an inch at a time. Dressed entirely in black, the slinking form slithers into the light, slowly unwrapped by the gloom in all its horrific glory. The mask, a grotesque hood of leather, covers the entire head. With small slits for eyes and mouth, the hood is crowned at the front with a blood-red, coloured horn. Like a unicorn but bent upwards, almost medieval in its design, it sits proud and stark against the black leather.

Sweating hard, his eyes bulging with the effort, a scream explodes from Thomas's throat, one muffled against the canvas. Pounding on the wall, desperately begging Amy to turn, Thomas knows it's in vain, yet still, he tries.

With Amy placing the phone to her ear, the fiend closes the gap between them, falling in behind her. The intruder goes to their belt, momentarily stopping above what looks like a sheathed knife, its fingers playing with the hilt, before moving on and removing something small, white, soft.

Confused, struggling with the limited view, Thomas's eye strains to see what they now hold. Far from a weapon, possibly a piece of paper...

His confusion is short-lived.

A white cloth is raised and brought into the light.

Turn around, goddamn it.

As if hearing him, Amy, now suddenly alert, turns only to be confronted by the intruder. She tries to act, but the horned creature is faster. While grabbing hold of her head with his gloved left hand, with their right, he smothers her face with the cloth. With Amy now at his mercy, her eyes roll over, her body goes limp.

The intruder, all business with his movements, expertly cradles her collapsing form while taking hold of her phone, terminating the call in one swift motion.

Breathing hard, Thomas backs away from the hole involuntarily. Now crying, he fights an invisible barrier between him and the wall.

You must watch, for God's sake, get back to the hole!

Pushing forward, straining, his mind screaming at his legs to move... Behind me, the sound of movement shocks him back to life. Turning, eyes wide with disconcertion, he focuses on the hallway. He tells himself he's alone; the sound was nothing more than his heart thudding or the continued rain, but still... his mouth, airy and silent, has lost all moisture, and his heart, all rhyme.

As sure as the rain slamming against the window and skylights, a loud creak creeps in from the hallway.

Someone's here.

15

10:55pm...

Suddenly, he's afraid. Like a child, lost, looking for his mother. And like that child, that same child he's never been able to outgrow, standing still, eyes wide against the gloom of the hallway, his body shakes through fear. The type of uncontrolled fear only children experience. The fear of the unknown, an unprepared and unwilling mind, unable to think, let alone move or act.

'Who's there?' Thomas calls, his voice though loud, quivers through fear.

Nothing.

The hallway before him remains unmoved, yet it trembles and pulsates with nauseating movements. It is his eyes, of course, a glazed throbbing distorting his vision, yet Thomas cannot move.

Wanting to return to the wall but unable to turn his back on whatever had made the noise, he decides to investigate. Not that he wants to, but the need outweighs desire.

Move you goddamn fool.

With the weight of iron, his feet finally get going. Stuttering and nervous, as if walking on uneven ground, Thomas crashes into the desk, shunting it, sending an empty coffee mug tumbling to the floor. Given the silence around him, its impact hitting the floor is nothing short of a bomb going off. It wrecks his already tattered senses as it sends an explosion of noise through the apartment, reverberating around the sloped ceiling.

Scurrying to the kitchen, he yanks a knife from the block, turns and approaches the hallway. Shaking in his hand, leading with it, the knife's shimmering blade cuts a line into the dim light ahead of him. Before proceeding any further, he flicks on the hallway light. Blinking before coming on, the bare glare does nothing to ease his wrung nerves.

Feeling pain streak through his hand and wrist, realising he's holding the knife too tightly, he loosens his grip and hisses with relief. Almost instantly, the handle becomes slippery in his hand, so Thomas is forced to wipe it with his t-shirt.

Stop stalling and start walking.

Surprising himself, he does just that – pushing forward along the hallway.

'I have a knife, you hear me, I have a knife, and I swear to Christ I'll use it, so come on out!' He shouts. 'Come on out, goddamn you, please.'

Ending the request with a *please* sends a shudder of impotence through him. His voice is weak and unconvincing. Choked by tears, his words echo uncomfortably through the apartment. He stops before entering the bathroom, grinding his teeth, unable to hear anything over the thrumming in his chest, the rain against the roof. Panting rather than breathing, creeping instead of leaping, Thomas peers into the room. While the hallway's light is sufficient to confirm as much, Thomas flicks on the light if only to kill the gathered shadows.

Empty.

Thomas moves to the bedroom. Again empty, the room's hollowness is now far more apparent than usual. Backing away, Thomas dashes to the end of the hallway and checks the front door.

Locked, with the chain-guard still in place.

Of course. What did you expect?

Closing his eyes, tears racing down his cheeks, Thomas falls against the wall. He attempts to steady himself, but the simple act of breathing has become difficult.

There's no one here.

Still shaking, hands quivering wildly, his legs weak, he pushes away from the wall and rushes back to the living area, the hole.

Placing the knife down on the desk, he all but falls against the wall. The thud is such, along with rocking the paintings against the plaster, it knocks the wind from his lips.

Breathing, he steadies himself.

Attempts to anyway.

Both Amy and her attacker are gone, and her apartment, though lit by lamplight, is empty. Eye glued to the hole, watching and hoping, a sudden surge of anger, brought on by the old familiar feeling of failure, clatters through Thomas.

He checks his watch.

11:01pm.

How the hell did he get in?

Minutes tick over, but the apartment is unmoved, frozen and shadowed.

You missed it.

You fucking idiot. You missed it, and now you're screwed.

The sound of the intercom buzzing has him jumping back from the wall. With shredded nerves, he takes one last look before leaving the hole.

Dashing across the room to the intercom, picking up the receiver, he slams, 'hello,' into the mouthpiece.

A crackled line greets him, and his uneasiness and fear return with an almighty vengeance, reaching into me, dragging him kicking and screaming from his wallowing stupor.

'Thomas,' Finally comes from the line.

'Yes?'

'Thomas, it's me, Peter.'

A gut-load of air bursts from his lips. 'What the hell are you doing here?'

'I couldn't stay away. Are you ok?'

'Come on up,' Thomas pants, buzzing him in.

Moving through the hallway, round the corner, to the front door, he unclips the chain guard. Unlocking the door's two locks, one standard lock and an unconvincing looking deadbolt, Thomas stops, looking at them with wide eyes. With no signs of tampering or damage whatsoever, Thomas is left perplexed and consternated. As such, watching through the peephole, he waits before opening the door.

The hallway beyond remains contorted and dark. Thomas waits for Peter's arrival, his breath heavy against the door. As if camouflaged, a skulking form shifts through the darkness. The hallway light, flickering, pops on.

A face on the other side of the hole looks back at Thomas, leaving him hissing, 'FUCK!'

Opening the door to the waiting Peter, his placid face quickly turns pale with worry. 'What's happened? Are you ok?'

'Just on edge, come on it.'

Following Thomas inside, he leads Peter through to the living area. He says, pointing to the hole, 'you can take a shift.'

Peter nods, removes his coat, folds it, and places it across the back of the sofa. At the wall, he presses his face forward, squinting into the hole.

'A man, a man took her. I saw him, watched him abduct her,' Thomas tells him, collapsing into the sofa.

'What did he look like?'

'He was masked.'

'Masked?' Peter asks, diverting his attention from the hole for a second.

'A leather hood, freaky too, a cross between a gimp and a Mexican wrestler.'

'Sounds like a fetish item, could be traceable?'

'Maybe... but Peter, I missed him leave with her.'

Looking over his shoulder at him, Peter asks, 'What happened?'

Rubbing his eyes with the thumb and forefinger, and for the first time tonight, Thomas feels the tightness of his muscles, the wrung in his back and neck.

'Amy came home from work, called her sister, and later sent her the text message, all according to plan. But, after that, well, things get complicated.'

'Complicated how?' Peter asks, his eye back at the hole.

'Well, she saw me.'

Turning from the wall, his mouth agape, Peter asks, 'saw you, saw you how?'

'She looked through the hole; we were looking at each other,' shaking his head, Thomas leans forward and looks at him. 'We spoke. I mean, we used a pad and pen, I thought I could save her, but it didn't change a thing. She called the police the second she was supposed to.'

'So, your intervention is part of the timeline,' Peter says, not as a question but a loose statement.

'Then, that monster crept up behind her, drugged her, I think, I mean I got distracted,' Thomas looks at him, waits for Peter's eyes lock with his. 'Peter, I'm positive someone was in here with me, like Amy, watching me. When I made it back to the wall, she was gone.'

Peter, thinking, asks, 'how did he get in?'

'Beats me, but there was no one here when I checked. With Amy, he just appeared from the hallway.'

You're never going to see her again.

A familiar dull ache returns, leaving his limbs heavy. Standing, pulling himself up, dragging his tired form, fighting against the need for sleep. His eyes flutter, he attempts to fight it, but the light around him spins, strobes, and flickers. Pink orbs flash before him, draining him. Returning to the sofa, dropping into it, Thomas rubs his weary face.

If Amy locked the door, how did that creep get into her apartment?

FIRST INTERLUDE

A BOY'S FIRST CRUSH

August 1986...

The boy was thirteen the summer they found the body in the tall grass behind his house. It had stormed the night before, removing the mugginess, leaving the morning fresh and bright. The early sun had brought a warm yellow light, eager runners, and a steady stream of dog walkers. It was as if obligatory, a man walking a trio of spaniels who discovered the body. He hadn't set out to disrupt the bloody scene, but the dogs, still hungry after their breakfast, raced to the messy remains with ravenous intent. Only when he finally gained control of the dogs, after dragging them from the scene, their mouths matted with crimson pulp, did he understand what he had found.

An army of concerned faces ascended upon the scene, taking up home mere meters from the boy's home. Men in uniforms, police and figures covered head to toe in white overalls. He watched it all from his bedroom window, excited by the circus, intrigued by the discharge of urgent energy as they scurried about the scene. The erection of the forensic tent, the tall green spikes stained red with blood, the boy watched it all through his father's binoculars with glued eyes.

Her name was Michelle Lu, and the boy loved her from the start. A law graduate from the city. Strong-willed, brilliant, and striking in both appearance and candour. The type of woman who would use long words without sounding pretentious. Her confidence and energy first hypnotised and amused him, well, that and her perfect face, hips, and glossy legs. And oh, how she liked to show them off, be it sunbathing outback wearing summer dresses and numerous bikinis.

So, for the boy, that summer consisted of humid days and sticky nights peeping in through her windows, which inevitably led to him rummaging through her trash. During these Moonlit trips, what he recovered surprised, educated him, and matured him to the world of women, their needs, their desires.

Michelle favoured a diet heavy on fruit and vegetables. She drank white wine most nights, and given the number of empty cartons of painkillers, the boy concluded she suffered from migraines. Michelle preferred makeup from Estée Lauder to other brands and used tampons instead of sanitary towels. She would like to knit scarfs and sweaters, though many of her attempts ended in failure. He found used balls of cotton wool, scraps of food, spent cans of Diet Coke, finished newspapers, spent crossword puzzles, junk mail, and used underwear. Though mundane to the common man, all of it was of great interest to the boy.

The boy considered whether Michelle was, in fact, leaving such items for him to find, a subtle sign, like a trail of breadcrumbs for him to follow. A challenge, as in, if he could be man enough, he could claim her as his prize. Then later, watching her parade behind her windows half-naked, lingering before showering, the boy took it as a stone-cold certainty.

One night, late and barmy, when watching her from the tall grass outback, the boy, sure he had been exposed, hunkered down as Michelle came to the backdoor in her nightgown. He was well hidden, but the way she stood gazing out over the garden, her gown fluttering with the breeze, the boy was sure she could see him.

She's doing it for me, he thought.

And so, with her display at the back door, the boy decided it was time to announce himself.

Nine days of preparing, waiting and yearning left the boy with stomach cramps. Plus, a permanent state of arousal left him weak-kneed and light-headed, unable to sleep or eat. Using scotch tape, strapping his small erection to his lower belly, the boy found he could move and complete simple tasks without the distraction. When it got too much, when the thoughts of Michelle left him weak, he'd bury his penis in a pack of frozen peas from his mum's freezer.

The wait, too, brought back the ghosts. Clattering around, howling into the night, keeping him from sleep. Chasing and pinning down stray cats had kept the ghosts quiet for a time anyway, but over the summer, watching Michelle, with *the want* and *need* to touch her, the ghouls had grown restless, demanding a response, screaming long into the night.

When it was finally time to sneak out late, the boy slithered from his window. Moving along the side of her house to the rear, the boy, almost giddy, scanned the back garden. No torch was needed for the trip. The moon, like a low spotlight, sat full in the sky. The lawn, blanketed in bright white light, shimmered like a sea of icy shards.

Perfect, he concluded – the night, the moon, the stillness in the air, the flutter at his chest. It was as if the world and everything in it had come to a halt. From the people, the critters, down to the shadows cast from the tall grass stretching across the lawn- it all stood in anticipation for him and Michelle to take centre stage.

The boy entered the home through an open window on the ground floor. Smiling, the boy was quick to conclude it had been left open, solely for him, for the night they were destined to meet.

Migrating from room to room, taking his time - drinking wine from a lipstick-stained glass, the boy moved on to inspect the line of photographs atop the fireplace mantle.

Legs shaking, the boy moved to the stairs and climbed into the shadows of the first floor. He moved to Michelle's bedroom from the bathroom, stopping to smell her perfume, body lotion, clothes, and underwear before mentally cataloguing them. He reviewed the selection of dresses, skirts, and high heels hung and stacked neatly in the wardrobe. Surprised, his arousal intensified with how her panties felt to the touch, how delicate and dainty, how they shimmered with lace and satin.

Running his hands over the bed, taking in the sensation of silk, savouring it, he stripped naked before crawling on top. Placing his clothes and boots down in a neat pile beside the bed, he stretched out across the cool duvet. Then, looking up at the ceiling, watching the flickering shadows, the boy wondered, like him, if Michelle had laid there, wanting, waiting for his arrival, night after night.

Unaware he had fallen asleep, the boy was dragged from a shallow, troubled dream by the sound of distant thunder.

Bolting upright in the bed, lightheaded, the boy struggled to let go of the dream, confused to find he had been crying.

Laughter, flirtatious and heavy mouthed, echoed up from the ground floor.

'You want me, don't you?" A woman asked, panting wildly.

It was her, Michelle Lu.

'Yes,' The boy replied, a cracked whisper of need.

'Oh god, I want to hear it. Tell me how much you need me?' She grunted, her voice closer, the stairs creaking beneath staggered, disjointed steps.

With laughter drawing nearer, accompanied by impatient moans, heated and stifled, the boy's erection grew with anticipation until it was engorged and spear-like, burning as if on fire.

'I want you; I love you; I love you....' The boy's words were ripped from his lips with the sound of a man's voice.

'I want you, fuck, I want you,' deep and horse, the man's voice was one of a rabid animal.

When Michelle and a man came crashing into the room, the boy was gone, as were his clothes and boots. Late twenties, over six-foot-tall, the man's build suggested he either boxed or played rugby. Kissing, giggling, pulling, and ripping at each other's clothes, they pawed at flesh, mouths engaged with wet, heated tongues on fire.

The boy was forced to listen from his hiding place beneath the bed. Covering his ears, squeezing his eyes shut, the boy was nonetheless tortured by the ragged breath of passion, the heat and melding of two bodies, the sound of raw sex.

Of course, the boy had seen plenty of people screwing before; his dad had made him stay up and watch those tapes – the German, blonde, big-breasted type. Remembering his dad's words, their discussions of sex, 'there's nothing wrong with just fucking, you don't need to love them all, I mean even pigs fuck for enjoyment.'

But not this.

Like wild animals, the electricity in the air, chasing and burning away the sweat, tortured him, seared his skin, strangling his heart.

When the boy crawled out from under the bed, he went unnoticed. Slipping into the shadows, watching them, disgust passed over him, through him, turning his stomach. He could feel it, the hate pitting, twisting his insides. Watching the man's furious pumping, the boy's hatred lifted to his chest, his heart, until the tears finally stopped, the ghosts were quick to return. With anger, clawing at the inside of his skull, banshee-like, they screamed, tearing open his mind, until they consumed him absolutely.

* * *

Waking sometime later, Michelle found the house cold and dark, and her lover gone. Sitting up, still groggy from sex, she called out, 'Jerry?'

Getting no answer, she swung her feet off the bed, stood up, and walked to the door, her legs still shaky, her skin sore around her mauled breasts and vagina. Still, it brought her a feeling of comfort, as did the sense of Jerry, the trickle, lingering inside her.

Leaving the bedroom, the darkness of the landing wrapped around her, stripping her of her warmth. The collection of shadows before her sent a surge of cold against her bare skin. Her eyes, wide and alert in the dark, scurried through the gloom for the light switch.

'Jerry?' Michelle tried again, the sudden cold bringing gooseflesh to her arms and back.

The boy waited in the dark, the kitchen knife still shaking in his hand. When the light finally flicked on, the boy remained hidden, eyes fixed on Jerry and the mess he and the blade had made of the once handsome man.

Can't fuck without a dick, his mind flared, jubilant, a smile breaking out across his young, stricken face.

'Oh god, Jerry,' she muttered.

Rushing to his ruined body, Michelle first stood, her shaking hands dancing at her sides. Slowly, at his side, she crumbled to her knees.

The sound of her quiet sobbing gave the boy reservation, but the ghosts and their torturous wails startled him out from his hiding place. Creeping across the kitchen floor, the boy stopped behind Michelle. Ahead of them, he could see her face in the reflection of the patio door. He waited until she looked up to find him staring back at her.

Before she could act, the boy moved in. With a quick swipe of the blade, he opened the side of her throat. Her hand shot up and clamped the wound, but blood began seeping out through her fingers in seconds.

Staggering forward, her words, her strained pleads sat choked in her throat. The boy, unconcerned, followed her as she crawled to the door, then outside into the back garden. Her tanned body, perfect a short time before, glistened with fresh, spurting blood, had turned her foreign to him, and the sight of it, her, sickened him to his core.

Though she tried, Michelle could not scream, managing gurgled whines as she made her way across the lawn, clawing at it, inch by inch.

Knife raised; the boy stalked into the shadows after her. Kicking her rump, the blow sent Michelle flaying forward on her face. Holding her gushing wound, Michelle rolled onto her back to face her attacker.

Using the heels of her bare feet, digging them into the lush grass, she pushed back, her face straining with the effort, but without the use of both hands, it was all but fruitless.

'I loved you....' his words caught in his throat.

Taking Michelle by her hair, the boy dragged her from the lawn into the tall grass behind the house. Dark within, their tips made silvery in the moonlight, the scurry of small creatures fled the scene, aware somehow of what would come next.

Alone with her in the dark, the boy took his time, and finally, somewhere in the night, he became who he was always meant to be.

When done, after stripping her of everything she owned: her womanhood, her dignity, her life, he felt energised, and finally, the ghosts, so quickly had they returned and how so angry, had been silenced, left satisfied, appeased.

Looking down at what he had done, her skin like marble, her body all bloody and rearranged, he didn't feel a thing. He did not panic, nor did he rush. Instead, a calm came over him, and an invisible energy new to him. It swept through his mind, chasing away the fog.

Taking his time, he cleaned up and amended the scene. He understood clearly that he would need to hide within his young body, to act like a child. He was good at hiding, pretending, a wolf in sheep's clothing. After that, he would learn to walk and talk like the rest of them, mature and grow, never forgetting the summer of 86, Michelle Lu, and the first time he fell in love.

PART TWO

RAINING CATS AND DOGS

16

Dave, apartment 2a...

Knocking for a fourth time, with Thomas already having waited for five minutes, his frustration has now morphed, forming as a throbbing headache behind his eyes. If not for the sound of movement from behind the door, Thomas would simply leave. Yet with it, as if to taunt him, his fragile resolve has him rooted to the spot. Anger at being ignored brings a percolation to his blood, leaving him uncomfortably warm, almost stifled inside his coat.

Stepping forward, thudding on the door with a closed fist, Thomas stands, his eyes glaring at the peephole.

A muffled, agitated voice comes from behind the door, 'yeah, yeah, hold on, will ya.'

With a click and a rattle, the door finally pulls open. In its place, an awkwardly shaped man shuffles forward, appearing from the dim light of the hallway beyond.

'Yeah, I help you with something?' The man moans.

'Hi, yes. I'm Thomas. I recently moved in upstairs,' he tells him, stepping forward, offering a hand.

'Yeah, I hear you banging around. Your mother ever teach you patience? Knocking like that, can't you see it takes me time to get up?'

'I'm sorry, I didn't know,' Thomas says, taken aback.

Thomas smiles uncomfortably but leaves his hand outstretched for the man to shake.

'Yeah, well, common sense doesn't cost a thing,' the man continues with a slurred and uneven voice.

Hesitating, the unkempt and dishevelled man, possibly middle-aged, steps forward and into the light. With the right side of his face appearing heavily sagged, like a stroke victim, his left eye droops open, exposing reddish flesh. Thomas tries to look away but finds he cannot. Instead, his eyes, as if pulled, are drawn to the man's loose skin, its ashy colour, and the pinks of his lower right eye socket.

And then there's the smell.

Along with the scent of beef burgers, mustard and onions on his breath, the man brings with him an overly sweet smell, the mouldy, one-week-from-an-infection type.

Awkwardly, his movement jarring and stuttery, he finally reaches out to meet Thomas's gesture. Taking Thomas's in his, shaking it, the man's hand appears crippled or stiffened with arthritis. Done, returning it to an odd, uncomfortable position at his side, his hand dances with an uncontrolled flutter.

Even with an unsteady lurch to his movements and his sluggish speech, with it being clear that the man is both cognitively and physically disabled, Thomas cannot help suspect the man.

Thinking back to the man, how he slinked in like a ninja, having watched him abduct Amy, then later, him cleaning the scene before taking her laptop and mobile phone, it is clear Dave is not the man he saw. In addition to all of that, his tracksuit, a black Adidas three-stripe, appears two sizes too big, leaving him drowning beneath it.

'The name's Dave. I help you with something?' He asks.

While his tone is now noticeably light, still cautious, he takes a step back, away from Thomas, into the darkened hallway.

'No, thank you,' Thomas says, thankful for the distraction, 'I just wanted to say hi, and if you need anything, I'm right upstairs.'

'I don't see me needing you for something, so....'

'Ok, well, it was nice to meet you,' Thomas says, starting to back away.

'Actually, wait, will ya. Come on in, I might have something for *you,*' Dave offers, stepping back.

'Ok, um, sure,' Thomas says.

Instantly regretting it, moving to the open door, pushing through gingerly, Thomas follows Dave along the narrow hallway. Here, the man's offensive body odour is elevated to a new and obscene level of sweetness. It stings his eyes, making them water, tainting the air, leaving it thick on the tongue, leaving Thomas teetering on the brink of vomiting.

Wobbling, almost limping, Dave's feet appear muddled, as if tied together with shoelaces. Trotting in behind the man, through to the living area, Thomas attempts to hold his breath as waves of sickening smells assault his senses. Gagging, Thomas forces back bile, it stinging his eyes, but thankfully it stays back, camped behind his pressed lips. Wanting to cover his face, Thomas makes do with him, wrinkling his nose.

Thomas throws his eyes over the room to distract his sense of smell. While copying Thomas's in layout, the man's apartment is blessed with high, flat ceilings. As a result, all surfaces, including the dining table, and the kitchen worktops, sit cluttered with magazines, books, old VHS tapes, empty food wrappers, and used takeout cartons of every conceivable food type. The coffee table, a large slab of cheap pine, now it would seem, serves as a graveyard for countless beer cans, Red Bull knockoffs and empty plastic, 1-litre cider bottles.

Finding his breathing has grown laboured, panicked, as if in need of fresh air, Thomas's eyes scurry to the yellow drapes lining the window. His chest struggles with the dullness of the room, its broody, murky, jaundice coloured ambience.

'You, ok?' Dave asks as a half-smirk curl with his words.

'Fine, thank you,' Thomas tells him, forcing a smile.

Diverting his gaze to the far wall, looking for paintings to match his own, Thomas sees none. Instead, the wall, smooth and covered, is wallpapered with light, faded eggshell strips. There, two tall bookcases flank a crusty old sofa. Stuffed full of old VHS tapes, scanning them, Thomas notes titles such as Friday the 13th, The Intruder, The Prowler, Final Exam, When a stranger calls, The Toolbox Murders, Prom Night, Slumber Party Massacre, Hell Night, Terror Train, My Bloody Valentine, and so on. From the golden era of *Slasher Films*, a mix of the seventies and eighties, all horror, all following a theme of young people, mainly women, being stalked and murdered in ever elaborate blood-soaked ways. Other cassettes sit dusty in blank, murky transparent cases, leaving the footage they hold a mystery.

Shuffling across the room to the far corner, Dave moves to an old, rusted filing cabinet. Calling over his shoulder, 'I've seen you, you're a busy guy, am I right?'

'How's that?' Thomas asks.

Agitated by the man's tone, the not-so-subtle insinuation in his words, Thomas shifts his weight, now anxious to leave.

'I seen the women, coming and going, pretty ones too, and the young fella, the fag in the suit,' Dave stops digging into the cabinet, turns and levels Thomas with concerned eyes. 'You aren't fags are ya, the two of you, I mean?'

'No,' Thomas says through gritted teeth. 'We work together.'

'Ok, well, that's good. Unnatural that, two men, I mean, London's full of em. You know what I'm saying, I can tell, faggots and queers, those fucking dykes that look like guys. I mean, it's bad enough we gotta share the city with those slant-eyed gipsies, let alone boy's going around dressed like girls. They'll rob you, you know, rob you and spit in your food if you don't watch em.'

'And you, you live here alone?' Thomas asks, forcing the words out to stop himself from screaming at the top of his lungs.

'Yeah, me, Charles and Diana,' Dave snorts, his head winking to his left.

In the far corner, suspended by a curved stand, a bronze birdcage is occupied by two squirrels. Squeaking, they climb the cage, round and round, over each other, in a marriage of frantic energy, stopping to bite the cage. Thomas notes the breaks in the cage bars, the apparent sign of failed escape accepts. It is now Thomas notes the unsubtle odour of old faeces. Sour on the eyes; it melds with the other smells, forcing Thomas on his heels.

'I got something you might like,' Dave says, holding up a small foil-covered sleeve of tablets, 'twenty-pound for four.'

'No thanks,' Thomas tells him.

'It's a good deal, cost you double online?' He moans, holding out the sleeve. 'I get it with my prescription, don't need them, though, just say I do. I got stacks.'

Looking at the sleeve, Thomas recognises the small blue pills. Smiling, he tells Dave, 'Thanks, but no thanks.'

'Your funeral friend,' disappointed, he turns back to the filing cabinet.

'My apartment, did you know the woman who lived next door?'

Turning, Dave smiles. 'Nice, like her sister, you know what I mean, right? 'Yeah, sweet little thing, nice and tight, you know what I mean.'

Shaking, his hands balled into fists, Thomas stuffs them into his coat pocket.

'She's missing, probably dead. You do know that, right?' Thomas says, his tone a little harder than he had intended.

Smiling, Dave says, 'I know, I hear everything.'

'Yeah, what did you hear?'

'Her sister, she comes, night after night, knocking at all hours, even though her sisters long gone. You know her; I see you follow her outside.'

'I heard her knocking, so I offered my condolences.'

'Yeah, your con... dol... ences, right,' Dave smirks, moving to the cluttered sofa. Sitting down, keeping one leg straight, he bends the other at an odd angle. 'I reckon she's a screamer, like her sister Amy.'

Hearing enough, wanting to leave, Thomas instead stays, keeping his feet planted to the spot. 'How do you mean?'

'Lilly being a screamer?' His smirk stretches into a smile.

'Amy,' Thomas stabs back.

Turning mischievous through his eyes, Dave's smile grows further. 'The night she went poof, I told the Police, but did they listen, no sir.'

'What did you hear?'

'A scream,' he says as if not hearing Thomas's question. 'Sent poor Charles all kinds of crazy, biting at his cage, shitting all over the place.'

'What time did you hear her?'

'Eleven-ish, yeah, sounds bout right, but things must have sorted themselves; she left here at 6am.'

Ready to leave, Thomas stops and looks at the man. 'She left here, alone?'

'Yes, sir.'

'Are you sure it was her?'

'Oh yeah, I'm sure. You see a gal like Amy, you'd don't forget her. That and that arse of hers. Like a peach, man, what I would do if I could....'

'And she left here alone, without a struggle?' Thomas interrupts.

'Yes, sir. I told the Police she had man trouble; you know what I mean.'

Stunned, Thomas attempts to take in this new piece of information.

She left, but how?

Looking at Dave suspiciously while questioning whether the man could be lying, Thomas instinctively considers him a suspect. Shaking his head in idiotic reflection, Thomas recognises there's no getting beyond the man's evident disabilities. Along with his long list of conditions, Thomas pictures him struggling to climb the stairs by himself, let alone be able to overpower and kidnap Amy. Her abductor was far bigger and nimble, someone who exercises and does so regularly and with vigour.

He could be pretending; it could be an act?

Thomas continues to watch the man. His sloping face, odd, crooked, angular frame, and slow garbled words.

He would need to be one hell of an actor. Plus, why would he?

Shaking such thoughts from his mind, Thomas asks, 'did you see anyone else the night Amy left?'

'Didn't see no one, heard the old puffin next door though, banging about. She's always knocking shit over. Snores to, I can hear her through the wall, sounds like an old man shitting, you know what I mean?'

Thomas watches Dave return to his feet, moving sluggishly to the squirrel cage and poking peanuts through the bars. Thomas attempts to process what the man claims to have seen, and, if he's not to be believed, he considers why he might lie?

It couldn't have been Amy. I saw her abduction.

Didn't I?

Ready to leave, Thomas thanks the man, suspicious of his story, and heads for the hallway.

'Hey,' Dave calls, stopping Thomas. Smiling, he waits for Thomas to turn back to look at him. 'You sure I can't sell you any dick-pills?'

* * *

Ms Harmony, apartment 2b...

The elderly lady kept Thomas waiting even longer than her neighbour. Knocking repeatedly, waiting, having heard her call out, 'I'll be right there, dear,' Thomas had stood waiting like a fool for near on ten minutes. Now sat on the sofa, watching the elderly lady shuffle across the floor on heavily swollen, bandaged ankles, her blue face mask and hairnet, Thomas understands why.

'She was a lovely girl, salt of the earth,' the old lady says, handing Thomas a cup of tea he has no intention of drinking.

Ms Harmony's apartment, identical to Amy's, is furnished with items from the 1960s and could easily be confused with an antique shop at a quick glance. Though overly scented by potpourri, it is a far nicer environment to visit than the dim, squirrel-ridden sweatbox of her neighbour. Along with the ornate umbrella stand in the hall beside the door, the apartment is furnished with items made from mahogany or oak, all thick and reassuringly sturdy. A bureau, side table, a glassed display case, matching but a little tatty with age, each sporting the tale-tale signs of years of house moves, the lugging from one removal van to another.

'Have you lived here long?' Thomas asks.

'Years, ever since my Henry died,' she calls from the kitchen. 'It's cheap, plus it's only a short walk down the hill to Bingo. Every Tuesday and Thursday for three years. That I believe, they call commitment.'

Returning from the kitchen with a cup for herself, taking a seat in the armchair across from Thomas, the old lady smiles, 'are you sure I can't get you a biscuit?'

'No, thank you,' Thomas says, looking down at his tea.

Milky and probably too sweet, it is already starting to congeal with pieces of skin forming on the surface.

'I am sorry, you caught me mid-wash. I like to take cold baths; it does wonders for my ankles. Look at me; what must you think?'

'It's fine, really,' Thomas tells her, fighting the urge to sneeze.

Wrapped in an oversized cotton bathrobe, hair in thick heavy rollers beneath the net, she looks at Thomas through two pink holes of ger sticky looking face mask of blue mush. Still, something in her face registers with him, a recollection from some distant time and place.

Thomas pauses to look at her. Something in those eyes of hers, in her voice, have him trawl back through his memory.

'I'm sorry, but have we met before,' Thomas asks.

'I don't believe so. Where is it you think we met?'

'I,' he again pauses. Shaking his head, confused and a little disorientated. 'Sorry, it's been a strange couple of days.'

'No need to apologise, my dear,' she smiles and takes a sip of her tea. 'You were saying you write?'

'Yes, my next book is about Pinegrove, about the disappearance of Amy Porter.'

'Terrible business, such a lovely girl. Worked for the NHS, long shifts, always working that one.'

'Did you know her well?'

'I did, yes, I mean she would drop in to water my plants when I go to stay with my daughter, she's an Actor, Carol Harmony, you've probably heard of her?'

'I have, yes,' he lies.

'She's appeared in Holby City, don't you know?'

Thomas smiles thinly.

'Here she is,' she says. Reaching over to a small side table, she picks up a framed picture and hands it to him. 'Isn't she beautiful?'

'Very,' again, he lies.

Though pretty, the woman in the photograph, in her late forties, plus-size, in Thomas's opinion, is far too ordinary-looking to ever make it in television. Her shoulder-length bobbed hair adds weight to her already overly round face. She is a sub-character, never the leading actor, not even in her own life.

Shaking his head, disgusted at himself for such a harsh review, Thomas hands back the picture. Looking down at it fondly, the old lady reluctantly returns it to the side table.

'I suppose, the loss of Amy, it must have come as a surprise to you?' Thomas asks, attempting to steer the conversation back on track.

'Of course, fine girl, tip-top, but the company she kept, well, that boyfriend of hers did her no good whatsoever.'

'James Ruck?'

'Yes, loathsome fellow,' she says with a shake of her head.

'Were you home the night she disappeared?'

'I was playing cards, solitaire, my favourite, but I heard a commotion, oh yes. The stomping of feet, screams, well I couldn't concentrate so, I went to bed, but could I sleep, no sir. I was worried, I really was, so I knocked on her door, but things had gone quiet by then. So, when I saw her leave, I was relieved, but when she never returned, I....' She drops her head.

'You saw her leave?'

Again, looking at him, her eyes turn glassy.

'Yes, I'm not ashamed to say I was busy around the peephole. I was worried when I heard her door slam upstairs, I checked, and it was her, leaving alone... After that, I never saw her again.'

"What time was this?'

'Six, six-thirty, yes, that sounds about right.'

'And you're sure it was her, and she was alone?' Thomas asks, sitting forward in his chair.

'Oh, yes, dear, she was alone, and it was her. I can still see her face now, her tears.'

My god, Dave was telling the truth.

'She was upset?'

'Mmm yes, I'd say, I could tell she'd been crying, and she was in a hurry too, looked like she had packed for a trip.'

'Packed?'

'She was carrying a bag, the overnight type. I just wish I knew where she was going, or better, to go back and stop her. Maybe I could talk to her, but I guess I'll never get the chance now.'

Thanking the woman, leaving before her stuffy perfume could lead to an outbreak of hives, Thomas leaves the cover of Pinegrove for the waiting rain. Not yet night, the early evening with grey, angry clouds do an excellent job of imitating it. Leaving the front entrance, Thomas is met at the porch by a deluge. Thick drops, bullet-like, thunder the porch roof and the path before him. A layer of surface water, alive against the cacophony, the million different drops springing back from the ground like the waves of an erratic frequency.

Frustrated by the weather, Thomas diverts his thoughts. With his tired brain creaking beneath the weight of the information he just received from both neighbours, with it being at complete odds with what he saw himself, he lets out a weary sigh. Where he had been suspicious of Dave and what he claimed to have seen, with Ms Harmony confirming it, he finds himself again at a loss.

She was abducted; Thomas saw it happen.

Yeah, so how was it she was seen by two witnesses leaving alone?

Thomas considers the possibility both Dave and Ms Harmony are lying, or at the very least, confused, but struggles to accept these as possibilities.

Unless they're in on it together?

What, like a conspiracy?

Thomas answers his own question with a weary, almost disgusted shake of his head.

None of this makes any Goddamn sense.

Through the booming rain, the harsh drumming, a low, torturous whine finds Thomas, dragging him from his thoughts. Turning to his left, attempting to trace the sound to its source, he scans the front of the house, the low wall and fir trees until they disappear along the side of the building.

A second plea, pitiful, like an injured child, finds its way through the rain. Flipping up his hood, an urgent surge has him move from the porch out into the shower. Darting to the corner of the house, peering around it, Thomas finds the narrow space beside the building to be rain-slicked and cloaked in low light. Pushed up against the structure, the line of bins sit, their tops pelted by the heavy rain. While intense, it echoes along the passage like the sound of a million little drummers pounding down on plastic, from beyond them, a low wail remains, punching through the downpour, like a backbeat of the damned.

'Hello?' Thomas calls.

Nothing.

The rain lashes in, slashing at his face, whipping his eyes like shards of glass. Shielding his face, Thomas scans the single row of bins pushed up against the brickwork, the fence panels on the right, and between them, the narrow space growing tighter.

Listening hard against the rain, a passing car at his rear threatens to wreck his senses, but as it fades to a distant hiss, the low moan ahead of Thomas returns—this time louder, more urgent, before pinching into a high-pitched shriek of guttural pain.

My god.

Stepping away from the wall, staying close to it, he moves towards the sound gingerly, his movements hesitant and stammering. Reaching the bins, stepping past them, he stops, eyes fixed on the ground. A blood trail, fading with the rain, faint at its tip, darkens as it tails away from the side of the house. Eyes on the stain, he follows it, along the side of the house, to the right, where it disappears beneath a narrow slit at the base of the fence.

Bending down, peering into the dark space, his view is restricted to a tiny slither of area sloping beneath the fence and back up as it climbs into the neighbouring garden. Listening hard, moving his ear closer to the fence, the low whine creeps through the panel with choked panting. Reminiscent of someone giving birth while simultaneously being hacked to pieces, it is enough to send a shudder of sickness through his bowls.

Standing up, turning on his heels, Thomas re-traces his steps. He leaves Pinegrove through the front gate and turns left on the street. Eyes on the neighbouring house, the windows and door at the front, finding them dark, he turns left again and slowly makes his way up the driveway.

With eyes still monitoring the house, the black windows, and the shadows therein, he moves into the narrow side passage beside the house. Mirroring Pinegrove, it is muddied by the weather, blotted and shadowed, instantly lending to hesitation and caution.

Following the continued wail of whatever had dragged itself beneath the fence, Thomas picks up the trail of blood, it smeared as it streaks across the path, disappearing again around the back of the house.

Approaching the corner, the cries intensify. Peeping around the brickwork, his eyes pick up the trail again, where it stops before the large bi-folding backdoors. There, Thomas locates the source of the cries. A cat, half of one anyway, severed above the back legs, the trail of blood now obviously the result of the poor animal having dragged itself home. Muddy and raw, the cat's intestines, having formed a gruesome pinkish tail of pulpy gob, appears like raw hamburger. Now weary of his presence, the fluffy grey and white Persian, its hair mattered and dirtied, edges closer to the door.

Who the hell could do this?

A fox?

They are common, regularly spotted stalking gardens, rooting through bins, and on occasion, even seen entering homes to steal food.

'Yes, it seems this area is the murder capital of the world, that is for cats and dogs, it is reported an alleged assailant is partial to both species.'

Recalling what Peter had told him, looking down at the feline, the savage yet accurate severing of the body, Thomas concludes the attack was carried out for a more deliberate, insidious reason.

Slowly, moving to it, he crouches down beside the cat. Reaching out a hand, he attempts to comfort the animal. Patting its head, he gets a hiss from the cat in return, not out of spitefulness but fear and confusion. Considering his options, Thomas quickly concludes leaving the cat in such a state is not an option, nor is leaving it for the owners to find. Having noticed the rugged treehouse, the slide, the covered sandpit, Thomas decides to spare the family, the children, of the horror – which, of course, leaves him to take care of matters himself. The thought alone turns his stomach, twisting it knife-like.

Still patting the head, brushing its wet, matted hair in gentle strokes, the cat's hissing fades, leaving only the sounds of groggy, faint pleas for help. Checking its collar and tag, 'Mr Sprinkles,' Thomas sigs in recognition- the name fits perfectly with the cat's grey fur, dotted with white patches.

'I'm sorry,' he tells the cat, wrapping his fingers around its neck.

Tightening his grip, stretching his fingers, looping them until they form a circle. Squeezing, the cat's cries pitch high but finally go silent. Now crying, staring down at the animal, Thomas closes his fist, crushing the throat, snapping the neck with a sickening crack.

17

8:01pm...

Having refused the loan of the 71 Capri, Peter did, however, allow Thomas access to his other car, a spacious two-month-old Audi A4. Equipped with all the latest mod-cons. Sat within the glow of the interior light, Thomas finds his breathing to be heavy, laboured, and pitched at his chest.

Lilly asking to see him had been unexpected and, well, unwanted. Not that he doesn't want to see her or spend time with her, but rather, the opposite; actually, it's just that he doesn't feel prepared for it. Man enough. Him going to see her, asking a series of questions; well, it's scripted to a certain degree, but this, her asking him to her apartment, is anything but.

Don't get ahead of yourself and start thinking she...

Shaking his head clear of the idiotic thoughts before they can form and take root, he climbs out from behind the steering wheel. Locking the car, Thomas cuts a line to the front of the building. While cascading off the roof in swirls, the rain falls straight like bullets out here in the open, soaks him in seconds.

Except for a stingy overhang, the front entrance offers nothing in the way of shelter from the downpour. So, Thomas is forced to press himself in close to the door, to the intercom. Still, the rain reaches in and pats his shoulders like heavy hands, matting his hair, dropping a chill through him.

Checking the directory, Thomas thumbs the button for flat 3 and waits.

'Hello?' crackles a voice from the speaker.

'Lilly?'

'Thomas?'

'Yes.'

'You're early.'

'The traffic gods were with me.'

A beat of silence.

'Come on up, first floor,' she says, finally.

With a ping, the lock disengages, the door pops ajar, and Thomas is finally allowed in out of the rain. Shaking off his hair, flinging rainwater about the place, he runs a hand through it, sleeking it back against his scalp.

Looking down at himself, Thomas is suddenly aware of how unprepared he is. Going out, doing social activities, interacting with women, all of it have each become a list of terrifying chores. Ghostlike, his appearance is unsightly and cold. An older, thinner version of himself. Pale and wrung, his face appears foreign to him, like a shade, a cruel joke. This is his existence now, lingering and shackled like the condemned. A bleak world where he is forced to live apart from the woman he once loved, his child; a world where he is truly alone.

'Thomas!' Comes a voice.

Lilly.

A sign?

Her voice echoes along the hallway, finding him, recalling his hand from the handle. Turning, he moves through the entrance hall. The pleasantly tiled square space furnished with a small sofa and mirror is lit by a hanging light—fake crystal showing all the hallmarks of an overpriced designer item. Still, the interior is warm and welcoming, decidedly more expensive than the small space he now calls home.

Climbing the stairs to the first floor, Thomas finds the landing lit by a matching set of hanging lights, though somewhat smaller. He follows the landing through to the rear of the building, where it narrows into a hallway. There, Lilly stands waiting for him at the open door of her apartment. Haloed by warm, welcoming light, her fiery red hair undone and loose around her face, like him, she appears conflicted, a mix of nervousness and borderline resentment.

Slowing his approach, perspiring, Thomas is suddenly aware of the pools of sweat gathering beneath his arms. He wants to scream, to run away, but somehow, his legs not only keep him upright, but they also push him forward.

Get a grip, *you're acting like some teenage boy with a crush.*

It's true, Lilly, like her sister, has had an effect, one he honestly thought was now lost to him. Mary hadn't simply taken his daughter in the divorce, it seemed, until now anyway, she too had stolen his ability to find women even remotely interesting, let alone...

Knock it off, for God's sake.

Moving again, he finds Lilly looking at him with wide, quite possibly, surprised eyes. They are such, that Thomas struggles to look at her. Her entire appearance, her effortless beauty, confuse him. Scare him. Her jeans and t-shirt are softened with a long-knitted cardigan, and her loose shoulder-length hair, dancing around the collar, together afford her an almost luminous aurora. Makeup less, with cheeks naturally tinted with a rosy hue, a natural warmth burns through her uneasy eyes, as if they are smuggling burnt auburn embers.

'So, you came,' she says.

'I said I would, didn't I?'

'You did, yes, so, I guess you better come in.'

Confused by her greeting, his stomach twisting in knots, Thomas follows her inside, through a small entrance hall to a warmly, lamp-lit lounge come diner. A rectangle in shape, a small kitchen juts off to the right, dividing the two rooms with pair of saloon-style swinging, batwing doors. Like her sister, Lilly's apartment is organically warm and welcoming. A scattering of plants, books, soft colours, and textures is lit by cosy low light. The pillows, rug, carpet, plants pots and ornaments, wrapped in teals, yellows, greys and greens, are softened by a team of perfectly positioned lamps. Wall art, scenery mainly, all boast exotic, treacherous, mountainous worlds. South America, Greece, and Northern Italy, each framed print is presented in black and white, lending an almost alien appearance.

'Please,' she gestures to the sofa.

Thomas eyes the three-seat sofa nestled within the inlet of a large bay window at the far end of the room. Beyond, a blackened, rain-stained window offers only darkness and mystery. As if reading his mind, Lilly says, 'believe it or not, ducks populate a steam down below, that is, when weather and time permits.'

Stepping around a long coffee table out front, Thomas takes up a position at the left end of the sofa.

'Drink?' She asks.

'Sure,' he tells her.

Watching her cross the room, Thomas notices her hips and the effortless way they sway from side to side. Pushing through the swing doors, Lilly disappears into the kitchen, the doors sweeping back and forth in her wake.

Finding his hands to have grown clammy, he quickly wipes them on his jeans. Ahead of him, on the rack beneath the coffee table, all but hidden amongst magazines, Thomas notices a book.

His book.

Dead Right.

Recognising it by the bold red and black artwork, a portion of the hardback protrudes beneath the May edition of *Artist's magazine.*

Has she read it?

Sitting back, he attempts to get comfortable. Crossing his legs, uncrossing them, he shuffles in the seat but freezes as Lilly returns to the room. Carrying two tumblers, each 1/3 filled with what looks like whiskey, she hands him a glass before sitting down at the far end of the sofa. Looking at each other, the silence quickly rushes in to form a barrier between them. Thomas takes a sip of his drink to fill the uncomfortable standoff but slurps at the glass through nervous lips.

Watching him, her lips puckered, Thomas observes the drink, neat whiskey, as a test. As warmth floods his cheeks and his throat, before dropping down to heat his chest, he instinctively closes his eyes. Opening them again, Thomas catches her smiling. In staring, her eyes have him transfixed. He studies her face as if unable not to. Like two small log-burners, he notes the autumnal notes of her eyes and how they marry the shade of her hair almost perfectly. He notices the nearly invisible downy hairs lining her cheeks and how they add a certain warmth to her face and her middle parting, lopsided by a slight quiff at her fringe. Tracing downward, Thomas eyes her slender, exposed neck. Not white or pale, her completion is instead creamy, tinted with pinkish hues, bronzed slightly by the flaring of freckles.

'Thank you,' Thomas tells hers, having to look away. 'For the drink, I mean.'

'You're getting water on my sofa.'

Assessing his wet clothes, he mumbles, 'shit, yes, sorry,' and springs to his feet.

Still looking at him, her expression is one of indecision. With a slight nod of her head, a sign he takes as a positive step, she places her glass down on the coffee table and joins him standing.

'Let me take your coat. I'll get you a towel.'

Placing the glass down beside hers, he slips off his coat and hands it to her. Nodding, almost but not quite smiling, she leaves the room.

Wiping his brow, he scoops up the glass and finishes the drink in two large gulps. Its heat is instant; the alcohol, very much needed, burning, subsides into an oaky haze in his chest.

Noticing a set of framed photographs scattered within a tall, rustic bookcase, lit with a small lamp on the middle shelf, Thomas moves to it, thankful for the distraction. Giving the door a quick glance before reviewing the photographs- a collection of memories, all happy, smiling, better days. Focusing on one, dressed in climbing gear, striking yellows and blues, Lilly and Amy sit perched upon a bolder at the basis of a mountain. The peak, its sheer slopes, sit choked in spotted, low cloud cover.

'Ben Nevis, 2016,' Lilly tells him from the doorway.

Turning to her, 'you climbed that thing?'

'Twice, yes.'

Joining him at the bookcase, Lilly picks up the picture. Looking at it, her wide eyes twinkle with sadness.

'Scafell Pike, Sca Fell, Great End, we like to climb, planned to climb Mount Olympus next year, I guess we never will now,' she says.

Her words, sorrowful and hurt, leave Thomas's throat tight. Placing a hand upon her shoulder, she lets it rest there, to his surprise. She doesn't flinch, nor does she recall away in disgust. Waiting for her to look at him, he smiles softly, 'we'll find her, ok, I promise?'

'Please don't promise... you can't, and you shouldn't,' she says.

Stepping back, his hand drops from her shoulder.

'Well, I won't stop looking, I can't now, I...' He tails away, his words lost.

How can I now go on living, not knowing what happened to her?

Looking at him, as if seeing the pain, recognising it to now live inside him, Lilly leads him back to the sofa. Sitting, she says, 'I've read your book.'

'Really?' Trying to act surprised, he joins her in sitting down. 'What did you think?'

'I liked it, I like light reading, so.'

She flashes a short, soft smile, still one enough to jangle his insides. Returning the gesture, Thomas watches her sip her whiskey. She again looks at him; her expression, now soft, is hard to read. All the while, her eyes, torment him, his stomach, having it loop over itself, a feeling foreign to him, one devastated by divorce and rejection.

'I prefer your work for the newspaper, *London's Lost Generation, The Great War, The missing children of the north.* If I'm not mistaken, you won an award for the latter?' She asks, though clearly already knowing the answer to the question.

'It was a long time ago. In truth, I got lucky even landing the job. They were good to me, afford me the luxury to write stories close to my heart.'

'And now?'

'Fiction pays more."

'Well, in your case, right now, not so much.'

'Ouch.'

Sipping her drink, him watching her, their eyes remain on one another. Seconds stretch on, him wanting to look away but unable to do so.

Speak idiot, speak.

'Tell me about Reggie Morris?' She asks, breaking the silence.

Reggie Morris.

Looking down, his throat tightening, he tries to breathe but instead gulps in air wildly, painfully.

'Another time maybe,' she says. 'How are you liking Pinegrove?'

'Apart from Dave, the pervert neighbour below me, fine.'

'Dave, yes, what a treasure,' she says.

'You know him?'

'Know of him, only what Amy told me. Suffers from hemiparesis, among other things, a true charmer.'

'I met him today and Ms Harmony.'

'The old lady, yes.'

'Did Amy know them well?'

'No, I mean both moved in after Amy, plus after the attack, well Amy wasn't so good with strangers.'

'That's interesting.'

'Interesting how?

'She, Mrs Harmony that is, told me she's lived there for years, I assumed longer than Amy. That reminds me,' Thomas says. 'Your sister was receiving letters from someone before her disappearance. Do you know who was sending them?'

'No, he always wanted to meet her at the same place, the turn off for the Holy Trinity Church, at dusk, but Amy never went. I did, though, Mike and me, but he never showed.'

'This Mike, he a friend?' he asks - the words leaping from his lips before he can stop them. 'I mean, it was good you didn't go alone.'

Looking at him, her eyes narrow, and a smile, though faint, pulls at the tips of her mouth. He considers telling the truth; the hole, the figure who took her sister...

'A friend, yes,' she says, looking at him. When he looks away, she fills the silence. 'I think it was a test.'

'A test?' He asks.

'To see if she would turn up, to see if the letters had worked. I have one here, a letter.'

Placing her drink down, jumping up, Lilly returns to the bookcase. Between two leather-bound hardbacks, she fishes out an envelope. Slowly, looking at it, Lilly returns to the sofa. Taking the cushion beside him, she passes Thomas the letter. In her eyes, he notices a shadow pass across them- a darkness, an inner sickness, rooted inside her, escaping her eyes as if unable to hide it.

From the envelope, he removes an 11 x 8.5-inch letter. Ivory, single fold, double thickness- the kind you won't find in the stationary aisle at your local supermarket. On the face of it, it seems to be the same type he'd witnessed Amy receive. This is further supported by a pressed violet dropping loose when opening the letter. Studying it further, the elegant yet light penmanship, the type that takes years to perfect, and the choice of words, a shudder of cold runs through Thomas. Taking a deep breath, Thomas reads:

My dear Amy,

You seem to have me at a disadvantage. Not one to give in to need, nor am I weak, never have I allowed anyone to have such a

hold on me, but my love, you are so very, very exceptional. Afraid you have stripped me of everything I knew to be true, my strengths, my plans for the future, rearranging them, changing them, changing me, I now understand this was my fate all along.

So, in you, I have seen the man I want to be, so I asked you again, implore you, please meet with me, or I will instead be forced to take matters into my own hands. The turn off for the Holy Trinity Church. Sunday, at dusk.

I love you.
Yours forever.

'Yours forever?' Thomas asks.

'We never did find out who sent them. Do you think the letters are connected?' She asks.

'Most certainly, yes. They continued right up to the night she went missing.'

'How do you know that?'

Because I can see the past.

'A contact of mine at the newspaper, they told me,' he lies but continues speaking. 'Plus, the letters were not postmarked or stamped, meaning they were hand-delivered by someone who has access to Pinegrove. Also, the fact they never refer to him waiting at Holy Trinity Church, to me, suggests he knew Amy hadn't gone.'

'Meaning?'

'He was watching her, closely and constantly,' he pauses. 'I think you're right in what you said, it was a test, a test your sister failed.'

18

2 days later...

Moonlight Toys, a filthy toilet of a sex shop, sits on the corner of Walkers Court, an area of Soho with tight one-way streets, dead ends and cobbled paving. Noting the redevelopment works throughout the area, the closure of other adult shops, and peepshows, Thomas wonders how long Moonlight Toys has before it disappears. Soon, with all traces gone, erased, scrubbed clean, it will be as if it had never existed, replaced with bistros, cafes, book shops, and new age jazz bars.

With parking being at a minimum and paid to park almost half a mile away, Peter elected to park his old Ford thirty or so meters from the shop, riding the curb beside a set of closed shutters. Watching the traffic warden shuffle her butt down the road, Peter estimates they have no more than twenty to twenty-five minutes before they get a ticket.

'It's a double yellow, so we better get moving,' Peter tells him.

As Thomas climbs from the car, Peter shifts Thomas a look, one he takes for apprehension, though he does an excellent job of masking it. Locking the car and straightening his long coat, Peter joins Thomas at the curb.

The rain and sharp chill chase them past the black painted façade and windows along the street. The words *OPEN* and *XXX* and *DVD* are abuzz with red neon. Several letters sit dark, sorrowful as if somehow, they know the fate awaiting the shop.

'So, we're really going in there. Walk right in the front door?' Peter asks, his pace slowing as they close in on the entrance.

'It will be alright. We're two guys looking at porn. You know how many guys go in here every day?'

'I don't know, how many?' Peter asks.

Stumped by the question, Thomas stumbles, 'I don't know, but it has to be a lot.'

Hesitating at the front entrance, which sits perpendicular to the corner. Thomas stares at the handle. This was what he was good at, once, going into a place, acting like he belonged. Now, looking down at his clothes, then at Peter's, Thomas recognises his mistake. The key is to blend in, not stand out like two out of uniform police officers.

'You, ok?' Peter asks.

'Yes, sorry, just a little rusty. Come on, let's look around, nice and easy like.'

'So, no go spoiling for a confrontation, no making a customer complaint?' Peter says, a smile pulling at his lips, an apparent attempt at lightening the mood.

Rolling his eyes, Thomas grabs the door handle but stops. To their right, along the road, lingering inside the inlet of what looks like a second door to the shop, Thomas spies a woman standing, smoking. Young and short, locked on him, her eyes are heavy and fogged but glint with recognition. Taking another long drag, she rubs her skinny arms, warming them. Her right arm is tattooed from shoulder to wrist, an amalgamation of cartoon characters, Loony Toons, Bugs Bunny, Daffy Duck, Tweety, Porky Pig, all connected by fading ink.

Pulling open the door, Thomas shuffles inside, Peter firmly behind him. Instantly, the smell of waxy leather, musk, and PVC plastic hit Thomas. Surprisingly, or unsurprisingly, depending on how you look at it, like stepping into a cave, the shop's interior is far darker than the storm outside. The music, fully charged, dark rock, the punk type, leaves the shop heavy under its weight. Though the music is low, it is still a hardcore assault on the ears- music full of blacks and reds, leather and spikes.

While not the first adult sex shop he's ever visited, it is, however, only the second. The first and only other, Annie's Adult Bookshop, a shithole near Kings Cross train station, long closed with all the redevelopments leading up to the 2012 Summer Olympics. He was seventeen and it was a time before the internet was widely used, a trip with a friend and his fake ID, which, as it turned out, wasn't needed. Two porn mags for £10, one named *Leisure-Ladies*, the other, *Lonely-Teens.* While being as respectful as such material can be, both publications were lurid with overly warm photography, glamorising the women, selling them as Hollywood megastars. The magazines found a home beneath his mattress, that was until his mother found them, and forcing Thomas to watch, burned them on the barbeque.

Moving through the shop, past a series of display shelves, Thomas is forced to divert his gaze from the team of male and female mannequins dotted about, modelling different outfits: fetish, sexy, leather, PVC, mainly black but all shiny, studded and cheap looking.

Bloody mannequins.

Horrible things, featureless faces, bald the lot of them, watching Thomas, tracking his journey through the shop. Thomas's mind momentarily goes back to William Telfer of Clydebank and his desperate escape from some nutcase posing as a dummy. Looking at them now, a chill runs through him. Expecting them to come alive, to lurch for him, Thomas diverts his eyes.

Looking around, he counts one male customer. Chubby and ball-like, looking over his shoulder, the middle-aged man smiles and nods as if saying, *'Hey pal, welcome to the club.'*

Already, his skin has turned itchy, prickled with heat. Moving through the shop, passing an extensive selection of sex toys: dildos, vibrators, different sizes, different colours, made from rubber, leather, plastic, and metal. One, monstrous in its scope, claiming to be modelled on a well-renowned pornstar, retails at over a hundred pounds though it looks barely human.

Stopping, turning back, Thomas finds Peter standing, inspecting the massive rubber penis.

'How does one use....' Peter starts.

'Bogart, we're here on business, remember?'

Shifting Thomas a look, rolling his eyes, Peter returns the penis to the display shelf.

'Help you with something, fellas?' A voice calls from the rear of the shop.

Turning, a burly man stands behind a glass counter. His leather trousers are completed with a heavily studded belt and leather waistcoat. His arms, muscular but wrapped in fat, are tattooed. Given his appearance, his pierced nose and ears, the ring in his lower lip, you'd think he would appear sleazy, but instead, his voice is warm, his tone is both light and welcoming.

'Just looking, thanks,' Thomas tells him.

'We got mags and videos in the back, shout if you want a demo,' he says, smiling accommodatingly.

Excellent customer service.

Thomas stops to inspect the items sitting proudly behind the glass of a thin cabinet/counter- a collection of whips, anal beads, plugs and clamps, gas masks, and other paraphernalia. More torturous than pleasure-giving, Thomas is clueless to their need and application. What is of interest is the series of leather hoods on display behind the clerk. The selection, all black, pulled, taught over head-mannequins, glare back at him. Like the one worn by Amy's attacker, the small eye slits and the zip-closed mouth holes leave him cold.

Moving on, in a hurry, Thomas pushes through an open doorway walled with hanging beads into a shadowed, narrow passageway. Closed doors line the walls on both sides. At the end of the hall, an open door, lit in dim light, is labelled:

MAGAZINES, VHS, DVD – IF YOU DON'T SEE IT, CHANCES ARE WE CAN GET IT – ASK AT THE COUNTER.

Moving along the passageway, Thomas stops before moving into the room. He checks a dark, skinny staircase on his right. His eyes follow its snaking path upwards before disappearing into the upper level. There he finds the same girl from before. Looking down at him, she is quick to retreat from view.

'Who is she?' Peter asks.

'A friend, I think.'

I hope.

Stepping into the dim room, passing through the second set of vertical beads, finding it unsettlingly quiet. Thomas stops to scan the space, allowing his eyes a moment to adjust to the low light. Cramped, low lit, the card tables running around the room's outer edge are topped with dirty plastic tubs stuffed full of pornographic merchandise. The overly tangy smell of cheap plastic and sweet musk quickly forms a film upon his tongue.

One customer, a lanky, balding man in long shorts, stands hunched over a tub of DVDs. His breathing, sweaty and heavy, appears fearful of their arrival. Looking over his shoulder at them, Thomas gives him a nod, but still, the man's uneasiness remains.

Ignoring the man, Thomas moves to the table to his left. Working clockwise, he scans the selection of goods. Already, an uneasiness, a film of grim coats his skin, his fingers, an invisible plague Thomas fears may never wash off. Magazines first: young, old, gay, white, black, oriental, mixed. All wrapped in sealed plastic, all boasting indecent, low grade, unflattering covers. After inspecting one from the first tub, *Posh Twats*, Thomas finds the plastic sheath greasy, sticky, and nasty as its front image. Quick to return it, slipping it back among a hundred others, Thomas wipes his hands on his trousers.

As they continue the tour, etching around the room, the lone customer slides sideways away from them, maintaining his distance. Tight to his chest, the man clings to a stack of DVDs like his life depends upon it. With another nervous sideways glance, as if fearful Thomas might steal the items from him, the man turns sharply and scurries from the room. Watching him leave, Thomas and Peter share a look before returning to the search. Thomas notes other genres listed under headings: Bondage, S&M, Teen, before moving on to DVDs: slutty babysitters, young men screwing old men, foot fetish. Horrible stuff, all of it, but from what he can see, all legal and mainstream.

'What are we looking for exactly?' Peter asks.

'Give it a minute,' Thomas tells him.

While he's not sure what he should be looking for, with the tip from Roadrunner being beyond vague, Thomas decides to remain in the room, browsing, hoping his instincts are correct.

'You boys ok in here?' Asks a voice from the doorway.

Bingo.

Before turning, Thomas flashes Peter a half-smile. At the door, a young woman peers into the room. While not who he was hoping for, Thomas offers her a smile. Returning the gesture, grinning wide, she slides into the room through the beads. Making eye contact, Thomas observes her as nineteen, twenty, twenty-one at a pinch. However, with the lack of clothes, her skinny, tiny frame, her flat chest, Thomas figures she could easily pass for someone far younger.

Maybe there is illegal stuff going on here after all.

Her denim shirt, Mickey Mouse crop-top and two-inch heels reek of prostitution. Her overdone makeup suggests insecurity, while her misty eyes hint at drug use or the first signs of cataracts, though Thomas suspects the former.

'Fine, thank you,' Peter offers.

'And you?' She asks, her eyes flicking to Thomas.

'I've been better,' he smiles.

'Well, I've got something for that. Do you want to follow me?'

'Sure,' he says.

Meeting her at the beads, he turns to Peter, 'I won't be long, I'll meet you back at the car.'

Peter's mouth drops open. Leaving him standing there, Thomas follows the girl from the room.

'Follow me, darling, this way,' she sings.

With her rump swaying above him, Thomas trails in behind, following her up the narrow steps, them creaking beneath their weight. With every step, her skirt lifts enough to give him a view of her buttocks and the thin, pink piece of material sitting nestled between them. Diverting his eyes, Thomas fixes his gaze on the steps as they wind up to the first floor.

At the landing, the fading light closes in around them, as does the paint-peeling walls and threadbare carpet. The cramped space doubles back into a hallway lit faintly by stingy wall lights, defused further by a layer of cigarette smoke. A series of doors lining the hallway on both sides sit closed. Beyond them, non-descript music echoes out, converging, leaving it a muddle in the tight space. Throbbing with heavy bass, it rattles through the walls, up through Thomas's feet, clouding his mind, removing his ability to hear.

Leading Thomas to the nearest door, she stops, one hand on the door handle, the other resting against his chest. Looking up at him, she asks, having to boom over the music, 'here we are. Now, before we get serious, you do have money?'

'Now, please don't take this the wrong way,' Thomas says, forced to shout. 'But I would like to see one of your friends. The girl with the tattooed arm?'

Taken aback, mouth twitching, she looks up at Thomas as if his words are an assault- like a slap to the face, one left without the decency of leaving a mark.

'Wonderful, thanks,' she huffs, turns and knocks on a door a little further along the hallway. 'Liz, one for you.'

Left alone, Thomas moves to the door and waits. His palms, having grown clammy, fidget at his sides with nervous energy. Hearing movement through the door, he readies himself. When it opens, the girl from before, with the tattooed arm, stands haloed in the doorway. At first smiling, but upon seeing him, her smile is ripped from her young face.

'Yes?' She shouts.

'I'm Thomas,' he tells her.

'What?' She moans, ready to close the door.

'Thomas, Thomas William,' he yells, stepping closer. 'But I think you already know who I am.'

'I, I don't know what you mean,' she says, her voice thick with an Eastern European accent.

Attempting to close the door, Thomas steps forward, stopping the door with his boot.

'Please, I just want to talk. I'll pay you for your time, ok?' He says.

Her grip on the door remains, but her narrowing eyes tell him she is at least considering the offer. Poking her head out through the gap, she checks the hallway.

'How much you got?' She asks.

'How much for an hour?'

She considers this and says, 'one-twenty.'

Yeah right.

'Ok,' removing his wallet, opening the billfold, he pulls out six twenties.

No wine for me tonight.

Handing her the notes, she takes her time to count them. Checking them for counterfeits, she holds them and studies them one by one. Happy, looking at him, still apprehensive, she rocks back on her heels. Finally, pulling the door open, she leads him inside.

The room is small, stuffy, and claustrophobic, but with the door closed, the pounding music, while slight, is muffled. The air, thick with artificial smells from a plug-in air freshener and the collective smell of men, as if competing, they permeate the air, staining it. The double bed is lit with pink tea lights at the back wall, wrapped around the cast iron headboard, while at both ends, dangling, is a pair of pink, fluffy handcuffs. The rest of the room sits within the dull light, almost apologetically.

'You could do with air-con,' Thomas tells her.

'We like to keep the heat turned up, wears out the johns,' she says, sitting down on the bed.

Dragging a chair from a small dressing table, Thomas sits across from her.

'Liz, that your name?' He asks.

She looks at him, her eyes working, considering how much to tell him. She is a pretty girl, be it hidden beneath two too many layers of makeup, but her green eyes, wide and intelligent, make up for it. It's a shame they sit all but hidden behind aggressively obvious fake lashes.

'Katerina, my name's Katerina,' she tells him. 'Liz is my working name; us girls all have one.'

'Katerina's a beautiful name,' Thomas tells her, sincere in his words.

Laughing, she flicks her head back. The light catches her eyes, setting them off against her short, blonde hair, cut close to her scalp. She almost has a boyish, pixie look, one many men pine for.

'You don't need to do that, compliments, you already paid me so,' she says,

'I wasn't, I mean,' he pauses. 'Katerina is a name I used in my first novel. It's often associated with the Greek word *katharós*, meaning *pure*.'

Her smile slips away, and for a moment, she looks guilty for mocking him. Taking her time, she considers her response.

'Fair enough,' she says. 'So, what is it you want to know?

'You called me,' he says. 'Road Runner, am I right?' he says, gesturing to her tattooed arm, he says. 'You can trust me.'

'Trust you, can I really?' She smirks.

'Yes, you can. I want... need to find out what happened to Erika, nothing more, your involvement doesn't have to be mentioned.'

Again, she looks at him, her eyes studying his. 'Ok, but this can't come back to me, understand?'

'Of course.'

'Ok, well, I knew Erika. She was... a friend. We used to work together.'

'Here?'

'Here, other places, but the point is Erika got out. She was just... two pretty for this place, this life, well, from the start. We were all surprised when she first arrived; all trim and tall, she looked like a fashion model, understand?'

'Sure, I get it, and she was popular?'

'With the johns, you mean?'

'Yes.'

'Very, they loved her, they all did. I remember when her profile first went live; I mean, within just twenty minutes, the phone was ringing off the hook. For the little time she was here, she made a lot of money, I mean, a... lot... of... money, a suitcase full, understand?'

'Anyone standout, any punters, harassing her, pestering, stalking her?'

'No, not that I know of.'

'Anyone acting strange, obsessive types, anybody scare her?'

'Are you kidding? Everyone who comes in here acts strange. Every time we open that door, we take a chance, fourteen times a day, understand? Sure, there are the quiet ones, the nervous johns, but you can't trust any of them.'

'Was there anyone, I mean, anyone specific Erika might have mentioned? Please think, it's important.'

With her eyes growing dark, her looking away, and her face turning bitter, it hits him. With him probing for information on Erika, he has overlooked the subtext in Katerina's answers. An amateur mistake made by a reporter out of practice and out of touch. In ignoring her plight, he has alienated, minimised, and insulted the young woman.

'Must be hard, this life?' He asks.

She takes a moment to consider his question, his words, but thankfully, she turns back to face him.

'It is, yes. We work hard, all of us, even the not so pretty ones.'

'I understand,' Thomas says, trying to think. 'You mentioned the name, Khaliq?'

She takes a moment. Clearly, the name alone has a hold over her. 'Khaliq runs this place and others across London. He instantly liked Erika, tried to mould her, but she was gone after six months. She got herself into the modelling game, found work too, then simply stopped coming back around.'

'This Khaliq, tell me about him?'

'Mean and demanding, but fair, I guess. 5.8" though he'll swear he's 6.2". Sees himself as a bodybuilder, but he's more fat than muscle. Claims to be rich and to have killed before.'

Porn shops doubling as brothels.

'And he and Erika went together, I mean, were they a couple?'

'For a time, but if you ask me, he was kidding himself. He was furious when she left, put his fist through the wall. Check for yourself, and you'll see, just out there,' she says, pointing to the door.

'And you think he hurt her?'

She considers this, nervousness creeping back into her features. 'Yes, I do. When she got out and away from here, she stopped seeing Khaliq, returning his calls, ghosted him, you know, and us, all of us girls, this life. She met someone else, not sure who, but she was in love, said she wanted a baby, she was looking at apartments with him, I know that much. Took photographs; she said he was brilliant.'

James Ruck.

'How do I get to speak to Khaliq?'

'Khaliq? How should I know, you're the investigator?' She snorts.

'I'm a writer, not an investigator....'

'That's not what your post said, former investigative journalist; that is what you said. So that was you, right? Or was it lies?'

Give me a break.

Sighing, rubbing his face, he looks at her. 'You're right, my mistake, but anything you can give me will help. You said he runs things from this shop?'

Again, she looks at him. Confliction stains her eyes, and the frail trust he had earned, Thomas fears now has been lost.

'He does, but he comes and goes...' she says, trailing off. Her eyes grow wide in discovery. 'He's running one of his markets soon; he'll be there, he always is.'

'What kind of market?'

'The underground type, illegal stuff... the darkest, trust me.'

'I'll be fine.'

'If you say so,' she says, rolling her eyes. 'But I swear, you give him my name....'

'I won't, and you'll never come into it, ok?'

'Like I say, if you say so. Now, you need to get out.' She tells him, standing up. 'I'll see if I can get you an address, but don't you come back here to speak to me, understand?'

'I understand,' Thomas says.

At the door, stopping him from leaving, she asks. 'What you said before about my name, meaning pure, is that true?'

Turning to look at her, Thomas finds her eyes in the glow of the tealights. Noting the change in them, now glassy, wide and hopeful, he smiles.

'Look it up. Like I said, it's a beautiful name. Clean, pure, blameless, innocent free from corrupt desire, from sin and guilt, and in a similitude, like a vine cleansed by pruning and so fitted to bear fruit.'

Turning from him, wiping her cheek, she smiles, one Thomas takes for a thank you.

'Fitted to bear fruit,' she stops to ponder the meaning. 'One day. Ok, well, you better get going, I have a client arriving soon, and he won't want to share.'

19

3 days later...

Peter's old ford rumbles through the deserted war-torn esque area of Millennium Mills. Situated at the south side of the Royal Victoria Dock, positioned between the Excel London and the Thames Barrier, the old nine-floor derelict sits within walking distance from London City Airport and the exclusive, recently built Britannia village in Newham.

Approaching the sprawling structure's chipboard fenced wall, they find a gated entrance to the grounds open but guarded by two hooded figures. Stepping out from the shadows, they quickly swarm the car, flanking it. Holding up a hand for Peter to stop, the one on the right steps out in front of them. When bringing the vehicle to a stop, the man steps round to the driver's window.

Winding it down, reaching his head out the window, Peter is first met by a torch beam, then the rain, made incandescent by light's sharp glare.

'Gentlemen, password please,' the man asks. His black hoodie and black jeans leave him a silhouette behind the torch.

'Calla Lily,' Peter tells him.

'Thank you,' The man says, removing the torch. 'You'll be searched on your way in. Good evening to you both, and please, behave.'

At least the password she gave me is legit; there's a start.

Stepping aside, the two men return to the shadows. Peter moves the car forward, the gears shuddering beneath his feet, biting with traction.

'Stay calm,' Thomas says, attempting to reassure the young man, though his own heart feels like a wrecking ball in his chest.

Passed the gate, a short slope leads them down to a parking area littered with rubble, overgrown shrubs and crumbling concrete.

'How on earth is this place still standing?' Thomas asks, his eyes roaming the darkened monstrosity.

'Believe it or not but the Mill's about to undergo a major renovation, part of a £3.5billion redevelopment of Silvertown,' Peter says, slowing the car, the head beams bathing the area in yellow light. 'Million-pound apartments, shops, gyms, cafes.'

'Another stain to cover. And markets like this will forward lay buried beneath,' Thomas says. 'Million-pound apartments, do you think people would still buy them knowing the horror this place has seen?'

Swinging the car into a tight spot between a burnt-out car and a massive slab of graffitied concrete, Peter shuts off the engine.

'I think everything deserves a second chance,' Peter says, eyes forward, careful not to look at Thomas.

Thomas considers this, 'maybe.'

Watchful, Thomas surveys the area through all four windows. Spatters of rain obstruct his view, but still, he can make out the vague outline of other cars. Beyond, the lower level of the sprawling structure is faintly lit. With both the night and weather competing to darken the area, London's lights leave an orange hue hanging over the decaying property as if poisoning the sky from the dock and the neighbouring residential areas.

'Ok, we look around and get a feel for the place,' Thomas tells Peter.

'And there was me thinking we'd go on a spending spree,' Peter says, smiling.

Thomas honours his response with a smile of his own and climbs from the car. The rain, quick to lash at his face, forces him to pull his coat together. Peter, locking the car, follows Thomas across the gravelly lot. Confused about where to go, Thomas is startled and relieved to spot another set of shadowy figures loitering at the corner of the structure. Like their friends at the gate, they too are dressed in dark clothes, hoods up, blackening their features. Using a torch, whipping it sword-like, one directs them around the corner.

Much like their way in, the area adjacent to the structure is a jumble of shattered cement blocks, craters and overgrown patches of poison ivy. As for the building itself, stretching out ahead of them on the left, partly cloaked, disappears, absorbed by the murky night. Even with the hooded goons guarding the place, with it shrouded in darkness, the site appears abandoned, and but from the occasional car, there would be no signs of activity whatsoever.

Glancing up at the building, Thomas shudders. The hundred or so windows, all hollowed out, the panes now smashed, leave the interior hauntingly dark. The walls at ground level, spray-painted with profanities and crude pictures, depict rape, murder, mutilation, the cruel and the vile, adding another level of grime. Thomas can feel it, on his skin, beneath his nails, so eager to dirty him, to darken his soul.

'Let's never come back here, ok?' Peter whispers.

'Agreed,' Thomas nods.

Ahead of them, a gaping entrance, once possibly a loading dock for trucks, is guarded by a further two men in hoodies. The pair direct them inside, their torch beams lighting the way, carving two cones of fading light into the structure's interior. A string of lights, bare bulbs on a wire, snake a line through the massive open space. Thomas traces them to a stairwell leading down into the guts of the building.

Following the lights, their feet in the open space slings echoes in behind them, chasing them across the damp concrete. Stopping at the stairwell, Peter joins Thomas in looking down, their eyes following the line of lights down to the lower level.

'I guess we go down,' Peter states, ominously, not as a question, but in horrified realisation.

Looking at Peter, his eyes holding no authority, Thomas steps forward and starts down, descending into the gloom. On the stairs, passing a departing customer clutching a brown paper bag stuffed with God knows what, the small man rushes past them with gusto, like a child might after visiting Santa's grotto.

The basement level is a sprawling cavernous place; its actual size cannot be determined due to the lack of light and the heavily soot-like malaise weighing down from above. A dimly lit pit of squalor, of which Thomas fears, merely breathing in its air may dirty him for the rest of his life.

Ahead of them, an area of tables and stalls sit clustered together, in rows, flea-market-like. Huddled beneath a network of lights, bare bulbs, each a murky orange, offering the faintest of light.

Beyond it, two rows of five shipping containers sit half in shadow, their fronts open, each covered with a curtain. A group of men sit around a table off to one side. Playing cards, their voices, low chit-chatter, sit back behind the market like a cackle of twisted crows.

Stepping away from the stairs, slowly, Thomas and Peter make their way to the market, shuffling in behind a customer. Extremely fat, his suit sits at least two sizes too small for him, his bloated, sausage-like hands finger the merchandise. His head jerks from side to side, from one stall to the next, an affliction Thomas takes as a cocktail of nervousness and excitement. Over his shoulder, shifting a look, uneasiness drops through his features. Turning, he skurries to the other side of the market, away from his pursuers.

Thomas attempts to walk like someone who belongs but is forced to stuff his shaking hands into the pockets of his coat. Having dressed conservatory in jeans and t-shirts, Thomas cannot shake the feeling that his and Peter's attire is both obvious and a poor attempt at fitting in.

I hope I am not taken for law enforcement.

I hope to blend in.

I hope to leave this place with both my life and soul intact.

He tells himself to not act contrived, easy to please, to try and come across as a seasoned buyer, but he feels the mask already slipping.

Twenty or so customers, primarily men, browse, shop, hunched over the tables, mouths open, eyes like that of a predator. Moving to the first table, feeling eyes on him, his skin prickles with gooseflesh.

'We got hard bondage, S&M, simulated rape, stuff harder than hard. I'll do you a discount for package deals,' a plump man reels off from behind the first table.

Thomas looks at him, almost disbelieving, his relaxed candour as off-putting as the contents on sale: VHS tapes, sleeves of DVDs, labelled and priced, but thankfully, blank of any imagery.

Moving on, they pass a stall selling dirty magazines. With labels such as *asphyxiation/choking/strangling, S&M/extreme-bondage,* the covers are grimy, perverse and sadomasochistic.

Next, and worse still, a large stall topped with dirty old cardboard boxes overflowing with blank VHS tapes with handwritten labels *scat/poop, snuff fantasy, spit/vomit/snot, transsexual, ugly/fat/old, water sports, fem doms (female domination), fisting/objects, gape/prolapse/rosebutt (extreme anal), hentai (extreme cartoons), incest, menstruation, rape fantasy, bestiality, body modification/piercing, face puking/rough, enemas/medical fetish, disfigured, necrophilia.*

Looking at the young woman standing behind the stall, no older than twenty, slim and attractive, shocked by her appearance, Thomas can only look at her, his mouth agape. She smiles as if knowing for sure he doesn't belong.

'Can I interest you, gentlemen, in a little, *Horse-cock-Dildo-Deep-Throat?*' She asks, still smiling.

She could be a movie star or model with perfect skin, high cheekbones, and flowing blonde hair.

'Tempting, but no, thank you,' Peter answers.

Stopping at the next stall, Thomas's heart lurches. Looking back at him is a row of mannequin heads, all masked, and while not the same, many of them bear a frightening resemblance to the one Amy's abductor wore. Like those on sale at Moonlight Toys, these appear somehow more extreme, macabre, visceral. Counting eight in total, all black and leather, where most are decorated with silver studs, zips for mouths, and tiny eyeholes, others have a far more exotic design. One has a blank face, strapping covering the mouth and eyes, reminding him of a tied straitjacket. Another, a horrific thing shaped like a dog head, is complete with a closed muzzle and neck chain. A second set made from latex is fronted with the worst of the lot, a plain hood broken by two small nose holes.

'Howdy,' the seller offers through a heavy Scottish accent.

He smiles at Thomas from beneath a tanned Stetson.

'Hi,' Thomas manages, all most choking.

The fat, topless man looks him up and down, his eyes roaming, enjoying what he sees. Rubbing his chest with short, stubby fingers, his nails bitten down to the nub, he smiles, 'You're a fan, I can tell. I've seen that look before, a mask-virgin, am I right?'

The seller's voice, well-read and soft, unsettles Thomas's stomach with its normality, and his smile, warm and welcoming, simply does not belong in a place like this.

'Yes, do you do others?'

'What are you looking for? I've got all kinds?' He smiles, a glint in his sunken eyes.

'I saw this video once,' Thomas stutters, his nerves apparent. 'There was this performer, who wore a leather hood, like these, except for a great big red horn on its front.'

'Red, um, sounds like a commissioned piece. Rex uses items with splashes of red.'

'Rex?' I ask.

'Yes, sorry, Max Rex. Extravagant, some might say a little strange but undoubtedly, talented, I think I might have a card here somewhere,' he says, bending down. 'Um, let me see, aw, here we are.'

Standing up, the fat man hands Thomas an old, crumpled flyer. His fingers, Thomas notices, are stained yellow, either from jaundice, excessive cigarette usage, or eating honey with his fingers.

The flyer is amateurish and garish, a small black piece of card, stained with God knows what reads:

> **YOUR DARKEST DESIRE - YOUR WORST NIGHTMARE - SEX AND DEATH - BLOOD AND WINE - FEAR AND UTOPIA - Items personally tailored as unique, one-of-a-kind toys**

'Mind if I keep this?' Thomas asks.

'You can borrow it, that is if you remember to bring it back?' The man's fishy pink lips grow, curling into another smile.

'Sure,' Thomas tells him.

'Anyone ever tell you, you look a little like Harrison Ford, from the '80s, Frantic, Blade Runner?'

'Not lately.'

'Shame about the beard. Don't hide behind it,' he smiles, his eyes lingering on Thomas.

Nodding, Thomas moves on, his skin on fire, crawling with the intensity of hives. Where his stomach had already turned over, the following table brings warm bile to his throat. Looking down at the selection before him, Thomas finds neat packs of polaroids, sealed in plastic, wrapped with rubber bands, categorised into gender, labelled with ages from fifteen all the way down to...

Swallowing hard, Thomas picks up a set. The wad, an inch thick, sits greasy in his hand. The top image shows a boy, too young to comprehend, which is thankfully censored by the rubber band wrapping. The seller, a wafer-thin woman with a hollowed-out face, stricken by drug use and bad choices, looks up at him from a deckchair, her black eyes of marble sliding from an old, worn paperback copy of Treasure Island. Far from thin, beyond frail, her form is cadaverous. Thomas disagrees with hitting women, no matter the crime, but he's fully prepared to make an exception for her.

'One-fifty a pack, I'll do discount for multi-buys,' she tells Thomas, smoking the remains of a roll-up cigarette.

'No, just looking,' Thomas returns the photos to the table.

'Too old for ya, we have younger, but it will cost you more,'

Shuddering, wiping his hands on his coat, he diverts his eyes from the woman and asks, 'Khaliq, you know him?'

'Sure, the big man, over there,' she nods her head back to the shipping containers, the table of card players.

Moving to the end of the aisle, the seller's eyes watch him until he and Peter break away from the market through a gap between two tables.

At his side, Peter whispers, 'What now?'

'I don't know. I um, I'm a little out of practice with all this,' Thomas stutters, seeing the men at the table turn to watch their approach. 'But we can't turn back now.'

From the table, they are met by a bald man whose face looks as if it's been dragged across concrete. Stout, fifties, wide as a truck, with a neck as thick as his head, he halts Thomas's approach.

'Gentlemen, can we help you with something? We got girls of all colours, all ages, what's your pleasure?' He asks.

'I'm looking for Khaliq?' Thomas says, his voice surprisingly firm.

'Never heard of him,' he says, the words blunt upon fat, bulging liver-like lips.

'You sure?' Thomas asks, the words springing from his lips as if unrestrained.

'I just said so, didn't I?'

Nodding, stuttering, Thomas eyes the rest of the men. One, possibly middle eastern, is far better dressed than the others. His shirt and jacket are sharp and well-groomed, like his eyebrows and slicked-back hair. However, his hard, tattooed hands, his bumpy face, lightly pitted, reminding Thomas of orange rind, speak of someone born into poverty and struggle. A jagged scar running across his throat adds credence to his observation. Even so, and where his fingers, wrists, and neck are all draped in thick yellow gold, his diamond-studded ears twinkle in the light, his eyes demand all attention. Dark, hollow, they lack even an inch of humanity.

Through a heavy accent, the man spits, 'he's in there, the second container.'

Thomas turns, his eyes following the man's outstretched finger to the containers. Nodding, Thomas steps away from the thick-necked man, moving to the row of containers, expecting something heavy or sharp to hit him from the rear at any minute.

What the hell are you doing here?

Strange to think now, now he's firmly inside the lion's den. It's always too late, the moment you realise your mistake, and now, surrounded by the worst we as a race can offer, does Thomas realise it.

Passing the first container, a low whimper escapes through the curtain. A dim light penetrates the material from inside, turning it ruby, leaving what sits beyond a mystery.

At the second container, hesitating, Thomas stops and turns to look back to the table. The same man nods, smiles, gestures with an outstretched hand to enter.

'After you,' Peter whispers at his rear, his voice high, a tremble to it.

With a heaving chest, gulping in air, Thomas finds it tastes like sweat, overly sweet perfume, and something else. As he pulls the curtain aside, he is quick to realise what this is.

'Hey man, what the hell!' Moans a startled man from inside.

Fat, pale, his skin glistening and naked. On his knees, panting, the confused and red-faced man looks over his shoulder with wide, wild eyes. Below him, his sweat streaked thighs wedged between those of a young black woman, a girl really, who lays sprawled out on a mattress. She looks up at Thomas, no more than eighteen, her eyes wide, hazy and heavy, punctuated by black circles. Her sprawled out arms, limp across the ground, are studded and bruised from extension needle usage. Possibly heroin, cocaine, methamphetamines, or a cocktail laced with God knows what.

Forced usage.

Stepping back, leaving her alone with the man, Thomas returns the curtain to its original position. The sound of laughter from the table, a mixture of rapturous and guttural, drags him away from the container.

Returning to the table, the laughing continues, even as Thomas snatches up a pen and a newspaper. Writing his number on a clear section of print framing the front page, he drops it in front of the man draped in gold, who Thomas is now sure is Khaliq.

'Tell Khaliq I have a business proposition for him. If he's not interested, I'll take my money elsewhere,' Thomas says, dousing the laughter.

Turning with Peter at his side, they head for the exit.

'Time to leave,' Thomas says, his voice shaky and pitched.

'You didn't leave your actual number, did you?'

Thomas looks at him, 'yeah, stupid?'

Shaking his head, Peter states, 'I'd say.'

20

1 hour, 14 minutes later...

With the dim lights of the old Ford's dash offering nothing in the way of comfort, the drive back from the market is one of silence and darkness. Their experience at the old mill, the things they'd seen, the vile and utterly evil, having taken hold, now sits between them as an uneasy stupor, growing, twisting with the night. A sickening feeling has now settled at Thomas's core, not one exclusively a result of the horror in what he saw, but one born from helplessness. The polaroids, the little faces, their bare bodies flash before his eyes, an endless montage that follows him when he closes them. Like his own private cinema, as if arranged by the devil, it plays over and over, staining his soul forever.

What started out as one missing woman, having turned to two, the case now opens before Thomas into something else entirely. Something far larger, horrific and insidious, Thomas struggles with what he's now supposed to do with the information.

I can't get involved with this; I mean, what can I do?

Wiping his clammy hands on his trousers, Thomas fidgets in his seat. With a hole burrowing through his core, deep inside, he is left empty, and his stomach flipping over with sickening cramps.

Turning to his right, Thomas looks at Peter in the driver's seat. It's clear the impact the evening has had on the young man; at times during their drive back, Thomas had stayed silent when hearing the soft whimpering of Peter crying. With his vacant stare, his dark and puffy eyes, the young man wears the evening's experience like a hollowed-out, sunken mask.

It will change Peter forever, and whatever securities he has, the blankets we all use to protect ourselves from the real world, if not gone already, soon will be. Thomas knows this all too well; it was why he traded non-fiction for fiction. The real world, the day-to-day horrors we see on every street corner are far more horrific than any story we can ever create. Fiction is fiction; it's why we all pay money to sit in the dark and watch masked men stalk and slaughter young babysitters, cheerleaders, and camp councillors, and why any true-crime documentary is always far scarier than any movie.

Thomas had wanted to reach out, place a hand on his shoulder, and offer him a few gentle words of encouragement, but he found he simply lacked the warmth needed. And like a great many things, Thomas regrets that now. A better person wouldn't have let Peter drive in silence, to cry like he did. And as such, Thomas's thoughts fell upon Amy, picturing her consoling Peter with her soft nature, with kind words of a woman who had seen hell, but had through it all remained good and decent.

Amy would have done that, but not me.

Mary, even Lewis would have done more, but not Thomas, the man he has become, the selfish, parent-avoiding, lonesome boozer who had stayed quiet when no one else would. With bitterness flowing through him, looking down, Thomas inspects the flyer in his lap.

Max Rex- items personally tailored as unique, one-of-a-kind toys. Fetish, Psycho-erotica, sex and torture.

Finding and noting the website at the bottom of the card, dragging his phone from his pocket, Thomas uses the internet browser function and searches. After a prolonged loading screen, Thomas is finally presented with a black page and a clickable icon button asking:

DARE YOU ENTER?

The words, dripping in a garish red, like that of cheap nail varnish, sits more like a stain on the screen. Thumbing the button, Thomas finds himself looking at an amateurish website, gaudy and lurid, spattered with blacks and reds, naked bodies and arty, blood-filled imagery.

Clicking on the gallery tab, Thomas is forced to wait as a series of square tiles are filled with static images of men and women dressed in leather and latex. They amount to nothing more than an orgy of mask-wearing brutes, sadomasochistic Mephistopheles. Horned, fanged, medieval demonology in all its horrific glory, all set against a backdrop of dark, dank cellars with exposed brickwork, chains and leather strapping hang over each scene like demonic Christmas decorations.

In some, half-naked women lay bound and gagged, tied to ugly looking contraptions. The rack, The Judas Chair, The Wheel, The Stake, The Pillory, and of course, The Wood Cross. Medieval torture devices, all constructed with an untidy hand, from ageing wood and roughly forged cast iron. Poor examples of historical items, each designed with the sole purpose of inflicting extreme pain, but not these. Imitations, laughable really, show the helpless would-be prisoners, each sporting an exaggerated look of terror and torture. Poor actors made to stand against the backdrop of a cheap set. Still, with the partly exposed breasts, the leather thongs, the exposed muscles of the leering men, all with one common theme- a distinctive red streak- be it a strap, a heel, a zip, a nipple, all act as a way of identifying the item as being one of Max Rex's extensive collection.

'Jesus,' Thomas moans.

Shifting his eyes to Peter, who, while saying nothing, has an expression that demands a response.

'Max Rex,' Thomas tells him, 'He makes bespoke sex toys, masks, all black, with splashes of red. I think it's a trademark. Anyway, it matches the mask the intruder wore, and well, it could be a lead.'

Pulling the car to the curb, shutting off the engine, Thomas joins Peter in peering out through the front windscreen, mouths agape. Where Pinegrove sits like a dark, gloomy giant to their right, two parked Police cars sit up the hill, their dome lights illuminating the night sky with neon blue swirls.

'This is the second time the Police have been out this week,' Thomas says, eyes scanning the scene.

Abuzz with activity, having gathered, a group of onlookers, rubber-neckers, line the street on both sides as it slopes upward. The crowd of hawk-eyed neighbours, with their coats pulled tight over their bathrobes, pyjamas and nightgowns, stand watching, drinking coffee beneath a ceiling of umbrellas.

'Do you know why?' Peter asks, his eyes fixed on the commotion.

Shaking his head, Thomas scans the mess of bodies. Rain distorting his view, the dark figures clump together like a solid body, heat from their gossiping mouths fogging the night.

'Let's find out,' Thomas says, opening the door.

Returning to the now-familiar rain, this time, somehow, it appears far colder – the type of cold rain that runs right through you. Shivering, together, they climb the hill. Ahead of them, voices, low but concerned, add to the mystery. While the cordon holds back the eager crowd, the two uniformed Police Officers tasked with the job stand busy fielding questions. The two officers do their best with tired faces and laboured hand movements. Still, the onlookers, a crowd of three people thick, demand information. Low chatter, moans, and even cries fill the night, but together sit hushed, almost muted beneath the downpour.

Beyond the crowd, the large, detached Victorian house sits lit from within. Every window burns yellow while the front flicks in and out of the darkness through waves of blue light. Shadows are cast across the house, dissolved, then re-cast. Like a Victorian zoetrope, the home dances back behind the glare. Exposed then hidden, the process is repeated over and over.

'My God,' Peter moans.

Turning to the house, Thomas instantly recognises the woman standing at the door. While donning her usual attire of a matching tracksuit and trainers, missing now is her friendly smile and poise, her cheerful smile energetic disposition. Instead, the woman stands as a mere shade, colourless, left with the appearance of ash. With her neatly applied makeup ruined, streaked with tears, she looks on in horror at the thing left on display on the lawn. Resting atop a tall wooden spike rests the head of the woman's faithful Great Dane.

* * *

Returning home, Thomas finds a lingering figure at his door.

'You look like you've been to hell and back,' Lilly says, stepping forward, placing a hand on his shoulder.

Her touch has Thomas flinching, sending him backwards onto his heels. With this, her look of concern only deepens. Looking over his shoulder, Thomas checks the stairwell, the landing and Amy's old front door.

Lilly smiles softly, 'Thomas, it's ok,' and waits for his eyes to meet hers.

'You better come in,' he tells her, moving to his front door.

Turning the key in the lock, pushing himself inside, he turns on the lights before proceeding into the dark space. The hallway, lighted with flickering, then stable bulb light, unsettles Thomas further. Stopping, his jittery eyes watching the hallway, while silent, his apartment awaits him with silence and deceptive intent. Finally, with Lilly placing a hand upon his shoulder, startling him, he shudders his way into the hallway, leading her inside. At the bathroom, Thomas, uneasy, weary, glances at her from over his shoulder and says, 'I need a minute, ok?'

'Sure,' she says, nodding.

Leaving him, watching her disappear into the living area, Thomas pushes himself inside the bathroom, all but falling through the opening door. He flicks on the light and closes the door in one quick motion. Alone in the bathroom, Thomas turns to the shower. Twisting on the faucet, he lets the hiss of its heavy flow fill the room.

Thomas's legs finally buckle, collapsing him to his knees. Unable to stop them, tears burst at his eyes, streaming, fogging the bathroom floor around him. In his mind, he sees them- the pictures, the children, the thousands of little Robins, the missing, the groomed, the abused.

How many remain in bondage, molested, and how many are dead now?

Pulling himself to his feet, he turns on the tap. In the mirror, misery tugs at his features, leaving his skin absent of all colour. Splashing his face with cold water, sleeking his hair back from his face, he looks at himself and asks glumly, 'what the hell am I doing?'

He sees it in his eyes, the lack of conviction, a lifetime of failure, the gutless man who chose freedom over a life with his wife and child.

Mary, she didn't love me.

His eyes can no longer hide the lie nor support it. Blame, shifted and reassigned for years, now falls at his feet- where it belonged all along.

Yeah, you keep telling yourself that.

A knock on the door, followed by, 'Thomas, come on out... please?' has Thomas shutting off the shower.

Opening the door, Lilly stands, staring up at him. Surprised by her expression, with its warmth, Thomas stands, almost dumbfounded by this change in her. Without another word, she moves in, lifts her face to his, and gently, very gently, kisses him. Her lips, closed and soft, press against his with just the right weight. Their sweetness is enough to, for a moment, shield him from the demons now occupying his world.

Pulling her lips from his, looking up at him, she says, 'I'm sorry, I, I don't know why I....'

'Thank you,' Thomas interrupts, smiling softly.

'Got anything to drink?' She asks, her voice now unsure and a little perplexed.

'Cheap wine?'

She responds with a scrunch of her nose.

'Brandy?' Thomas adds.

'Cheap wine it is,' she smiles.

Turning off the light, shaky and a little unbalanced, he follows Lilly through to the living area. Moving to the kitchen, Lilly calls over her shoulder, 'Where am I going?'

'The fridge for the wine, glasses in the cupboard above the sink,' he says, slumping down into the sofa.

Closing his eyes, locking himself in darkness, his reprieve lasts only a moment. Before him, from the dark, he is tortured by the image of a young boy. No more than eight, his dull, dark eyes, lifeless now due to what he has been made to do, don't plead for him to help but rather condemn him for doing nothing.

Joining him on the sofa, the shifting of the cushion beside him snaps open his eyes wide and stark. Looking at Lilly, her concerned eyes on his, she places down two wine glasses and a chilled bottle of white. Snatching up the bottle. Thomas goes straight for the screw lid, twisting it off with a crackle, dragging the two glasses closer.

'I'd say let it breathe, but....'

'It'll still taste like dogshit,' he spits, filling the two glasses, sploshing some over the sides of both. Pushing a drink across the table to her, he lifts the other and downs the contents. Sharp and dry, piercing alcohol floods his throat, burning it. Pouring himself another, he flops back, exhausted.

Looking at him, giving him a minute, Lilly asks, 'where were you tonight?'

Thomas looks at her and considers telling her the truth, all of it-where they'd been, the hole, seeing Amy taken.

'A lead.'

'Amy?'

'Yeah, I mean, no, not really, Erika.'

'Erika, you're looking for her, really?' Her tone is now noticeably different.

'Yes,' he says, looking at her. 'I think your sister's disappearance and hers are linked.'

'Linked how?'

'Well, think about it,' he says, sitting forward. 'Amy and Erika are two extremely different women with different backgrounds and careers whose lives converge because of one common factor.'

'James?' Lilly asks, her eyes sceptical.

Nodding his head, he says, 'bingo.'

'How?'

'Fuck knows, haven't got that far yet, but there's a connection, there has to be.'

'And tonight?' She presses, eyes wide, expecting.

'The horrible and the vile.'

'Don't do that, don't shield me from what you've found, I have a right to know....'

'I have this recurring dream, I'm sixteen, and I'm standing looking at my old school, frozen, deafened by the wail of the approaching fire engines,' he starts, cutting her off. 'The flames, well, they've already done the devil's work, and I'm made to watch, forced to listen to the screams of those stuck inside. Six children, a teacher and the elderly janitor all die. I know this, but still, I stand there, unable to move. Reggie Morris, a bullied and ill-tempered fourteen-year-old boy, would take the blame. You see, he was seen returning to the school shortly before the fire took hold. When his diary was found and examined, the depth of his torture and pain became clear upon reading his words. Well, after putting two and two together, the case was closed, leaving Reggie to live on after death with the infamy of a mass murderer. His family were run out of town, of course. Black, overweight, with glasses far too big for his face, Reggie had been bullied all his school life, so I guess he never stood a chance. A ticking timebomb, they said. Well, the thing is, I witnessed the whole thing, from the tree line, past the tennis courts. I saw Reggie go in, but not before the fire started, but after. The boy, the school had wholly neglected, bullied and fucked over, had gone back in when no one else did. Now, in the dream, I realise I can move but to my shame, I choose not to. Later, I would write about Reggie, about what I saw, how he couldn't have set the fire, and that he died attempting to save the people who tortured him his entire life. But still, Reggie is dead, and me, I'm left as a man who once had the chance to do something.'

'I read your story, but Thomas, you were a kid; if you had gone in, you'd be dead too, you must see that. I mean, what could you have done?'

He looks at her, 'It's not a case of *could* of, I *should have* tried.'

Looking at Lilly, her eyes and expression bring tears to his eyes. Sliding across the sofa, she takes his face in her hands. Kissing him again, this time, her lips more demanding than before.

Pulling back from her, not thinking clearly, he says, 'Lilly, I need to tell you something.'

'You're not divorced, and that you, in fact, intend to move back in with your wife?' She smiles, kissing him again.

Again, pulling back, he looks at her. 'Lilly, I need to tell you, Amy, I've seen her.'

Her head snaps back, her eyes flicker and narrow.

'What I'm going to tell you will sound crazy, I don't understand it myself, but you must listen to me, listen and follow the steps I give you, ok?'

'Ok,' she says, her face now awash with sickening confusion.

Taking a deep breath, he drags himself up from the sofa. He knows this is a deal-breaker, but he also knows he can no longer keep it from her. Moving to the wall, looking through the hole, he is relieved to have a point of reference. Though dark, Amy's belongings are yet to be removed in her timeline- the rug, the bookcase lined with books, the fresh plants are all still present and visible through the hole.

Turning back to Lilly, 'Amy's things, who removed them from her apartment?'

'Me and dad, why?'

'So, there should be no reason why they should still be there, next door?'

'No, I mean, what do you mean?'

'Come here, please.'

Standing up, Lilly steps around the coffee table to join him at the wall. Stepping back to give her room, Thomas finds her eyes with his, 'There's a hole in the painting, at the sail, through it you'll see Amy's apartment, please.'

Looking at him, Thomas can see the cogs turning in her mind by the rapid movement of her eyes, the lids fluttering. Stepping up to the wall, clearly uneasy, she moves her face to the painting.

'It's dark but give it a second for your eye to adjust, then tell me what you see.'

Reaching up on her toes, tight jawed, she presses her eye to the hole. Slowly, her eye growing wide against the canvas, her breathing intensifies.

'Her things, I, I don't understand, me and Dad moved them,' she says, turning to look at him. 'Has someone new moved in?'

'Come with me,' he says, taking her by the hand.

Thomas drags her from the wall, from the room, down the hallway, to the front door. Lilly digs her feet into the carpet outside the apartment, pulling Thomas to a stop.

'Tell me what's happening, I don't...' She pleads.

'I will, but you have to come with me, ok?'

Her grip on his hand tightens, and with a nod of her head, she lets him lead her through the front door, inside Amy's old apartment. Quick to close the door behind them, the darkness of the hallway closes in, leaving Thomas fumbling for the light switch. Finding it, after a moment of panic, he flicks it on. As the hallway light springs to life, Thomas steers Lilly along the hallway, around the corner, into the living area, all the way feeling the growing resistance in her grip.

Turning on the light as they enter, the living area is as cold and vacant as Thomas's previous visits. Letting go of her hand, Lilly moves to the middle of the room, spinning silently, scanning, eyes wide, her mouth a growing hole. Stopping, turning to Thomas, red-faced, she asks between bated breaths, 'what the hell is this?'

'I, I don't know, I mean, a void, a window in time, a wormhole, or possibly, a time-loop,' he stutters.

'A what, a time-loop?' She spits.

'Einstein's general theory of relativity supports it, I guess, I've tried to understand it, but, I mean we follow it around, *time* I mean, and the hole, somehow, allows us a window into it.'

She looks at him sceptically.

He takes a slow, deep breath and levels his eyes on hers.

'A window in time, like a fracture in this reality,' he pauses. 'I can't believe I'm actually saying this, but, well, it's time-travel, crazy as that sounds, and the how and why, I don't know. But, on the other hand, it could be the greatest discovery in human history.'

With this, tears well in his eyes. The enormity of it, the responsibility and the expectation.

'You could make a fortune, showing it to the world.' Lilly says, looking down.

'We do that, and we'll never find Amy,' Thomas says, surprising himself, the words leaping off his lips instinctively. 'We make it known Amy's abduction was witnessed, and he might just disappear into the wind, vanish, and Amy with him.'

Looking at him, and while her eyes show the signs of her yielding, her tone remains defiant.

'You were watching my sister all this time,' she pauses. 'You could have told me. I could have seen her one last time, and you stole it from me.'

'You're right, but Lilly, at first, I didn't know what I was even looking at,' he pleads thinly.

'Yes, you did, so don't lie to me. In seeing my sister, you saw your next book – the guy who cracked the case when all others couldn't. Does it bother you Amy's probably dead now, and you could have saved her, does it?

'I tried to save her, I did, but... I saw him, the guy who took Amy; I saw it happen,' he tells her.

'Who is he?'

Seeing her question as an opening, an opportunity to, in some small way, start to repair the damage his lies have caused.

'He wore one of those leather masks, a wrestler's hood, or a gimp mask, the type that covers the entire head, so I couldn't see his face.'

'A gimp mask?' She asks, her face confused.

'Yes, well, sort of, but it was different, more medieval, macabre....'

'Like a horror movie?' She asks, a tremble in her voice.

'Yes, I'm sorry. Somehow, he got inside this apartment, which appears to be impossible. He crept up behind her, drugged and took her, then left with her.'

Tears form in the corner of her eyes, blinking, she is unable to stop them from spilling down her cheeks.

'You were right about me, Lilly; I did see your sister as a lottery ticket, my next bestseller. I figured, in solving Amy's disappearance, I'd save my career, that's what I thought, but that's not how it is now,' he says, attempting to breathe. 'In saving your sister, I realise now, I might just save myself, my soul, whatever's left of it, anyway.'

Surprising himself, in telling the truth, admitting to his motivations, he finds breathing, though slight, comes a little easier. Watching Lilly, giving her a moment, her eyes working. He fully expects her to leave, to see through him and his reasoning, but instead, while hesitant, she takes a step toward him, closing the gap between them. Now, with the softening of her brow, expecting her to kiss him, he is again surprised, relieved, and slightly disappointed when she instead drops her head.

'I can't change it; I tried with Amy, she saw me, the night she was taken, I mean, we communicated. I tried to save her, I did, if we had another ten, fifteen minutes... but the past is the past, everything I did, still led to her being taken.'

Looking up at him, her eyes wide and buttery, warmth returns to them. They are enough to elevate her face to a point where it pains Thomas to even look at her. The feeling in them, the hurt and confusion, leave him speechless, his soul achy and heavy.

Stripped of her makeup, her protective shell, her strength and resolve, Lilly stands before him like no woman has before. The pain upon the surface, her need for help but reluctance in accepting it, her love for her sister, her shop and the warmth of its products, finally spark the respecters in his mind, firing them, charging his heart with energy new to him, a feeling lost, hidden beneath years of denial and fear.

Wanting to hold her, to kiss her, reaching down with his head, the shriek of his phone buzzing at his pocket stops him short. The sudden shrill is quick to bring space between them, like somehow, being caught by our parents, Thomas backs up sheepishly. Removing the device, not recognising the number, Thomas answers it regardless.

'Hello?'

'Thomas?'

Katerina.

'Yes?'

'I've got info on Erika. Will you meet me?'

'Sure, where?'

'Lincoln Hills, there's a place up there. You'll know it when you see it. Friday, 10pm?' She says, her voice hesitantly distant.

'Is everything ok?' He asks.

'Yes, sorry... will you meet me?'

'Sure,' he agrees.

'Ok... ok, great,' she says, her void flat, detached.

'Are you sure everything's ok?' He asks again.

A beat between them.

'Of course,' she finally says, 'see you then.'

Being greeted with the dial tone, he shuts off the phone.

'Who was...?' Lilly asks, looking up at him.

'A lead,' he says, cutting her off.

'And?'

He looks at her.

'Don't shut me out,' Lilly says and follows it up with. 'Please.'

'Ok, well, a friend of Erika, I'm meeting her Friday night.'

'Where?'

'Lincoln Hills, and no, you're not coming.'

'Lincoln Hills, you shouldn't go either.'

'It will be fine, remember I've done this before, interviewing undesirables, its....'

'Stupid and dangerous.'

Though he smiles, he knows deep down, she's right.

21

4 days later...

Darkness surrounds them on all sides. A black shroud hugs the car with a tight grip. The headlights cut them a path through the woods, be it as a faint stream.

'You know this is stupid, dangerous, right?' Peter asks from the driver's seat.

'I've been told, yes,' Thomas moans in response.

Ahead of them, Lincoln Hills, a forested area some three miles north of Beckley Green, waits for them behind a mask of darkness. The narrow road, snaking back and forth, serves solely as a gateway to a place all but forgotten, a derelict, now alien to the world around it. Having scouted the area earlier in the day, the remote small picnic area, shop, and cafe now sits as a castoff, gutted and vandalised. Once an isolated hideaway for hikers and families, the benches out front, the small wooden fort and noticeboard are now chard black, broken, and overgrown with weeds, leaving the remote spot on the brink of being reclaimed by the surrounding woodland.

'Someone's behind us,' Peter announces. 'It wasn't there before, and I'm sure I saw the shape of a car pull out from an inlet.'

Turning to look over his shoulder, two small spots of light flicker through the trees, distant and disappearing, reappearing with every turn in the road. The forest, the thick border of black sitting back from the road by steep ditches and wild bramble, make it almost impossible to track the car.

'Let's just relax. It's only a car; there are turnoffs all the way up this hill,' Thomas tells him but finds himself leaning forward in his seat.

Rolling up his jean leg, revealing his sock bulging with a sheathed knife.

'We're not stabbing anyone, are we?' Peter asks, eyes wide on the blade.

'Of course not; it's simply a precaution.'

Checking the side mirror, tracking the trailing headlights, them blinking through the trees, Thomas watches them grow as if closing the gap.

'Ok, pull into the next inlet. We'll let them pass and see what they do. It could be Katerina, but let's be sure.' Thomas says.

Peering forward, Peter swings the car to the left into a shallow layby. Shutting off the engine, killing the headlights, in unison, they together turn to look out the back window.

The lights, growing still, stuttering between the trees, disappear and reappear, disappear and reappear, and disappear behind a bend in the road.

'Where did they go?' Peter asks.

'Let's give it another minute,' Thomas says, unable to mask the apprehension in his voice.

Nothing, the road, winding below them, remains dark.

'What do we do?' Peter asks.

'Nothing. Let's not jump to conclusions.'

Still, they watch for the coming car.

Nothing.

Nodding, Peter brings the engine back to life. Continuing up the hill, Peter steering the car through the night, Thomas fights the overwhelming desire to turn and look over his shoulder. Making do with the side mirror, seeing no signs of a car behind them, the uneasiness, however, clings to him, chasing them along the road.

Nearing the crest of the hill, the tree line thins to make way for a small lot. Beyond it, the lone, weather-beaten, darkened structure appears out of the night, sorrowfully like a wounded dog or an unwanted turd on the lawn. Where the daylight had given the abandoned area a certain sad, melancholy appeal, the darkness of night, the deep pockets of black clotting the land, lend it a deceptive, ominous mask. Beyond, the hills, heavy with trees, stretch out like a rugged carpet of black pitted shadows.

Peter pulls the car into the small, gravelled lot. Across from them, a large SUV, black and tall, sits cold, its interior dark.

'Looks like she's here,' Peter says.

Thomas eyes the car - new and German, sitting on expensive, diamond-cut 22-inch rims, and considers if it fits Katerina.

Someone could have given her a ride?

It's reasonable to expect she doesn't trust me, so there's no need to panic.

Parking the car, shutting off the engine, Peter joins him in scanning their surroundings- the SUV, the nearby structure and its scantly lit, hollowed-out interior. The trees beyond, and the rain filling the space between.

'We should turn around and leave,' Peter says, eyes wide. 'This place reeks of death.'

Turning and looking at Peter's pale face in the shadowed light, Thomas quickly understands his fear. Thomas feels it, too; his stomach knots with what feels like undigested gristle.

You leave now, and you'll never find out what happened to Amy.

'You can stay here if you want, it's fine, but I need to speak to her. So, to me, it's worth the risk.'

Peter pauses, rechecks the area, and nods in agreement. Then, like a child sat up in bed, watching the wardrobe in the dark, his eyes blink back at Thomas, trusting him to keep him safe.

They climb from the shade of the car, out into the night, the rain, the unknown. Scanning the area, from the dark SUV to the lot's exit, to the café's interior. Thomas watches for the approaching car from before but finds only a wall of black at the treeline.

'You were right. I don't see the car's headlights anymore,' Peter says.

Thomas traces Peter's eye line to the dark road from which they came and beyond, as it slopes down, is swallowed whole by the night. Thomas watches and listens, longing for a stillness, a place where he can think with reason. Finally, the rain, soaking him through, flooding his senses, clouding his ears, leaves Thomas with one conclusion.

Peter's right: we should leave.

Instead, ignoring his inner voice of caution, he says, 'let's get this over with.'

Crossing the lot, rain all about him, Thomas stops at the front entrance. A set of double doors hang loose, pushed inwards, creating a grotesque metal jaw of sorts. Leading Peter inside, out of the rain, fighting his sodden jacket, Thomas allows his eyes a moment to adjust to the darkened shapes, the heavy gloom blotting at the corners. He tries to focus, but the rain, still present, hitting the thin roof in sheets of heavy thuds, leaves his fear teetering on the edge of despair.

'Hello?' Thomas calls, instantly regretting it.

His unsettled voice, bouncing around the dark space, only adds to his discomfort. Be it that, or his cold, damp clothes, like his legs, Thomas's hands tremble wildly.

'Down here,' answers a voice from an open but shadowed door behind the counter.

Across from them, located at the far side of the small space, the door, a dark rectangle, offers only uncertainty.

'Is it her?' Peter asks.

'I don't know; it's hard to tell.'

The rain against the gutted structure had muffled the voice, yet it still sounded female-like. Slowly, crossing the floor to the counter, around it, Thomas leads Peter to the waiting door.

Peering inside, Thomas finds a short hallway leading to concrete steps. The darkness and ambiguity it offers bring Thomas to a stop.

Excellent, a basement.

Out of eyeshot, possible from an adjoining room, a small portion of the lower level is lit, being it faint, by a small cone of light breaking the gloom with yellow light. It does little to remove the thudding at his chest, nor does it answer the concerns plaguing him, freezing his feet to the spot.

Leave, get the hell out of here.

Thomas and Peter share a look, both seeking reassurance in the other. Watching Thomas flounder, unravelling, Peter asks, 'Thomas?'

Thomas's eyes dart back to the waiting basement, back to Peter, to the exit, Peter's car beyond. Now solid and overwhelming, the pull of leaving sends a sickening wave through his stomach.

Ready to leave, to retreat like the coward he is, he is stopped by an image from this past.

His school.

The fire.

Reggie Morris.

Licking his now dry lips, Thomas shakes his head, struggling with the conflict. It is all he can do as his fear, his common sense, directly competes with this new historical notion of salvation.

Thomas turns back to the cold concrete steps, the guts of the structure waiting below them, his eyes bulging with pressure.

'Thomas?' The voice calls again from below.

This time clearer, now confident the voice belongs to Katerina, Thomas takes a series of deep breaths. Gathering his courage, what is left of it anyway, he starts down, closing in on the soft light and fighting the darkness as it closes in around him. At the bottom, he stops and waits for Peter to join him before continuing forward. A dank passageway awaits them. Narrow and concreted on all sides, the wet walls appear slimy from rainwater leaking down from the storm above. The ceiling bleeds white chalky drops from hidden fissures, splashing the concrete ground before them. Thomas fixes his eyes forward on the faint light seeping out from a room at the far end of the passage. A beacon or a trap, plunder of ruin. Regardless, he must continue.

Meters from the open door, growing louder with every step, a series of muffled moans leak out into dim light. Peering inside, lit by a single portable lamp, its faint light leaves most of the room in shadow. Stopping in the doorway, blinking hard, Thomas struggles to comprehend what he's looking at. Before him, in the middle of the floor covered in clear plastic sheeting, a woman is tied to a chair.

Katerina.

Stepping into the room, moving to the helpless woman, hearing Peter calling out, 'No,' before he can act, Thomas is struck across the back of the head. In a snap of pain and light, his world turns black and cold.

* * *

With a flicker, heavy as if weighed down, Thomas opens his eyes. Laying on the cold, wet, hard floor, he is met with a pain in his head, all-consuming, like nothing he's ever experienced before.

Why am I lying on the floor?

Attempting to move, he finds his hands are unresponsive. The pain in his head is likened to being electrocuted. It rattles around his skull like a crazed rubber ball before shooting down his spine.

Are my hands tied behind my back? How did that happen?

Looking up, groggy, his vision is hazy and flared due to a portable lamp positioned close to his face. The floor of the small concrete room is covered with a plastic sheet; it creaks beneath the weight of heavy, moving feet.

Surrounded by three men, the first Thomas recognises instantly, leaving his heart plunging. The middle eastern man from the market, the one drenched in gold, is joined by the bald, thick-neck, too from the market, and a tall third man with eyes too small from his skull-like face. A fourth stands over by Peter, and like the others, Thomas notes to be wearing black gloves.

Thomas seeks out and meets Peter's eyes. Laying on his side, hog-tied and fearful, the whites of his eyes speak of utter terror.

The men step back and part, giving Thomas a view of Katerina. Still tied to the chair, only now can he take in the horror of her condition. Beaten, her face swollen, she appears hardly conscious. Behind her, in the corner, sits a long metal trough.

'Let her go,' Thomas croaks.

He is answered by a kick to his ribs. A second kick harder has him crawling for the door. Thomas screams through the pain, through clamped teeth on his lips, leaving the taste of blood upon his tongue. His shriek is enough to drag Katerina back to the present. Looking at Thomas, to Peter, her eyes grow, bulge wide, almost bursting.

The thick-neck bends down, grabs a handful of Thomas's hair, and yanks him up onto his knees. Screaming through gritted teeth, only to be searched, the man's hands are heavy on Thomas's clothes, deliberate; it's clear the thug is seasoned to this sort of thing.

Please don't find the knife.

Moving down his body, his chest and rib cage, down to Thomas's legs, every touch sends streaks of pain through him, jolting him.

'Look what we have here,' the thick neck removes the knife and tape from his sock, ripping it clear, tearing hair from his shin and calf.

Shit.

Stepping aside, the man makes way for who Thomas is now sure is Khaliq.

'Khaliq?' Thomas asks.

With dark, lifeless eyes, Khaliq answers with a nod. His lavish gold jewellery shimmers in the lamp's light, as does the smooth new skin of the scar at his throat.

'I didn't know what to make of you at first. Strutting in like you did. Kat here gave you the location for our market and the password, but she is yet to cough up why. She's a tough fucker; I'll admit it.'

Thomas looks at her, her eyes pleading for him not to divulge the truth; why she had decided to betray Khaliq.

'Are you Police?' Khaliq hisses.

'No.'

Considering this, Khaliq looks down at Thomas, his dark eye unmoving.

A beat.

With the nod of Khaliq's head, an unspoken order, the thin man moves to Peter. Helpless, Peter's eyes track his journey and grow wide when they can no longer follow the man any further. At his back, looming over Peter, the man reaches down and takes hold of his hand. With a snap, he breaks the forefinger on the left hand with a sickening crack.

Clamping his eyes shut, Peter screams out in pain, a terrible high piercing wail that proceeds to bounce around the small room, leaving Thomas on the cusp of urinating himself.

What the hell have I got us into?

'My God, no, please....' Thomas starts.

With Khaliq nodding a second time, the middle finger on the same hand suffers the same fate, followed by another howl from Peter.

Red-faced, Khaliq stomps across the floor, his boots heavy on the wet plastic, splashing water into Thomas's face, his eyes. Taking the helpless Thomas by the hair, his tight grip tugging at his scalp, Khaliq looks down at him, his eyes cold and unsympathetic.

'We'll break his fingers, his toes, all of them, I'll fucking feed him his own, understand me, you stupid fuck. Are you the fucking Police?'

'No, I'm a writer, you have to believe me, I....' Thomas protests but is quickly silenced by a solid fist to his injured side.

'Fuck this,' Khaliq grunts.

Bending over Thomas, attacking him, hitting him square in the face... once... twice, the second blow splitting open his lower lip. Taking hold of his collar, dragging him, the now exasperated Khaliq hauls Thomas across the room, sliding, scurrying on his hands and knees. Thomas tries to get up but cannot. His withering form, weak and wet, sabotage his now limp and depleted resolve.

Slung against the trough, Khaliq kicks Thomas again, his boot savagely snapping his head to one side, leaving his mouth bloody. Light flashes across his flicking eyes, and darkness... and light... darkness... light..., but somehow, he manages to stay conscious, well, barely.

'Hold this fool,' Khaliq tells his goon.

Stepping forward, the thick neck is quick to join them. Eager, wrapping his bulbous fingers around Thomas's neck, he yanks Thomas forward, bending him over the trough.

Think God-damn it, fucking think.

A flash of steel, a tearing of Thomas's jeans at his rump, and a burst of cold air fills the space, spreading inside the material, tightening his testicles, reducing them to walnuts.

Disappearing for a moment, Khaliq returns, holding a black leather holdall. Dropping it down beside Thomas, unzipping the bag, the thick neck slackens his grip on Thomas's neck enough to allow him a clear view of the opening.

A dildo.

The biggest he's ever seen.

Big enough to kill someone, at least 15-inches long and as fat as a can of baked beans.

Probably modelled on an ogre.

Obviously giddy, still a little groggy, and nauseous, fresh bile warms the back of his throat.

'I hope you like anal sex,' Thick-neck snorts into his ear, his breath surprisingly fresh and minty.

They're going to rape me... no... God, no...

'I'm not Police, please, god, I'm a writer, god please,' Thomas pants.

'I'm sorry, no lube, I'm afraid,' Khaliq tells his captive, readying the monstrous toy.

Moving it to Thomas's rear, lining it up, hard rubber is pressed in against his anus. Lingering there, as if toying with Thomas, it circles the rim.

Now crying, sobbing uncontrollably, bile rising, sprays from his quivering lips. The trough takes most of it; the rest splashes the floor.

Thomas pushes up with everything he's got. All inner strength, up through his legs, back, screaming with the explosion of energy.

He doesn't move an inch.

'You struggle, and it's only gonna hurt you more. So, relax, you might just like it,' Khaliq whispers, pressing the dildo in between his ass-cheeks.

SPEAK, FOR GOD'S SAKE, SPEAK!

'Erika, Erika Sobo!' He screams.

The pressing at his anus stops.

'What about her?' Khaliq asks, his tone now decidedly different.

'Oh god, ok, listen, I'm investigating her disappearance... I'm a writer... I used to work as an investigative reporter.'

'Bullshit,' Khaliq scoffs.

'No, it's true, someone took her,' Thomas pleads. 'Someone took her... her disappearance is linked to another.'

A beat.

Thomas stays silent, listening, praying. With a jolt, his head is dragged back, away from the trough, and his rump, now exposed, hits the ground, slapping cold plastic. Khaliq takes a knee before him, his face close to Thomas's, his breath meeting his.

'Talk,' Khaliq spits.

'Ok, ok, like I said, I'm investigating her disappearance and another woman... I believe them to be linked.'

'Who?' Khaliq presses.

'Amy Porter, Erika was having an affair with her boyfriend, a guy called James Ruck.'

'James Ruck, I know the guy.'

'He's dead, but there's a link.'

'Where is she? Why hasn't she been found?' Khaliq asks, still not entirely convinced.

'I don't know....' Thomas starts.

'You don't fucking know?' He asks through gritted gold and bright white teeth and spits a laugh in Thomas's face.

'James was planning something, ok, before her disappearance, he had her keys cut, and her mobile phone stolen, both were found at his apartment.'

Khaliq goes to open his mouth but stops short. Instead, he looks at Thomas, studying him. 'Are you a good investigator, Mr William?'

'Yes, I got here, didn't I?'

'Yeah, you got here, almost got yourself fucked too.'

Thomas takes a moment before speaking, knowing his following words will either get him killed or set free.

'I'll find out what happened to her, I promise, you have my word,' Thomas tells him, looking him in the eyes.

'Your word means shit to me; I don't know you. You come walking into my market, on the word of this slut, believing I had something to do with Erika going missing?'

Khaliq's words are cold and bitter, yet Thomas recognises the hurt at the mere mention of Erika's name.

'She's just worried; Erika's her best friend; she figured I could help. I needed to meet you, and your market seemed like the best way.'

Again, Khaliq looks at Thomas, sizing him up. Finally, his eyes flick to Katerina's pale face, streaming with tears, pleading.

'Who is Erika to you?' Thomas asks, attempting to gain back his attention.

Khaliq pauses before responding. Thomas can tell the situation has now changed and recognises an opportunity to get out of this place in one piece.

'She's one of my girls, was, I run a small network of high-class girls, the £500.00 an hour type, Erika was born for it, beautiful, but she wanted out, wanted to be a model, wanted away from it. So, I hooked her up with photographers like Ruck, the motherfucker,' he hisses.

Shaking his head, looking down at the dildo in his hand, he tosses it back into the bag. Taking a moment, his jaw twitching, finally Khaliq again looks at Thomas.

'I'll ask you again, how good of an investigator are you and don't bullshit me, don't cross me, understand?' He asks.

'I was good, once, but that was a long time ago, but I'll find out what happened to her.'

'And him?' Khaliq asks, nodding his head at Peter.

'My assistant, he's helping me, and he's doing it for free.'

Khaliq looks at Peter, back at Thomas, his eyes working, his mind thinking. Finally, he looks up at his thick-neck friend, and with a nod of the head, the man approaches Thomas.

'Hey, wait...' Thomas starts, a quiver again returning to taint his words.

Turning Thomas over, with a snip, his wrists drop free of the cable ties. Like him, Peter is freed from his bonds. Sitting up sheepishly, he cradles his damaged hand in a painful grimace.

'You investigate Erika, but you stop with me and my girls, understand?' Khaliq tells Thomas. 'This was business, nothing personal, but given what you're doing for Erika, you get a pass this once.'

'I understand,' Thomas tells him.

'This world, my world, it will stain you, you won't come out clean, no one does, no one,' Khaliq says, his eyes finding Thomas. 'Others like me, worse, we don't like people poking around. They catch you; they'll kill you.'

Hands shaking, Thomas pulls himself to his feet. With pain tearing through his side, hunched over, he coughs up a mouthful of blood. Needing the wall for support, he waits for Peter. Shaky on his feet, they converge at the door. Thomas lets him leave through the doorway before turning his attention to Katerina. Closing her eyes, tears race down her cheeks towards the duct tape at her lips.

Using the doorframe for support, Thomas turns back to look at the now standing Khaliq.

'I need something from you,' Thomas says.

'You making demands?' Khaliq asks, smiling.

'I need your word; your word Katerina will be ok.'

Laughter breaks out from the goons, yet still, Thomas holds firm in his request.

'You know what I deal in, yeah? Well, my word doesn't mean shit.'

'It does to me, searching and saving one life, can't be at the expense of another.'

Khaliq looks at him, his words, his reasoning triggering something in his eyes.

'I was snooping, and snooping sometimes gets you hurt, but she misses her friend, nothing more.'

'Fine,' Khaliq tells him with a flick of his hand.

Nodding a thank you, Thomas follows Peter out the door.

'Hey, writer,' Khaliq calls over Thomas's shoulder.

Turning slowly, wincing, he looks back at him.

'She's dead, right? James Ruck killed her, didn't he?' Khaliq asks, his eyes glazed and full.

'Probably, they normally are, but I want to know for sure, you want to know for sure, and I won't stop looking until I find out what happened to her.'

'James Ruck,' Khaliq says. 'He used to hang around with others like him, photographers, amateur filmmakers: films, cheap-crap. I used to stock it, but no one bought it. Gangbang, queer-shit, hookers and teens mainly. If I were you, I'd start there.'

'Can you help me with that?' Thomas asks, very aware how now he is pushing his luck.

As if recognising this, another smile creeps across their face.

'You thinking we're in some partnership now, that it?' He asks, laughing.

Thomas just looks at him and says nothing. Khaliq's smile slips, and across his face, a flash, nothing more, Thomas again sees the hurt clinging to the man. They share a moment, Thomas and the kingpin, an unnatural, silent understanding. Nodding in return, Thomas gives Katerina a soft smile, a thank you, and an apology and leaves her alone with her attackers.

22

The next day...

Katerina lays hog-tied, helpless, and fearful, and Thomas, a statue of fear and inadequacy, can only stand and watch. Naked, her body glistening with sweat, her mouth muted with a ball gag, her sorrowful moans while matching her bulging eyes, plead to Thomas.

Before him, as if it had been a lie all along, her face changes.

Not Katerina.

Lilly.

GOD NO!

Clearly beaten, spotted purple and bruised, her body a quivering wreck. Thomas wants to rush to her, but he cannot. Now standing behind a sheet of glass, he is forced to watch. Lilly lays out of his reach on display beneath a single bright spotlight.

Funny how I hadn't noticed the glass panel before.

A thick shadow hugs the room on all sides, draping a black veil over the world beyond, so black, it is both final and absolute. From it, *he* appears, the horned beast.

HELP, SOMEONE, FOR GOD'S SAKE, HELP!

Though masked, he is naked. Tall, muscular, impossibly toned, his penis, a low swinging pipe of meat, is as horrific as it is impressive. As he approaches the helpless Lilly, his shaft grows with every step, becoming monstrously engorged.

Thomas pounds his fists against the glass screen but to no effect.

Still, the fiend draws closer.

Sensing his arrival, fear streaking across her taught face, her eyes grow wide, watering them, staining them with a terrified, radish, red hue. Then, at her side, looming over her, his horn casting a long shadow, the fiend pulls at her binds, and in an instant, they gently fall away, as if they were made from tissue paper all along.

His hand moves to his now enormous and pulsating penis and goes at it with rhythmic strokes. No longer afraid, Lilly looks up at the man, then back over her shoulder at Thomas, her hazy eyes seeking out his. Though still Lilly, her smiling face is now different, altered somehow, darkened and foreign.

Sliding her legs open in anticipation, while her moans are for him, they in turn act to taunt Thomas. Then, bending over her, studying her offering, the masked man produces a knife from somewhere, a long and jagged thing, a horrific tool of death and slaughter.

He traces a line along the inside of her right thigh with the blade, cutting her thinly, leaving a red streak in its wake. With him moving to the left leg, her squirming beneath him, Lilly shivers with child-like excitement against the cuts to her pale skin.

Why can't I look away?

Closing her eyes, her chest heaving, crawling atop her, the masked man readies the knife, his penis.

Please, let me look away. Please shield me from this, please...

The attack begins, and it does so in a shower of red, guttural screams and the carnage of wild, frenzied slaughter. The man slashing, Lilly withering with a mixture of euphoria and agony, blood now soaking the bed, it spilling over the sides, splashing the floor. Only now is Thomas finally released from the nightmare, sparing him the torture of Lilly's grisly demise.

Jerking awake, jolting upright in his chair, the laptop's screensaver bright in Thomas's eyes. Lined with sweat, his clothes stick to his skin like clingfilm.

A dream. No, a nightmare.

My God.

Rubbing his face, and clawing the hair from his eyes, Thomas continues to be plagued with images of Lilly and the masked man. As if burnt into his skull, the blood-soaked bed, her body being savagely taken apart, plays out before him.

And the fiend's dark eyes.

The huge blade.

His pulsating-cock.

Fuck!

The worse nightmare he's ever had now stands as a warning of a possible fate awaiting him. Wincing in pain, holding his bruised torso, Thomas reaches across the table for more pain pills. Opening the lid, dropping two into his hand, adding a third for safe measure, he knocks them back with a glug of red wine.

Running his finger across the laptop's trackpad, the screen blinks back to life. A paused video shows a woman, gagged, surrounded by men, the act frozen mid-gangbang.

And you wonder why your dreams are so horrific.

Checking his phone, sliding it back across the desk, he reads another message from his mother:

> **Mum:** *Hi Tom, it wouldn't hurt to call your mum once in a while. If you need money, don't be afraid to ask, just call me, please. Mum.*

Reading her message as both concerned and another not so subtle way of rubbing his nose in it, Thomas decides against responding. Instead, with his breathing finally levelling out, he gets up and heads for the hallway. With the nightmare still clinging to his shadow, Thomas turns on the hallway light before moving to the bathroom.

Light on, he shuffles to the sink. Diverting his eyes, he hopes to avoid his own reflection but fails almost instantly. Dull eyed and pale, misery leaks from all areas of his face. With the image comes the memories of Mary, her labelling him as gloomy rather than uninspired and unfulfilled.

Looking back at himself, recognising the traits, he sees a man who lingers on the *what-ifs* instead of, *I can.* He sees it now, the time he's wasted, the blame he's shifted. Misadventures, missed opportunities, rejections, dejections, put-downs, cast-offs, cheated, ridiculed, sackings, let-downs, no-shows, anti-climaxes- he's used it all to covert his shortcomings. Firstly, there is his agent, the twenty-eight-year-old intern turned director of Thomas's career. While intelligent with a list of qualifications to boot, she is yet to write anything of meaning.

'Me, an editor, has not the time to write her own stories, for I spend my time correcting your mistakes,' she had said.

Not believing her at the time, he now considers it with a sickening realisation. Accepting her reasoning surprises him, as if now, for the first time, he is allowed the clarity needed to be rational. It makes him think back to Mary, whom he blamed for everything from his insecurity to his failing Libido. Hell, he even blamed Robin, her birth, labelling her arrival as *poor timing*. Looking at himself now, it's a strong word, but he hates what he sees. The man he has become, the waste of his best years, the nights spent drinking wine alone, are each a crime, and Thomas, with painful recognition, sees this now. With it comes a sickness and shame and a level of sadness, even for a dreary soul like his.

Splashing his face with cold water, Thomas moves onto his teeth. Brushing them removes the stale, pungent taste upon his tongue. Rinsing his mouth with Listerine, burning in seconds, he spits it out with angry disdain. Still, the taste of blood from the night before, the nightmare, remains.

Leaving the bathroom and returning to the laptop, Thomas does so with a gut full of consternation, or is it constipation? Regardless, the screen with its horrors waits for him at the desk. Sitting down before it, he focuses on the content. Clicking the back button and returning to the sites home screen- X-Creeper.com, Thomas is presented with row upon row of videos. Just one of a never-ending stream of adult sites. And while they claim to be legal, mainstream, even ethical, they all follow a consistent theme- women of all ages being treated as objects, as commodities, for the gross desires of men. *Solo, girl-on-girl, extreme bondage, group sex, rough sex,* all concluded with women made to smile, to moan out in pleasure, to demand it harder, and with rapturous vigour, scream with enjoyment.

Hours of trawling through sludge, the worst the internet can offer, led Thomas to the 2014 Global Slavery Index. A trade of young girls, many vulnerable, exploited, kidnapped- those exported from poor rural parts of counties such Romania, Albania, and worse still, India, Pakistan, China and Bangladesh, where women in their millions are being trafficked for sex. As startling as it is vile, Thomas was forced to absorb the information, the almost staggeringly impossible statistics. India alone is home to more than fourteen million victims of human trafficking, where 95% of these people are forced into prostitution. This is a breeding ground where these same girls later become traffickers themselves, and in doing so, close the cycle of victim and perpetrator.

Sat looking at the laptop, the seemingly endless videos, alone in his dark apartment, Thomas is struck by the enormity of it all, the task ahead of him. Where one woman's disappearance led to two, he now sits on the edge of something far-reaching, far larger than he could ever have imagined.

Too large.

A rabbit hole with no end.

The legal sex trade, with its blurred lines of right and wrong, acts as a doorway to a bottomless hotpot of crime, exploitation, abuse, rape, and murder. With a limited time and using basic search parameters, Thomas managed to find a network of squalid brothels, the pop-up type, like the ones at the market where paying men abuse girls, all under the nose of their bosses. And then there are the faces of hollowed-eyed girls. Young, attempting to be sexy and alluring, but unable to mask stares of expressionless pain, as if the work, the acts they are forced to do, has simply stripped them of who they are, ripping out their souls, killing their hope, their plans for the future.

Thomas found, unbelievably, mainstream internet sites and marketplaces selling sex through their personal ads section, in essence, helping the facilitation of prostitution. While some were forced to close such avenues with the arrival of the anti-sex trafficking bill in 2018, other sites continue still to flirt with the law.

Having again called and spoken to James's father, Ricky Ruck, Thomas wasn't surprised to learn James had for a while worked as a cameraman for several different pornographic websites. However, only later in his career did James move solely into still photography. Cars, fashion, model shoots, but also spreads for adult magazines. It would seem whatever he could get, though he would claim to be *sought after* and *in demand.*

It was apparent, though open with the information, Ricky wasn't about to add shame to his son's life and, now in death, about to speak ill of him. Still, there was an unspoken truth between them- that his son James was an amateur photographer working within the porn industry, and because of this, led in some way, a shady life. Like Khaliq, Ricky named several of James's friends who too made money filming sex, model shoots, cheap shit glossed over to look professional.

Closing the internet browser, Thomas opens a new Word document and begins stacking the facts:

James works as a cameraman making porn films with his friends.

James turns to still photography and later begins dating Amy.

Freshly out of the escort business, Erika tries her hand at modelling.

She meets James, and they start a relationship.

The whole thing blows up, and Amy finds out.

James and Erika spilt.

Erika falls pregnant, tells James.

Her phone and a copy of her house keys were found in James' apartment – Erika was quoted as fearing James, believing he had something planned.

Erika disappears along with her Mini.

In a seemingly unrelated incident, James is killed in a traffic accident.

Stalked, Amy is kidnapped from her apartment.

Sitting back in his chair, rubbing his face, feeling the tightness in his muscles, Thomas considers options.

Like you have a choice.

He goes to his phone. Opening it, scrolling through the list, down to the number of his old friend. Dialling it, hoping she'll answer, and praying, like the last time they spoke, she doesn't tell him to go fuck himself, or worse, that he's a sell-out and fraud.

* * *

Hildur is late to arrive, and though Thomas is expecting it, annoyance tugs at him, nonetheless, darkening his temper. Not having seen her for over two years, and after failing to respond to her numerous messages, it had been a surprise she agreed to meet him at all. Still, the endless waiting only adds to his growing frustration.

So, forced to wait, Thomas watches the passing world through the steam fogged window. Beyond, the city appears to him as it always does; busy and angry, dull and hinging on infection and disease. Due to the continued rain, the roads appear like sheets of icy glass. An endless stream of cars hiss past, spraying water to the curb outside the window, smogging the street in ashy plumes. Worse still are the people, the army of faceless zombies, who huddle beneath umbrellas, who walk the streets in waves, cowering beneath a dejected grey veil of low cloud cover. In reflection, given how badly he acted when leaving his job at the newspaper, Thomas accepts this as a timely return to the city.

Bum fidgeting, as if unable to find the perfect spot, Thomas scans the coffee shop, the different customers, their faces, their smiles. The air is full of the sounds of hissing steam and the clatter of plates, backed with an underlining of nauseous chit-chat. Thomas focuses on the smoke rising from the all-chrome barista machine, the young staff abuzz around it, in a hurry to meet the queue of orders, all the while, the uneasiness remains. Here in the city, everyone and everything moves at a different pace; well, that's how it seems to him anyway.

A speed he no longer understands.

If he ever actually understood it in the first place.

This world, the hustle, louder than he remembers, is now lost in a loop of controlled chaos, rushing around fast, too fast, leaving it a blur about him. It is as if he is stuck in a glitch, out of sync, no longer in tune with his surroundings. With this unfair exclusion, Thomas feels bitterness, resentment, anger... and shame.

Returning his gaze to the window, peering out through the dying light, he takes note of the passing cars, if only to occupy his mind. Their dark windows and the occupants are masked behind the rain. Next, he tracks two women hunched together beneath an umbrella a little too small for the both. Then a pregnant teenage girl, smoking a cigarette, drinking from a can of Tennent's Super T beer. Lastly, he notices a homeless man dirtying the street across from him. Hunchbacked and filthy, the rain streaking his grimy face in stripes.

Finally, Thomas spots Hildur crossing the street with her usual gusto. Pressing through the rain, passing through the bodies, Thomas notes the cigarette, her pinching it dead before entering the coffee shop. Collapsing her umbrella, easing in through the entrance, her eyes find him from the door. Thomas plants a smile on his face, one to meet her gaze, and though she meets his gesture with one of her own, it is thin, transparent to how she feels.

Here we go.

Moving through the crowded space, weaving and bobbing, he loses sight of her momentarily. Reappearing from behind a row of suited men stood at a table in the room's middle, brushing rain from her short, cropped hair, she steps between two tables, sliding over to his window table.

Rising to meet her, he says, 'thanks for coming.'

'Thomas,' she says, sitting across from him at the window table. 'You're looking rather dishevelled, if you don't mind me saying so.'

Thomas notes her ageing, strained voice and how it now appears to creak and croak.

'I do, actually,' he says, forcing a smile.

Her eyes widen when they settle on his crust covered split lip and grow further as they take in Thomas's overall condition. Finally, they look at one another, eyes locking, familiarity returning with feeling, and the eager remnants of long but not lost resentment.

A long beat.

Both sizing up the other.

'I got you a latte, extra milk,' he smiles.

'Fuck off,' she snaps, though her tone is far lighter than her words.

As she takes the seat opposite him, Thomas slides a cup across the table to her. With steam rising from the black coffee, she removes her leather gloves and clamps her hands around the cup, smiling against its warmth.

'I had a feeling you'd need my help at some point,' she declares proudly. 'But I'm trusting you with this information. You do remember loyalty, don't you?'

'I do, and I'll be in your debt.'

'Again,' Hildur adds sharply. 'You'll be in my debt again.'

'Again,' he agrees.

'James Ruck, the police looked at him, I mean, seriously looked at him. They found Erika's fingerprints all over his apartment, her phone and a cut copy of her keys, but as he and Erika saw each other, this he could easily explain away. Around the time of her disappearance, pings from a mobile phone tower had him positioned somewhere outside of town. The Police are confident Erika Sobo was with him, but they found nothing after searching the area.'

'This area out of town, where is it?' Thomas asks.

'A wooded area and lake out near Marlow, the Police believe he stopped there for over an hour. They think they stopped there for a time, they found tyre tracks matching James's car, but it never led to anything.'

'A burial site?'

Hildur looks at him, eyes narrowing, wanting to say something, but instead responds with, 'the Police did follow that line of thought, but they've looked but never found anything. After that day, Erika was neither heard from nor seen again.'

'So, he had motive and opportunity,' Thomas says. 'Amy Porter, her laptop and phone were accessed the night of her disappearance, do you know why?'

'It would appear, to delete files. Online searches, stuff like that,' she pauses. 'You really think these two disappearances are connected?'

Shrugging, exhaling deeply, Thomas watches her go back to her coffee. Shaking her head, a sly smile spreading, she again goes to say something but stops before the words can form. Looking at her, Thomas notices the flecks of grey in her hair, the ones able to escape continuous dyeing. She looks older, too- the skin over her face and neck hangs a little bit looser. Her eyes, greyer than he remembers, sit enlarged behind her red thick-lensed spectacles. For as long as he can remember, Hildur had looked the same, like a photograph, frozen in time. Once a strong woman in her early fifties, one with a flair for colour and originality, seeing her now, Thomas notices the change. Where her skin was once blessed with an olive hue, it now appears translucent, almost anaemic. He, too, sees it in her hands, the slight, almost hidden tremor to them.

'How have you been?' He asks.

'Fine. How's the book coming along?' She asks, sipping her drink, hot steam fogging up her glasses. 'I was expecting you to release one last year.'

'It's, not...' he sighs. 'No new ideas, not even bad ones.'

'So, what's this all about?'

'I don't know, it started, I mean, it seemed like the perfect....' He says, stopping short.

No longer can he refer to it as just another story, another project.

Leaning forward, her eyes seek out his. 'You can always come back and work for me; the doors always open?'

Her hand reaches out across the table, taking his. This surprises him, almost startling him back from her touch.

'Hey,' she says softly.

'I know, one day maybe,' he tells her, backing away.

'And Ann would love to see you. You should come on by the house, she may be an old stubborn bitch, but my Ann can still make mean enchiladas.'

He looks down, unable to meet her gesture. The smile he offers is both thin and drained of all colour.

'Forty percent of all pornography depicts violence towards women, crazy but true. And videoed child sexual exploitation, child porn, is now one of the fastest-growing online businesses, can you believe that?' He says, his eyes welling with the enormity of the task.

'It's nothing new; sex sells,' she says, sipping her coffee.

'I'm not talking about *just* sex or am I referring to the young woman trying on bikinis on social media. I'm talking about trafficking, exploitation, abuse.'

'Tell me, do you watch porn, do you masturbate?' She asks coldly, taking him by surprise.

'What, I...'

'We're all part of the circle, we watch it, it's free, but we condemn it. The demand is there, and it's only growing. Where sex was once enough, now, well, the mainstream has changed; the line has been broken. Cities like London, our societies' pinnacle in property, culture, and structural infostructure, sit on a layer of utter depravity. I'll tell you another thing, the dark world you speak of, the one below our feet, the once tabooed, is no longer reaching up from the sewers. It's invading our televisions, music, walking every street corner. No longer is it isolated to the untrodden and impoverished,' she says.

'I've seen it, the chicken-hawks, perverts, the desperate... the children... the countless women,' Thomas stutters, choking back tears.

'Not all women are victims; some sell it, endorse it, even make it, and not all of them want to be saved, believe it or not, some like what they do, it's a career, a way of making serious money,' Hildur tells him.

'Come on, Hildur,' Thomas moans.

'Dismiss it, go ahead, but just remember, you're blind if you can't see beyond your own nose,' she pauses as a heat warms his face. 'But it sounds like a story to me, an important one too, one which needs to be told.'

'I don't do that anymore,' he tells her, his eyes fixed on the table between them.

'Have you ever considered the reason why you can't write a decent second book?' She asks. 'Maybe, just maybe, you're not supposed to?'

Her words have his head snapping back, his eyes rushing to meet hers.

'Like I always say, fiction is fun, but it's the truth....' She starts.

'It's the truth that matters,' Thomas finishes.

'Damn straight,' she smiles. 'How far must we travel; how long must we wait. How many seasons, watching the passing of time, growing old in its shadow. Round and round- how long until we find ourselves at the circle's end, back at the start, the place where we belong?'

'William Blake?' He asks.

'Actually, it was you,' she says. 'There's a great writer in there, You Thomas are still there, you just need to find a way to bring him back.'

He smiles softly, unable to meet her eyes. So, she waits for him. Patient as always. A true friend. One he only now recognises as such.

Lifting his eyes to hers, he reaches with his hand, sliding it across the table to her. With hesitation, she meets his gesture.

'Oh, and the friends you asked about, you might want to look into Simon Finch and Morgan Teller. Two long-standing school friends of James, then business partners,' she says.

'Business partners?'

'Film making and production, adult material mainly, low-end stuff.'

Is this who Khaliq had meant?

Thomas recalls Khaliq's words.

'He used to hang around with others like him, photographers, amateur filmmakers.'

'Ok, Simon Finch and Morgan Teller?' He clarifies, making sure he has the names right.

'Yes, it appears James fell out with them some years back, but interestingly, in the weeks before Erika's disappearance, they reconnected. They traded messages daily but stopped when Erika fell off the map.'

Nodding, energised by the new information, Thomas smiles and says, 'thanks, I do appreciate this, you know.'

'Let me know when you finish the story, but finish it, accurate and true, the young ladies of this city, the missing children, the abused, deserve nothing less.'

Watching her leave, letting his eyes follow her outside, along the street, past the same homeless hunchback, all the way until the city and crowd, the rain and gloom, reclaim her. Thomas pictures her heading back to work, to the office he once worked. His mind drifts back to the large bullpen, his cubical and computer, the summer afternoons when the sun would cover the entire floor with a warm, golden blanket. And at Christmas, the office decorations, the large tree at the room's centre. He's missed it, all of it, but only now, seeing Hildur again, does he recognise by just how much. He misses Della, the plucky twenty-one-year intern who would flirt with Thomas in a non-sleazy, de-ageing kind of way. He misses the view from the garden on the roof, the twenty-pence cappuccino from the machine on the third floor. And now, to his surprise, he misses writing copy, digging into a story, following it to its conclusion. He too misses Hildur, the weekends he spent with her and Ann, drinking wine, watching old films, and how she'd read his work, tear it apart but print every word just the same.

Damn, Hildur, still taking me to school.

Smiling, one of warmth in seeing his old friend, quickly fading in bitter remembrance. Deciding to leave, Thomas is stopped before leaving the table by the buzzing of his phone. He checks the phone's screen, the number displayed, not recognising it, he answers regardless.

'Hello?'

'Hello, you sent me an email?'

'Max Rex?'

'Yes, you mentioned a large sum of money?'

'I did. Thanks for calling. I'm interested in commissioning a piece, a one of a kind?'

'Ok, how much you got?'

'How much do you charge?'

'£1,000.00 gets you entry-level, £2,000.00 gets you something special.'

'£2,000.00 will be fine.'

'Good. I'm having a soiree Saturday at 10pm. I'll send you the address.'

'I was hoping to do business....'

'I only do business with those I know, fellow fornicators, those I can trust with my art.'

Taking a deep breath, sweating hard, hating even speaking to such a person over the phone, Thomas says, 'Fine, send me the address.'

23

4 days later...

The warehouse, one of many, looks disused and rundown. Out of the row of metal structures, each lit out front by faint, yellow overhead lights, is warehouse-17 which shows any signs of life. Below the roofline, a red glow emanates from a series of long slit-like windows, bleeding into the night like devilish eyes.

Peter pulls his Ford into the lot, slowly moving along the row, the headlights searching through the persistent rain for a free spot.

'There's a lot of people here,' Peter moans, his strapped fingers loosely guiding the wheel.

'Probably a highlight of the pervert calendar,' Thomas says.

'Not everyone here is perverted,' Peter tells him. 'Here we go.'

Finding a spot, a short stretch from the entrance, Peter yanks on the wheel, steering his car between a small convertible coupe and a white panel van.

'Sure, they ain't,' Thomas tells him. 'How're the fingers?'

'Still broken.'

Noticing a slight tremor to his voice, Thomas places a hand on his shoulder.

'Why don't you stay here,' Thomas tells him.

Turning, eyes glassy, Peter looks at him, and while his face sits wrapped in shadow, his eyes he can tell consider the offer.

'I'm not scared, I'm just...' he starts,

'You're what?' Thomas asks.

'Shitting bricks,' he says.

In the dark, the young man smiles, one forced but one powered by resolve.

When he reaches for the door handle, Thomas stops before exiting. 'I do appreciate this, your help.'

Peter's face, still shadowed in the faint glow of the dash, looks back at Thomas. 'I know.'

'But you don't have to, this world, the shit and grime, it doesn't have to be yours?'

'Your stories, your books, your work before, they mean something to many people. I think you miss that now when you self-analyse. Your words have helped people, and they can again,' Peter says.

Seeing Peter's eyes glaze over in the ambient light, Thomas's well with warm, salty tears. What had upset Peter so, well Thomas cannot be sure, but in his state of mind, where they are, what they might see, he is unprepared and ill-equipped to ask at this time.

Following Peter outside, the fresh evening rain acts as a cold slap to the face. The stretching of his wounded side has Thomas mashing down on his teeth. Though being patched up and medicated, discomfort remains. With the chill through the rain, Thomas is left shuddering under its downpour. Lack of food, sleep, and overexposure to the horrors of this world, plus almost being anally raped, all now conspire against him, leaving Thomas a wreck of lifeless muscle.

While they accepted what Thomas and Peter told them, a vague story of them falling from their mountain bikes, it was clear the nurses had remained suspicious throughout their treatment. Regardless, the nurses had seen to their injuries: two bruised rips for Thomas, two broken fingers for Peter. Of course, the wounds would heal, but like an itch under the skin, stubborn dirt beneath the nail, the scars of what they saw at the market, the look of terror in Katerina's eyes, he fears will be harder to forget.

Closing the car door, flipping up his collar, Thomas cuts across the lot to the warehouses. Offering minimal protection from the downpour, ducking beneath the stingy overhang at the front, he stops to wait for Peter outside the rusted shutter of a long out of business meatpacking company.

Hunched against the torrent, Peter rushes to join him. Together, they move along the front of the shutter to the next warehouse, and the next, finally, arriving at warehouse-17, they take up a position beneath a lit neon sign. Lipstick red, it shocks the night with its garish inking.

MAX REX - The Ossuary - All things fetish, taboo, the unspoken...

'You sure this is the right place?' Peter asks, though his words tease, this tone remains glum and monotone.

Shifting him a look, Thomas passes the shutter to a lit, sheet metal door. Breathing heavy, each gulp pained with his damaged rips, beneath the glare of the overhead light, at the mercy of the heavy downpour, Thomas takes a moment. His eyes flip from the intercom to peter, who stands with a look of discomfort as if in need of the toilet. Pressing the button, like Thomas, Peter is startled as a crackle creep out from the intercom, cutting open the night.

'Yeah?' A slow voice asks from the speaker.

'The names Thomas. Max, is expecting me?'

'Thomas, what?'

'William, Thomas William.'

A long beat...

Peter looks at him, eyes wide, his skin flush and pale in the glare.

With a ping, the door pops forward.

Ok, you can do this.

Panting, laboured, Thomas stutters but pulls the door open. With Peter at his rear, stepping forward, they are presented with a tight hallway. Lit by a line of bare red-light bulbs, the hallway runs away from them, its tail long and dark. Music booms, rattling through the sheet metal walls. Heavy rock, the worst type, all rage and screaming, like the background music to hell, fill the air with dread, suffocating it.

Moving forward, Thomas's eyes are drawn to the framed posters on the left. The one-sheets capture different leather/latex wearing creeps, all lurking, abhorrent and cheap. On his right, wall-mounted glass display cases, shallow and slightly lopsided, contain sex toys of the exotic type. Crude and poorly put together, they border on the horrific and the obscene. First, an unnaturally large rubber strap-on, decorated with red leather strapping and buckles, has its shaft laced with razor blades. A second, a leather bra with spiked cone nipples, their tips painted red.

A third has him stopping to stare. A bondage-style mask/hood, leather, wholly black but for a red zipped closed mouthpiece. While not exact, the tightening of his stomach, the shrinking of his penis, tells Thomas he could be close; that Max Rex could be Amy's abductor. He glances over his shoulder to Peter, who stands stunned, eyes fixed on the mask.

Moving on, the mask watching them leave, Thomas and Peter approach the two heavyset, well-dressed men waiting for them at the end of the hallway.

'Good evening, gentlemen,' one offers. 'If you would be so kind, arms and legs apart, please.'

Thomas and Peter are frisked with heavy, thorough hands, yet unintrusive. The larger of the two men, a jacked-up skinhead with steroid abuse written across his eyes, hums with surprising elegance as he works his way down Thomas, patting his chest and his arms. Moving down his sides, pain is sent surging through Thomas's midriff. Wincing, Thomas is again surprised by the man's acknowledgement of this, apologising with what appears to be genuine sympathy.

Moving lower, the man's giant-like dinner-plate size hands cup Thomas's legs as they slide down. Clamping each leg tightly but thankfully stopping above the knee, Thomas meets the man's smile as he stands up, gesturing to the large metal sliding door on their left.

With Peter joining Thomas, pulling the open for them, the bouncer nods a smile and says, 'gentlemen, have yourselves a good evening.'

Stepping through the opening into the converted warehouse, the booming music rushes in, hitting them with the force of a slap to the face. It is such that it stops Thomas before he can proceed any further, as to scan the open space, to climatise himself to the dark, and well, opaque scene. A network of concrete pillars, each wrapped in what looks like latex, run from floor to ceiling. On some, vertical running red fluorescent light tubes leave it hazy and heavy with shadow, leaving the massive open chamber with an air of weighty oppression. Pockets of people clutter the floor. Where some stand chatting silently against the music, others either sway to the music or act with far more vigour through frantic head-banging, hip-thrusting, and body manipulation. Men, women, young and old, all in erotic dress: leather, PVC, latex, little to no clothes, naked, some with whips and buckles, but all conceal their faces behind leather hoods, gas masks, and warped versions of the classic masquerade type. Those unmasked wear makeup, some crudely applied, while others, expertly so. Drag queen-esque, with creativity and flair, but darker somehow, leaving the eyes like small black olives, peering and leering.

He could be here, Amy's abductor; he could be any one of them.

Considering this, a cold chill creeps in beneath Thomas's skin. Searching the bodies for a matching body shape (slender and tall), movement (cat-like), and sex (male), scanning the masked faces, Thomas struggles with the awkward light. With the booming music and red lighting, his vision is hindered by wild flickering shadows generated by hundreds of tall, black wax candles.

Disconcerting still is the large, four-poster bed's dotted at the edge of the floor. Each bed is draped with dark velvet curtains, leaving what lay behind them a mystery. One to their left sits with its curtains open, where a well-built black man, stacked with muscles, dressed only in a shiny, diamond-encrusted eye mask, waits on the bed, propped up on one elbow. His eyes, peering out through the mask, watch the dance floor, searching, waiting for someone to come join him. As a well-dressed man in a suit and tie takes up the offer, snapping the curtain shut behind him, Thomas diverts his eyes to a series of large-screen monitors anchored to the pillars. Each display the same rolling footage of snakes, black like oil, coiled together in a clump – a mating ball, they wither and fuck, like yards of riving rubber tubing.

Stepping forward, his mouth now dry, Thomas leads Peter through the warehouse. Through the crowd, Thomas spies a long, mirrored bar taking up most of the far wall. Overhanging it from above, an office of sorts made from two shipping containers connected, running side-by-side. Sitting high, perched on metal struts, the facing side is entirely glassed. Thomas counts at least five shadowed figures standing behind it, looking down, their faces each a black smudge.

Passing through groups of naked or half-naked people, the costumed and scantily clad, deeper into the room, Thomas catches the eye of three identically dressed women. Matching red leather bra and knickers, black stilettos. Tall and slender without an ounce of fat, all three are model-like but hide their faces behind red leather eye masks. Each holding a studded dog chain at their feet, three men sit crouched on all fours, their heads covered in black, eyeless, mouthless hoods, matched to the leather, spike collars around their necks.

'And you are?' Asks a muffled voice to Thomas's right.

Turning, Thomas finds a tall man, trim and lean, naked except for a black gas mask, staring at him through narrow eye slits. Though shadowed by the mask, still, they shimmer with what looks like cat-like contact lenses. The man traces an invisible line from his navel with a roaming hand, down to his chest, stomach, stopping as his finger disappears within a heap of dark pubic hair.

'I'm new,' Thomas tells him. 'Where's Max?'

'Mmmmm, new, fresh fish... he's up there, watching, of course.'

His gaze follows the man's outstretched finger, following the line to the glass office, to the one dark figure standing front and centre.

Thanking the man, eager to get away from his burning eyes, Thomas gets walking again, weaving between people, away from the man and his stiffening penis.

Arriving at and stopping before it, Thomas stands wide-eyed, staring at the party's centrepiece. Propped up from the ground, a blindfolded, morbidly obese woman lays atop a wooden plinth. Lit by a single bare bulb, sprawled out on the back, the woman's fatty blubber threatens to spill over the edges.

My god.

A small group have gathered around, each holding something. Moving closer, noticing her skin, where portions of it appear black, Thomas is quick to realise the group is holding black marker pens. Passing them, watching as they take turns in colouring sections of her bloated skin black, stunned, he looks at Peter. Busy ogling a petite blonde as she leads a suited man to a vacant bed, he finally turns and finds Thomas waiting for him. Thomas cannot help but smile; Peter's face, a mixture of shock, excitement, and 'Oh man, I've been caught,' turns to one of fear as a spotlight drops down on them from the heavens. Blinding, Thomas is forced to shield his eyes with his hand.

And the music goes silent.

Along with everyone else, the obese woman pops up onto one elbow to look at the pair.

'Good evening and welcome,' comes a voice, loud, God-like, from above. 'Are you here to join my flock, or are you lost, a transitory, someone in search of their metamorphosis? Or perhaps a false Sheppard, here to infiltrate and taint the water?'

Struggling with the light, he looks beyond it, but Thomas's vision is reduced to dark, blurred shapes.

'I'm here to see Max,' He calls back, still guarding his eyes.

'And so, you have found him,' the voice booms.

The low chatter of words breakout from small pockets of the crowd, hushed whispers, those of a collective, pinging across the floor, chased around with giggles, claps of excitement.

'Like I said on the phone, I'm here to do business with you, nothing more.'

'Business, business, there will be time for business, but first, before I allow you through, like all who came before you, you will take and pass the test,' the voice says, cultured, his tongue curling around every word.

The warehouse again goes silent. The giggles, claps, and jeers fade away as if everyone, but Thomas and Peter know what will come next.

'Thomas, we should leave,' Peter moans.

Ignoring him, Thomas shouts, 'what goddamn test?'

A beat – in the silence, fear creeps inside Thomas's mind.

Yeah, we should leave.

Ready to turn, run, fight his way out if he must, words from the rafters anchor him to the spot, running his heart cold.

'Your young companion, take him in your mouth,' the voice says expectantly.

'Take him in my....' Thomas mutters, confused.

'Fellatio, my dear boy. I want you to suck his cock.'

'No, sorry,' Thomas splutters, the words blurting out as blunt groans.

'Either you do it, or you'll leave; it is that simple.'

'Fuck off!' Thomas shouts.

Turning to Peter, Thomas gestures towards the exit but comes face-to-face with three heavy-set men. Clones of the guards at the door, having taken up positions behind them, block any idea of an escape.

'Don't fight, assimilate, yield, join my flock, please,' Max continues, his loud voice coming from multiple speakers.

Turning back to the spotlight, to the place beyond it where Thomas is sure Max is standing. Though assured behind the booming voice, something in his threats, his words have Thomas convinced the man is all words and no spine.

'I work for the Daily Reporter. I'm doing a piece on the killing of two women, each perpetrated by a man wearing one of your commissioned masks. My story is ninety percent done, my editor wants to send it to press, but I figured you might want to have your say before your work is associated with a serial murderer.'

A long beat - silence.

The spotlight disappears.

'At the bar, take the stairs to my office,' Max calls, his tone now decidedly different, almost weary.

Momentarily, Thomas's vision is spotted and blotted with black, soot-like patches. It takes a moment to clear, but as it does, the music returns to flood his eardrums, further unbalancing him.

Focusing on the office above the bar, Thomas starts moving around the plinth—the obese woman tracking their journey, smiling through a bloated, greasy face. She's not alone; eyes from across the floor peer out at them from behind sneering masks.

With Peter in tow, Thomas tackles the metal, grated steps. Looking down to his left, the barman, a thick wedge of muscle, tattoos, and hardship, tracks their ascent. Climbing higher, his attention turns to the office through its glassed front. Three silhouetted figures peer out at them, their heads moving in silent unison as they climb the steps with them. One of which leaves the glass, disappearing into the shadows beyond.

Max?

Another suited bouncer stands waiting at the top of the steps. Wide, his chest pushed out, he watches their ascent with steely concentration. With his right arm extended, an outstretched finger directs them inside the office.

Passing him, Thomas turns and moves through the door. With it closing behind them, the music is reduced to faint rhythmic thuds and whines. Four finely dressed men, one woman, and a bounce stand waiting inside, while a seventh person sits watching from an armchair. Wearing leather trousers, a leather waistcoat, and long leather gloves, with long talons at the fingers that tap the chairs' bronze-plated arms. Sitting cross-legged, his booted foot twitches with the beat of the music. His face pancaked with white makeup, is finished with skinny black painted eyebrows and lashes, a thin moustache, and red lipstick, mimicking *Clark Gable* in *Gone with the Wind.*

'Max Rex?' Thomas asks.

Smoking a cigarette through a vintage, black and white holder, sitting extended from his left hand, the man watches Thomas through a veil of thin smoke.

'That was quite the entrance,' he smiles, his eyes lingering and clingy.

'Thanks to you,' Thomas says, scanning the room.

The room around them is an utter contradiction—sleazy sex paraphernalia such as hooks, and pulleys hang from the ceiling. The painted black walls, studded with spikes, is wrongly paired with ornate red leather sofas, an antique bronze drinks trolly, and three large ageing painting on the back wall.

'True, true,' Max smiles. Looking at the paintings, he asks. 'Do you like it?'

Each trimmed with carved, heavily bronze frames, the three paintings could be best described as 16th-century porn. Sex, sodomy, orgies, all on fading yellow canvases.

'Marquis de Sade, 18th century,' Peter says.

'Yes, yes, well done, my boy,' Max laughs. 'Artist, writer, fornicator, prisoner.'

'Rapist, paedophile, nutcase,' Thomas adds.

Max's eyes working, move over Thomas like crude oil. But, given his makeup, Thomas cannot read the man's expression.

'You said something about money before?' Max says.

'I also remember telling you about a man I'm looking for.'

'Who... wears... my... masks, yes?' His smile is now evident.

'Possibly. Full leather hood, tiny slits for the eyes and mouth....'

'Sounds mundane...' Max snaps back.

Stepping forward, pointing to his forehead, Thomas concludes with direct aggression, 'with a red fucking horn.'

'A horn?'

'A great big one, yeah,' Thomas tells him, 'You made it, didn't you?'

There is a beat of tension between them, bubbling, growing. Finally, standing up, Max rises slowly from the armchair. The unnaturally tall man straightens out his waistcoat before taking a long drag on his cigarette. Gliding to the window, his movements almost bird-like, Max gestures for Thomas to follow.

Joining him there, where Thomas had seen his makeup as the reason for his broad grin, up close, he sees Max as the owner of an unnaturally big mouth. Too big. The grin upon it, oblique and wrong, is demon-like in the low light.

'He's here, the horned man you seek, down there with my flock,' Max whispers.

'Who is he?' Thomas asks.

Turning to Thomas, lifting one eyebrow, he grins, 'he calls himself, *The Great Deceiver*.'

'Satan?' Peter asks.

'What's his name?' Thomas presses.

'I don't know. He didn't tell me. A lot of my customers don't.'

'And did he pass your test, or was that just for us?' Thomas asks.

Max smiles in return.

'Thomas,' Peter says.

Not hearing him, Thomas takes Max by the arm, alerting the bouncer into action.

'Careful now,' Max whispers.

Looking over Thomas's shoulder, Max gestures for the bouncer to remain where he is with a wink and nod.

'Thomas,' Peter repeats, now louder and more urgent. 'For God's sake, look!'

Turning to Peter, his face troubled in the dim light. Following the line of his finger, through the glass, down to the crowd below, Thomas sees him. Standing alone, upright and stark, hands behind his back, his horn rising up to meet Thomas's stare.

The Great Deceiver.

'Stay here and get a description!' Thomas calls over his shoulder to Peter.

Leaving the office, pushing the bouncer aside, Thomas takes the stairs two at a time. Bounding down, he crashes into a guy dressed in a leather boiler suit at the bottom. Grunting, the man is pitched forward into a pillar, spilling his drink.

Turning, scanning the floor, Thomas's eyes work hard to find him amongst the clutter of bodies. Instead, dancing people, naked and leather-clad, pass before his eyes, blocking them. Moving forward, scanning the shadows, the pockets of space and darkness, pushing people aside, he spots a swelling in the crowd, it parting, bodies bumping.

There you are.

Thomas catches a glimpse, nothing more, a moving shadow, the leather hood, the horn, then it disappears again, ducking behind a pillar.

Charging forward through the crowd, he starts after him. At full speed, barging a woman aside, followed by a couple, interrupting their embrace, Thomas's bludgeoning weight knocks them both to the ground in gasps, either in pain or from exhausting sexual release.

Ahead of him, Thomas spots The Deceiver again, moving out from behind a pillar, slithering snake-like to the exit, disappearing through it; the darkness is greedy to accept him.

Pushing past bodies, 'MOVE!' Thomas screams, but the music leaves his voice mute. Shoulder barging a guy to the side, knocking him on his rump, Thomas pushes forward, ignoring the pain in his ribs. Finding a clearing in the crowd, he sprints full pelt to the exit. With the door sliding shut before him, sticking out an arm, ramming it through the closing space, a scream bursts from his throat as the door clamps in. Bouncing back, the door pulls open, and in its place, the doorman stomps forward.

'What the fuck are you doing....' The doorman starts.

Pushing him aside, holding his now injured right arm to his chest, Thomas moves into the hallway and along it. Closing in on the door, it pulling shut, Thomas can only watch as the world beyond narrows to a slither of light, leaving the end of the hallway dark and uncertain.

Pushing harder, tearing forward, away from the music to the door, bursting through it, out into the cold, wet night, the door slams shut behind him. Silence is quick to wrap itself around him, lurching Thomas to a sudden, jarring stop. With the adrenaline draining away, the brittle cold rushes in to jab at his lungs. As if in competition, the pain in his arm burns like warmed coal, joining his injured rib, blisteringly so, throbs his vision in waves of pinkish nausea. Not broken, far from it, but the tissue of his forearm, tender, brings a wince of stuttering breath when touched.

Scanning the area, the dark lot, the night beyond, his heartthrobs through his eyes. While rain pounds the pavement, his heart, likewise in his ears, rattling through him, jarring his teeth together. Parked cars shimmer, the exterior lights lace with the raindrops, leaving them shimmering like a million tiny shards of glass across the hoods and windscreens. Pockets of shadow fill the different spaces between them, any one of them a possible hiding place. Being pelted by the rain, now feeling it, Thomas moves out into the lot. Walking between the two rows of cars, eyes squinting, peering through the downpour, searching between the vehicles, straining against the darkness.

A noise creeps in from the night through the rain, bringing Thomas to an abrupt stop. His eyes dart from one car to the next, to the line of warehouses.

Nothing.

The thunder of the rain, heavy and drumming, dancing all about him, wrecks his senses. A second sound, a cackle of metal scraping, has his eyes snap to the row of shutters. Eyes straining through the downpour, he cuts between two parked cars, watching the structures. Returning to the warehouses, hugging the wall, Thomas shuffles along their front, his eyes darting about, his heart jumping with every thud of rain against the sheet metal roofing. Each warehouse is fronted with heavy closed shutters and dark brick, shiny from the rain, a structural design repeated over and over. Thomas stops abruptly, passing one shutter to the next, arriving at number 14.

The shutter of warehouse-14, slightly raised, hangs open, leaving a two-foot black gap at its base.

This is it... he's in there.

24

Thomas tries to take in air, but his breathing has intensified through ragged and inconsistent gasps. In truth, if not for the rain, Thomas would think the world had stopped. Impeding him with its glare, the overhead light cannot breach the darkness, leaving the interior black and absolute.

Moving to it, approaching it from the right, hunched over, Thomas peers into the dark space. Seeing nothing, he listens and still hears only the rain, both outside upon the concrete and inside, rattling the metal roof in concussion-like waves.

Hesitation again takes hold, leaving Thomas a floundering fool, teetering on the edge of retreat. Crouching lower, pressing his head forward, he somehow, against the resistance of a coward, manages to push his feet to the opening.

Still, he sees only darkness.

I really don't like this.

It could be a trap.

Duh, you think.

Rocking on his feet, forward and back, forward and back... a new sound, a clattering of something falling and cracking against concrete. Moving before he can protest, his feet have him shuffling into the darkened space beyond. Dipping low, his flexing torso and numerous injuries drag a whimper from his pressed lips.

Inside and out of the rain, now standing, Thomas allows his eyes time to adjust before proceeding further. The light recedes, and the darkness, brooding, gathers around him in seconds. While light filters in through the stingy elevated windows, it cannot penetrate the clotted gloom, leaving the far side of the warehouse dark and deceptive.

Narrow strips of light stretch across the floor from the windows at ceiling level, while faint light drops down via evenly space small skylights. Muted shapes sit on the edge of shadow, allowing only a suggestion of what lays beyond.

Now moving, his steps slow but cautious, Thomas crosses the damp and puddled floor. Beneath his feet, a layer of grime, filth, rotting bird shit, and litter leaves the surface precarious. As such, his steps are stuttering and gradual, and his eyes, shuddery, move between the concrete pillars, searching the space between.

Ahead of him, a sound brings him to a stop. The wet cold rushes in with it, chattering through his teeth before dropping down, leaving him weak and somehow exposed.

'Mr Williammmmmm... I seeeeeee youuuuuu.'

Snapping his head from side to side, his eyes wide and frantic, Thomas scans the space between the pillars, struggling, each an inky pocket of danger.

'You've been looking for me, yes, soooooooooo many questions,' the voice hisses in from the dark.

'Who are you?' Thomas asks, his voice a soft whisper.

A stunted laugh comes from the darkness, one of confidence and knowing.

'That Mr William is the mysterrrrrrrry,' the voice says, now closer.

'The Great Deceiver?' Thomas asks.

Thomas's eyes, agitated, continue to roam the floor before him, the pitted black shadows, the still dark.

'You want to know, don't you, all about me? I can take many forms; I can be anywhere; I can be anyone. I have hidden in plain sight, the mundane and the generic, the man who passes you on the bus, he who tips his hat in greeting.'

'You're a coward hiding behind a mask,' Thomas spits.

'Very good, very good, it appears I underestimated you.'

'You know me?' Thomas asks.

'Mr William, I've been watching you for some time.'

'Like you did with Amy?'

'Hmm,' is followed by another short laugh, but also movement. 'How do you know that?'

With words leaping to his lips, Thomas manages to stop them before speaking to them, before blurting out the secret; the hole, seeing Amy, witnessing the abduction.

Considering his options, trying to think, Thomas recognises the need to move and venture into the darkness ahead. So, breathing wildly, fists clenched, he pushes himself forward towards the black shroud. The once hidden shapes slowly reveal themselves as a team of giant stacks- wooden pallets towering towards the high ceiling. Ahead of him, within the columns, a snap-like cackle is chased from the gloom by a flash of electric blue.

Eyes focused forward, closer, he edges toward where the crackle had originated. The rain slamming into the structure's metal shell, now all most deafening, ravages his senses, forcing his eyes to jump about, from stack to stack.

Screw this.

An inner drive has him charging forward, between the palettes, a snap decision, nothing more, into the darkness, his fists ready but shaking. A second pop brings him to a stop. Looking around, his search becoming a ragged series of head swings, he moans, 'where are you?'

The faint sound of shuffling ahead of him tugs at his ears, his nerves. Turning, twisting on his heels, Thomas is slow and laboured. Lifting his arms like dead weight, they take an age to rise.

He sees nothing but the darkness all around him as it closes in, wrapping itself around him.

So, he waits.

Unwilling to move ahead, unable to go back, he finds himself in no man's land.

Where you've been your entire fucking life.

His frustration and fear are replaced with anger, anger at himself for being so goddamn inept.

A noise has him spinning again on his heels. To him, it sounds like the movement of feet, the sound of passing, but he can't be sure...

A crack of bright blue light blinds him, turning everything white. With it, pain slides through him in spasms, thrashing at his limbs, leaving him rigid, pulling his muscles tight. A second loud electric burst surges through him, dropping him to the floor, to his knees, before dumping Thomas on his back.

Unable to move, Thomas lays looking up at the dark lofted ceiling.

At his attacker's mercy.

He's... got a... goddam... taser.

Cursing through gritted teeth, riding the electrocution, it sizzling through his veins, Thomas vaguely catches sight of his attacker. Watching him through wavy, bright white flashes, Thomas's vision and consciousness flicker in and out. As his shadow moves around him, Thomas tries but cannot track him all the way. His eyes, like the rest of him, are frozen and rigid. It is a fear so intense he is simply unable to react to it.

Bending down to meet Thomas, producing something from his belt, his attacker flashes steel across his face. A knife, huge and ugly, its tip drawing a line from Thomas's temple, down his cheek to his mouth.

Thomas gasps, his heart all but stopping, as the man's masked face appears above him. His tongue slithers out from the mouth slit and dances around it with excitement. Dipping down low with the horn, he strokes Thomas's left cheek with its tip. Pulling back, smiling through the mask, his dark, olive-like eyes, loaded with menace, peer down at Thomas, black with the absence of light.

'I'll ask again. How did you know I was watching Amy? How did you learn of my mask?'

Thomas stays silent.

'No, cat got your tongue, well, I have something for that,' he purrs, his voice dripping with venomous joy. 'Open wideeeeeee.'

Thomas tries to move, but his body is stark-still, like hardwood, and his limbs, unresponsive and useless, appear numb.

The knife slips in between his lips without any resistance. Gently, The Deceiver navigates the blade deeper. The taste of metal floods Thomas's mouth. Crawling along the roof of his mouth, the knife tip is plunged deeper but stops before his tonsils and throat.

'Thomas!?' Calls a voice from the entrance.

PETER!

Unable to move or speak, Thomas is forced to watch as The Deceiver turns his attention to his young friend.

Sliding the knife clear from his mouth, wiping the blade dry on Thomas's jacket, The Deceiver snaps to his feet. Knife in hand, ready and huge, he darts away, disappearing from view.

Thomas tries to scream, his throat straining, but manages only a low murmur.

'Thomas!?' Peter calls a second time. 'Are you in here?'

Fuck... no... God, please.

A shuffling from a stack to his left is followed by the voice of his attacker. Frail, a pained whisper, it calls back, 'here, I need help.'

'Thomas, is that you? Where are you?' Peter's voice is now uncertain but again has drawn closer.

'Here, I'm bleeding,' The Deceiver whispers, beckoning Peter into his trap.

NO!

Again, Thomas tries to scream, to move his body but remains silent, prone, helpless, perthitic. His eyes, straining to see, stretching them in their sockets, is allowed a limited view of the area around him, nothing more.

'Thomas, tell me where you are. I'm blind in here?' Peter stutters, his voice now ragged and urgent.

I'm here, goddamn it!

But so is he.

My god, Peter...

Pushing up with everything he has, screaming silently inside himself. While his body remains limp and heavy, he does sense some feeling. Slight, a twinge at the tips of his fingers, a dull numbing, faint at first, returns to his hands and arms, allowing him the feel of the cold concrete beneath them. Dragging his hands up his body, centimetre by centimetre, along the ground, Thomas finds he can fold them at the elbow. Pulling them up to his armpits, lifting his head, pushing it up from the concrete, his neck muscles, working again, go taut, like hard rubber ready to snap. What could be mistaken as a lost child, Peter approaches as a blurred form, following a similar route to the one Thomas took only minutes before.

'Peter...' Thomas mumbles, his tongue numb and bulbous, his words low and stifled at his throat.

Stopping before him, fifteen meters from where he lay, it is unclear whether Peter is looking at Thomas or if something else now has his attention. Hands flat against the floor, pushing through gritted teeth, like some vampire from an old black and white movie, slowly he begins to rise, his spine all but snapping from the strain. Up onto bent elbows,

Thomas pushes again, his wrists creaking with the effort. Through his hands, his core until finally, Thomas gets himself into a seated position.

Panting, Thomas finds the effort it took to get his back off the floor has resulted in urine streaming through his jeans, warming and soaking his thighs.

'Peter... he's...' Thomas tries a second time.

From the right, the shadows shift, and a lurking form darts between the space of two stacks. It is still unclear if Peter clocked it, but his approach is slow and stuttering, his head swinging wildly from side to side.

Closing his eyes, mustering every bit of strength, Thomas screams, lungs burning, 'PETER, WATCH OUT, HE'S HERE!'

Leaping from the shadows, knife raised, The Deceiver charges at Peter. Stunned and slow to react, Peter turns, but his attacker is on him before he can comprehend the situation.

Falling back, Peter lands on his rump. Using his feet as a shield, Peter's face is one of lucid terror. The Deceiver, stalking forward, slashes wildly at Peter's feet, who is now backtracking, screaming with every fresh slash of the blade.

It is unclear whether the screams are for the knife meeting skin or merely out of anticipation of it- it's deafening all the same. Regardless, it's enough to have Thomas moving, pushing forward onto his hands and knees. Crawling, slowly gaining traction, closing the gap an inch at a time, Thomas is forced to watch on, helpless, as Peter struggles to fend off his attacker.

Move goddamn it.

With one last burst of energy, emptying his lungs, his reserves, somehow, Thomas manages to spring to his feet. One step... two... three, he charges forward, head down. Thomas stumbles almost falls, his legs wavy and elastic-like beneath him.

Closing in, somehow remaining on his feet, he rams hard, shoulder first. Expecting pain, closing his eyes in anticipation, Thomas is instead surprised by a searing burn-like slash at his lower gut.

Staggering to a stop, light on his feet, the pain is accompanied by a fuzzy haze that quickly drops over him. The combo threatens to buckle him at the knees but manages to somehow stay upright.

Opening his eyes, he finds The Deceiver standing before him. His eyes, dark pits beaming out through the narrow slits of his hood. His tongue, snake-like, slithering, protruding from the mouth hole, licks the upper zip.

With a surge of warmth flooding his clothes, his waist, looking down, Thomas watches as the lower portion of the shirt turns red. His vision wavers, and finally, his feet buckle beneath him, dropping him to his knees.

The Deceiver, breathing hard, panting with excitement rather than exhaustion, lifts the knife again, its long blade dripping blood.

My blood?

Did he cut me?

With his arms limp at his side, propped up on his knees, Thomas looks down at a slash across his abdomen, the torn shirt, and finds two fleshy red lips of skin hanging open, spouting blood. Thomas tries to move, but his mind and body feel detached- an out of body experience.

I'm going to die.

Thomas waits for the end to come, for death to rush in and steal the life from his chest. Closing his eyes, waiting and expectant, he is instead met by a loud shriek. Banshee-like, it tears open the night, reverberating around the warehouse.

Opening his eyes, Thomas sees The Deceiver, backing away, hobbling with a small knife protruding from his thigh. Turning, he slashes his knife at the now standing Peter, tearing open his jacket arm, whipping a trail of blood over the floor. Continuing to back away, The Deceiver turns and heads for the shadows, limping and dragging his impaled leg.

Collapsing beside Thomas, holding, nursing a cut arm, hissing in pain, Peter asks, 'are you ok?'

Looking down at the five-inch slash to his shirt, flinching, Thomas fingers the raw fleshy wound across his lower abdomen. Snapping his teeth together, the gash stings with fiery intensity.

'It will need stitches,' Thomas tells him. Looking at Peter, Thomas levels him a look, one of gratitude. 'Thank you.'

'No, thank you, knife-in-the-sock-trick, I learnt that from you,' Peter says, first smiling, now wincing.

25

4 days later...

The act of simply getting up out of bed is enough to drain what reserves Thomas has left. He had decided against answering the intercom, at first anyway, but, with its persistent wail, it dragging his nerves jangling to the surface, shuddering his teeth together through anger, he decided to get up.

Gripping the edge of the mattress, needing it for support, he pulls himself up to a sitting position. The action, while short, brings a hiss from his pressed lips. Sweeping his legs over the bed a little too quickly, he flinches and moans as his stitched wound pulls and contracts. Pushing himself up from the damp, sweat-stained sheets, the muscle fibres of his back tweak and wrench with the effort.

Unsteady on his feet, but they will, in fact, support him, shuffling, he starts across the floor. Though slow, the movement feels like the stitched line could tear open, spilling his guts out across the bedroom floor. While only a short distance, the pain is nothing sort of child-birth-like. The painkillers, having worked their way out from his system, leave him to suffer alone, dulling the pain only slightly.

With every step, the freshly patched stomach flexes and pulls, and while he will swear, he is leaking, the dry bandage tells him that he is, in fact, overreacting. The heavy strap wrapping his midriff would stop it, of course, he knows this, but with the nightmares now becoming a consistent fixture when he now sleeps, not content with staining his nights with torture and blood, with them haunting him even now, he is otherwise convinced the bandage will fail.

Even now, a nightmare clings to him, taunting him and his fragile psyche. He can still see it as if burned into his retinas- him tied to a hospital gurney, awake and lucid, at the mercy of The Great Deceiver. Yet, standing over him, proudly, like some medal of honour, he wears a set of hospital scrubs. The mask, different somehow, its horn bigger, looms over Thomas. The eyes, twinkling with the bright glare of an overarching operating theatre lamp, beam down at Thomas with eager anticipation.

Moving about Thomas, busying himself in preparation for surgery, Thomas's surgery, he hummed, dancing around the bed in mocking jubilation.

'Hello Mr Williammmmmmmmmmm,' The Deceiver sang, a sing-song tone to his voice.

Though impossible, Thomas can still smell antiseptic, disinfectant, and the omnipresent scent of death. It drags him back to the nightmare, to his capturer, and how, in the dream, he had struggled to track his movements. Though he couldn't see, he, in fact, knew with certainty, his head was fixed in place by heavy leather strapping. That's the thing with dreams, while offering an insight into what we shouldn't know, with this knowledge and forethought comes fear and foreboding.

Disappearing for a moment, his abductor's absence was filled with the clatter of metal, the squeak of old wheels. When he returned to the gurney, he did so with a sheet covered metal trolley.

Again, Thomas knew what waited for him beneath. Overt and obvious, the lumps and ridges beneath the sheet needed no label. Still, when he whipped the sheet clear like some goddamn matador, the trolley's contents dragged a shrill scream from Thomas's lips.

Taking his time with each, savouring the moment, The Deceiver presented each item with the gusto of an over-exaggerated salesperson. Tools and implements of varying sizes and shapes were offered up to Thomas one by one. Cold steel, shiny and spotless, glinted with every twist, swipe and slash. Lancets, endocarps, Rongeurs and scalpers, scissors and forceps, clamps and retractors- all polished, new, unused. There were dilators and speculums used to access narrow passages or incisions and suction tips and tubes for removing bodily fluids.

Thankfully, Thomas woke before his captor had the chance to use any. Yet, the nightmare has left him sweat-covered and cowering within his own skin—a scared, shaking, shrivelled little man who is now forced to shuffle instead of walk.

Grinding and mashing at his teeth, sweat is quick to pool beneath his arms. An odour, he notes, has already taken up residence beneath his t-shirt, leaving him praying it's not Lilly wanting to come up.

Pressing the receiver button, he speaks into the intercom, 'Yes?'

'Thomas, it's me.'

Mary.

Wonderful.

Without saying another word, Thomas lets her in. She'll remark on his appearance, his injuries, and no doubt, the sweaty hum of his clothes. So, Thomas considers it a good thing he stopped caring what Mary thought of him long ago.

Is that right?

Agitated by this, he continues to shuffle, sliding his way to the front door. Getting there takes him an age. Upon opening it, Mary stands, arms crossed, resting on her pregnant belly. Her expression, stern as always, melts away when she takes note of his condition.

'Jesus, Tom, what happened to you?' She asks.

He considers his response. Lie or the truth? Looking down at himself, his topless, bandaged torso mottled by fading offish yellow bruises, Thomas recognises lying would be futile.

'Come in, please,' he tells her.

His shuffling legs are slow and arduous, following him inside, along the hallway. Unlike their customary eagerness, chasing him into the living area, her boots instead follow with a level of reserve, a sudden apprehension.

'I'd offer you a drink, but I can't right now, the doctor says stretching might tear the wound, plus you'd only refuse one so,' Thomas tells her as he moves to the sofa.

Sitting down, teeth together and grinding, he gestures for her to do the same. Eyes on him, Mary sits beside Thomas on the sofa, a little closer than expected or likes. Her presence, like always, fills the room with a nervous lull, draining Thomas of all energy.

Placing her handbag down at her feet, she straightens the hem of her dress at her knees. Perched on the edge, a hand on her engorged yet neatly proportioned stomach, she levels him a look and waits for an explanation.

Deciding it will be easier to just give her one, he says, 'it was work, I'm rusty, I got blindsided, I'm not as young as I used to. Need another reason?'

Still, she looks at him.

Her expression is hard to read—the anger in her eyes mask all other emotions living there.

Exhaling, Thomas looks down.

'I was attacked, stabbed. A flesh wound, but it needed stitches,' he says.

'Who attacked you?' She asks.

'I don't know; he was masked.'

''That it?'

'Ok, I was stupid, reckless, almost got myself killed, not to mention my colleague. So, I guess I'll just add it to the list of failures, the long fucking chain hung around my neck.'

She opens her mouth to speak but stops short, the words hushed at her lips, unable to form. Instead of responding, she returns to her handbag. She removes a small, folded sheet of paper from it, and with an outstretched hand, she passes it to him.

'What's this?' He asks.

Mary simply nods and drops her head.

Looking down at the piece of paper, slowly unfolding it, warm tears flood his eyes. A drawing of a man hand in hand with a little girl holding a violin. The picture is underlined by the words:

> **My daddy is a writer. He is very famous, and his book is in the library. Mummy won't let me read it, but Lewis has. My Daddy is very busy. Important people are always busy. Mummy tells me this is why I don't see him. I love my daddy. I hope he loves me too**

Obviously written with the help of her mother, Thomas's throat nonetheless tightens, along with his eyes, well and blur.

'Signed, Robin,' he sobs.

'Thomas, court proceedings have already started, custody will soon be awarded. You do know I can't have Robin dragged into' she pauses. 'Well, whatever it is you are involved in. I'm sorry, I am.'

Though he tries, he cannot look at her. But, of course, she's right, and things, it would seem, have now come to a head. Absence from the proceedings and, well, his daughter's life, while having helped him with his book, only shielded him from his greater responsibility.

'Whatever this is,' Mary says, looking at the corkboards, the photos, the crazy scattering of the displayed information. 'Wherever this rabbit hole leads you, finish it ok, your daughter needs you, and I'm not going to do this anymore, this back and forth. Look at yourself, Thomas, look where you are, for Godsake.'

Looking at her, wiping his cheeks, his words are plead-like, 'Not now, Robin can't see me like this.'

'Then fix it,' she says, her tone now decidedly softer. 'If the courts rule against you, I won't intervene, understand, Robin and I will move on.'

'I will, I promise,' he tells her, his eyes trying to find hers.

Looking at one another, her eyes linger, but her lips say nothing. Retrieving her handbag, she stands, and for a moment, Thomas is concerned she might fall. He reaches out for her, but she, in return, offers only a smile. While warm, it is one he sees as profoundly hurt. Her eyes, glassy and red, leave him to question what it means. Once, she had loved him, that he knows for sure, even his work, that is when he worked for the newspaper. Now, seeing her exposed, shedding her hardened shell, he is left to wonder, even by some small measure, whether she still holds any love for him.

'Things weren't that bad between us, were they?' He asks.

Mary takes a moment before turning back to face him. When she does, with the colour leaving her face, she fixes her eyes on him.

'Our lives became predictable and uneventful, sterile and colourless,' she tells him, honest but said through glassy eyes. 'But I love... loved you, deeply.'

Love or loved?

Thomas realises it no longer matters when looking at her, her protruding belly, her new wedding ring, the tremor running through her hands and chest.

Pulling himself up from the sofa, grimacing in standing, he looks at her.

'Mar, I just want to say, you're right, about everything, and I'm sorry. And, Lewis, he's a good man, though I'll forever hate him for that,' Thomas smiles, bringing a burst of short laughter from her lips. 'He's a better man than me. You deserve that. Robin deserves that. Whatever happens, however, this thing ends up, please know that I've never stopped loving you, both of you.'

Mary pauses, her eyes alive with both emotion and surprise. Obviously concerned by his words, Thomas contemplates telling her more. As if seeing this, she nods, smiles, and goes, leaving him alone once again.

26

3 days later...

'And who is this?' Lilly asks.

'Peter, he's been working with me,' Thomas tells her.

Turning to Peter, who smiles, she asks, 'And have you, like me, told Thomas he should be at home resting instead of being out?'

'I have to be here,' Thomas snaps, annoyed at the fuss.

Looking at him, considering his words, she nods and says, 'So you know, I'm only here because you think Erika and my sister's disappearances are linked.'

When they arrived a short time earlier, the erected marquee was all but empty. Now, the scene is abuzz with activity and people swarming inside, queuing to collect maps, whistles, torches, and hi-vis vests.

Arriving with two fellow officers, PC Burke makes his way through the crowd to the middle of the tent. Along with his handlebar moustache, Thomas recognises the tall, assured man from the news by his sharp crewcut and bullish deportment. With mounting pressure from Erika's family back in Sweden, the police have finally stepped up their efforts. Along with making fresh appeals for leads, they asked for volunteers to help search a specific woodland area in Marlow where James took Erika when she disappeared.

'Ladies and gentlemen, thank you for coming out,' booms Burke, his voice deep and hoarse from years of giving orders and cigarette smoke. Shaking his head, rainwater is flung from his close-cropped hair and bushy moustache. 'What we're looking at here is a search of a large area across varied and challenging terrain. The weather will make it difficult; the rain appears here for the rest of the week, so we've narrowed the search area down to two square miles. It's vast, but it's close to Erika's last known location, a petrol station north of here. We will be working in teams, so please follow the lead of my officers. If you see something, anything at all, a piece of clothing, an area of disturbed ground, an unnatural pile of foliage or twigs, if it catches your eye, use your whistle and let the lead officer know, ok? The colour of your vest aligns with my officers, so let's get moving. Thank you.'

Leaving the cover of the Marquee, returning to the rain and sloppy mud, Thomas joins an amassing collection of strangers: The Police, family and friends of Erika, random people, well-wishers, reporters, tag alongs, sycophants, and quite possibly, The Great Deceiver.

As the large group fan out, putting on their vests, Thomas watches their faces, taking in their forms and how they each move. He checks for anyone with signs of an injured leg, a limp, a hobble. With it being six days since the attack, the stab wound to their thigh would be far from healed. It would show, Thomas is sure of it. So, he watches them, all of them, the different people and their gaits, but in the rain, the dimming light, they appear to him as a blur, non-descript and faceless.

He could be any one of them.

How would I know?

Slipping on his vest, one arm after the other, slowly as to not tear his stitches, he follows Lilly and Peter out from under the cover. Pulling the hood over his head, he shivers inside his coat as the cold afternoon rain envelopes him.

Above his head, a helicopter rattles across the sky, tearing open the low, grey ceiling. Police, navy with its top painted yellow, circling back around, its blades churning with laboured whines. Arching his head, Thomas tracks it until it disappears behind the treetops to the northeast.

'Thomas, Thomas William?'

Thomas turns to find a man standing, looking at him, a half-smile draped across his face.

'Yes, how did you know?' Thomas asks, edgy, not recognising the man.

'I've seen your picture online. It's me, Ricky, Ricky Ruck, James's father?'

The short but well-built man chiselled and handsome, sports designer stubble and, quite possibly, a weave beneath the hood of his gym sweatshirt. Obviously, a bodybuilder, his imposing width is undercut by a casual, welcoming expression.

'Sorry, hi, how are you?' Thomas asks.

They shake hands, and while short in stature, Ricky's large hands wrap around Thomas's.

'I'm good, you know, can't complain. I thought I'd come out, do what I can. It's the least I can do, right? I mean, if my son did....' His voice breaks off, cracking under the weight of his words.

'I understand,' Thomas tells him, taking the soft approach. 'Erika and her family, they'll appreciate you coming out.'

'Thank you,' he nods. 'But if my son, if he....' Ricky says, trailing away.

'Let's just look for Erika. The other stuff, we can sort out later, ok?' Thomas says, placing a hand on the man's shoulder.

Nodding, wiping his face, he smiles and looks at the vest in his hand, 'Team pink,' He laughs, 'Team wuss, right?'

Not liking the man's candour, his turn of phrase, Thomas simply smiles. Watching him walk away, he can see so much of his son in him. The swagger at his shoulders and his clothes lead Thomas to label him as a stereotype- the Ralph Lauren Polo wearing, fake Breitling type.

For Godsake, the guy lost his son.

Surprised at his own self-correction, Thomas watches the man disappear into the crowd, loathing himself for judging the man so harshly. Still, Thomas studies his legs, his gait. With no signs of a limp or injury, Thomas is forced to exclude him as the man who attacked them, that and the fact he's a least a foot shorter. The voice, body shape and eyes all fail to match Ricky. His broad shoulders are alone enough to rule him out as the masked attacker.

This leads Thomas back to James and how he fits into the case.

So, if James killed Erika, who the hell is the man in the mask?

Thomas considers this.

Simon Finch and Morgan Teller?

James's two friends, who Thomas is yet to track down.

The same two individuals who had been in contact with James right up until Erika's disappearance but then stopped suddenly when she did. Thomas also considers if James is actually dead. As in, he faked his own death. Stupid, Thomas knows this, but the two cases, Amy and Erika, their link, still alludes him.

Turning, Thomas follows Peter and Lilly past the marquee to a clearing twenty feet down a shallow slope to where a group of orange vests have gathered. A mean-looking blonde officer stands waiting at the head of the group, waving them in with a twenty-inch-long black flashlight.

Her tightly drawn ponytail, her cold, puckered face, and steely eyes fail to match her soft tone. 'Hello, I'm Officer Johns. If you can all follow me, please. We'll take this track down past the creek. It's a short trek but still, let's all try and stay together.'

As a group, they follow her. A team of orange vests, marching in silence to the cacophony of falling rain, splatter the muddy wet trail before them.

'Do you think we'll find anything?' Lilly whispers.

Looking at her, Thomas smiles, 'Why are you whispering?'

'I don't know,' she again whispers, smiling.

Shaking his head, 'I don't know. James stopped here and stayed for a while, so it's a possibility Erika is out here somewhere.'

'You mean her body, right?' Lilly asks.

'Yes, she's been gone too long to be found alive,' Thomas tells her glumly.

'And you think that's the case for Amy?'

With Thomas offering no answer, she diverts her eyes away, out to the trees on their right and the dull grey sky beyond them. Walking in silence, their group snake a line along a narrow dirt path. Like the weather, the mood is quiet and sombre. Thomas considers what they might find: evidence, clothing, signs of a shallow grave, a body? He considers if James Ruck could be responsible. His actions before her disappearance were indeed suspicious, with motive and opportunity-James wouldn't be the first man to kill his lover because of an untimely pregnancy. And as such, coming back to it, Thomas is left with an impossible question to answer. How does Amy's disappearance factor into the story if James killed Erika?

With Peter out in front, they follow the line of people along the small creek on their left. Both the rushing of the stream, the soft patter of water foaming the stones, and pebbles are all but drowned out by sheets of rain hitting the water.

How can the two women in James's life disappear, and how can he have nothing to do with it?

A thought occurs to him, one which is as far-fetched as James staging his own death. James's old friends, who he talked to before Erika's disappearance- could be involved. Could James have paid them to get rid of both Amy and Erika? Even with James's untimely death, would they still honour the request?

Thomas concludes it is simply too much of a coincidence, and James was involved somehow, no matter the level of involvement.

Thomas stops to look at the creek. Its narrow stream, widening in areas pelted by the rain, appears deep in parts. Its dark waters, mirrored with a gloomy sky creeping through the trees, made all the darker by the rain distorting its surface.

Erika could be in there?

Hell, she could be anywhere.

As they move deeper into the woods, following the creek down a modest incline, the trees close in all around them, darkening the trail. With the path-breaking away from the stream, the group are steered to the right, Johns waving her enormous torch. A slight climb and the trail narrows further as it carves a line through a sea of spruce, large oak and willow trees. The canopy overhead brings a reprieve from the rain, be it at the cost of light. Gloom and shadow work in tandem to blacken the world below.

Glancing about, Thomas's eyes working the foliage to his left, the right, seeing movement everywhere, his pace slows. The forest is moving, which he knows is impossible, but where the shadows and the unknown were once safe, benign, now means only to deceive him. Through the wind, the trees creak loudly, like breaking bones.

Will I ever feel safe again?

As if hearing the wail of his inner torment, Lilly looks over her shoulder, instantly setting him at ease. Her smile and eyes are nothing short of light, pure and shining, and possibly salvation itself.

Finally, the heavily dense woodland opens into a clearing. Overgrown with waist-high grass, littered with unruly brambles, poison ivy, nettles, and groundsel. The rain, the sorrow in the birds' chirps, and the brood of clouds lining the treeline across the clearing leave a miserable, almost darkly overt and cadaverous film over the scene.

'Ok, everyone, our search starts here, so lets all fan out. Take it slow, be patient, be thorough,' Johns calls. Her words all but muted against the rain. 'If you see anything, anything at all, use your whistle and alert me. If in doubt, blow your whistle. If you get into any trouble, you blow your whistle. Ok, let us snap to it.'

Looking at Thomas, Lilly rolls her eyes, bringing a smile to his tired, troubled face. Her eyes linger a moment longer than they should, meeting his directly, before sliding away, returning to the task at hand. The group, twelve strong, look at one another before spreading out. With his gaze remaining firmly on Lilly, who has the power to keep the wolves at bay, Thomas follows her into the grass.

They march forward in a line as a group, the soggy ground sticky beneath their feet. Flicking on the torch, dropping the beam into the grass, he starts his search.

Cursing his decision to wear trainers, leaving his boots at home, the loose mud is quick to wrap around his feet like a cartoonish sock, making it hard to move. Shuffling rather than walking, the terrain not allowing much else, the constant shifting, sliding, re-balancing, pulls at his stomach, his healing wound. Placing a hand to it, feeling the bulge of the bandages, the ache of damaged tissue, fearing he might fall, Thomas slows his pace to a plodding crawl.

Pressing in deeper, pushing through the tall spikes, with every step, the displacement of the sloppy mud, excrement like stink, is energised and released from the ground.

As Thomas covers his nose and mouth with his sleeve, a whistle rings out, sending a shock of activity through him, jolting his muscles awake, pulling at his dull wounds.

Looking out across the clearing, someone over to the left stands looking, an outstretched hand pointing, the whistle pulled tight to the woman's lips.

Making her way through the grass to the woman's location, closing the gap between them, the line of volunteers stopping, each of them turning in unison to face the whistle-blower and the approaching Officer Johns.

'What do you think it is?' Asks a voice from Thomas's right.

Turning, finding Peter standing, looking past him, his eyes fixed on the commotion.

'It's ok, it's a dead dog. Let's carry on!' Johns calls.

Appearing from the treeline, the group has maintained a relatively consistent line, now crossing into a picnic area at the far side of the forest. When the weather permits, the isolated spot is scenic, even romantic. A quiet hideaway, alive with nature and colour. But not today. The constant rain, the gloom from the clouds, the greens, yellows and blues are dulled, muted to greys and bruised purples. With the sad, depressed expressions worn by the volunteers, the spot sitting before Thomas appears as nothing more than a body disposal site. Morbid, yes, but when searching for the remains of a missing person, coming to a remote spot so deep in the forest, one shadowed and darkened by heavy rain, well, it's challenging to picture it as anything but a killer's dumpsite.

Plus, Thomas's wet clothes aren't helping matters. Soaked through, the cold has already seeped into his bones, leaving a solid rigidity to his joints. No longer walking, he trudges across the wet grass, falling behind the group with every step taken. Before him, Thomas spots three wooden benches, one litter bin, and a small, gravelled parking lot. Overgrown grass, unchecked weed growth, litter and broken glass carpet the area. While not precisely treacherous, it leaves him with a fresh wave of trepidation. Beyond that, a lake and small island sit back behind high banks and a dotting of willow oaks circling its edges.

The continued rain, now far heavier and louder, lends to the idea of lower-hanging clouds. They appear mere meters away as if, by reaching up, Thomas could touch them. He won't do that, can't, not because of its impossibility, but in fear he might have a heart attack if it were to happen. Perspective is a funny thing- how the mundane can be grotesquely altered by mood, weather, the time of day. Everything appears dark to him now, dark and deceptive, and lurid at the seams. A creeping horror, subtle, itches at the edges of this new world, one where the lines between the real and the nightmares plaguing him each night have well and truly converged. He knows this, but still, he cannot separate them, nor can he rationalise his anxieties.

A crack of thunder tears him from his thoughts, and while it shouldn't, the jarring jolt sends a shudder of stiffening pain up his spine. A second whip of thunder, though impossible, now appears far closer, as if inches from his head.

Thomas searches the sky, the rolling clouds, for the helicopter. The heavy low ceiling and torrential rainfall make him conclude it is no longer in service.

His eyes return to the lake. Recalling what Hildur had told him, that the Police found tyre tracks at a picnic site- he considers if this is, in fact, *the* picnic site.

Are there others? I mean, how many can there be?

Continuing forward, while unruly and needing landscaping, the ground is far easier to negotiate than the bog-like sop from where they came. The damage has already been done with sodden socks and trainers, long soaked through, cold seeps through Thomas's clothes. For the most part, his raincoat has protected him, but with the constant, sharp angle of rain, it now fails, leaving his jeans and jumper beneath damp and clinging to him like wet wallpaper.

Leading with his torch, the beam seeking out beer cans, the scattered remains of a McDonald's takeout bag, its contents soaked and spooned about the first of the three benches. This pattern continues- rubbish and spent fireworks, smashed beer bottles and used condoms.

This would sure make for an excellent place to assault someone.

It's secluded, quiet, and any approaching car could be seen from at least a quarter of a mile away. The road leading to the lake, though narrow, is visible right up until it disappears over the crest of a distant hill. At night, the bright headlights of an approaching car would be unmissable and traceable. Reviewing the distance, and by no means exact, if a car should appear on the horizon, Thomas estimates someone would have at least three or four minutes before it would reach the site.

Maybe it's the fretting weather or the grime and filth beneath his feet, but the whole area, the lack of wildlife, the quiet through the trees, leave this place reeking of death as if it was always destined to become a place for the abandoned and the decomposing.

Stopping at the lake's edge, Thomas looks out across the water. Like a movie, but one lacking any natural colour, the dark water sits waiting, spiked with the rain, all but confessing to what it holds.

James stopped here, why, to bury Erika... in the lake?

Waiting for Peter to join him, Thomas asks, 'do we know if the police dragged the lake?'

'Not sure, but it would be easy to hide a body in there. What about her car?' Peter asks.

'Missing, like her. None of this makes sense,' Thomas says. 'Erika tells James she's pregnant, he drives her out here, what then, he kills her? Dumps her body somewhere and then goes through the bother of doing the same with her car. With her phone and the copied keys at his place, the guy must have been an idiot. And not forgetting how Amy fits into all this. If James killed Erika, who's the asshole in the mask, who attacked us?'

Quiet falls over them as they both ponder what they know. Looking at the lake water, watching as it laps gently along the shoreline, its surface fluttering against the rain, a blast of a whistle shocks them into a collective groan.

Shrieking across the lake, the second blast of a whistle scatters the birds from the trees. Checking the line, the different faces, the wail comes from somewhere ahead of them, past the lake and the tree's underlining the sky.

'Another dead dog?' Peter asks.

'I hope so,' Thomas moans.

The wail of another whistle rings out, and another, and another; long, urgent bursts from somewhere distant. Turning, Thomas scans the tree line, his eyes searching for the source of the screaming; all the while, his gut twitches with knowing; *this isn't another dead dog.*

27

8:16pm...

'They found a knife, shovel, duct tape, black bin bags and lime to mask the smell of decomposition; in essence, a kill and disposal kit,' Thomas says.

'So not another dead dog?' Peter asks.

Thomas shifts him a look and goes about pouring the three of them a glass of red wine. Filling each, pushing two across the coffee table, Thomas snatches up his and takes a drink. Together, they watch him, the eagerness of his lips. Gulping, he smiles.

'Sorry, thirsty,' he tells them.

'We can see that,' Peter says, bending down to take a glass.

Taking her glass and taking a sip, Lilly says, 'how did you get this information?'

'An old friend,' Thomas says, meaning Hildur. 'The police have traced the items to a DIY store in town, Grey's Lumber and Supplies,' he looks at Lilly, steadying himself. 'The purchases were made using Amy's credit card.'

'What?' She asks, her face contorting.

'Thirty-one days before the trip out to the lake, which is important because the store's CCTV footage is erased every thirty days. Whoever purchased those items knew this.'

'James?' Peter asks.

'Well, it wasn't my sister,' Lilly spits.

'Quite.' Peter responds. 'Grey's lumber, I'll look into it; there has to be a link to James.'

'It means he was attempting to cover his tracks,' Thomas pauses, not for effect, but due to the sickening feeling coursing through him. 'He was framing Amy, or at the least, pushing the evidence her way if the Police ever dug into Erika's disappearance.'

As a group, they fall silent.

Lilly, twitching in her seat, sips her wine. Her eyes grow dark, hatred sweeping through them. While Thomas wants to go to her, reach across the sofa and take her in his arms, he doesn't. Partly because Peter is present, but mainly because he feels ill-equipped to make such a gesture.

Only those who have genuinely suffered can heal those who are damaged.

Words Thomas recalls from his early work. Considering them, he is quick to push them from his mind. Taking another drink of his wine, he says, 'the items are being tested for trace and DNA evidence, but it appears from preliminary findings, they are unused.'

'Unused?' Peter asks, eyes snapping wide.

'That's what she said,' Thomas tells him, settling back on the sofa.

'Let me get this straight, James buys these items to use in Erika's murder and the disposal of the body. They drive out to the lake, but for some reason, he doesn't end up using them, so what, he dumps them. Erika still disappears; what am I missing?' Lilly asks.

They look at one another.

There are no clear answers now.

'The lake,' Peter starts. 'If she's in there, there'd be no need for the items.' Peter proposes.

'James turns up fully intending to kill then bury her, seeing the lake might have altered his plans.' Lilly considers, falling back into the sofa beside Thomas. 'Still, it feels like a bit of a stretch.'

'Hildur believes the Police fully intend to search the water, but the lake is one of many, so it will take time,' Thomas says.

'What about her car? It, too, is missing. If we can trace it, it might lead to something?' Peter muses.

'It's possible,' Thomas considers. 'I remember the Police making a statement to the effect it was last seen at a petrol station, might be something?'

As if to leave the question hanging in the air, they again all fall quiet. Drinking his wine, Thomas watches Lilly as she sips the rioja. He smiles as she scrunches her nose in distaste.

'No good?' Thomas asks.

'It's terrible,' Lilly laughs.

Turning his attention to Peter, Thomas asks, 'and you?'

'Not one to complain, but it is truly awful,' Peter spits out a laugh.

Lilly too laughs, and Thomas, unable to resist, joins them. Wincing in pain, fearing his wound might tear, Thomas's discomfort brings an end to the laughter.

'Are you ok?' Lilly asks, a smile still pulling at the corners of her mouth.

'It does hurt, you know,' Thomas tells her.

'We know it does,' Peter says. 'My friend, that is why it's so funny.'

My friend?

Thomas smiles, unable not to. Though he acknowledges how and why both Lilly and Peter had come into his life, the horrors interweaved in it, he cannot help but be thankful for the time they have given him.

As if seeing this herself, Lilly's smile again grows, not like the one before, but one of appreciation, as if by somehow reading his mind, she too agrees that through this horror, some good may still come from it.

Peter, Thomas notices, has grown uncomfortable. Looking around, Peter stands. Gesturing to the door, Peter means to leave them alone; Thomas recognises this and offers him a smile.

'Would you mind if I head next door, I want to check on something?' Peter asks.

Thomas nods and says, 'sure, the door should be unlocked.'

Nodding, Peter leaves, disappearing down the hallway. A second later, the front door closes behind him.

'I've never said thank you for what you're doing for Amy,' Lilly says, her eyes on Thomas.

'And you don't have to,' he tells her.

Still, her eyes stay locked on him. They appear to be searching for something.

'Promise me, please,' she pauses, now looking down. 'Promise you won't go and get yourself hurt again?'

Reaching out, Thomas takes her hand in his. She looks at him, her eyes shiny, so he brushes her red ringlets, still a little wet from the rain, away from her face, from her troubled eyes. Cupping her cheek in his hand, feeling her soft glow, she closes her eyes and nestles in against it. A warmth surges through him, and for the first time in the longest time, he has hope for the future.

Thomas is startled by a banging on the adjoining wall. In unison, they leap to their feet. A second set of rasps from the other side send a flutter of dusty plaster down the wall.

Peter!

With Lilly in tow, Thomas bolts for the hallway, along it, pushing against the pain searing across his gut, out the front door. Moving to Amy's apartment, in through the door, moving as fast as possible. His wounds pulling and tugging drag a moan through clenched teeth, yet he doesn't stop.

Peter, he finds, stands against the wall, his eyes fixed on the painting.

'You need to see this,' Peter calls.

Relieved to see he is ok but now awash with tiredness and fatigue, Thomas rubs his face with heavy hands.

'It's you, but someone else is there with you, hiding,' Peter declares, his mouth muffled against the wall.

His words bring a sudden stop to Thomas's feet. 'What, who?'

Stepping back from the wall, making space for Thomas, Peter says, 'I don't know, but I saw him; someone is definitely there with you.'

Moving to the wall, Thomas slams his face against it, rattling the painting. As his apartment comes into view, he sees himself, his future-self sitting within the glow of the desk lamp. With his back to the hallway, Thomas's future self speaks into his mobile phone with what looks like agitation, possibly, anger.

It is now Thomas sees it.

In the hallway, a shifting form makes the dark space swell with presence.

'Who is it?' Peter asks.

Stepping forward, as if being unwrapped by the shroud, a masked person enters the room.

Thomas recognises him instantly.

The leather hood, the horn, and the snake-like movement of his body are enough to leave Thomas numb.

Unable to speak, disbelieving what he's seeing, his eyes straining with the effort and now sweating hard, Thomas wants to close his eyes but cannot.

Thomas, through the wall, slamming the phone down, turns red with rage. Thomas watches himself sling a glass of red wine across the room, shattering it over the floor. Crying, his future-self slams his fists into the table.

Thomas's attention moves to the horned intruder. Like before, dressed entirely in black, he slinks in from the shadows with the movement of a cat, or liquid, sliding in unnoticed. Closing in behind the seated Thomas, the intruder removes something from his belt.

Lifting it, it shimmers with steel.

A bowie-knife.

Horrific in size, of at least ten inches, he prepares it in his hand, his fingers wrapping around the handle with anticipation.

'Get up, goddamn it,' Thomas screams at the wall.

As if hearing him, his future self looks at the smashed glass on the floor. As if in recognition, looking up at the hole, his face is quickly drained of all colour.

Turning, slowly rising from the chair, Thomas is quick, but The Deceiver is quicker. Jabbing the blade once into Thomas's stomach, burying it in deep, helpless, Thomas can only watch on as he is savagely attacked. Falling against his attacker, Thomas watches himself fall. Collapsing, dying, he crumbles in a heap at The Deceiver's feet, blood pooling all about him.

Stepping back from the wall, his mouth airy and silent, his eyes pull wide with disconcertion.

'Thomas, what is it?' Peter asks.

'He, he killed....'

'Killed who?' Lilly moans.

'Me,' Thomas says. 'He killed me. I'm next.'

SECOND INTERLUDE

DECEPTIONS

October 1994...

Shuffling into the bathroom, her clothes pulled tight to her chest, Jessica flicked on the light before closing the door. Then, placing her clothes down beside the sink before dressing, she found her reflection in the mirror. The dark eyes peering back at her, her smeared makeup, red skin, and her breasts stained with paw marks were unrecognisable. Once pretty, luminous, Jessica was quick to recognise how job-hopping, failed dieting, sunbed use, and time had aged her. A cheerleader in her university days, the once spritely, plucky, tanned socialite had become and seemingly overnight, a top-heavy blonde, all chest and no waist, a waste of her degree and the natural beauty inherited from her mother.

'Nice tits, a good shag, but not a girl you'd take home to mum,' is how her ex had described her.

But David had been different.

A lumbering trucker, David was naturally overweight as he was balding. Yet, where Jessica saw these as a handicap, he carried himself with all the grace of a man happy in his own skin, one thankful for life and the time he is given on Earth. While a hard worker and good earner, David was mundane and beige in his existence. He was the opposite of what she wanted, what she needed. Still, David had clung to her, happy, content, though all too aware of her detachment, the hours she kept, and the secrecy applied to her mobile phone.

'This is the last time?' Jessica said.

Her reflection, staring back at her, was unconvinced.

An all-too-common ritual.

Her mask of indifference, contradicting her words, forced warm tears to her eyes.

Deepening her tone, she repeated the words, 'this is the last time.'

Again, her words are shallow, almost mocking.

Closing her eyes, she saw him, felt him still inside her- Ray, her lover. Ripping at her clothes, the thrust of his tongue, the emptiness when he was done.

Vomiting, careful to avoid matting her hair, her retching was accompanied by tears, another ritual. Then, she cried for her David, herself, and how people now look at her, fearful they would soon see through the charade. Then, as a collective, her friends, past lovers and colleagues would come together to laugh at what she had become- a shade of a once-promising young woman.

Then, as per her routine, she pulled herself together. She washed her face and then brushed back her hair. Finally, she redressed, grimacing due to a cluster of finger marks across her breasts. Red and sore, her nipples were left puffy from Ray's enthusiasm.

She first slipped on her panties, the matching bra- black lace, scant, items designed with no thought of comfort. Next, she fastened the bra strap, wincing as she adjusted the cups over her mauled breasts. Pushed up, bulging, the bra cups struggled to contain her size- another design choice of men.

She studied herself in the mirror, hating how the underwear made her look. Instead of being sexy, the design failed to complement her body, leaving her looking cheap.

What do you expect, Ray gifted them?

Moved onto her dress, dropping her feet inside, pulling it up, firstly, up her legs, over her hips, she locked place by resting it upon her breasts. She looped the straps over her shoulders and fastened the dress at the side.

Moving on to her makeup, straightening it out, she was again stopped by her own reflection. Gone was the once pretty face, replaced by a simple, ordinary mask. Her skin showed the first signs of sagging while her neck sported a new layer of fat. The mirror adds ten pounds, but the mind, more so.

Her eyes, dead, haunted, held her gaze as if searching for something.

'This is the last time.'

Like always, no longer able to maintain her stare, losing the standoff, she dropped her head. Then, with her focus on her wedding ring, tears again flooded her eyes with the thoughts of David.

Loyal, kind and straight.

'He doesn't deserve this,' she cried. 'This is the last time.'

Turning off the light, upon leaving the bathroom, she found a chill had spread through the hotel room. Ray laid where she had left him, sprawled out on the bed, his clothes scattered about the floor. His muscular form was made more so by the shadows created by the lone side lamp.

She stopped at his side to collect up her heels, her purse but lingered there before leaving. Looking down at her sleeping lover, revulsion rose from her stomach, forcing her to cover her mouth, not in the apprehension of vomiting but in fear of waking him.

While their meetings had been reduced to hotel visits every other Thursday, they had at least managed to retain the passion. Well, for a time anyway. The night had started off like all the others- exciting, the air, his touch, laced with electricity. Then, in minutes, as if it was never there, it faded into a distant memory, leaving her alone with a snoring man and a guilt-filled pit in her stomach.

In her mind, she sees it- the lurid act. Him ripping at her clothes and bra, him taking her nipple into his gaping, hungry mouth. Him licking it, sucking deeply, him gnawing on it like a dog would a toy.

'This is the last time,' she whispered.

Where she expected the familiar vacuum to come rushing in, stripping her of her strength, to her surprise, and for the first time, need and failure was replaced with nausea. This, she took for a sign, one of many the night would offer her.

Leaving the hotel room, careful not to wake him, Jessica did so without looking back. Where it abandoned her before, the strength needed finally made an appearance. It energised her with options, with hope, with power. A power to choose, to act. To live a life without being afraid all the time. And it felt beautiful, truly, and liberating.

Passing through reception, the usual night clerk, a plump lady in her fifties, had been replaced by a younger, more presentable model. Where the older woman would smile without judgement, her younger colleague, a skinny blonde with a tight ponytail and high cheekbones, sneered through an expression laced with, 'aw honey, bless your heart.'

Jessica breezed through the front sliding doors with a new sense of clarity, and a smile, though the feeling was foreign to her. The October night greeted her with a light chill and breeze, a freshness accompanied by the smell of earlier rain, pine through the trees, and fallen leaves. It felt fresh, pure, born anew, and it brought warm tears to her eyes.

Looking out across the lot, with the air tugging at her, she smoothed her dress against her thighs. Across the lot, her five-year-old Fiat, though wet from the rain, for once, appeared almost clean.

'I'll clean you tomorrow,' she said aloud, smiling because she for once believed her own words.

Climbing in behind the wheel, closing the door, Jessica found she could breathe for what felt like the first time. Looking at Ray's Mercedes, all new and ice white, she considered slashing the tyres. Smiling, recognising she neither knew how to or had the tools to complete such a wild and reckless act, she turned the key over, bringing her fiat to life.

Leaving the lit parking lot, Jessica turned her car onto a desolate two-lane. The quiet stretch of road, disappearing between deep woodland, along with the darkness of night, was quick to swallow her small car. Although the drive home would usually take fifteen minutes, Jessica found she was in no rush. David was away driving and wouldn't be home until the weekend, so she settled back in her seat.

Maybe I'll stop off and get a cheeseburger.

Unlike Ray, David didn't care how she looked. When she was ill the Christmas before, when she gained all the weight from steroids, David's view of her was unflinching.

'A cheeseburger and fries,' she decided, smiling.

Following the road, as it weaved through one corner to the next, hitting a straight, the headlights raced to close in around an object at the side of the road.

A person, short, hunched over, grew in the headlights.

Slowing the car, peering out through the side window, Jessica was concerned to find a woman, alone, making her way along the dark stretch of road. More concerning was her condition; pregnant, her belly protruded out from her loose, open hoody.

Passing her, Jessica watched her shrink in the side mirror. Based on her clothing, her petite frame, Jessica took her as young, seemingly vulnerable, and most certainly in need of help.

'You can't leave her out here, not now, not this new Jessica,' she told herself.

Smiling, flicking on the indicator, Jessica pulled the car to the side of the road. Winding down the passenger window, watching the woman's approach in the mirror, Jessica noticed the woman's sudden change in pace. Slowly, obviously worried by Jessica's sudden stop, the young girl gave the Fiat a wide-berth, stepping into the gravelled road-siding.

Leaning across the passenger seat, peering out through the open window, Jessica called to the woman, 'hey, it's a little late for a walk?'

The woman, stopping, looked in at Jessica but said nothing. Her small face, cloaked behind a curly fringe, sat mostly dark within the hood. Narrow shouldered, with a loose hoodie and baggy jeans, the girl could be a teenager, and as such, Jessica's concern for her well-being grew.

'You shouldn't be out here by yourself. Let me give you a ride?' Jessica asked.

Still mute, the woman nervously checked the road, ahead of Jessica's Fiat and behind.

'Please?' Jessica pleads, surprising herself by her need to help the young woman.

Checking the road for a second time, nodding, the woman approached the passenger side door. Pulling it open, her struggling with the weight, the cabin was filled with light. Climbing in, folding awkwardly with her bump, a sharp chill followed the woman inside. Closing the door, dousing the interior light, the young woman sat, head down, a cold silence all about her.

'I'm Jessica. What's your name?'

'Lucy,' the woman said, her voice barely a whisper.

'Nice to meet you. Where to?'

'Town?'

'Town it is,' Jessica smiled.

Pulling the car back to the road, pressing her foot to the pedal, Jessica settled back, and with a smile tugging at her cheeks, she asked, 'how far along are you?'

'Excuse me?'

'Your pregnancy, how far along are you?'

'I'm not pregnant,' the woman said, eyes forward, fixed on the road.

Glancing at her pronounced stomach, 'I'm sorry, I thought,' Jessica stopped, falling silent, confused.

Driving in silence, uncomfortable, her rump fidgety in the seat, Jessica racked her brain for something to say. The young woman beat her to it.

'I wonder if David would forgive you,' the young woman asked, her voice decidedly different.

Blinking, Jessica turns to the woman. Looking back at her, her face lit by the light of the dashboard, Jessica's mouth dropped open in realisation.

Not pregnant.

Not even a woman.

But a man merely pretending to be one.

'Not for cheating, no, but for the abortions... one... two... how many are too many?' He asked.

With eyes fixed forward on the road, Jessica stayed silent.

'Look at me?' He says with a soft voice, his tongue curled around each word.

'No,' Jessica responded, tears forming in her eyes.

'Now, now, please, look at me.'

Slowly, turning her head halfway, she slid her eyes the rest of the way.

'Thank you. Now, I want you to pull the car to the side of the road,' he instructed.

'Why?' her voice shaky.

'Well, now, I can't tie you up whilst driving, can I? That, my dear, would be dangerous.'

* * *

Waking sometime later, Jessica did so in darkness. Groggy, heavy, it felt like her mind had been wrapped in cotton wool. She tried to think, to focus, but it was as if the power of thought had been stolen from her. Shivering, cold down to her bones, Jessica tried to move but found her arms and legs unresponsive and heavy. Blinking against something soft, Jessica tried to think back, to remember.

I was driving, wasn't I, but driving where?

Movement, the shuffling of feet, stole her attention. Attempting to call out, like her ability to move, her sight and voice had been taken from her.

Again, attempting to focus her mind, a streak of pain sparked and flared in her skull.

So, I was driving, yeah, driving home, home from...

And finally, she remembered – the dark road, the pregnant girl... the man and his dark eyes.

I can't see because I'm blindfolded.

I can't move because I'm tied up.

I can't speak because I'm gagged.

I'm cold because I'm naked.

Fear took hold, leaving her in a state of utter panic. Then, screaming out through her gag, stifling it to a muffled cry, her moans were finally silenced with the sound of a voice from a place beyond the blindfold. Gentle, cultured, assured by not arrogant, his tone and cadence spoke of education, control, and experience.

'Good evening, my dear. Don't fret, you will be confused and drowsy, for this will soon pass. Try to remain calm, control your breathing, for you are in safe hands; you are with me now. I do apologise for the restraints, but unfortunately, such measures are required. In time they will be removed, but for now, I will remove your blindfold, so please allow your eyes time to adjust.'

As a leather, gloved hand removed her blindfold, Jessica's frantically blinking eyes were eager to drink in the light. Above her, a naked bulb hung low, blinding her from the rest of her surroundings. As the glare subsided, she was able to focus on the shadowed man standing over her.

'I've been watching you; did you know that?' He asked.

Attempting again to move against her binds, her movement entirely restricted, tears were quick to well and blur her vision.

'Now there, don't cry. There's no need for tears.'

Stepping in closer, blocking the light, with the man's head acting as the moon would when completing a lunar eclipse, his face comes into view.

Not a face.

A mask.

No, worse, a full head leather mask. Studded, shiny, it appeared and smelt as if freshly waxed. It dipped lower, his sunken eyes peering out through small slits, his breathing heavy through the tiny nose holes. Sat behind the open three-inch zipper, his tongue slid out to lick the metal, enjoying the taste, her reaction beneath him.

Her eyes, growing fast, bulged wide as a terrified scream was stifled at her gag.

'You don't like it? Well, it's my first,' he said, a lone finger tracing a line around the edge of the mask.

Utter fear, primal and dark, took hold, tearing through her mind. Frantic, Jessica screamed, her lungs burning from the effort. Her eyes stretched and strained in their sockets, searched her surrounding for something, anything. Still, it was him and his dark eyes, looming over her, and his voice, calm and soothing, who answered her.

'Please, try to calm down,' he pleaded.

Her nipples went turgid against the cold air, her stomach lurched. Unable to hear him, Jessica continued to fight her binds, screaming with muted moans.

'Please, listen to me, try to be calm,' he continued, his words both soft and understanding.

But only fear spoke to her. So, delirious, she continued to resist, for a time anyway, right up until her abductor let out an almighty roar, 'LISTEN TO ME!'

His tone was enough to silence her.

Her stomach, bowels, squirming, threatened to give way. If not bound, she would have been paralysed by fear. Instead, eyes locked on his, she was forced to watch him bend over her, his face dropping lower and lower.

'You will be quiet, and you will do as I say. This is your one warning. Scream out again, act like a child, and I will see you suffer a death beyond hell, beyond your worst nightmare. Now, do we understand each other?'

And just like that, he had her complete attention.

Staying silent, she lay frozen, watching his gloved hand return to wipe away her tears. His fingers lingered there, moving to her lips, gently caressing, playfully but deliberate. In their wake, her eyes spoke of absolute terror.

'You are heavenly, an angel? So natural in the way the light catches you, so beautiful, timeless, and I imagine most men miss that about you. They might, but not me, no, my dear, I see everything you are, what you can be... what we can be together. Now, I'm going to remove your gag. Remember my warning, and I, in turn, will act like a gentleman. Nod if you understand?' he asked.

She nodded in agreement. When her gag was removed, Jessica coughed wildly as she drank in large gulps of air. Closing her eyes, blocking out the monster leering above her, Jessica saw her husband in her mind. Again, tears returned, warming her cheeks as they slipped off her face.

I can do this. Be good, and you'll get to go home.

Home to David.

I'll never hurt you again; I love you, and I'm coming home, I promise...

She could see her loyal husband and the future still possible for them. A detached home outside town, white picket fences, a dog, a garden with children playing.

Jessica's body was found two months later. Sprawled, naked, shaved head, her brains bashed in. Time and the warm autumn heat had worked together, leaving the body bloated, the mouth sagged open like a gaping hole; a freeze-frame of some unspeakable horror had been left as if in a perpetual state of terror, alone, forever screaming silently.

PART THREE

THE MURDER OF THOMAS WILLIAM

28

37 days before Thomas's murder...

The road into Amersham is aggravating enough without the shadow of pending death looming over you. Not satisfied with the endless stream of speed cameras perfectly placed to impede the driver with their deceptive intent, the road into town is lined with an assortment of large, envy hungry, expensive homes. Sprawling houses, mostly brown brick, no two alike, most if not all, sit back from the road behind neatly kept gardens. Other, larger, more expensive properties are hidden behind conifers or high walls with gated entrances. The type which leaves Thomas dull, bitter and regretful. Worse still, along with heavy, bustling traffic, Thomas has the weight of a ticking clock for company.

37 days.

Wanting to have left earlier, he was forced to stay home while the locksmith took most of the day fitting two new locks: a standard Yale deadbolt and an Enforcer-4, heavy-duty double lock.

I like to see the creep get through them.

Somehow, still not convinced, he attempts to divert his thoughts. But, instead, his mind goes back to what he saw- the intruder, the blade, and him dropping to his knees. Thomas sees the blood and his skin going pale. He sees himself dying, his body going limp, his dreams, aspirations, his future ending in the most savage butchery.

37 days.

Knowing this, knowing the exact moment he dies, is numbing, paralysing. After watching himself get stabbed, Thomas remained at the hole. Having watched the intruder drag his limp body from the room, down the hallway, into the bathroom, after watching him leave, he hoped, he prayed. However, still, his future-self never reappeared. Finally, and when he couldn't watch anymore, he returned to his apartment. Peter had remained in Amy's apartment, at the wall for some time, and when he finally joined them, he was quiet, lost in thought, almost reserved, then cried.

'I won't get to see my little girl grow up,' Thomas had moaned.

Beside him on the sofa, with a hand on his knee, Lilly said softly, 'don't say that, the futures not been written, we can change it.'

'Like I did with Amy, everything I did, she still got taken, murdered all the same,' he told them.

'That's the past. The past has happened, we can't change it, but the future, the future can be rewritten,' Lilly had said passionately. Defiant, glancing at Peter, her eyes pleading for support. 'I'll stay with you. We both will right, together, we can....'

'LILLY, STOP!' Thomas shouted, his voice mean and piercingly loud.

As an ugly silence fell over the room. Lilly, pulling back from Thomas, removed her shaking hand from his lap. Then when Peter left them alone, Lilly took Thomas by the hand.

'The futures not written. We can change it,' she told him.

'Maybe, I don't know. What if time is a loop; we follow it around, thinking we have control over our lives, but instead, we're mere dots, predestined to reach a place in time?'

'But you don't know for sure.'

'I tried to save your sister, everything I did, and still, she was taken.'

'I know you think it's hopeless, but Thomas, the hole, Amy's disappearance, this whole nightmare, none of it makes sense. Erika, James's death, and you... coming into my life....'

Looking at her, her eyes, for a moment, Thomas felt the darkness drain from him, replaced with a warmth, a feeling he thought had all but abandoned him.

'Love,' he started in response, his voice breaking. 'Something I thought was now lost to me, a part of my life, left to the past.'

'I won't lose you too, you understand me, if I have to stand guard all night, every night, I will, that son-of-bitch has already taken enough from me,' Lilly said, setting his heart ablaze with thunder and colour.

Whether it was her tears or the strength of her words, her inner power, Thomas vows to fight, do all he can to find the killer, uncover the truth of both Amy and Erika's disappearances, and if he's lucky, somehow survive the inevitable.

Traffic slows, which instinctively elevates his heart rate. When you don't have long to live, queuing traffic is enough to have him wanting to scream until his lungs explode. Instead, Thomas takes his frustration out on the steering wheel instead. His knuckles turn white as he grips down on it, the leather creaking beneath his fingers. With the rain, heavy like the traffic, the line of cars, buses, lorries, white vans before him sit at a crawl, like a line of ants marching home.

Finally, after another ten minutes of crawling, the Sat-Nav crowns proudly, 'you have reached your destination.'

Thomas flicks the indicator to the right and waits for a break in the traffic. The slow, steady stream of vehicles continues as if blind to his request to leave the road. Growing impatient, Thomas nudges forward, pushing the hood closer to the white centre line. A young man driving a new Porsche thumps down on his horn, startling Thomas, bringing him to a stop. Giving Thomas the middle finger, passing him as slow as possible, as if to let Thomas read his lips, he mouths the words, 'fucking prick.'

To stop them from shaking, Thomas's grip on the wheel again tightens to the point of being painful. Growing warm beneath his clothes, he flicks on the air-con and adjusts the set of blowers, angling them towards his face.

Finally, with a short break in the traffic, Thomas mashes down on the accelerator as a tall Volvo SUV flashes its lights. Too eagerly, perhaps, as he stalls the car, bringing it to a skidding stop across the oncoming lane. An elderly lady glares at him from behind the wheel of the Volvo. With lifted eyebrows and a shaking of her head, she labels Thomas in no uncertain terms as stupid or unsuitable to hold a driving license.

Waving her an apology, restarting the car, he shunts it forward, off the road, onto the driveway, stopping before the eight-foot-tall, solid wood gate. Winding down the driver's window, rain splashing in at his face, Thomas reaches out to speak into the intercom. Pressing the button, static and a wince-inducing buzzing greet him.

Finally, the line clears, and a voice, soft and well-spoken, comes through the speaker, 'Hello?'

'Hi, it's Thomas William. We spoke on the phone?'

'Oh yes, Mr William, you're late. I remember agreeing 3pm?'

'Yeah, well, I got unlucky with the traffic, sorry.'

'I see. Well, as you are here, please come in.'

The gates pull inward on electrically powered hinges to reveal a large three-story house. The driveway, circular, loops from left to right, passing an oversized double garage, the main house, and a modest annexe before returning to the gate.

Squeezing his foot down on the accelerator, Thomas pushes the car through the opening gate. He angles it to the left and begins to circle around a perfectly kept lawn of bright green. While trimmed with flowers at its edge, a stone water fountain demands all attention at the centre. Water spurts from the mouth of a young man- clearly a centurion, his elegant dress, his shield and raised sword suggest the Roman era.

Driving past the garage, Thomas eyes a Land Rover, Mini, and an aggressive-looking Audi wagon. Although all appear new, with license plates registered within the last year, the combined cost of the three, Thomas calculates to be enough to finance the purchase of an average home.

Pulling the car alongside the front of the house and shutting off the engine, Thomas climbs out into the rain. Through its steady downpour, he darts across the bricked paved driveway to the house. The front door, heavy oak and dripping in bronze fittings, is finished with a huge knocker in the shape of a Roman Eagle. Rapping on the door, the solid wood unflinching, he waits as a blurred figure appears through the frosted side panel, growing as they draw in close.

The door opens, swinging inwards, and in its place, Thomas is greeted with a smile, be it a thin one. Where he envisioned her to be far older, James Ruck's mother is an attractive, alluring, youthful-looking woman in her early fifties.

With intelligent yet cold, sneered eyes, she levels him a look, one he takes for agitation or surprise, 'Thomas?'

'Yes, Mrs Ruck?'

'It's Tott now, but please, call me Michelle. Come in, please.'

Holding the door open for him, Thomas follows her into a grand, tiled foyer. Mosaic and intricate but subtle, the colours muted and in keeping with the light grey walls.

'You have a beautiful home,' he tells her.

While she smiles over her shoulder, Thomas takes it as one laced with impatience. His eyes move to the staircase running up along the left wall and the open landing below the entrance. Again, the Roman theme continues here. Each depicting a different battle, the panel clad walls are lined with large paintings framed in copper. A set of tall Tuscan Roman amphora floor vases add to the overall theme. Naturally aged, with small handles towards their tops, they line the entrance hall on both the left and right.

'Thank you,' she says, leading him through the foyer, to the right into a medium-sized study, come library, of panelled wood and filled bookcases.

Following Michelle over to a set of armchairs positioned at a slight angle at an open fireplace, taking her lead, Thomas sits and takes a moment to scrutinise the woman's appearance. He struggles with what he sees. Michelle sits in the perfect spot between the two and does so almost arrogantly, neither slim nor overweight. Curvy and voluptuous, her dress pulls tight at her breasts and rump. Black, sitting above the knee, he imagines the dress and ones like it are in daily use.

Probably worn to simply control men like me.

'You understand the investigation is still open, so I won't speak about specifics, nor will I aid you or anyone else in darkening my son's name,' her words, though strong, assured, come from smiling lips.

'I understand,' Thomas says.

'Still, my heart does go out to the poor girl's family. Losing James was awful,' she says, again her expression failing to match her words. 'But we have closure in his death. For her mother, well, I imagine it must be like the torment of the damned, that is if Swedish women are allowed to *feel* for themselves.'

'Amy too is missing,' he tells her.

'I was under the impression she just upped and left. Depressed, or was it repressed? I'm sure James's passing would have had a terrible effect on her.

Crossing her legs, tanned, smooth and polished as if greased, she looks at Thomas. A test, Thomas recognises. Her eyes slide from his, down his shirt, stopping at his belt, lingering before venturing lower. Sure, she is an attractive woman, but after sharing time with a woman like Lilly, looking at Michelle Tott and women like her, he feels nothing whatsoever.

'I'm sorry for your loss,' he tells her, hoping to regain her attention.

'Thank you,' she says, her eyes lazy in returning to his.

'Your son was a photographer?'

'Among other things, yes.'

'Other things?'

She again levels her eyes on his, considering his question, his pressing of the point.

'Well, James liked to dabble, from painting to archery, acting to directing. He finally settled on photography, but in truth, he was never any good at it. However, we, myself and his stepfather, supported him through it all, of course. Yes, my James was a dud, a little, how can I say, profligate, yes, I'll be the first to admit it, but he's no killer.'

What son has ever received such a glowing review?

Where he intended to be cordial, his candour light and sympathetic, the way she looked, her tone leave him unable to maintain the charade.

'I understand he spent time in the porn industry, cheap films, under the counter-stuff?'

'I see, right to it. Like I said, I have no intention of discussing each little thing my son did, let alone bask in his mistakes.'

'I understand, but your son did make those types of movies, he and his friends?'

'Yes, yes, another failed venture. James dipped his toe and found the water was too hot. Young men make mistakes, am I right?'

'How's that?'

'Well, look at you, a once published author, but not now. A married man, but not now.'

'You've researched me; I'll take it as a compliment.'

'You do that, every little win, bully-for-you,' she smiles.

With anger starting to percolate, Thomas decides to abandon all caution and courtesy. 'Do you think your son was capable of murder?' He asks.

A sneer drops through her face. Her eyes flick wide, then narrow in contempt.

'Like I said, my James was no killer.'

'Not according to the Police; I hear they interviewed him.'

'And yet there was no arrest, no charge,' she says, her eyes narrowing still. 'I watched a few, my son's films, his and those halfwit friends of his, Simon and Morgan.'

Simon and Morgan- their names just keep coming up.

'Those films are poor taste, crude, but I guess men go for the grainy type,' she continues. 'Whores, the lot of them, they'll open their legs for anyone if it means getting a moment in the spotlight, so don't ask me to pity them. But, my son, my James, the idiot he was, the mistakes he made, those women, all of them, they were still below him.'

This has her smiling- her words, the power she has over men, beam through her eyes.

'I'm sorry I bothered you,' Thomas tells her. Getting up, he steps away from the chair. 'Thank you for your time.'

'And the woman in his life, Amy, plain as they come, whatever he saw in her, I'll never know. She was what he called his 'constant,' his 'home,' but there were always others. Others, like Erika, pretty but unremarkable. Sure, my James was no saint, Erika wasn't the only girl he saw on the side, he takes after his father in that regard, and if you ask me, the likes of Amy, well, she should be thankful my James ever graced her with his eyes,' she says, her smile growing malicious.

Looking down at her, words failing him, he watches her hands move to her legs. Gently, her fingers trace a line along the seam of her dress before gently, only an inch, pulling it up her bare legs, exposing her tanned thighs.

'Your son was no Casanova, nor was he ever really a photographer, even if he wanted to be. On the contrary, he was a lecher and a coward,' Thomas says, looking her up and down, his disdain now exposed.

'Is that so?' She grins.

'But I guess we shouldn't hold it against him. I mean, the apple didn't fall too far from the tree. No job, no children left to raise... what good are you, Mrs Tott? Good day to you,' he tells her, leaving, stripping her of that smile.

29

30 days before Thomas's murder...

'Thomas, did you hear what I said?' Peter asks from behind the steering wheel.

'Yes,' Thomas says. 'Sorry.'

Again, counting the minutes until his death, having phased out, Thomas turns his head to look at Peter.

'James did some work for Grey's Lumber back in 2018, photographs for their catalogue, stuff for the local paper, so it's conceivable he knows their CCTV procedure. So, it's traceable, right?'

'But not to the items,' Thomas says. 'There's no way to prove James was the one who purchased them.'

Pulling his old Ford into the gravelled layby, Peter shuts off the engine, leaving the Capri perched upon the crest of the hill. Peter sighs deeply, one Thomas takes as a mixture of frustration and exhaustion.

'James can't get away with it,' Peter says, looking at Thomas. 'Death is too good for him.'

Thomas looks at him, nods, but says nothing. The young man needs words of encouragement, of hope, but Thomas, heavy with regret and pessimism, knows with certainty he is not the man for the job.

Turning, unable to look at him, Thomas winds down the window. Twisting the old handle and bringing it down in short shunts rather than one smooth motion, Thomas eyes the narrow road ahead. It curving down, zigzagging its way back to town, and the sharp incline to their left, which presumably leads to the hill's peak. The steep sheer is such, Thomas is forced to dip and arch his head through the opening to see the top. Rain splashing his face, his eyes trace a set of narrow concrete steps up through the foliage, twisting as it climbs with the continuation of the ascension.

'I figure we park here and make out way up on foot,' Peter says.

'You sure this is the place?'

'I have it on good authority that it is. A bungalow in Simon's mother's name, the thing is, she's long dead, which leaves the whole thing reeking of criminality.'

Having researched Simon Finch and Morgan Teller, their identities and location had remained elusive. Left frustrated, he tried Linkedin, Company's House, and even their social media pages but found all to be inactive or out of date. When Thomas returned to Hildur for help, she struggled to find anything concrete. Which finally led Thomas back to Khaliq. His call to him went as he hoped though talking to the man who almost raped him left Thomas nauseous, his skin itchy with what can only be described as hive-like welts.

'Hello?' he said when answering Thomas's call.

'This is Thomas William.'

'How the fuck did you get my number?'

'I need an address for Simon Finch or Morgan Teller.'

'Yeah and? Get a phonebook.'

'But you do know them?'

'Yes, I've sold their stuff, but....'

'Look, there is a definite link between them and Erika before her disappearance. If I am to look at them further, I need to see them. Can you help me or not?'

There was a beat while he considered the request, possibly Thomas's tone. Khaliq's breathing, heavy, sounded raspy and agitated, filling the phone line with deep rumbles.

'I haven't used their cheap shit in years, but I think I still have an address somewhere.'

'An address for what exactly?' Thomas had asked.

'How the fuck should I know,' he scoffed.

Khaliq had come good and provided Thomas with an address, be it an old one for Simon Finch, but had been unable to provide a use, if any, for the property.

'I still think we should have called them first.' Peter says.

'The last time we did, we were ambushed, twice actually, so no, we go up, have a look first, ok?' Thomas says.

Peter pauses and shakes his head so slightly it is almost invisible. 'Aren't you scared?'

Thomas smiles. 'Sure, I am Bogart, shitting-bricks.'

Echoing Peter's words from nights before, recognising this, and after a long beat, Peter smiles and nods in agreement. 'Knife in the sock?'

Smiling, Thomas looks at him, 'Of course, you?'

'Never leave home without it.'

Climbing out from his seat, flipping up his hood, Thomas steps away from the car. Moving to the steep bank, he stops before starting up the concrete steps. Exhausted just looking up at the climb, the sleek path, the frail metal handrail, the task in hand leaves Thomas dejected and exhaling deeply.

Locking the car, doing up his long beige peacoat, Peter closes it on a royal blue roll neck made of cashmere. His continued well-turned-out, classical appearance, paired with the almost effortless way he matches colours with textures, dark cotton and tweed, again leaves Thomas sour with his inadequacy and, well, his age.

Grunting frustrated breaths, moving around to the car's front, Thomas joins Peter at the steps. Starting the climb, wide enough for them to walk side by side, Peter waits for Thomas on the third step before resuming. Gripping the metal handrail and using it for support, each step is a burden for Thomas. Still healing, his wounds, the sensation of new skin stretching at his stomach, flexing with every movement, churns at his bowels.

'From what I gather, Simon Finch and Morgan Weller are two a-class wannabes. Childhood friends of James, they stayed friends through university. Like James, Simon studied film and photography. But, while James ventured out into still-photographs rather than film, Simon never progressed further than a cameraman,' Thomas tells Peter.

'And Morgan Weller?' He asks.

'A low-level producer who started out making documentaries, mundane stuff, amateur and crap. Now, he's churning out cheap adult films, a little outside the mainstream by all accounts. But, of course, they'll claim the ratty and grainy look is a design or artistic choice, rather than their lack of talent and financial backing.'

Halfway up and blowing through his lips, Thomas allows Peter to take the lead as the steps narrow, angling to the left. With a gap opening between them, Thomas attempts to pick up the pace. Still, his wounded lower stomach and labouring heart now act to sabotage his efforts. Chest throbbing, heat searing up from his sweaty feet, he stops, holding his wound. Looking up at Peter through the rain, his eyes following the steep angle, the slick and puddled concrete, and the grey cloud ceiling waiting for them at the top of the climb. Grinding his teeth, bearing them, Thomas pushes on up to meet Peter. Looking down at him, Peter sports a worried expression, one plastered to his wet face, stricken with rain and concern.

Joining him, falling against the railing, panting and sweating, the world around Thomas slows into a sickening spin. Taking a moment to collect himself, he finds Peter has now gone quiet. Staring off in the distance, past the houses and trees below them, Thomas notes the shadow now hung over the young man's face, his eyes, and a darkness he fears now lives within him.

'I had a dream last night, which is strange for me, you see I don't dream, ever, never have. Even when I was young, not one, until last night,' Peter says, eyes fixed on the horizon. 'Sat in a chair, I am forced to watch a film. What starts out as a vintage cartoon evolves into little more than a sleazy piece of pornography before changing again, escalating into something far more devilish. A girl, a child really, naked and tied....' Peter pauses. 'Well, you get the picture. Of course, I want to look away, but somehow, I know, if I do, even for a moment, I will lose my mind. So, I'm left with the choice, either I watch the horrible footage or look away and lose my mind. Torture or insanity, those are my options, yet I cannot decide.'

Thomas places a hand on Peter's shoulder but says nothing. No words can heal what he's already seen, what he yet might see again.

'Does it get any easier?' Peter asks.

'No,' Thomas says, taking a moment. 'And if we're lucky, it never will.'

Turning, Peter looks at him.

'The horrors of this world, the grime, the abuse, the savage, should always affect us. So, the fact it does means something.'

Peter responds with a nod of the head, and together, stride for stride, they again continue their climb.

Slow, painful, panting again in seconds, Thomas needs the rail for support.

'Don't worry, on the way back, you can slide down the handrail,' Peter says.

And while he offers a smile, it's a thin one, his tormented face unable to display any natural warmth.

'Don't joke, you might need to carry me,' Thomas tells him, a smirk japing at his cheeks.

The final ten or so steps are torturous on his feet, his wounds, with each one bringing a burning to his calves and thighs.

Finally reaching the summit, chest heaving, Thomas joins Peter at the curb. A row of detached, single-story homes sits back behind sloping lawns. Drab and failing, the structures are made all the more sombre by the dark grey sky and heavy rain. A dotting of trees does their best to break up the monotony with a bit of colour, but with the continued wind and rain, their limbs hang low and semi-bare. A layer of pine needles carpet the road, but instead of a fresh crunch underfoot, they squelch like soggy Shreddies.

Accessing his phone, checking the image he found online, Thomas points to a detached bungalow over to their right.

'There it is,' Thomas says.

Its gravel driveway, looping up from the road to the side of the house, disappears beneath a darkened carport. Though not precisely rundown, the place does border on it. The windows at the front are either blacked out or drape covered. With the fading light, the bungalow appears dark and empty. If not for the cars on the driveway, Thomas would take the house as abandoned.

'It might be a little dire, but the view is at least....' Peter starts.

Thomas joins him in tracing the steps back down to Peter's car, the snaking road, and beyond, the spattering of greens and the grey of concrete. They appear locked in constant struggle, though the new world, urban and beige, seems to be winning the fight.

Turning back to the bungalow, the job in hand, Thomas eyes the dark windows. Stepping out into the road, Thomas takes the lead and approaches the property. A rickety chain-link fence runs alongside the driveway on the left, all the way to the rear, where a large SUV and a worn 2008-plate Porsche Boxster sit parked. The sound of muffled music, faint at first, escapes the structure, barely audible through the drumming rain.

'Sounds like someone's having a party?' Peter declares from the rear.

Approaching the front door, a PVC frame with frosted panels at the top and bottom, like the windows, the hallway beyond sits dark with questions. Standing looking at the buzzer, ready to press, Thomas's outstretched finger hovers an inch from the button.

Don't stall, Thomas. Get on with it and ring the bell.

A voice from his left has him retract his hand. Startled, Thomas turns to his left to find a man looking at him. Having appeared from the side of the property, his sudden arrival is far more unsettling than his thin appearance.

'Can I help you, fellas, with something?' The man asks.

Thomas smiles and asks, 'we're looking for Simon Finch and Morgan Weller?'

Holding an e-cigarette in his hand, the man, in ankle-biting chinos, loafers and a tight pink Fred Perry polo, edges back on his heels. Thomas instantly recognises him from his Facebook profile picture by his perma-tan, fake and overdone, designer stubble and neatly trimmed eyebrows.

'Who's asking?' His voice, wavy, matches the mess of highlighted curls atop his head.

'We're friends of James Ruck and Amy Porter.'

'Sorry, you've got the wrong address,' he smiles before sucking on the e-cigarette.

The vapours reach out to meet them, staining the air with mint and cucumber, lingers as the man leaves, hovering there like an exorcised spirit.

Moving away from the door, walking back to the driveway, Thomas turns and watches the man shuffle back down the driveway, towards the rear of the house, disappearing through a gate.

'That was Morgan Weller, right?' Peter asks.

'Yeah, that's him,' Thomas says, unable to hide the bitterness in his voice.

'What are we going to do?'

'I've got an idea, but you're not going to like it,' Thomas tells him.

'We're going to break in there, aren't we?'

'Yes, Peter, yes we are.'

* * *

A clump of trees across the street, three houses down, gives them a good view of the bungalow. Though not fully shielded, the closely-knit tree branches, looping and interconnected above their heads, provide a little respite from the rain.

Having watched Weller leave the house with another man, possibly Simon Finch, and two young women, Thomas and Peter remained crouched within the treeline. When the pair returned in the SUV with a further two girls and a third man, Thomas and Peter had stayed hidden. With the SUV pulling out of the driveway, its tyres hissing against the tarmac, Thomas cannot be sure who is left inside. While it appeared the same number of people who arrived had also left, with the darkening sky and the coming of night, Thomas is left unconvinced and jaded.

Looking at Peter, his face a dim smudge in the transitory light, Thomas tells him, 'you're staying here, ok.'

'Why?'

'I need you to alert me if they come back. You see that SUV, you call my mobile, I'll have it on vibrate.'

'And you'll just leave if I call. You're not going to stick around, and....'

'And get stabbed again? I'm not planning on it, but I have to go in there; you understand that, right?'

'I do,' Peter nods. 'There comes a time in every man's life when he needs to step outside and face the wolves at his door.'

Thomas nods, though not quite matching the task in hand, he recognises Peter's sentiment, quoting the words from his first novel.

Standing up, letting the cold rain shift through him, it drops through Thomas's shoulders, sliding down his back to his heavy legs. Having been crouched for over an hour, his thighs have grown numb and unresponsive. Giving his legs a moment to allow the blood to circulate, he again inspects the street. The placement of the streetlights results in allowing the darkening sky to fill the space between, and with the bungalow sitting perfectly between two lampposts, it hangs back, masked by the dying light.

Shuffling at first, stepping out from beneath the trees, rain splashing at his face and hair, soaking him through in seconds. Head down, Thomas pushes forward to the driveway. Confident the deep shadows offer him adequate protection from any onlookers, he climbs the shallow slope to the front of the property. Slowing his approach, watching the windows, he hears no sounds from the dark home, no music like before.

Moving again, sticking to the chain-link fence, the gravel crunching beneath his feet, the occasional stone flips and scatters about him. Passing beneath the carport, switching to the side of the house, Thomas steps away from the fence. Creeping alongside the house, past the same crappy Porsche, Thomas stops at a rear gate. Hearing the rain drum down against the carport's plastic top, he flips the handle upward. As the gate pops back an inch, pushing it inward, Thomas peers through the growing space. Watching the house for movement, like the ones at the front, the windows sit darkened from the inside. He studies them but sees nothing. While not yet dark, Thomas recognises time is not on his side- the night will soon arrive, and with it, only darkness and shadow. So, scanning, Thomas spots a set of concrete steps at the far side of the house. Leading down to the ground, disappearing out of sight, a tightness reaches in, stealing his breath.

Great, another basement.

Thomas moves to the steps, snapping to it, cutting across the garden, sliding past the rear windows and patio door. Narrow and steep, the steps drop into shadow, offering just a hint at the door waiting at the bottom. Wet, the concrete appears greased, so he slows his approach to avoid falling. Still, his feet splash through the sheets of water collected upon each step, leaving his socks damp and weighted.

At the door, wooden with a single glass panel, Thomas tries the handle. With a pop, it opens into more darkness. Thomas sighs in relief, stepping inside, with the rain receding into a dull, suppressed pounding, it chases him into a dim hallway. The deep cold returns, falling over him like a blanket. Not from the rain or his wet clothes, but due to the uneasiness of the unknown.

Taking a deep breath, puffing out his chest, Thomas moves into a small room piled high with boxes. The basement's layout is train-car-like, with all rooms set out in a row, one after another. With a lowered ceiling, PVC strip curtains, the kind you'd find in a walk-in fridge, hang in each of the doorways, leaving what sits behind a dull, foggy mystery.

A quick scan of the first room, a dank space, Thomas labels it as a storage room of sorts. While evening light sneaks into the basement through a series of small slit-like windows at ceiling level, the area before him is clotted and dark. Along with the boxes, which there are numerous, the stuffy room holds a tightly packed clothes rack and a network of shelves stacked full of what looks like thousands of DVD cases.

Removing his phone from his pocket, activating the torch feature, Thomas first inspects the metal shelving unit. DVDs, stacked by title, all porn, cheap, the low-budget type, the covers are nothing more than a printed piece of paper with a faded coloured image of a young woman in a bikini, folded and forced into the sleeve. With titles: *Grandpa's dirty secret, ON but still turned ON, Piss-Pals...* it is clear these men, while not satisfied with making adult movies, produce depraved, grotesque and inhuman films. And there are thousands of them, all neatly stacked, all ready for shipping. A second unit, fully stacked with blank DVD cases, labels and postage envelopes, speak of a sizable operation.

Why would anyone want to watch such a thing?

Shaking his head, disgust now taking over, Thomas moves on. Scanning the different outfits clustered together, bursting, the collection threatens to collapse the flimsy-looking aluminium clothes rack. Nurse, schoolgirl, nun, teacher, police officer, latex and lace, all unimaginative, skimpy, used and worn, sticky and stained and sordid.

Crossing the room to the doorway, he stops, bringing his phone's torch up to highlight the contents of a large open trunk. Full of sex toys, dildo's mainly, most of which are large and aggressive looking. Chains, whips of different sizes and shapes. Ropes, handcuffs. Among the clutter, all but hidden within beneath, his eyes fix on something. A cold chill runs up his spine, sending a tremor through him, leaving his hands shaking wildly. His heart, skipping, dances against his chest. He reaches into the dark space and pulls the item up from the trunk's depths. Shifting it in his hand, Thomas inspects the leather mask. Eyeless with a red ball gag built into the design, flipping it over, he finds the word *MAX* stitched chaotically in red cotton.

Max Rex.

My God, this could be it.

Simon or Morgan, really?

Considering this, returning the mask to the trunk, he moves to the doorway. He passes through into the next room using his fingers, peeling the strips apart like curtains. Running the torch beam across the room, a wet room/come makeshift changing room of sorts, he finds a toilet and shower sitting to the right, partly exposed by a half-drawn shower curtain.

Stepping to a door on his left and opening it, he throws the light inside a cramped, dark space and a staircase leading up to presumably the main house. Closing the door, stepping across the room, one step.... two... three, he reaches the next set of hanging plastic strips. Passing through them, letting them slide over him, their contact leaving him shaky, he enters the last of the three rooms. Sweat and the scent of men taint the air, making it stuffy. At first, Thomas takes it for a bedroom but quickly sees it for what it really is, a sex dungeon for the depraved, a movie set for the cheapest of adult films. A double bed sits against the far wall, with light boards and tripods set up around it. In the far-right corner, further light-boards, backboards hint at a shoddy, half-assed attempt at a photo studio.

Crossing the room, he spots a desk and computer sitting within a deep alcove, its monitor alive with the motion of a generic screen saver. Approaching it, leading with his phone's torch, he sweeps the beam across the desk. Flipping open a ring binder, Thomas reviews the thick wedges of files. Each is stapled with a Polaroid, resumes, hundreds of them, male and female. Contact details, age, weight, height, all standard stuff, that is, until you reach the bottom of the one-sheet. Experience, past works, and a place for the candidates to list their tolerance levels. Heterosexual, bisexual, homosexual, bondage, anal sex, and so on. All pointless, of course, given the industries rule of- *the more you'll do, the more work you'll get.*

Thomas stops, his eyes fixed on the profile of a young man, the photo. Nineteen, skinny and short, his slight frame is offset by a large penis. His name, Lee Martin, and his stage name of *Lee So' Hard* takes up the upper portion of the one-sheet, circled with a heavy pencil.

Closing the binder, turning, and leading with the torch, Thomas is startled, dropping the phone as it begins to vibrate in his hand. Bending down to retrieve it, the torch beam shining upwards, blinding him, he quickly flips the phone over. His eyes, still wrecked by the direct glare of the torch, flare his vision with incandescent spots of yellow and red.

Slowly, as the blinding hue subsides, he sees Peter's name lit by the display. Panic gets his blood pumping. Darting back the way he had come, smashing through the plastic flaps, he hustles through to the last of the rooms, where he comes to a dead stop. Headlights streak in through the slit windows, sweeping from the front to the rear.

SHIT!

Standing frozen, Thomas hears the rumble of an engine go dead and watches as the headlights go dark, sharply followed by the thud of car doors being slammed. He needs to move, he knows this, but he's conflicted about which way he should go.

Staring up at the low ceiling, he attempts but fails to trace the sounds, the heavy footfalls of booted feet, to predict their route into the bungalow.

Fantastic, you're trapped, way to go.

He returns to the middle room, backtracking, his skin beginning to prickle, his eyes now throb with the increased blood pressure, almost blinding him. Frantically, he searches the room for options. Finally, fixing on the closed door, recalling the staircase beyond, he darts to it, yanking the door open, moving to the darkened staircase, ready to climb but pauses on the bottom step.

The dark door is abruptly framed with yellow light and movement, passing across the narrow strip beneath it. To underline it, laughter rips out through the floor above, echoed by the thuds of stomping boots and the booming of loud voices.

Thomas is forced to backtrack, away from the stairs, his eyes fixed on the door above.

'Get the lady a drink,' a voice says.

Another shadow passes over the door.

The handle twists.

The door pulls backwards, whining on its hinges.

Jumping back, closing the door, Thomas spins, his eyes scanning the room for a way to escape. Behind him, heavy boots start their descent, thumping down the stairs, creaking the wood beneath them. Paralysed, all Thomas can do is stand, rooted to the spot.

Shit or get off the toilet, Thomas, but do something... anything.

30

8 seconds later...

Morgan Weller is the first to enter via the closed door. Thomas recognises him by the same chinos and polo shirt from before. A young black man born with broad shoulders and excessive height and a young-looking brunette who can't be any older than nineteen follows him into the basement. Her youthful face and petite frame contradict her dark and sultry makeup. Her crop top is as short as her skirt, leaving her belly-button-piercing glinting in the dim light.

The second act of the amateur-porn-duo, Simon Finch is the last to enter. Well-dressed in skinny jeans, a designer shirt and a waistcoat, in his early thirties, along with being thin, too thin, he is aggressively balding and gaunt. He walks with the air of someone with money, but Thomas knows better- Finch is nothing more than a walking credit card, one with little to no credit left. Moreover, his juddering movements speak of another affliction- cocaine use, heavy and often, further supported by exaggerated hand moves and him excessively wiping his nose.

With an almighty buzz, light flashes, blinking intermittently at first, before showering the entire basement level in bright white light via a team of fluorescent tubes at the ceiling.

'You can get showered and changed in here,' Weller says. 'But you are shaved, right? Klaus told you yeah, we don't like fuzz here.'

'We like to maintain a fuzz-free zone,' adds Finch.

Now in the light, the brunette appears far younger, possibly as young as sixteen, who nods along with blurry, star-filled eyes.

'Jez here will take care of you; he's one of our best performers,' Morgan tells her, gesturing to the tall black man.

Thomas fears for her safety, understanding what will happen now, given the size disparity between the guy and the girl. Her head reaching his lower chest, the girl follows Jez, Morgan, and Finch to the room with the bed. Thomas lets out a deep breath, watching them through a narrow slit in the shower curtain. Crouched low, his knees pressed hard on the tiled floor, eyeing the small room for a way out, Thomas considers whether now is *the* time to leave.

It's Jez, the lead performer, who re-appears first. Now shirtless, more skinny than well-built, he ambles past Thomas leisurely, whistling to the tune of *she'll be coming round the mountain.* Thomas continues watching him until the young man disappears through the plastic stripes into the first room.

Thomas's eyes move to the closed door ahead of him. He pictures the dark stairs beyond, climbing them to the ground floor, and considers whether he can reach the door before being intercepted.

If you're going to go, go now.

Thomas's phone buzzing for a second time loosens his bladder, leaving him a wreck. He needs to urinate and fears he may very well wet himself if the pressure continues to increase like it is.

Checking the phone, recognising the number belonging to StarKiller, he lets the call go to voicemail.

'Klaus recommended you, highly, he said you were pretty, but I think he sold you short,' Weller's voice again, loud enough to carry to Thomas's hiding spot. 'We're gonna start with the basics, ok, photographs for the website.'

'So, let's get them clothes off. It will be hot, sexy, trust me, babe,' Finch pitches in.

'All of my clothes?' She asks, her voice tiny.

The two men laugh.

'Yeah, babe, it's cool, just relax with it, no hassle, ok?' Weller adds.

'Ok, sure, I thought we would take it slow, is all,' she says.

'Look, it's like getting ready for a shower, you take off your clothes, we take pictures, we move on, ok?' Finch's voice, slimy, worm-like, is laced with annoyance.

The girl has now gone silent.

'Klaus told you what we do here, right, what we put to film? Asks Weller.

Still nothing from the girl.

'Klaus should be clear on the specifics; if he wasn't, well, it's on him. We service a particular area of the market. Abuse porn, hardcore blowjobs, it sounds worse than it is ok, we'll lay it on thick on camera, but it's all an act, all part of the illusion,' Finch says.

'Illusion?' The girl asks, sounding like a child.

'Look, the guys out there pay to watch the rough stuff, forced and brutal, some go as far as simulated rape, sick shit, it's hard to stomach, but it's mainstream now,' says Finch.

The girl now appears to be sobbing, though from where he's crouched, Thomas can't say for sure.

So, get out there and help her?

'Look, we take care of our girls, there's a line, and you'll never be asked to cross it. It's gonna be hot, sexy, trust us, ok?' Weller says, almost moaning with frustration.

Thomas doesn't get up, nor does he rush in to save the nameless girl. Instead, he remains cowered behind the shower curtain. Instead of doing something, he closes his eyes to the soft sounds of the girl undressing. With the reel's clicking, the whine of the flash, bright strobes of light, blinding, illuminate the plastic flaps as the photographs begin.

Jez reappears from the storage room, now naked, his long dick swinging between his legs- he strides across the room, eager to join the party.

'Jez knows what he's doing, follow his lead ok, nice and smooth, sexy like, ok?' Weller tells the girl.

'Ok,' her voice, sweet but raspy, is low as a whisper.

From this concealed position, Thomas again spies the door across from him. His way out.

Now would be the time to leave.

Yet still, he remains crouched within the shadows. Removing his phone, he punches in a message and sends it to Peter.

Thomas: *Hiding. They've not seen me. I'll be out soon.*

The clicks and pops of the camera have now been replaced by the sounds of sex. Loud, aggressive grunts from the man, chased from the room by miserable low whimpers from the girl. Closing his eyes, he sees the girl, her slight frame, underdeveloped form, her drug-induced eyes. As the groans grow louder, far from pleasure, the escalation in her moans is not through enjoyment but discomfort and discombobulation. To Robin, the girl's face changes before his eyes, be it a slightly older version of his daughter. The image brings warm bile to his throat, burning it, watering his eyes.

Some hero, hiding in the shadows.

Dismissing any thoughts of courage, him sitting, hiding, amounts to nothing more than cowardice.

You make me sick, fucking sick to my stomach.

Yeah, tell me something I don't know.

'Say you're a whore,' one of the men asks.

'I'm, I'm a whore,' she whispers.

'You like big dicks, don't you?'

'Yes.'

'Yes, what?'

'I like big dicks.'

'Damn right, you do. Jez, get it in her mouth, I want the bitch throwing up.'

* * *

'Slurp that shit up,' Weller tells the girl.

Listening to the men abuse the girl, for what now seems like the longest time, to his shame, through it all, Thomas stayed hidden.

'Bitch mop it up,' the girl is ordered.

The girl now gagging, brings a rapturous bout of laughter from the men.

Thomas again shifts his eyes to the two exits.

You need to leave right now.

Still, he stays unmoved, frozen like some terrified rabbit caught in the headlights of an onrushing car.

You had your chance to do something, to be a man, but you blew it. Instead, you sat here listening while those assholes subjected her to God knows what.

He considers what he could have done.

What was I supposed to do- there's three of them and one of me? There was nothing I could do.

He rolls this over in his mind. His conscience chases him, a better part of himself, trying in some way to convince the coward in him, until one name appears in his mind, reminding Thomas of the man he is, of who he's always been. As if on cue, Reggie Morris comes to mind, to remind him, to taunt him.

'Told you, easiest £200.00 you'll ever earn. Now, take a shower, clean yourself off, we go round two in fifteen,' Crowns Weller.

Shit.

Through the slit in the curtain, Thomas sees the girl appear from the plastic flaps. Naked, her body puffy and sore in some areas, is purple with bruises in others. Her mouth and chin gleaming with wet vomit, she shuffles across the room, her arms covering her breasts and vagina. Thomas slowly rises to his feet, watching her, tracking her shuffling, limping approach. Her shadow passes over the curtain, briefly filling the slit in the plastic.

Pulling the curtain aside, whipping it across Thomas's face, the girl steps forward. But, before she can act, he reaches out, grabs her by the waist with one hand, and with the other, he manages to stifle a scream before it explodes from her lips.

Twisting, pushing her against the back wall, still gripping her mouth, Thomas turns and grabs the shower curtain, pulling it back, closing them in behind it.

Squirming against him, she cries out, a muffled plea for help silenced against his hand.

'Quiet, please,' he whispers. 'I'm not with these guys. I'm here to help.'

Big help you were ten minutes ago.

To his surprise, she nods beneath the weight of his grip.

'Come on. Let's get a move on. I can't hear water running,' calls a voice from behind them.

Simon Finch.

Reaching up, Thomas feels around with his free hand for the shower faucet. Finding the tap, turning it, cold water rains down from the showerhead, soaking them both. Flinching, shivering in seconds, her wide eyes on Thomas, she remains silent, yet her eyes, weeping, stay wide and stained with red lines.

'Good, you got five minutes, ok sweetheart, times a wasting,' the voice calls, tailing off as it again disappears into the neighbouring room.

'I'm leaving,' Thomas whispers. 'You can stay, or you can come with me. I'm going to remove my hand, please don't scream, ok?'

With her nodding, the look in her eyes is enough to convince him of her obedience. Removing his hand, watching her, he asks, 'are you with me?'

Her response comes in the form of her nodding, crying, her body shaking against his.

'Ok, follow me, stay close, ok?'

Taking her by the hand, he turns to the curtain. Peering around it, though seeing no one, laughter echoes out from the room with the bed. Leading the girl out from behind the curtain, they cross the room. Water dripping in behind them, her wet bare feet slapping the hard floor, the sound as it chases them from the room is nothing short of an explosion going off. It's not, of course; it's the pressure of the situation, leaving every noise, even her low breathing, to sound like thunder in the small room.

Sliding between the strips of plastic, Thomas navigates the girl through to the storage room. Heading towards the rear passageway, the back door, their progress is brought to a halt by a voice to their left.

'Who are you?'

Snapping his head around, Thomas finds Jez standing, mid-digging through the trunk of sex toys.

'We're leaving,' Thomas tells him, his hands now fists, ready but trembling.

Jez, looking at the girl, his eyes roaming over her battered skin, pauses not to consider Thomas's request but in reflection. Dropping his head and backing away, Jez nods sourly.

Pulling the girl to the passageway, along it, and out the door, the rain meets them like a barrier, stealing Thomas's breath. Gasping for air, turning, the girl stumbles out behind him. Shaking wildly, falling against Thomas's back, it is now Thomas notices the blood oozing down the inside of her legs. With the girl's knees giving way, dropping her to the ground, Thomas quickly snatches her up in his arms. Straining against his wound in the process, grunting, turning, Thomas carries her away from the door. Pushing up through the rain, he climbs the steps to the rear garden.

Moving along the dark windows at the rear, out through the gate, Thomas turns the corner and hurries down the driveway. Panting through bared teeth, the pain from his stomach wound burns as if seared with an iron poker.

Out from under the carport, away from the bungalow, Thomas moves to the road. Peter rushes to meet them from the shadows. With a face of utter confusion, his mouth and eyes each a gaping hole.

'Jesus, what's going on...' Peter starts but goes silent at the sight of the girl.

Moving into the road, Thomas carries her to the curb opposite.

'Get the car ready; she needs a hospital,' Thomas tells him.

'Thomas, look,' Peter says, staring off over Thomas's shoulder.

Turning, Thomas spots Weller, tearing down the driveway, his loathers spitting wet gravel ahead of him, into the road. Sliding to a stop, as if unable to cross the street, glaring, Weller booms, 'yeah, run, you fucking pussy.'

'Take her,' Thomas says, passing Peter the girl. 'Get her to the car, I'll be along in a minute.'

'Thomas?' Peter asks, confused yet still taking the girl into his arms.

Removing his coat, covering the girl, Thomas says, 'go, I'll be right behind you.'

Watching Peter back away while struggling with the loads, seeing him disappear down the steps, Thomas turns back to Weller. Red-faced, eyes ablaze with rage, Weller remains back at the driveway.

Fucking coward.

'Do you know who I am?' He barks.

'Yeah, a fucking asshole, the type of guy who watches porn with his dinner,' Thomas says, leaving the man laughing. 'Funny? Yeah, well, I can do one better. How about bottom feeder, paedophile, saprophyte, you know what that means or need me to get you a dictionary?'

Thomas leaps from the curb before Weller can respond, possessed by an impulse, a fit of inner anger unfamiliar to him. Sprinting at full pelt, forgetting the pain at his stomach, across the road, towards Weller, who, as expected, starts to back up.

Eyes growing wide in surprise, the retreating man is tackled by Thomas at the waist. Spearing the man, pitching him back, Weller is creamed across the gravel, with Thomas sprawling atop him. Thudding the ground, a burst of air from Weller's gaping mouth warms Thomas's face with hints of sweetened coffee.

With the man wiggling beneath him, moaning, Thomas slams a punch into Weller's face, splitting his nose open with an explosion of blood.

'Get the fuck off me, Jesus, help!' Weller screams.

At the house, Finch appears but hesitates before approaching.

'I saw what you did, what you were doing to her!' Thomas screams.

'Look, we're making a film, ok...' Weller gasps. 'Fuck, get him off of me.'

'Asshole!' Thomas spit, punching the helpless man for a second time.

'Hey, stop,' Finch, now fully engaged, moves towards the commotion.

Seeing this, Thomas quickly rises from the ground and starts in at him, stomping down the ground between them, but slides to a stop as Finch produces something chrome and heavy. Pointed at his face, Thomas finds himself staring down the wrong end of a revolver.

'I don't know who the fuck you are, but if you take another step, I'll put a hole through your face, understand?' Finch shouts, his voice cracking under the weight. 'Now, the girl you took, she's contracted to us, so you need to bring her ass back up here, understand?'

'Not going to happen.'

'You, her father?' Finch asks. 'I think you've got the wrong idea; this is a business; we've broken no laws. She's of legal age, consenting, it may appear brutal, but it's just how the industry is.'

Thomas glares at him, wanting to reach for the gun. 'Just business right, that's all it is,' Thomas spits back.

'That's right.'

'You and your friend here, abusing girls, making them eat their own sick, having them shit themselves, that's business to you, asshole!'

'You need to leave, now,' Finch tells me, cocking the pistol's hammer.

Strangely, Thomas feels no fear. The two men, the pistol, offer nothing compared to what they've put the poor girl through. And then there are the countless others, hundreds, possibly thousands, made to do God knows what for little to no money.

'Why make films like that?' Thomas asks.

A smile creeps across the man's face, amused but slightly confused by the question. 'Why'

'You deaf, yeah why, why the fuck would anyone want to watch that!?' Thomas screams, making his throat raw.

'Are you serious? Guys love it and believe me, the need is growing; I mean, have you been online lately? Do you watch tv, everything's sexualised, adverts, even goddamn cooking shows, sexy sluts making brownies? In their nighties, the whole goddamn world wants it. And let me tell you, sex and just sex is no longer enough.'

Looking at the man, feeling all energy seep down through his legs, Thomas drops his head. Pushing Weller away with his boot, Thomas closes his eyes.

'Look, I know why you're here. It's about James, right?' Finch says, lowering the gun to his side.

'James's mother, she called you, didn't she?'

'Look, we had nothing to do with that. What James did, I mean, he tried to involve us, but....'

'Involve you how, what did he want you to do?' Thomas asks, watching Weller closely as he climbs to his feet.

'Look, James was my friend. Understand, we go way back.'

'Tell me, what did he want from you?' Thomas presses, his voice cracking into a sneer.

'To get rid of Erika, ok, to kill her, she was pregnant, he said she was going to ruin him. So, we told him, no, I mean, we grew up with the guy, but he had become an arrogant prick, got that from his dad, thinking he was going to be some big-time movie director, we all did back then, dreams of fucking Hollywood, awards, but look at us now, shit happens.'

'Did James kill Erika?' Thomas spits.

'Look,' Finch snaps, exhausted. 'I tell you this, you fuck off and leave me and my business alone?'

'Fucking tell me, or I by god I'll...' Thomas shouts, no longer able to control the devil rising up in him.

A tension-filled beat between them.

Staring down the drive at Thomas, Finch, shifting a look to the now sheepish Weller, cracks first. 'I don't know, truly I don't, but he sure had every intention to, even said he'd found the perfect spot picked out for her, by a lake. He used to take her there, back at the beginning, when he was piping her. Said she'd feel comfortable out there, out in the woods, said it would be romantic, almost poetic. Fucking prick, what did I tell you, but that was James. I mean he even wanted to screw her one last time before dumping her in the ground.'

31

25 days before Thomas's murder...

Poking his head inside the door, Thomas finds Emily to not only be awake but sat up in bed reading. Beside her, in the corner, Peter sits slouched, mouth open, asleep in a chair. Peter's snoring, while present, is both light and unoffensive. An open copy of *The Hollow Man* sits across his chest. A John Dickson Carr novel from the 1930s, a locked-room mystery, is like Amy's abduction in its most basic sense. Thomas assumes, along with other such books, are now research material for his young friend.

Knocking on the door, gently, as not to wake him, the girl looks up from her book, first to Peter, then to Thomas.

'Hey, it's ok. I'm with Peter, may I?' Thomas asks, gesturing for himself to enter.

Shifting a second nervous look to the sleeping Peter, her eyes snap back to Thomas.

'My name is Thomas William,' he adds, offering a smile.

'You're the one who pulled me out of there?'

'Well, me and Peter.'

With a soft nodding of her head, an action he takes as, *you can enter*, he steps into the room. The girl, Emily Lynn Hart, has her own room, which is surprising given the state of the NHS. Thomas suspects this is due to the inner trauma sustained rather than her outer injuries. Still, with the rain lashing against the lone window, the solitary side lamp, if not for the sleeping Peter, the room would be cold and dark. As there are no *get-well cards*, Thomas speculates the magazines, chocolates, and fruit to be gifts of Peter.

Looking at her, now without the makeup, while eighteen, Emily could quite easily pass for fifteen. She has the girl-Friday appeal with her short hair, fluffy and unkempt, and if it wasn't for her lips and big round eyes, she could easily pass for a teenage boy.

'He's nice, Peter; he's not left my side... he's only been kind to me.'

'Yeah, he's good like that,' Thomas agrees, his eyes moving to him.

Her guardian angel.

Smiling, Thomas concludes the girl to be in good hands.

'They say I should be able to go home in the next few days, once the stitches... inside me have taken time to set. No permanent damage, the doctor believes I'll be able to have children...' she says, looking down, tailing off.

Thomas is forced to blink back the anger from his eyes, or is it tears? Looking at the young girl, her petite shoulders, hips- thinking of her with Jez, recalling the sounds of him pillaging and purging her of her innocence and youth, her very soul, a hatred, new to him, settles at his core.

In his mind, he sees them, the young faces, the innocents, those forced to smile whilst being abused. An endless revolving stream, the starry-eyed, the drug-fuelled, the jacked up and energised. Then there are the vacant stares, those dull eyes void of a soul, young women and men, children, the faces that Thomas knows for a certainty, will stay with him forever, haunting his shadow.

Even the pushers and the performers, men like Jez, who too are victims of the industry, now occupy his mind. Now seeing it, breathing in the filth, Thomas knows he can no longer simply sit on the side-line as a spectator. Ignorance is no longer an excuse, nor is inactivity. Those of us who *can* do something *must* do something. His hands are dirty now, dirty and forever so, and there's simply no way to get them clean by continuing on like this. Ignorant and blind, that's him, but not anymore. Like those who see a crime and continue up the street, those who turn up the television when they hear a woman cry rape. Looking at Emily, feeling her pain, Thomas feels a shift at his core, be it a sickening twist, a knife pushing in deep, but still, one he takes for change.

Yeah, if I manage to survive, right?

Thomas tells himself that there is still time, reminding himself to continue his fight, but he still rues his mistakes, the blind alleys, the dead ends, his loves and loves lost, and the time wasted. It is as if now, this burden of time only serves to remind him of what could have been.

Approaching Emily, with a glum shadow dropping over him, he gestures to a plastic chair beside her bed and asks, 'may I?'

'Sure,' she tells him, still looking down at her lap, 'Did they hurt you, Simon and Morgan?'

'No, and they won't be contacting you again,' Thomas says and waits for her eyes to meet his before continuing. Removing his phone and finding Erika's saved photograph, he shows it to the young woman. 'Ever seen this woman? Her name is Erika Sobo. She's from Sweden.'

Looking at the phone, her eyes move over the screen but stay vacant.

'She's beautiful. But no, sorry. Is that who you were looking for?' She asks.

'Yes, but I am glad I found you.'

From his pocket, he removes an envelope and hands it to her. 'I'm not looking to tell you how to live your life, far be it for me to give life advice,' he pauses. 'It doesn't matter how you found yourself in that situation, and if you want, you can go back to it, but in the envelope, you'll find a name and number of an old friend of mine. He works helping young people like you, a good man, someone you can trust. So, if you want out, a new life, he can help you.'

Removing a folded piece of paper, opening it and reading, her eyes well up.

'And the money?' She asks, thumbing through the small bundle of twenty-pound notes left in the envelope.

'So, you can book into a hotel, get takeout, a change of clothes.'

Wiping away her tears, she looks at Thomas through glassy eyes. 'This is too much.'

'Please, you'll be doing me a favour. Trust me, I'd only spent it on cheap wine,' he tells her, smiling warmly. His eyes, for a moment, drift away. 'And that nonsense is in the past for me now.'

Now awake, Thomas finds Peter looking at him from the chair. His eyes are glazed, possibly due to waking or something else, but in hearing Thomas's words, he nods softly. Knowing precisely what the look on his face means, Thomas returns the gesture, smiling. Thomas hopes Peter knows just how much his help has allowed him to see his own strengths, his weaknesses. He should tell Peter, thank him, while he still has time, but he won't, can't, so he hopes through his weary smile, Peter knows just how much he appreciates the man he is, for the time he has spent at his side.

'You might want to stick with this one,' Thomas tells Emily, 'He might just make you a better person.'

Getting up, moving to the door, Thomas is stopped before leaving.

'I, um, this is not what I wanted, a life for myself, I mean,' Emily whispers.

Turning to face her, smiling softly, Thomas levels her with his eyes. 'No one does, no one, but if we're lucky, we get the chance to turn it all around, to change our lives, to rewrite our fate.'

'Is that what you're doing, changing things?' She asks.

Thomas notes hope in her voice, as if in agreeing with her, somehow, it'll make her journey back to the light that much easier. Thomas pauses to consider it.

'Yes,' he tells her.

'Never too late to turn it all around?'

'Never,' Thomas smiles in leaving, wishing he could believe it, feeling the weight of his pending death sour his hope.

His heart.

His soul.

32

22 days before Thomas's murder...

For the first time in a long time, words flow onto the page. Finally, sitting two-thirds complete, but with no type of conclusion, it is at least an accurate account of the disappearance of Amy and Erika from the facts uncovered as far. He resisted the urge to include opinions, preconceived notions, unsubstantiated reasonings or theories, and as such, his work is hollow, lacking no hint at a conclusion.

Did James kill Erika?

Thomas is now sure of that, but the link to Amy's abduction remains a mystery.

Hell, if there is even a link at all.

Jaded, Thomas drags himself up from the desk. Stepping away from the table, Thomas stretches, but the ache in his muscles remain.

You need to sleep.

He checks the time.

8:17 pm.

He considers calling it a night, turning in, and getting an early start tomorrow, but he knows a peaceful sleep will not be waiting for him there. Nightmares keep him awake, his pending death aside, nightmares are now the great worry. They grow darker with the night, horrible and sexual- masked intruders stalking him, Lilly, Mary... even Robin. Cold sweats, heart-attack pains in his chest, he wakes to the sound of a scream ripped from his own lips every time.

The phone ringing at the desk has Thomas turn to it wearily. Like the nightmare, the phone calls are now a constant thing. Picking the device, the screen ablaze, and as per the routine, the number is withheld.

Posting his contact details on ArmChairDics had been a bad idea, he gets that, but he was desperate. In fact, he still is. A few tips came through, nothing of note, but on the whole, honest people contact him and still do, with theories and suggestions.

These calls, however, are the opposite.

They follow a common theme- silent or heavy breathing throughout the day but mainly at night. On occasion, the caller will whisper, low and inaudible.

Thomas considers letting it ring but knows that this is no longer an option for him with time running out. Though he has no way of confirming whether the calls are linked to his investigation, they could be idiotic trolls for all he knows. However, still, he is tethered to them, nonetheless. Recognising the need for every little bit of information, every lead, even if it is the sound of heavy breathing, Thomas answers the call. Returning to the desk, sitting before his laptop, he lifts the receiver, placing the phone to his ear. He says nothing and instead listens.

Silence.

Which is nothing new.

Breathing, low and deliberate, reaches out from the darkness, burrowing its way beneath Thomas's skin, jabbing at his nerves.

Slamming down the phone, ending the call, letting go of the breath pitched at his lips, he closes his eyes.

Opening them, the laptop screen waiting for his return, the cursor blinks the name *Erika Sobo.* With his attention firming fixed on Amy and upon recognising the neglect he has shown to Erika, relegating her to little more than a minor character, Thomas decided, and rightly so, to give her a voice of her own.

Twenty-four, olive skin, while naturally a brunette, Erika donned a caramel, blonde tone before her disappearance, which elevated her Sunkissed skin. Thin rather than slender, but with hips perfectly suited to tight Levi's. With a family back in Sweden, she had come to the United Kingdom in May of 2017, looking to become a model. This she achieved, for a while anyway, leading her to Khaliq, then James. Speaking to the few friends who returned his calls, while both spoke highly of her, they had echoed their dissatisfaction with Erika's choice of men.

Nevertheless, it was clear that Erika loved James and planned a future for them to be together. James met her friends and her mum via facetime, he even set up an Easter egg hunt for her friend's twin toddlers. James and Erika went on weekend breaks and shopping trips and viewed at least three apartments in the city. But, in the end, like Amy, he too conned her, working them both, promising them the world, only to lose them both.

Discussing Erika's disappearance, her friends were eager to highlight her social media presence, or more to the point, lack of it. Erika was a constant user of Facebook, Snapchat and Instagram, but in the days before her disappearance, with James having stolen her phone, her updating was restricted to when she was home where she had access to her laptop. Since her disappearance, however, there has been no posts, likes or share. In fact, there has been no activity at all.

Reviewing her Facebook page- where Erika's friends had first left concerned comments, appeals for information and pleas for help and tips, the posts since have darkened. Frustration, fear, and the inevitability Erika is, in all likelihood, now dead.

'Erika, where are you, hon?'

And.

'If anyone has seen Erika, please DM me – this is urgent.'

And.

'My thoughts are with Erika's family.'

Thomas searched for but failed to find anything from James. No posts, no messages of support, or for information. Nothing. This again leads to the idea James, in some way, is responsible for Erika's disappearance, or at the very least, echoes the man's cowardice. Even his father posted a message, be it short and to the point, but his son, through it all, had stayed silent right up until his death.

Inevitably, assholes and trolls quickly reared their heads, with posts claiming Erika to not only be alive and well, but in hiding, simply craving attention in her disappearance. And there are those far more insidious, those people who used the internet to torture Erika's friends and family. One profile popped in the wake of her disappearance, claiming to be Erika, followed by a series of posted comments mocking her friends and family, James, and lifestyle choices. Venomous stuff, toxic and vile, the words of the insecure, resentful and uneducated. When the profile user failed to answer even one of five personal questions correctly posed by Erika's friends, the profile was taken down and flagged as an imposter.

A new Facebook page has since been set up in Erika's name. One created by her friends, dedicated to her disappearance. Clicking on it, Erika's warm face looked back at Thomas from the front page. Makeup free, the breeze tossing at her hair. Golden sand stretched out behind her, meeting and melding with the ocean, backed by a sky of stark blue. It haloed Erika perfectly, bringing life and warmth to her face. Her smile, not one for the camera, Thomas recognised was for the someone who stood behind it. Her eyes beamed, focused on a place above the lens, and her smile, while slight, oozed with feeling and a playfulness that brings tears to Thomas's eyes. Having ignored Erika, Thomas now feels shame in it and vows to do more, dedicating time to her and Amy.

For a second time, his mobile phone startles him from the table, the screen bright and jarring in his eyes.

Another withheld number.

Answering it, the familiar breathing from the other side finds him but is now accompanied by a low cry. Like a small bird, almost child-like, Thomas recognises the pleas of a helpless animal, possibly a cat.

Shaking, the phone twitching at his ear, Thomas forces his eyes shut as the cat begins to shriek. He should hang up, but he owes it to the poor animal to listen. The sound of water, the plunging of the animal, it struggling beneath the surface. In and out, again and again, the caller dunks the cat beneath the water until finally, the howls subside into the ragged murmurs of the dying. As the line goes quiet, which Thomas is thankful for, a new malevolence rushes through the line to greet him. From the silence, a bell pings through the line playfully, deliberately. And a voice, low and vile, drips with menace – it calls to Thomas.

'*Ding, dong, bell, pussy's in the well. Who put her in? Little Johnny Thin. Who pulled her out? Little Tommy Stout. What a naughty boy was that to drown a pussy cat? Who never did any harm? But scared all the mice in the Farmer's barn.*'

Again silence.

Thomas stands frozen.

After what seems like the longest time, finally, the line goes dead, and Thomas is spared the torture of his stalker.

The intercom buzzer sounds, shocking Thomas to his feet. Muttering, he moves to the receiver. All but ripping it from the hallway wall, he says 'Hi,' but doesn't recognise the voice on the other end.

'Thomas William?' Comes a strong female voice.

'Yes, speaking.'

'Detective Inspector Lena Hayes. Can I speak with you?'

'Ok, it's a little late,' he protests.

'It won't take long, thank you.'

A little angered, shifting his weight, he buzzes her in.

Moving along the hallway to the front door, Thomas watches her approach through the peephole. Not alone, a man follows her up from the stairs. Waiting until they've arrived at the door, he studies them for a moment. Removing the guard chain, he works down the door, one lock at a time.

Opening the door, struggling with its weight, Thomas finds Hayes, a small, stout black woman sporting a short, tidy afro tinted with just a hint of grey. She smiles, a perfectly rehearsed routine, he can tell.

'Hi, Thomas?'

'Yes.'

'This here is my partner, Sergeant Shaw. Can we come in?' She says, and in tandem, they show Thomas their identification.

Thomas takes his time to study their IDs. While still smiling, Hayes waits for him, though her expression shows signs of wavering.

'Thank you for seeing us,' she says, expertly breaking the standoff.

Holding the door open for them, leading them into the living area, he turns to face Hayes. She quickly snaps her eyes from the corkboards, back to him, but not before Thomas manages to catch the slip of her smile.

The two officers fan out. Shaw moves to the corkboard where he stands, his tall frame dipping low, seemingly interested in collecting information. Thomas takes him for a rugby player or regular gym-goer with his suit jacket struggling to contain his broad shoulders, chest, and upper arms.

'My research,' Thomas says, gesturing to the corkboards. 'I'm a writer.'

Shaw turns to look at him but does so with a flat expression. Thomas sees the workings in his eyes, the cogs turning. His short-cropped crewcut and lack of facial hair give him a boyish look, which lends to the idea his muscles and bodybuilding are a way of compensating.

'I see. We're actually here on a different matter,' Hayes says, her smile now gone.

'Ok,' Thomas says, her words pushing him back a step.

'Timothy Rice,' she says, almost accusatory in her tone.

'Never heard of him,' Thomas says, not recognising the name.

'I see,' she says, eyes fixed on him. 'You're a member of the website, ArmChairDics.com, you post on their forums, is that right?' But, again, her words are more of an accusation than a question.

Looking at her, to Shaw, whose attention has turned to the laptop at the desk and papers scattered about it.

'What's this about?' Thomas asks, finding his stance is now both pensive and defensive.

'How about StarKiller, recognise the username?' Hayes asks.

'Starkiller, yes, I know him.'

'And you didn't know his name was Timothy?'

'Was or is, what's happened?'

'Well, Timothy is why we're here, Mr William. We assumed you were friends.'

'Look, stop with the cloak and dagger act. What's this about?' Thomas demands.

'He's dead, Mr William, his mother, found his body yesterday morning in their basement, hanging, an apparent suicide.'

Thomas's mouth turns dry, 'my God. You said *apparent*?'

'Well, I have a few concerns with the scene. But, being a crime writer, you'll know the processes we must follow before we make any firm ruling either way. I understand the two of you have been in contact?' She asks.

'He was helping me, I mean, I'm writing a book about the disappearance of Amy Porter and Erika Sobo, we found him online, through the forums, all he wanted to do was help, a lot of members do.'

'What was he helping you with exactly?' She presses, her narrow eyes studying him.

'This apartment, the history, Amy Porter, she's my neighbour, I mean, she was, well before I moved in here.'

'I see. Were you paying Mr Rice at all, or was he working for you for free?' She asks.

'For free, why?' Thomas asks but snaps at the snooping Shaw. 'Do you mind?'

Shaw looks at him for a long moment, shifts his partner a glance, but returns Thomas's notepad to the table. Thomas reads the words on the page and feels his chest start to compress under the sheer weight of the moment.

I can't do that. Please listen to me. Tonight, you disappear. That's all I know. Either by your own volition or someone takes you

'Either by your own volition or someone takes you,' he says, quoting the text. 'What does that mean?'

'I write fiction so....'

'I thought you said you were writing about Amy Porter and Erika Sobo?' Hayes asks.

Thomas notices her eyes, narrow and cold, and how they study him without an ounce of sympathy or fairness.

'Doesn't mean it's not fiction....' Thomas starts, but again she cuts him off.

'I see, like a drama, I get it, I bet you'll sell a tone of copies,' she says, stepping closer. 'Mr William, are you familiar with Jack Unterweger, the crime writer....'

It's Thomas's turn to interrupt her.

His tone is heavy and harsh.

'And serial killer, yes, and I resent the accusation,' he says, the room spinning in sicking sways around him.

'Yes, that's right, the crime writer who became a killer himself....' Shaw adds.

'I want you to leave,' Thomas snaps, his words biting.

'Ok, thank you for your time,' she smiles, turning.

Following her partner from the room, she stops before the hallway to look over her shoulder at Thomas.

'So, you know, I'll be coming back, and when I do, we'll get to the bottom of this sick little story of yours. You have a goodnight, Mr William. I'll be seeing you.'

Dipping forward to tip an invisible hat, she follows Shaw down the hallway, leaving Thomas alone. Alone with the ghost of StarKiller to haunt him.

33

20 days before Thomas's murder...

'And who did you say you are again?'

'Thomas William, I'm a writer, and I really need to see your CCTV footage.'

The clerk, an enormous middle-aged man with a pumpkin for a head, stares blankly back at me. His sunken eyes are like little marbles set deep within his skull; they blink and flick from Thomas to Lilly, then back.

Reading his name tab, Thomas softens his tone, 'Look, Craig, I'm not asking to take it away or make a copy, just to the see it. A woman is missing, and all I know is she was here, her car was here, and now she's gone.'

Craig's beady eyes again move from him to Lilly, to a place beyond them, scanning the small shop and the other two customers.

'The Police already took a copy. She never even came inside, never got petrol. She parked her car out front, nothing more,' Craig moans, his voice whiny, almost petulant.

'But if we find her, with your help, Mr William here will name you in his book; you'll be a hero,' Lilly tells the man.

With narrowing eyes, Craig looks at her, the cogs, be it slow, clearly working behind them, but still, Thomas is forced to place his hands on the counter to stop them from shaking.

20 days left.

'Five minutes is all we need ok, you queue up the date, and we'll scan the information, easy?' Thomas adds.

'I could get sacked,' Craig moans.

'No one's getting sacked, Craig; you're doing the right thing here. You're helping us find a missing person; you'll get a goddamn medal,' Lilly crowns, an urgency to her voice.

A brief smile flashes across the clerk's face, his eyes shifting back to Thomas, Lilly, across the shop, out to the petrol pumps outside. Following the man's gaze, Thomas spots Peter walking the lot, taking photographs, as he would put it, 'snooping.'

Nodding finally, Craig gestures for them to follow him with a whip of his large, round head.

Moving to the right of the cashier desk, rounding it, Thomas heads through a doorway leading to the rear. Together, they shuffle into a cramped and stuffy hallway before packing into a small office behind the man. As Craig takes a seat before two monitors, Thomas and Lilly stand and watch as he cues up the footage.

Scanning the small room, Thomas finds a topless woman smiling back at him. Young, big-breasted, her hair in ringlets, the glossy film of the poster, the makeup of the young woman, and the apparent lighting do nothing for him except offer a reminder of the industry awaiting further investigation.

If I ever get the chance?

Dismissing the tatty old poster, he finds Lilly watching him, her eyes narrow. With eyebrows raised, a smile tugs at one end of her mouth.

'Caught you,' she whispers.

'No, I...'

Craig both interrupts and saves Thomas from finishing his sentence. 'Here we go. This thing works like a VCR, play, pause, rewind. I've paused it a little before she first arrives.'

Standing up, squeezing through them, he looks at Thomas with heavy, dowry eyes, 'five minutes, ok?'

'Thank you, Craig,' Lilly tells him, watching him leave.

Closing the door behind him, leaving them alone, Thomas snaps to it, dragging a second chair to the desk of monitors. Sitting down, Lilly joining him, he shuffles his knees beneath the desk. Studying the antiquated equipment, locating a series of buttons on a flimsy control panel, Thomas presses play, bringing the frozen image to life. Black and white, grainy, recorded with a frame rate of two seconds, the footage stutters and jumps. The service station's exterior is visible via a high, widely acute angle. Cars of different shapes come and go, as do people of varying descriptions, moving from their cars, vans, motorbikes to the shop and back in a blur of stuttering motion.

Small compared to other larger chains, the petrol station offers three pumps and a small convenience shop offering the essentials like bread, milk, booze and for some, cigarettes. Vehicles pull in from the left side of the lot and then depart from the right. At the top right of the image, almost out of view, three parking spots sit empty.

Pointing at the screen, her finger tracking, Lilly says, 'that's her mini.'

A dark-coloured Mini pulls in from the left, identifiable by its top painted with the Union Jack. Passing the pumps, it slows, its form shuddering to a stop. With it reversing boot-first into one of the parking spaces, Thomas finds himself moving closer to the small screen, eyes wide, fixed on the Mini. Minutes later, a dark, possibly a black two-door coupe pulls in alongside her mini.

'James?' Thomas asks.

'Yeah, that's him,' Lilly tells him, bitterness pulling at her words.

Stepping out from the Mini, Erika, removing what looks like an overnight bag, moves to James's BMW. Jumping in, Erika and James are both concealed from view, the distortion of the video, the lack of clarity, masking what lay behind the car's windows. After a while, James's car pulls back, turns and leaves the lot, disappearing from view.

'So, James did pick her up,' Thomas says.

Eager on the buttons, Lilly forwards the footage. A collection of sputtering images, cars and people zigzagging in and out of the frame, rain all the while helping to distort the image.

Eyes on the monitor, Lilly asks, 'how'd your daughter like the lamp?'

Lamp?

Thomas looks at her, confused.

'My shop, the one I gave you?' She adds.

'Aw yes,' shaking his head in recognition. 'Not given it to her yet, I will, it's just....'

'Just?'

Looking at her, surprising himself, he says. 'I've never been good at, well, being a dad, changing nappies, the crying, so as Robin got older, there was this inevitable gap between us, and though I try, I can't shake the feeling I make no difference to her life.'

'I'm sorry, Thomas, about losing Robin, I mean.'

'Thank you, but I think my grieve is a lie; it's nothing more than self-pity.'

Looking at him, thinking, Lilly runs her hand across the desk, over to him, interlinking her fingers with his.

'And I think you're far too hard on yourself,' she tells him. 'Tell me about her?'

The question, while simple, has Thomas taken aback. He goes to speak, but words fail him. In his mind, he sees her, outback, digging for worms, wearing only a pair of wellies, dirty knees, and that old Iron Man t-shirt of hers. Up until now, strange to think, but he honestly believed he hadn't taken in such details. In fact, he remembers it all. The crying, the laughter, the successful and the not so successful nappy changes, the worry, dentist visits and tears, her lengthy hair like that of her mother. Robin looks like her too, pretty and destined to be beautiful, but adventurous and funny. Thomas recalls the way she eats spaghetti, slurping and spraying, and the way she smiles when eating her dessert.

Turning, finding Lilly looking at him, like him, her eyes are misty with emotion. Awaiting his response, patient, she smiles softly.

'My daughter,' Thomas pauses. 'Robin, she's light, pure and heavenly, and I never saw it.'

'But you do now,' Lilly says.

Her words, kind, too kind for a man like him, bring with them a surge of energy, hope.

'My father worked all the time when Amy and I were growing up. With my mum not working, being a driver, my dad needed to pull doubles just so our family broke even. Looking back, I don't remember him leaving or his absence. I just remember him playing with us on the weekends, making forts in the garden, walking the dogs down by the stream. You do your best, and you try- it will be enough, trust me.'

'If I survive, right?' Thomas grins thinly.

Rolling her eyes, she turns back to the footage and continues to plough through, mashing down the fast forward button.

Thomas considers her words, her attempts at reassuring him.

'You're close, with your parents, I mean?' Thomas asks.

'Yes,' she says, her eyes focused on the monitors. 'The four of us, me and Amy, were the perfect family.'

'*Are*,' Thomas reminds her. 'You are the perfect family.'

'Yes,' she says, nodding, thanking him. 'And you?'

'I have an over barring mother. No brothers, no sisters. My father died when I was young, the Falklands.'

'I'm sorry,' she says, looking at him.

'HMS Sheffield. Twenty men died when it sank; my father was one of them.'

'A sailor?'

'No, a chef who died in the galley.'

'So, he died a hero,' Lilly says, not as a question, but as a statement of fact.

'No, I'm afraid, nothing so grand. He died slicing melon for the breakfast rush.'

'But he died doing what he loved, in the service for others?'

He fixes his eyes on her. Her words, her reasoning, flow into him.

'Yes, in the service of others,' he nods, his hand squeezing hers. Wiping tears from his cheeks, he says, 'wow, that's a lot to live up to.'

He takes a moment, and Lilly, at his side, waits for him. Thinking of Robin in such a way, his parents, where he'd expect an air of despondency to rush in, he instead finds only calm. This is new to him, a level of almost acceptance. He again clears his blurred eyes before returning to the monitor display to the blur of stammering footage. Thomas's eyes fix on the top right corner, to where the three parking spaces are located. Pressing play, Lilly reviews the passing cars...

She resumes the footage... and halts... resumes... and halts...

Slowing the tape, bringing it back to a two-second shunt, Thomas and Lilly draw closer to the screen. Through still raining, moving through the lot, a dark blob shudders into view, then stops beside the Mini.

James's car.

The tailpipe puffs out a cloud of grey smog. The car, like James, is nothing more than a nice suit, a suit with empty pockets and crappy lining. The engine sits idle, the vehicle sitting motionless.

The passenger side door opens, the footage shudders forward, and a figure climbs out from James's car.

'It's Erika,' Lilly moans.

Saying nothing, watching intently, Thomas follows Erika as she slams the car door, moving around the back, returning to her Mini.

Climbing in behind the steering wheel, watching James reverse and leave the petrol station, though faint through the windscreen, Thomas watches Erika drop her head, burying her face in her hands.

'So, James dropped her back here, I don't understand. This is the day she went missing, the last time anyone ever saw her?' Lilly says.

Confused, Thomas tries to think.

'Yes, she disappears shortly after this footage was captured,' he says, still watching Erika, who has disappeared behind the sun-visor.

'Doing her makeup?' He asks.

'Yeah, she looks upset, so I'd say she's straightening herself out.'

Seemingly done, Erika's driver's door pops open. Climbing out, she hurries across the lot to the shop, stopping at a payphone fixed to the shop's exterior wall.

'What is she doing?' Lilly asks.

'Making a call,' Thomas answers, but he is forced to elaborate with Lilly shifting him a look. 'Her mobile phone was missing; James had it in his apartment.'

Picking up the receiver, Erika quickly slams it back down within one frame, turns and trots back to her car.

'Couldn't have been important,' Lilly says, her eyes following Erika.

Climbing back in behind the steering wheel, starting the engine, Erika pulls forward, the Mini cutting through the lot to the exit, its union jack top fading within the noise of the frame.

Leaving the shop, they do so in silence, in thought, the footage adding to their confusion. The petrol station's open roof offers a canopy from the rain, so before proceeding further, Thomas stops and turns to his right—to the payphone. Thomas finds a laminated note tapped to the receiver, moving to the sole unit, hung against the wall beneath a plastic domed shield.

So, I guess it explains Erika slamming down the receiver.

'Out of order!' He calls over his shoulder to Lilly.

Away from the phone, leaving the cover of the open roof, walking across the lot, Thomas walks to where it meets the road. Stopping at the roadside, rain pounding the ground around him in heavy pellets, he waits for Lilly and Peter to join him before pointing to the right.

'James went right, heading back home,' he says. Turning to his left, he adds. 'But Erika went left, further into the woods, alone.'

* * *

'In here,' Thomas calls from the passenger seat.

Nodding, Peter drags the wheel to the left, skidding his Ford from the sleek road into the Service Station. Far bigger than the one before, this BP station sits three miles up the road on a large plot of land perfectly positioned before it forks towards the M25 and a path leading deeper into the woods.

Peter pulls the car to a stop behind a closed car wash, the wheels slipping. Thomas springs from the vehicle, eager and energised.

'I'll be back in a minute,' he calls, shutting the passenger door on his words.

Jogging alongside the car wash, through the lashing rain, he passes the row of sixteen pumps. Cutting across the lot to the side of the main building where a set of two vacant semi-closed payphones wait. Standing before them, beneath the overhang of the service station's roof, he pulls his mobile phone from his pocket, scrolls, selects a contact and presses the dial button.

'Hildur, it's me,' Thomas says, out of breath.

'Thomas. I'm guessing you want another favour?'

'Yes, sorry.'

'Will it get me into trouble?'

'Well, depends on how careful you are.'

Thomas hears her sigh, a huff and a puff, but more significantly, 'Ok, what is it?'

'Along with two numbers, both payphones, I'm going to text you a date and a window of time. I need you to find out if any calls were made from these two phones, and if so, I need the numbers dialled?'

'Oh, just that, you understand I need to use my contacts to get such information, and the trouble I could get in by simply requesting it?' She moans.

'I know, I wouldn't ask if I didn't think it was important.'

A pause, but through the line, Thomas notices the easing in her breathing.

'I know you wouldn't. Ok, Thomas, I'll get on it now.'

'ASAP, Hildur, please.'

'I said I'd get on it, didn't I?' She snaps.

'Thank you,' he smiles.

About to end the call, pulling the phone from his ear, the sound of her distant voice stops him.

'Thomas, Thomas?'

'Yeah?'

'So, are you going to come back and work for me or what?'

Smiling, he tells her, 'Hildur, you know what, I just might. And like you said, there's a story here, an important one, one bigger than the disappearance of two women.'

'What, really?' She asks with excited surprise.

'Speak to you soon, Hildur, and thanks,' Thomas grins, ending the call.

Formulating a message, along with the numbers listed on the payphones behind plastic coverings, Thomas adds the date Erika went missing, with a time and hour on either side of her visit to the petrol station before. Sending the information in one SMS message, he returns to Peter's waiting Ford.

Climbing in out of the rain, having already soaked him through, his wet clothes cling to him uncomfortably. Rainwater drips from his unruly fringe, streaking his face. Pushing the hair from his eyes, he finds Peter from the front seat, Lilly from the rear, looking at him expectantly.

Calming his breathing, he starts, 'ok, so James picks up Erika, I think fully intending to kill her.'

'Because of the murder kit found,' Peter adds.

'So, let me get this straight, James plans to kill Erika because she got herself pregnant, he buys, what a kill kit? Drives out to meet her, then what, he decides against it?' Lilly asks.

'I think so, yeah,' Thomas says.

'Yeah,' Peter agrees, nodding, eyes locked with Thomas's.

Lilly stares at them, unconvinced.

Noticing this, Thomas explains, 'ok, let's look at what we know. James and Erika met out here and then went off together in James's car. James had already taken her phone, believing she couldn't be traced, and with a copy of her keys back at his, after he's done with her, he can go back and stage the scene. Anyway, they meet, he takes her out to their old hook-up spot, where he fully intended to kill her. We know this because of the items found out there. Now, I don't think he buried it that day, but before, in preparation. I wouldn't be surprised if he parked his car right next to it – remember, it was found near the parking area near the lake. It's isolated, remote, and Erika felt comfortable there.'

'The perfect place to ambush her,' Peter adds.

Nodding, Thomas continues, 'they weren't out there long, which again lends to the idea he took her to the picnic stop at the lake. Now let's look at James- for someone who uses his phone almost all the time, the day she disappeared, along with Erika's, James left it at home.'

'Like you said, so they couldn't be traced,' Lilly says, her eyes flickering, working through the information.

'Yup, because he knew the phones would be traceable when pinged against phone masts. What he failed to plan for was vehicle number plate recognition- both his and her vehicle were picked up heading out of town,' Thomas says.

'So, why didn't he kill her? He put in all the effort so he could?' Lilly asks.

'God knows- change of heart, he came to his senses, bottled it,' Thomas pauses, considering something new. 'Maybe she wasn't pregnant after all, or maybe, she finally saw him for what he was and decided to simply walk away. The truth is, we may never know, but he orchestrated it to get her out there, and for some reason, he changed his mind.'

'And Erika heads off in the opposite direction,' Peter says.

'Ok, so where?' Lilly asks.

'I don't know, but after he dropped her off, not having her phone, she attempted to use the payphone back at the first petrol station.'

'But it was out of order,' Lilly says.

'Yes, so I'm guessing she stopped here, on her way to somewhere, and made the call. I have a friend running a check on the payphones now. If she called someone, we'll find out who.'

'So, what do we do now?' Peter asks.

Thomas opens his mouth to say 'wait,' but stops when he sees Lilly looking around, back and forth through the front and back windscreen.

'Lilly, what is it?' Thomas asks.

'It was near here, I'm sure of it, where James was killed, a mile north from here. Amy said he got out of the car, white as a ghost. It was as if he saw something in the woods, something that scared him enough to get out of the car.'

'Erika goes missing near here, then weeks later, he brings Amy out to the same place, what to kill her?'

Thomas considers this, confusion growing. Turning to Lilly, whose expression is now a mask of utter horror, he asks, 'you said they were away for the weekend, do you know where?'

'I, I don't know,' Lilly mutters.

'We need to find out, don't we?' Peter asks.

'Yes, we do, and in knowing, I think it might just solve this whole Goddamn nightmare,' Thomas declares.

34

18 days before Thomas's murder...

From the passenger seat, Lilly eyes the road and nods in agreement. 'Yes, this is where Amy parked, where James was killed.'

Pulling the car to the side of the road, Thomas wrestles with the wheel as the tyres slide across soppy gravel, loose mud, crunching stones into the ground.

'We have about three hours of daylight, we see anything, note it, mark it, if it gets too dark, we can always come back first thing tomorrow,' Thomas says.

Lilly nods her head in agreement and fastens her yellow, silky looking raincoat, flipping up the hood to cover her head. In catching Thomas looking at her, she asks, 'What?'

Wanting to say how lovely she looks, he instead says, 'nothing, sorry.'

While she appears to take enjoyment in this, in his discomfort when it comes to her, he doesn't mind. In fact, it fills his stomach with butterflies and fireworks.

Looking out through the driver's window, the tree line across the road sits back behind a wall of rain, falling in diagonal sheets. Fully intending to set off earlier, the rain from the night before continued into the morning, and by lunchtime, it had become a deluge. Finally, running out of daylight, they had decided to head off into the woods regardless. Peter had planned to join them and said he still might, but they had decided to leave without him with their spontaneous leaving just after 4pm.

Climbing from the car, zipping up his coat, pulling up the hood, he closes the door and moves to the boot. From the shade inside, he removes two flashlights and two ponchos.

'Picked them up this morning, pound-shop,' he says.

Offering Lilly both, while she gratefully takes the light, she declines the poncho.

'I'm good with my coat, thanks,' she smiles.

Dumping the ponchos back inside the trunk, he joins Lilly at the roadside. The road, shiny and sleek, pelted, still shows the signs of the accident. Black tyre marks scar the surface like bruises as if demanding the world never forget it.

'She had parked this side, and James crossed here, right?' He asks.

'One minute he was there, the next, he was gone, is how Amy described it.'

'And it was this side of the road, the woods, he was heading towards?'

'Yes. It was raining like today, and they were arguing.'

'Do you know what about?'

'Erika and James, the affair. Amy told him it was over, it upset him, but still, why would he get out? Amy said it was as if he saw something in the woods.'

Puffing out his chest, checking the road, he says, 'let's find out.'

All clear, they cross, Thomas leading the way, moving against the rain at his face. The treeline ahead is densely filled, but the trees are thin, primarily silver birch, white all the way up to green and orange heads.

'You said before, you don't know where they had been for the weekend?' He asks.

'Amy never said. They intended to spend the weekend together but started back the same day they left. She tried to forget what he did, but her love for him had gone.'

Nodding, recognising this himself, seeing how Mary's love faded so abruptly, he shuffles on, down a slight decline, stopping to hold out a hand for Lilly. Refusing this, she joins him in the ditch without the need for his help. Again, and even in the rain, the gloom of the clouds, Lilly finds a way to make him smile.

'I've been thinking about what you said before, about James's intentions with Erika,' Lilly says, stopping before the trees. 'Though

CCTV didn't show it, for all we know, James caught up to Erika and killed her just like he planned. And Amy, he could have planned the same, made up some crap about a weekend away and brings her out here.'

Thomas considers this, his eyes fighting against the downpour; he sees nothing but trees and a loose end in Lilly's theory.

Why did he get out of the car?

Beyond the trees, between them, he sees nothing of note, nothing to warrant James's odd behaviour, nothing which resulted in James leaving the car, leading to his death. Yet still, there is a silence between them, a deep hollow, a place where shadows converge and scheme.

Moving into the woods, the ground, a collection of loose foliage, though wet, is far from soggy, making traversal easy enough. With the evening fast approaching, the darkening sky and the canopy of trees leave the light below dim and defused, dying with every second. Though reduced by the tree limbs overhead, rain seeps through as a light shower, lone drips, and a fine mist.

The conditions lead Thomas to click on the torch, dropping a warm yellow cone of light at the ground before his feet. Lifting the torch, flicking it, the rain slashing at the beam with what looks like shards of ice, Thomas sweeps the light from left to right.

Looking at Lilly, following her lead, Thomas pushes forward, using the beam to lead the way. Finding pockets of dandelions and blue bottles, they press deeper into the brush, weaving between trees, avoiding patches of poison ivy.

'After this, when this is over, what will you do?' Lilly asks.

'I don't know,' he says honestly.

'What will you do about the hole?'

'Fill it in,' he says, looking at her through the rain.

'You're not at all curious about how it came to be?' She asks, stopping, staring at him.

'No, not really. There's no way of knowing what the hole is and where it came from, but no one should see their future, it's a curse, and it can't continue.'

And what of Timothy?

With the Police still yet to follow up on their earlier visit, with the investigation into Timothy's suicide remaining open, his death now lingers hauntingly within him. Another limb to the same tree, splintering from the case, growing wild but with no answer. Shaking his head, he pushes on, attempting to focus. Ahead of them, the density of the forest thins, making way for a set of trails. Forking off in four directions, Thomas leads Lilly forward, taking the path that best fits with the direction he was heading when he was killed.

The path, flanked by deep foliage, spreads out into a clearing. Thomas imagines the spot was once scenic and peaceful, complete with a small lake, now sits secluded and overrun with bramble and wild weeds. Instead, darkness looms large, the water now boggy, muddy, like thick oil, matches the grass, patchy, balding, dead. A collection of common Alders, trees with a fondness for water, line the bog, slowly dying, their trunks dark, their wilting leaves brown and dry.

An uneasiness stirs and flutters inside him, leaving him cold and hollow.

The place reeks of death.

Dark, sombre, deceptive.

The trees, the blackened bog splattered by the rain, the sound muffled and dull, are accompanied by a dead crow sitting part submerged in the slop. Broken beer bottles, crisp packets, and trash litter the area, while an old traffic cone protrudes partly from the mud at the far side. There are no sounds of birds, or insects, only the rain, the movement through the trees, and the distant hum of occasional traffic from the road.

Moving around the bog, Thomas anticlockwise, Lilly the other way, watching the slop as he goes, the smell of dead leaves and animal shit makes an appearance, stinging his eyes like sliced onions.

Meeting Lilly at the far end of the bog, her dour expression matches her tone, 'nothing.'

'I don't get it,' Thomas moans, turning back to look over his shoulder, back the way they came. Even from where he's stood, back through the woods, he can see the road, be it at a distance. A clear line of sight is achievable if caught at the right angle, even with the rain.

'There's nothing to see; from where he was, there's nothing here,' Thomas says, frustrated.

'There's something back here,' Lilly says but stops, eyes peering through the trees north of the bog.

Following her line of sight, at first, he sees nothing but the mesh of trees and foliage. Moving closer, adjusting his position, distant slithers of colour come into view between them.

'I'll be damned,' Thomas hisses.

'Could it be what James saw?' Lilly asks.

Looking over his shoulder, he says, 'I'm not sure. I mean, if you catch the angle right, maybe.'

'You hear that?' Lilly asks.

Turning, they attempt to trace the faint thuds, metal on metal, as it creeps through the trees.

'Let's go get a closer look,' Thomas tells her.

Eyes fixed on whatever it is hiding behind the trees, side-by-side, they start away from the bog along a dirt road. Rain rushes down to meet them as the tree cover recedes slightly, reduced to looping and curling overhead as a loose awning.

'What's stopping a stranger from kidnapping Erika? After making the call, I mean she could have driven anywhere,' Lilly says.

'She never left this area. Number plate recognition would have flagged it,' Thomas says as his eyes spy flashes of red through the trees to their left. 'I think there's a car back there?'

'A mini, Erika's?' Lilly asks, looking herself.

'No, I don't think so, different colour.'

Coming to a narrow country road, clotted with shadow, though asphalt-covered, its width barely enough to accommodate one car. Still tracking the object, they turn left onto the tarmac. Moving along its high banks of wet foliage, their already limited view is stolen from them.

'It's a house,' Lilly says, her head craned, looking over the bank, through the trees.

They stop at a turn-off marked with a sign stating: *Eagle's Birch.*

Eagle?

Reviewing the sign, the bronze eagle above the words, something is jostled free from his mind. Thomas isn't sure, but it begins itching at his memory.

'I guess we better see who's home.' Thomas says.

Nodding, leaving the road for the driveway, the house before them sits all but hidden from the world. A Swedish lodge of the future, how a home would look if made by Apple, the house sports sharp lines and arrogance in its design. Moving up the drive, it is impossible not to be in awe of the overall build. Obviously inspired by camping, the roof, A-framed, like a tent, a perfect upside 'V', its two points drop down into the earth act as the primary support for the structure. Over two levels, the inner section is cube-shaped, fully exposed by the glass at the front and back. Modern white surfaces are lit strikingly by a sprinkling of light sources across both levels. Clinically bright, the entire interior sparkles like whitened teeth.

'We shouldn't be here,' Lilly says. 'We don't know who lives here.'

Slowing, Thomas surveys the area. He eyes the double garage to the right of the house, and a spotless red BMW M2- a two-door teenage boy's wet dream- sits shimmering in the dye light.

Listening, straining against the rain, the previous sounds are now far more prominent. Metals, heavy and forced, thunder against one another. Thomas traces the sounds along the driveway, past the house on the left, where it fades with the limited view.

'Stay here, ok. I'll go and speak to the owner; they may have seen something,' Thomas tells her.

She looks at him and shakes her head. 'I'll come, but let's be careful, agreed?'

'It'll be fine,' he says, forcing a smile.

Where the woods and the bog had filled him with dread, this house, with its ultra-modern design, the clinically white interior, the bright lights, should set him at ease, but it doesn't. The clean and affluent don't always mean safe, and Thomas quickly reminds himself of this as they continue towards the house.

Stopping at the shallow stoop, Thomas peers in through the glassed front. Open plan, a lounge/diner and a kitchen area, all minimalist, clean, but sterile, are lit by a team of hidden spotlights on the ceiling. The ground floor is afforded a slight orange flicker from the log burner at its middle but does little to warm cold white surfaces, walls, and floor.

Locating the doorbell- a video doorbell of the future, Thomas presses the button but hears nothing from inside. Pressing it for a second time, Thomas dips his head closer to the glass, his eyes scanning the ground floor to the open staircase leading to the upper floor.

Fogging the glass, snapping his head back from the door, Thomas quickly wipes it with his coat sleeve. But instead, he manages to smear the patch, ruining the panel's perfect reflection.

'Thomas, someone's coming,' Lilly says, jolting him back from the door.

Following her eye line to the left of the house, he, too, hears the approaching sounds of crunching gravel beneath heavy footfalls. A man shuffles into view, appearing from the side of the house, half-shadowed by the failing light.

35

'Thomas?' The man asks.

'Ricky, Ricky Ruck,' Thomas says, not wanting to sound confused but failing. 'How are you?'

Ricky steps forward. Sleek with grease, pulling off blue plastic gloves, he smiles. 'Sorry, I was working out back'.

'Working?' Thomas asks, attempting to give himself time to think.

'I've got a hog due to be delivered in two weeks,' he smiles. Seeing the confusion on their faces, he adds. 'A chopper, motorbike, I make them custom.'

'So, not a wild pig?' Lilly laughs, nervous and obvious.

Smiling, Ricky's eyes linger on Lilly a little longer than Thomas likes.

'What are you doing here?' Ricky asks.

'We're here by chance, really. We've been walking the woods, investigating James's death,' Thomas tells him.

'James's death was an accident, Mr William, but I appreciate you looking all the same. No one else has. You're soaking, come in, please. I'll get you both a towel, a warm drink,' Ricky gestures for them to accompany him.

They follow him around the side of the house, along the sloping roof of the structure, to a side door. Ricky leads them inside and out of the rain, into an anti-room of sorts, a utility/wet room equipped with a shower and white goods.

Removing two large bath towels from a neat stack beside a sink, Ricky hands them one each before scooping up one for himself.

Removing his hood, Thomas wipes his wet face dry and moves on to his matted fringe. Watching Lilly, she does the same, and Ricky, now rubbing his damp hair dry, watches her with keen eyes.

Like father, like son.

'If you wouldn't mind removing your shoes, I'm something of a dirt and germaphobe,' Ricky asks.

Nodding, Thomas bends down to undo his laces. His right foot first, then the left, removing his shoes, Thomas places them to one side. With Lilly doing the same, they follow Ricky into the main house.

While fully exposed to the darkening clouds outside, the glassed front and back manage to leave the ground floor surprisingly airy. While it is warm, the open log burner providing natural heat across the floor is far from cosy. Positioned at the centre of the room with curved sofas encircling it, the burner spouts flames, their fingers lapping and dancing around chunks of timber at its middle. Heat reaches out from it, but the white, almost alien textures and furniture only act as a tonic of ice against the flames.

Closing the door behind them, the sound of rain outside all but disappears, reducing it to a slight patter against the glass, be it muffled. It leaks into the house, but it's quickly smothered by the gentle pops and crackles of the burner.

'Can I get you both some tea?' Ricky asks, moving to the open kitchen.

Like the rest of the house, glossy white, modern and expensive, its white granite surface sits polished and clutter-free. Unfortunately, while perfectly aligned, the white tiles scream surgery and antiseptic.

'Please,' Lilly says.

'Thank you,' Thomas adds.

Removing two mugs from a set of drawers, Thomas watches Ricky as he drops a tea bag into each.

With no need to boil a kettle, Ricky adjusts the handle of a fancy looking faucet, the tab producing boiling water instantly.

'Is it him, the man in the mask?' Lilly whispers at his side.

'No, different shape, height, it's not him,' Thomas whispers back.

But he does call himself, The Great Deceiver remember?

Watching him, dunking and re-dunking the teabags, he discards them in a bin, hidden with the worktop. Thomas observes him as short and wide, broad at the shoulders.

The guy looks like a goddamn bulldog, not the slender spectre who abducted Amy, who attacked Peter and me.

Leaving the kitchen, first handing a mug to Lilly, Ricky passes Thomas the other. Smiling with two rows of teeth to match the interior of his home- bright white, one shade below blinding.

'Thank you,' Thomas and Lilly echo.

Still, he stands looking at them.

'Ricky, I meant to apologise. I went to see your ex-wife,' Thomas says.

'And you survived to tell the tale?' He laughs.

'Barely, but yes.'

Turning, moving back to the kitchen, Ricky goes about fixing himself a drink.

Sipping his tea, warmth quickly floods through Thomas, followed by sharp sweetness to make him wince.

'Sorry, I forgot to ask and went ahead and put sugar in both. My mind lately, since James... well, it's been all over the place.'

'Which is understandable,' Lilly tells him, smiling, sipping her tea, seemingly happy just to be out of the rain.

'You're Lilly, Amy's sister. I mean, you look like her,' Ricky asks, again his eyes eager and lingering.

'Yes. I'm sorry for your loss,' she says, diverting her eyes to me.

A beat.

'And for yours, Amy was a good girl, an angel, and she was too good for James right from the start.'

Lilly nods, looking down, like Thomas, obviously a little uncomfortable by his candour. While Thomas agrees with what he says- him rubbishing his son's name, his tone not just surprises Thomas but unsettles him.

As Ricky goes back to finish making his drink, Thomas turns to the wall. From the front of the house, it runs all the way to the kitchen. Neatly plastered and painted an off white, its length is lined with framed photographs, breaking for the side door they entered. Neither cluttered nor intrusive, the pictures, a collection of memories captured in black and white, elevate the décor above the plain and the surgical. Drinking his tea, the sweetness setting his teeth on edge, he is drawn back to the pictures.

'So why go poking around the woods? I mean, my son died crossing the road?' Ricky asks from the kitchen.

Poking?

Interesting choice of words.

'Well, Erika was last seen near here, so,' Thomas says.

'Is that right?' He says with a short, stunted laugh.

Drinking the tea, scanning the photographs, tiredness falls over him. Rubbing his face with his free hand, he notes a series of shots showing the house at varying degrees of its build. From a hollow wooden skeleton surrounded by stacked lumber and grizzled machinery, the pictures progress to a finished image of the all-glass home Thomas now stands in. There are shots of different motorbikes and classic cars, some mid-rebuild, others complete, all chrome and shiny. While he notes the photographs of James, as a baby, all the way through to adulthood, a great number of other pictures show Ricky with an assortment of different women.

Still reviewing the collection on the wall, feeling a vibration from his pocket, Thomas removes his phone and answers the incoming call.

'Thomas, it's me, last favour, ok, but I have the information you asked for,' Hildur barks down the line.

Stopping, Thomas's eyes lock, freeze on one photograph. An older image from an earlier time shows the bog outback and an old tractor stuck in the mire, all but sunken. A group of men stand frozen in time, wrestling, hauling it clear with a rope and winch.

'Thomas, are you there?' Hildur snaps, jarring Thomas away from the photographs.

'Sorry, yes, what did you find?'

'Well, only three calls were made from the two numbers, period. The first was to a Miss Katie Lynch, the second to a Mr Trevor Clyne, and lastly, one call was made to a Mr Ricky Ruck.'

His blood runs cold.

'Thomas, did you hear what I said? She called James's father the day of her disappearance; you know what that means don't you?' Hildur asks.

'Yes, thanks, Hildur. I'll need to call you back.'

Terminating the call, his eyes return to the photograph from before. He eyes the bog and the tractor almost hidden below the mud. It stays that way until a loud crash, echoing through the room, tears his eyes from the wall.

'Thom...as I feel....' Lilly stammers, her cup shattered at her feet.

Collapsing with wide eyes, Lilly drops to the floor like a rag doll. Thomas tries to rush to her but finds his heavy legs unresponsive. While his mouth opens, it is silent and voiceless. A growing numbness quickly spreads through his chest, legs, and arms. Finally, the combined effect drops him to his knees, the floor, in a messy sprawling heap.

Facedown, Thomas's cheek pressed against the cold tiled floor, he looks at Lilly, who looks back at him, her eyes wide, fear coursing through them, agitating them.

He looks for Ricky but finds he is unable to move his head. In fact, he cannot move at all – his entire body paralysed, numb and distant.

'Lil...lly, weee neee,' his ability to speak too has been stolen, leaving him to communicate through mumbled moans and low grunts.

The tea, that's why it tasted so sweet.

A movement to his left, urgent feet moving across the tiles, leaves Thomas cold, stopping his heartbeat and stealing it from his chest.

If I could move, I can...

Feet appear at his side.

Thomas is rolled over, flung onto his back.

Above Thomas, looming, his face now different, darker, Ricky looks down at him. His expression is mixed, almost annoyed. Moving again, all business now, he quickly takes hold of Thomas by his ankles and pulls.

Dragging him, past the plush sofas, past the kitchen area and dining table, Thomas tries to reach out with his hands to grab hold of a table leg, but his limbs are unresponsive.

Panic swirls within him. An icy panic of uncontrollable fear.

Being paralysed, he screams, but his words are hushed at his lips.

You idiot, fucking idiot, you walked right in, and now you're going to die.

36

Thomas is dragged through the opening at the folding-rear doors. His rump first bangs up over the lip of the door, followed by his shoulders, his head. A surge of pain cracks his skull as his body drops and again as his head slams the paving slabs outside the door. The impact knocks his head sideways, flashing white strobes of light through the vision. From this new perspective, with the rain lashing at his face and eyes, he cannot see where he is being taken. Instead, he is forced to look at the passing treeline, the dense forest of greens and browns, and something else, something hiding, peering out from cover. Thomas tries to focus on it, but it is gone in a blur of movement.

As he is again dropped, this time from the patio slabs down to sharp gravel, Thomas manages a series of unintelligible groans. Dragged, his head bumping along the bed of sharp stones quick to scrap his skull, Thomas is aware of a dull yet distant numbness returning to his fingers, his toes.

I need to stall him.

Yeah, but you can't talk, remember?

Dragged from outside to inside, the rain stops, and the light recedes. Thomas can make out a workbench topped with machine parts, raw chunks of metal from his fixed angle, a garage or workshop of some kind, all set before a wall of tools. To the right of the workbench, inside his cone of view, is what looks like a homemade forge complete with a cement stove and iron hood.

His legs are dropped, and his feet slap the concrete floor. Thomas can hear Ricky moving around but cannot place him. His moving feet dissipate, and if not for the rain pounding the concrete, Thomas would be left in silence, alone, waiting for Ricky's return.

Ok, so he's going for Lilly, so you've got two minutes, three tops.

Again, he tries to move, and while his arms and legs are unresponsive, he now feels pressure in his head and neck muscles. Straining against the numbness running throughout him, he pushes upward with his head, his neck taught from the strain.

As if controlled by an external source, like a videogame controller, he manages to twist his head, inch by agonising inch. Looking up at the ceiling, like the main house, it is tent-like, its peaked tip is blotted black above the hanging light. Lifting his head an inch from the ground, twisting again, his eyes desperate to understand his new surroundings, find more tools, car/bike parts, oil drums and red-metal storage cabinets.

Movement in his peripheral brings a stop to this, stopping his heart momentarily. Quick feet shuffle across the concrete, the rain shifting as someone moves inside the workshop, and words whisper in from behind Thomas.

'Thomas, can you move?'

Though recognisable and given his current state, the voice leaves Thomas struggling to place it.

'Thomas, can you move?' The voice repeats.

Peter?

A burst of hope shoots through Thomas, energising his limps.

Appearing at his side, looking down at Thomas with glassy, wild eyes, Peter drops to his knees. Wrung with anxiety, his face glistens with a pale, white sweat.

'Jesus, can you speak?' Peter asks, a growing urgency in his voice.

As Thomas tries to speak, his panic-stricken face drops down to meet his lips.

'He... dru...gggged us, can't... movv... vve,' Thomas stutters.

'Well, I can't lift you all the way, so you'll need to help me,' Peter stresses before stepping behind him. Scooping his arms under Thomas, looping them under his armpits, with a grunt, Peter heaves. Thomas is hauled up to a sitting position as if on a pully.

With one hand on Thomas's back, Peter, now crouched at his side, takes hold of Thomas's chin with his free hand. Twisting it to face him, Peter says, 'I am sorry about this,' and rams his index and middle fingers into Thomas's mouth, past his lips, over the tongue and down his throat. As his fingers press in further, deeper, reaching his tonsils,

Thomas's insides shift. Heat rises from within, from his gut to his throat. Warm, fresh vomit spurts from his lips, down his front, over his lap and trousers. As if a switch has been flicked, the heavy haze across his eyes begins to fade.

The feeling of blood pumping returns, rushing through his limbs, stabbing the weight of pins and needles at his fingers and toes.

'Call, call the Police; he took my phone,' Thomas mutters.

Peter looks at him. His expression is lucid with worry. 'I left it in the car.'

'Shit,' Thomas groans, trying to move. 'Lilly, we need to go get her.'

'We will, but we need to get you out of here fir....' Peter starts before the words are ripped from his lips by the scream of a gunshot.

Piercing and loud, it shatters the stillness of the evening before boomeranging around the workshop, rattling around Thomas's skull with teeth-gritting pain.

Warmth again washes over Thomas. Stunned, he is quick to note why. Showered in blood, shocking in both its volume and dark shade of ruby, Thomas turns to look at Peter, whose mouth has dropped open in silent surprise.

Peter fumbles at a ragged wound at his shoulder. Glistening, spouting crimson, he slumps over, hitting the concrete beside Thomas.

'Peter?' Thomas asks, his voice frail and cracked.

'He, he's coming,' Peter whispers, eyes wide, the words dying on his lips.

Sluggish and awkward, Thomas drops his hands to the floor. He attempts to push himself up but finds he has neither the strength nor the motor skills. Thomas is instead struck across the back of the head, sending a streak of white pain across his eyes, chased away by a sudden and cold blackness.

His eyes flicker, the weight pulling at the lids, leaving him with an overreaching threat of passing out. A lazy haze of pain tugs at him, pulling him under. Fading, the world dulls all around me, the black edges closing in.

Thunder snaps from the heavens, hateful and final, slitting the world above with a primal roar. Snapping open, Thomas's eyes grow wide, blinded by a startled haze.

Did I pass out?

Thomas finds himself lying on his side. Peter, looking across the floor at him, now pale and ghostly, stares at Thomas with a death gaze, and if not for him blinking, Thomas would take him for dead. Peter's young face, now alien and contorted, is a mask of glassy anxiety. Laying within a pool of blood, it is both extensive and appears copper-like in the firelight.

He's fired up the goddamn forge.

How long have I been out?

With movement and shuffling, quick feet appear from Thomas's left. Ricky's feet. And Lilly's limp body dropped down beside him.

Dropping her feet first, Ricky moves away, again disappearing. Looking at Lilly, her drugged, shiny eyes locked on his, Thomas sees fear within them and the freighting reality of pending death. Straining, Thomas reaches out and takes her hand in his. The effort required all but drains him of all reserves. Looking at her, then Peter, dying in front of him, Thomas rues their chance at escape. With a loud clatter of metal, with the darkening of the workshop- Thomas resigns himself to death. A lifetime of failure and shame, all culminating, leading him here to the killer.

I should have gift wrapped myself.

Bitter and powerless, he lays in wait.

It could be the name of my autobiography.

He might stay this way if not for Lilly and the single tear escaping her left eye, it circling around her nose on its way to the ground. And, as if on cue, movement at the workbench alerting him to Ricky's location. With the clatter of metal, the hum of a machine of some kind coming to life, Thomas puts his plan in place.

'Erika... she's... out in the bog, isn't she?' Thomas asks, his voice barely enough to reach up above the racket over by the bench.

'You stupid fuck,' Ricky laughs with his back to them. 'James and Amy turning up for the weekend had me scrambling, I'd admit it. I had that dumb bitch's car dismantled outback.'

Finally, a lightbulb pings on in Thomas's skull.

'He saw it, didn't he, James, her Mini, the roof painted with the union jack? You knew he'd take the blame, your son?' Thomas says more as a statement than a question.

'Hum... just so you know, I intend to dismember you and combine your remains with molten metal to weigh you down.'

His words, harsh and final, bring terror to Lilly's eyes. Thomas's bowels, matching her reaction, squirm and roll over.

Keep him talking, Goddamn it.

'And Amy, why her?' Thomas asks.

Ricky turns, his eyes glaring,' What the fuck are you talking about?'

'I know what you did. I have evidence, a digital copy at a secure location,' Thomas bluffs.

Ricky says nothing but instead laughs, as you would to a child. He turns from his captives and continues with what he is doing. Carrying a chunk of metal over to a large metal drum, he dumps it inside before heading back to the workbench to collect a second chunk. Repeating this action, now with the third piece of metal deposited inside the drum by a handle on its side, Ricky drags in the large metal stove. Putting on a pair of gloves, the heavy-duty kind, Ricky opens the stove's door, releasing a wave of incredible heat. It quickly spreads out across the floor, leaving eager flames to roar from both sides of the furnace.

'You hear me; everyone will know what you did,' Thomas continues, desperation tainting his obvious words.

'You lie,' he says, unconvinced.

Collecting a long metal pole from the tool rack above the workbench, its crescent-shaped end fits perfectly around the drum. Pushing, Ricky forces the heavy drum inside the stove, where flames quickly reach out and dance around it before retracting the tool and closing the door.

Though confused about what this means precisely for them, Thomas recognises the mortal danger they are now in. He lets go of Lilly's hand, palms down on the cold concrete floor, he pushes himself upwards. Straining, all but failing, he somehow finds the strength to drag his heavy body up to a sitting position.

Turning, Ricky looks down at him. Seeing his condition, Thomas panting like an old dog, a smile creeps across his face. Garish in the glow of the firelight, the man's laughter is one of a man who knows the truth and fully intends to mock Thomas in his final moments.

Looking at Lilly, her eyes, red, pleading, bring warmth to Thomas's chest, strange considering the situation. Dropping his head in defeat, Thomas starts to cry. Whimpering, circuitous, Thomas whispers to himself, the words, 'Amy, Erika, dead, the bog, murderer,' all hushed but audible.

Laughing still, Ricky approaches Thomas, taking a knee at his side. He looks at Thomas, amused and curious, his smile playful. 'What, what would you like to say?'

As if unaware of his presence, head down, Thomas continues, 'Amy, you killed Amy, Erika, the bog, buried, both, murderer.'

'What?' Ricky dips his head in closer, his ear edging closer to Thomas's mouth, laughing all the while

The laughing stops with a sickening thud.

Falling back, collapsing beside Thomas, rump first, Ricky stares back at Thomas with wide eyes, his mouth sagging open and growing.

'Knife in the sock-trick,' Thomas tells him, which is met by a cracked laugh from Peter.

Looking down, dazed, Ricky's hands go to his side and the growing red patch seeping out from the protruding knife at his ribs. Doe-eyed, he takes the blade in his left hand and slowly pulls at it. The long slither of silver slips from his shirt, expelling a gush of blood in its wake. A whine, high and pitched, escapes his lips.

Holding the knife, his child-like expression changes back to the cocksure asshole from before.

Grunting, 'motherfucker,' Ricky pulls forward. Using his right hand for support, he readies the knife. Poised to strike, the pending attack is halted by two legs from his rear, wrapping around his waist.

Lilly's legs.

Lilly uses her thighs to bite down on Ricky's torso, squeezing him like a hungry python. Ricky roars with pain, blood spilling from his wound around her clamping legs. Pulling him backwards, he struggles atop her, squirming. With the knife in hand, waving it around like a mad man, blindly he searches for her with the blade, desperate and wild, he screams like a dying banshee.

Rolling to his left, Thomas reaches out and grabs Ricky's boots. Pulling at them, he drags himself up his body, clawing at his trousers, legs, and belt.

Groaning, Thomas reaches out and makes a play for the knife but instead clamps his hand down on the blade itself, its lower edge slicing into his hand and the fleshy skin of its palm.

As Thomas screams and retracts his hand, rolling, Lilly tilts to her left, sending them all sideways. They land on their sides with a thud,

Thomas and Ricky come to rest in some kind of perverse embrace, whilst the knife, springing loose from Ricky's grip, clatters the concrete.

Scrambling for it with an outstretched hand, Thomas's fingers crawl at the ground, inching closer. With his right hand, Ricky sends a fist into Thomas's wounded stomach. A second punch has a gut full of air bursting from his lips, leaving Thomas with pain searing through him, and as such, it is like being injured all over again.

As Ricky readies a third fist, Thomas waves a feeble hand before his face. Closing his eyes, he prepares himself for another blast of pain. Instead, a high-pitched shriek shatters the carnage.

With her right arm wrapped around the man's face, Lilly claws at his right eye with her middle finger. With it hooked inside, pressing her finger in, blood pools around it as it roots in deep.

Now all but given up on the knife, Ricky still screaming, instead lashes about in wild, animal-like waves.

Growling, Lilly booms in his ear, 'either you stop moving, or by God, I'll fucking rip it from your skull?'

And like that, like a good boy, Ricky stops moving.

37

13 days before Thomas's murder...

'I hear you'll live,' Thomas says from the doorway.

'Is that what they're saying?' Peter asks, peering over a worn copy of *LA. Confidential.* 'I'm quite the stir around here; the nurses are extremely attentive.'

'And the arm, I understand it's two inches shorter?' Thomas smiles, entering the hospital room holding a tray of original glazed Krispy Kreme doughnuts.

Crossing the room, Thomas places the treats down upon the bedstand in front of Peter. Thomas stands looking down, taking in his condition. Clearly wrecked, with an arm in a sling, puffy purple bags underline his eyes, still, the young man sports a smile.

'How's the hand?' Peter asks.

Looking down at his bandaged hand, Thomas grimaces. Stitched, healing, but still sore, flexing his feels send a wave of pain up his arm.

'Well, typing is proving arduous.'

'*Literally* shedding blood on the page,' Peter smiles, 'How very Shakespeare.'

'Quite,' Thomas says.

A beat between them.

Their eyes lock, the horror of what they've seen, how close they'd come to death, all of it, pour out through them. Turning his head, Peter diverts his gaze to the window. Blinking back tears, he wipes his cheeks with his one free hand. Thomas gives him a minute, and surprising himself, he reaches out and places a hand upon the young man's shoulder.

The rain upon the lone window, rather than mocking Peter, instead does its best to mask his tears.

'What's, what's the news?' Peter asks with a tight throat.

'They've drained the bog,' Thomas says. Removing his hand, sliding it into his jean pockets, he drops his head. 'They've recovered the remains of at least one female and a car, be it in pieces.'

'Erika?' Peter asks.

'They haven't announced anything official yet, though it does appear the car parts found do match her Mini. From what I've learned so far, it will take time to fully identify her. It appears he dismembered her then set her body parts in block mould with melted metal, you know, as to weigh it down, just like he told us.'

'He was going to do the same to us, wasn't he?' Peter asks.

'Yeah, he was. He drops the dismembered body into a mould, then pours in the melted metal, and when it's cool, he sinks it in the bog, like an iron anchor,' Thomas tells him.

'So, James was innocent,' Peter says, as a statement of fact, not as a question.

'Well, I wouldn't say innocent. James took Erika out there to kill her, he had every intention to do just that, but I think when it came to it, with them talking, maybe he learnt she wasn't pregnant after all, or he saw sense in what he was about to do, either way, he dropped her off, completely unaware she had been speaking to his father behind his back. It wasn't the first time Ricky cashed in on his son's success with women.'

Peter looks at him, his eyes wide with questions. 'Are their others?'

'Dead? We don't know, but it's clear between them they were sharing women. I mean, the pair were in competition.'

'Competition, what does that mean?'

'They found a spreadsheet on Ricky's hard drive, Ricky versus James, father versus son. One point for a blonde, two for a brunette, three for a redhead.'

'Jesus,' Peter hisses.

'It gets worse. Extra points were awarded for age, breast size, sex acts, well, you get the picture.'

'My God. And Amy?' Peter asks, looking at him, hopeful.

'Nothing yet, but there are other bogs, lakes, so it's only a matter of time. I've passed on everything to the Police, the mask linked to Max

Rex, links to Amy, everything except the hole. They're searching Ricky's property now, the grounds, sheds and lockups,' Thomas says, turning again to the window.

'I'm sorry, Thomas, I really am, but at least now you're safe?'

With what should have been a relief, finding the killer, solving the case, and getting a second chance at life, Thomas's world is instead left hollow and cold with them yet to find Amy. Wiping tears from his eyes, Thomas takes a moment before turning from the window.

'Spend time with Lilly, with your daughter, and finish the book,' Peter says, his voice soft.

'You don't need to worry about me,' Thomas says, his voice now struggling.

'Both Erika and Amy, their stories need to be told. You owe them that; you owe it to yourself,' Peter tells him.

Turning, Thomas finds Peter's glassy eyes watching him. With concern staining them, Thomas offers him a smile in return. Nodding, Thomas tells him, 'thank you.'

From the corridor, a shadow appears at the open door. Sliding into the room, her trainers squeaking against the linoleum floor, Emily offers a shy smile.

'Hey Thomas,' she says.

Along with sporting a sundress and a clip in her short fringe, there is a new colour to her skin, her eyes. A new energy, a new lease of life. Somehow, through it all, thankfully, she's been allowed a second chance, a return to what she is, a girl and nothing more- one with options, one full of hope for the future.

Smiling, she looks at Peter, who smiles in return, one of warmth beaming through his eyes. Entering the room holding a stack of old paperbacks, Emily moves to his bedside.

Moving around the bed, heading to the door, Thomas gives them both a smile.

'It's good to see you up and at em,' Thomas tells her.

Placing a hand on her shoulder, he squeezes and heads for the door.

'We did some good, didn't we, Thomas?' Peter calls from the bed.

Stopping at the door, turning to Peter, his eyes wide, Thomas recognises the depth of his question. He, too, feels it, the need for an answer that will make sense of it all, some resolution to make it all better, one to chase away the nightmares, the dirt from under their nails. No plaster, no going to bed with a glass of warm milk and waking the following day with the wounds all mended. Change and healing take time, and while Thomas knows, for him anyway, it may take the rest of his life, Peter doesn't deserve to hear that. For a man like Peter, what the man he strives to be, he deserves better than the truth.

'Yeah, we have,' Thomas says, though not believing his words.

Thomas knows hauntingly, for himself, that it will only be over when they find Amy.

Until I find her.

'I'd like to work with you again,' Peter asks. 'If that's ok with you?'

Before leaving, Thomas turns and smiles. 'I hoped you would.'

38

3 days before Thomas's murder...

'And you believe this Ricky Ruck killed Timothy Rice?'

Thomas sits, his face pinched, his expression pained. Rubbing his eyes, unable to remove the layer of frustration and exhaustion from them. Hayes and her silent partner, Shaw, stare back at him with expectant eyes from the sofa. To break their gaze, Thomas stands up from the desk and moves to the corkboard. Pausing before speaking, attempting to select his words carefully, he instead flounders. Linking Timothy's death to Ricky Ruck is tenuous at best, but there is a connection; there must be, though Thomas has yet to find one that makes sense.

'You said yourself you had concerns with the scene. Ricky Ruck killed his son's lover and possibly his girlfriend, Amy Porter. Everything I've discovered has led back to him, though I'd admit there are still some grey areas,' Thomas says, his words bordering on protest.

'But you said Mr Rice was investigating this place, Pinegrove. So why would Mr Ruck kill him?' Hayes asks.

Her oval-shaped plump face, stoic and pensive, has a look Thomas takes as her natural mask.

Turning his head, Thomas's eyes shift to the wall, the painting, and the hole. He considers the connection, and while preaching it, he recognises the lack of any real supporting evidence tying Ricky Ruck to Timothy.

'I... look, I don't. I'm trying to help,' Thomas says, rubbing his face. 'I didn't know Timothy, we spoke a few times, and he offered to help me.'

'Help you with your book, for free, you mean?' Hayes asks, almost accusatory.

'You already know he was,' Thomas says.

Thomas pauses. Breathing deeply, he sighs with exhaustion.

Still, her eyes watch him. He can tell that they are judging him, though he now no longer cares.

'Look, he seemed like a good kid. Smart, and yes, he was helping research my book. He had passions, hobbies, and well, in my opinion, he didn't appear suicidal,' he says.

Still, the two Police Officers look at him. Doubt hangs between them, doubt, and lingering questions. They stay silent for a moment longer than they should, an apparent attempt at letting Thomas stew.

'The day he died, Timothy came here.' Shaws says, breaking the silence. 'Why?'

Thomas looks at him, 'what?'

'Mr Rice came here; his mobile phone pinged off a local mast,' Hayes adds, her eyes narrowing. 'What did you talk about?'

They continue to scrutinise him with piercing eyes, cold and apathetic, as you would an insect within the sphere of a magnifying glass.

He came here?

'We didn't speak, I mean....'

'You didn't speak to him, or you didn't see him at all?' Hayes asks.

'I, um,' again flummoxed, Thomas blunders his way through a response. 'He may have come here, but I never saw him.'

'And the phone call?' Shaw asks, eager with the question.

Hayes, shifting her partner a look, turns back to Thomas.

'Call, I never received a phone call?' Thomas protests.

'He called you from here, from Pinegrove, the call lasted for three minutes, and you don't remember it?'

It hits him.

The telephone call he received when hiding in the shower before escaping with Emily. The call he let go to voicemail.

'Mr William?' Hayes asks.

'I don't recall that. I'm sorry, I really am, but I don't know what else I can say to help.'

They look at him, calm and cool, studying him. Looking at Hayes, whose eyes glisten with activity and thought, Thomas offers a weak smile, one born from discomfort.

Closing her notepad, Hayes gives Shaw a frustrated look. Pulling themselves up from the sofa, Hayes leading the way, she offers Thomas a thinly false smile. Disappearing in seconds, when removing a business card from her pocket, when handing it to him, her face turns stern, her lips pressed.

'We'll be seeing you, Mr William,' she says.

Nodding her head as if tipping an invisible hat, she smiles and starts for the hallway.

'Mr William, you remember me mentioning Jack Unterweger?' She says, looking over her shoulder.

Of course, the crime writing turned serial killer of women.

'I remember the insinuation, yes,' Thomas says.

'Very good, Mr William, the insinuation, I like that,' she says, nodding, her words sharp and icy. 'It is written, Mr Unterweger thought a lot of himself, saw himself as genius, but the truth is, he wasn't half as smart as he thought he was. Through all his schemes, his lies, he still got himself caught.'

'I'll keep that in mind,' Thomas says. With her turning again to leave, Thomas stops her in the hallway. 'If you don't mind, seeing that it's an important factor, what's my motive to kill Timothy?'

Turning slowly, as if to take her time to answer, when she looks at him, her face holds a new level of disdain that is quick to leave Thomas flat-footed.

'A motive, well let me see. How about this- snooping, he found out something about you, a secret maybe?'

'Sounds a little farfetched, don't you think?' He asks.

'Well, I don't know. Let's see, you move into an apartment building where only weeks earlier, a woman in the neighbouring apartment went missing. You then, being a writer, start to write a book about it. Coincidence? Sure, you're a writer, just not a very good one, one who needs inspiration because he has none of his own. You see, I've read your work Mr William, researched you, your failures, your marriage, and to me, it looks like you needed an idea, a nugget you can turn into a pot of gold. How's that sound?'

'So let me get this straight, not satisfied with murdering Timothy, you've also got me pegged as Amy's abductor?' He asks, stunned.

'Maybe you're right, just my farfetched imagination. But, on the other hand, maybe I should be a writer,' she smiles. 'I guess we'll just have to wait and see.'

Departing, they leave without saying anything else, as if to leave her last words to linger. Her warning taints the air with the desired effect, leaving his mouth dry, his blood boiling.

Slamming the door, watching them leave through the peephole, Thomas quickly goes to his pocket. Retrieving his phone, Thomas dials his voicemail. Skipping through three messages left by the woman handling his custody case, four from his mother, he finally settles on the one left by Timothy.

On the day he died.

'Thomas William, the writer, it's me.' Timothy starts through the phone. 'I'm over here at Pinegrove, pick up if you are home. I'm a little confused, the building appears to be owned by twin sisters Grace and Marlene Edwards. They started renovating the building into apartments back in 2018, fully intending to live here themselves... yeah, sorry, I thought I heard something. Anyway, I can't find any trace of them. It appears they disappeared... Thomas is that you....'

The line goes dead.

What the hell was he talking about?

Stomping back along the hallway, Thomas stops at the bathroom before returning to his laptop.

Unclipping his belt and sliding the zipper down, he drags his jeans down his tired legs. Struggling with his strapped hand, as his ass hits the seat, his mobile phone wails from the living area.

'Christ!' He groans.

Yanking his jeans back up, he fastens his belt as he leaves the room.

Returning to the living area, struggling with his zipper, feeling it crumble in his hands, he stops short in recollection.

His eyes find the wall, the hole.

My broken zipper... I remember...

'Lilly,' he says aloud, recalling seeing this very moment before.

Rushing to the table, searching the cluttered top, he finds a pad and pen.

Now, what to write.

Considering this, his mind blank, finally it hits him.

You've already seen it remember.

Writing the note, holding it up:

She's at the front door
If you leave now, you'll catch her
Don't let her get away

Stopping, now concerned, he questions why and how this has still occurred.

But I stopped Ricky; the future has been changed, hasn't it?

39

The day of Thomas's murder...

Finally finished, the cursor flashing back at him, Thomas sits looking at his laptop without an ounce of achievement. Empty and unfulfilled, he lacks any sense of contentment, and it troubles him.

It's done, finished.

Yet still, somehow, he knows this isn't true.

With the story taking so much of him, and now having to let go, putting it to rest, without finding Amy, without a body, he recognises moving forward will forever be impossible. The thought of this, not having closure, his mind permanently open to the mystery of the case, scare him; no longer is he in control of his own destiny. Where before he knew of his pending murder, though now safe, a life of uncertainty, open with questions, scares him more than death.

Getting up from the table, standing and stretching, Thomas crosses the room to the window. With night having closed in, dropping its shroud down over the world, the roads below sit rain sleek and empty. Only the scattering of lights offers signs of life, be it distant and misanthropic.

His phone buzzes at his pocket.

Mum again.

> **Mum:** *Hi Tom, just checking in. Hope all is ok. I miss my granddaughter. I miss my son. Please call. Love mum.*

Guilt sweeps through him. She is alone, widowed, and I, her only child, treat her like a stranger. He writes his response:

Thomas: *I'm sorry for shutting you out. It's been rough, but that's no excuse. I promise to be better.*

Leaving the window, Thomas moves to the wall. Standing before the corkboards, his eyes roam over the cluttered items. Firstly, Khaliq and Katerina. While his distaste for the pimp, drug and dealer of paedophilia dealer remains, with Thomas having spoken to Katerina early that morning, for now anyway, Thomas is happy he can put Khaliq and his business to one side. Though Katerina had, returned to work within days of her beating, the man had stayed true to his word, and Katerina had been left alone.

Moving on, fixing on a photograph of Ricky, and though he tries to fight it, a tightness returns to his chest. He and his son James stand together, topless, tanned, and muscular, arm in arm. Covered in foam, possibly in Ibiza or someplace, surrounded by bikini-clad girls, the two men could be mistaken for brothers.

Since his arrest, according to Hidur's sources, Ricky has remained tight-lipped and resolute while recovering in hospital. Although a confession isn't needed, of course, the evidence found in search of Erika is both overwhelming and damning. As for Amy, nothing had been uncovered or announced linking him with her disappearance.

How and why would he kill Amy?

What am I missing?

Erika had gone there to seek his council. Instead, after she rebuffed his advances, he attacked, assaulted, and killed her in fear of getting caught. Though appalling, the murder, and his actions after the fact, though incredibly grizzly in how he disposed of her, are all too common. But Amy and her involvement simply does not fit.

Unless Amy found out what he did?

Considering this, once again, Thomas returns to the corkboard and stacks the information from the beginning:

James Ruck works as a cameraman making porn films with his friends, then turns to photography and begins dating Amy.

Amy starts receiving letters from an unknown someone.

Freshly out of the escort business, Erika tries her hand at modelling. She meets James, he uses her as a model, and they start a relationship.

Amy learns of the affair – James dumps Erika, and he and Amy make a go of it.

The whole thing blows up when Erika falls pregnant. She tells James, who, in fear of ruining his life, starts plotting to kill Erika.

Her phone and a copy of her house keys were found in James' apartment. Erika was quoted as fearing James, believing he had something planned.

James purchases tools used in the disposal of her body.

Worried, Erika begins communicating with Ricky Ruck.

James meets Erika outside town, plans to kill her, but learns Erika's pregnancy was nothing more than a bluff. So, changing his mind not to kill her, they go their separate ways.

Erika visits James's father. He attempts to seduce her, but when she refuses his advances, he rapes and kills her – believing his son would be suspected. Ricky disposes of her body, along with her dismantled Mini in the bog outback.

Leaving his father's house, possibly upon seeing Erika's dismantled mini through the trees, he gets out to investigate but is killed.

Which leaves Amy.

Thomas considers this and how her abduction fits into the puzzle.

Amy decides to leave Pinegrove, and her stalker's behaviours escalate.

Amy is kidnapped from her apartment.

StarKiller investigates Pinegrove and turns up dead. Suicide but suspicious.

Thomas returns to the desk and sits down. His eyes fix on the letter before him, the one Amy received from her admirer. Collecting it up, removing the folded piece of paper, he again reads the words written:

My dear Amy,

You seem to have me at a disadvantage. Not one to give in to need, nor am I weak, never have I allowed anyone to have such a hold on me, but my love, you are so very, very exceptional. Afraid you have stripped me of everything I knew to be true, my strengths, my plans for the future, rearranging them, changing them, changing me, I now understand this was my fate all along.

With everything he knows about Ricky Ruck, the man he is, the stock he comes from and later bred, finally, it hits him.

Someone else took Amy.

Someone with access to Pinegrove.

Someone who could get in without leaving signs of forced entry.

His phone ringing at the desk startles him, squeezing a 'holy shit' from his pressed lips.

Answering it, he tries to control his breathing.

'Thomas?'

'Hello?' He asks, not recognising the voice.

'It's Sue, Sue Wright. I'm handling your custody case?'

Sue Wright?

Finally, it clicks, and Thomas matches the tiny voice to the small, dumpy woman.

'Sorry, how are you, Sue?' He stutters.

'That's quite alright, but Thomas, I do have some bad news.'

'Ok.'

'You do recall me stressing the importance of your attendance; well, the court heard the case in your absence. As a result, Mary and Lewis have been awarded full custody.'

'But Mary, she came to see me. She was understanding of my situation?'

'Yes, she even spoke for you, but failing to show up, again, well it wasn't looked at favourably, I'm afraid. You have the right to appeal, but I think we need....'

Slamming the phone down, Thomas picks up his wine glass and slings it across the room, shattering across the floor, staining it with red slashes. As tears swell in his eyes, blurring his vision, slamming his fists down on the table, the contents are rocked atop it.

Hopeless, it's all fucking hopeless.

Something falls over him, a feeling, no, more like deja-vu. His eyes fix on the smashed glass, the red streaks.

His blood runs ice cold.

This is what I saw- my future.

He recalls this very moment, him seeing himself slamming the phone down, flinging the glass across the room, and him, the slinking shadow, sneak into the room behind him. Like his intervention in Amy's timeline, thinking he had changed things...

Just like with Amy, you haven't changed a thing.

Swallowing hard, Thomas listens but hears only the raspy sounds of his baited breathing. Turning, rising slowly, too slowly, his legs all but failing him, he comes face to face with the intruder.

The Great Deceiver.

A flash of silver.

Thomas screams a stifled shriek.

Warmth floods his shirt.

Sliding down him, collapsing, dying, Thomas hits the ground.

THIRD INTERLUDE

ENDGAME

December 2020...

He was alone. So very alone. For so very long. In his solitude, he had grown disillusioned and uninspired. All budding ideas had died early in their conception, unable to challenge or hook him long enough to see them grow.

After months of searching, stalking, hunting, the nights roaming the streets, the bars, nightclubs, year after year, he all but given up, resigned to an empty life; one where the artist, the great performer, would totter about alone.

Where the trolling phase, the searching, the selecting, once excited him, it had only dulled with time. While the search still offered a level of enjoyment, a familiar emptiness had taken hold, rotting him from within.

Even his murder of Maggie Rowland the year before had done little to exorcise his suffocation. He had taken his time with her, kept her captive for a week, but like so many others, she failed to keep him engaged. Sure, he loved Maggie, but she lacked depth and forethought, and more importantly, ambition.

Then Laura Bates, the teenager some six months later, and her enthusiastic, line-backer boyfriend. He had planned great things for her, but having her imprisoned, bound and gagged, with her weeping for her dead boyfriend, her pleads, her weakness had merely led him to kill her more quickly. Instead of energising him, he was left with a dull ache at his core, one he knew would only deepen.

Later, when drawing upon his deepest fantasies, using theatrics and deception, he targeted the Lynn family – the perfect husband and wife and twin daughters, then the luring of William Telfer. But, again, he gained nothing except experience. Even when Mr Lynn begged for his life, his daughters, and their third child still growing inside his wife, when he pleaded and cried, The Great Deceiver only felt detachment. Mr Lynn might have been a doctor, educated and wealthy, his pretty wife loyal even when he wasn't, but as a pair, their marriage was nothing more than a thin pretence, a wasted life. They had been weak, especially in death. Turning his stomach, their shortcomings gained them a death sentence, swift and violent.

Mr Telfer and the ad for a laptop for sale, while being nothing more than a bit of fun, a distraction, it was nothing more than self-indulgence. Again, The Great Deceiver was left unsatisfied.

He had taken jobs, those unsupervised, allowing him time alone to ruminate and fantasise. He took to driving a taxi, picking up women, dropping them off home, hundreds of them. Still, only two had been worthy of further inspection. Libby Rose and Claire Delacroix, both young, beautiful, educated, but plain, their characters lacking the fire he required, the heart, and depth. He watched them, dedicated over one hundred hours to each woman, and for time, even lived in the basement of Libby's family home.

He had bailed on both projects before his plans could fully form.

He had become what all those in law enforcement fear. A bold adversary, one who is self-controlled rather than reckless. Not just clever, but ingeniously cunning. He was all these things, but still, he was alone, and therefore, he knew with sickening certainty, he would never reach his full potential.

So, he resigned himself to a future forever searching for the one, 'his endgame.' He would stalk, linger in the shadows, and rip the life from the local wildlife, but always alone.

Until one afternoon.

It appeared before him like a lighthouse might through the sea-mist. A light in the dark. An angel shining in the night.

Pinegrove in all its glory.

A decaying monument to a grander time, a shadowed giant left, like him, to wallow among the sycophantic dullards, those with money, important jobs, busying themselves with children, puppies, flat-white coffee, and dreams of summers spent at Disneyland.

A dark tapestry of history and change, interwoven almost but not entirely, bleached by the modern world around it. Shadowed, ignored, and left to die a slow death, but not anymore. These days, no one believes in miracles, the impossible, but they will. When he was done, the old house would be studied, written about, and remembered. Like him, it would live in infamy.

After taking control of the building, infiltrating its inhabitants, devouring them, he set about altering the terrain, creating his theatre. With its hollow walls and deep, dark pockets, with a little work, the building would form the perfect launchpad for future projects.

Then one day, he saw her. Amy Porter. The last original, unique woman in London. Watching her walking along the street in her hospital greens, rain plastering her uniform against her olive skin, sleeking down her long brown hair, he was positive he had never seen anyone look lovelier.

He tracked her from the rain to a coffee shop, where she drank a pot of tea alone. Her downbeat demeanour was both intoxicating and heart-breaking in equal measure. Watching her from across the shop, transfixed, with plans beginning to form, life once again swept through his bones.

Unaware of his presence, blind to the calling of fate, her destiny sitting mere meters from her, Amy sipped her tea, satisfied with the rain-swept streets being her only entertainment. A choir of hissing cars, the thrumming of rain on concrete, with her taking enjoyment in the commonplace, all he could do was watch on, transfixed. When a smile pulled at her face, with her finding joy in the weather, he knew without hesitation, deviation, or question, Amy Porter, was the one.

As she moved to her phone, searching at least two different property sites, it all became clear – what he was to do, his future, and their future together.

And so, it began.

Like a switch being clicked inside him, his mind and mental acuity had him planning and fantasising. Like it once did, the trolling phase excited him, invigorated him, giving him direction and purpose.

From identification to stalking, stalking to cataloguing, he was quick to invade her world. He memorised her diary, every tick, her loves and hates, those she gave time to, those she did not. He, too, tracked her work patterns, her friends, her sister Lilly, and her boyfriend, James Ruck- the wannabe filmmaker turned cheap photographer. He suspected Amy knew of her boyfriend's numerous deceptions, the women he would frequent, on some level but had decided to fight for the relationship. Not out of love, no, but in fear of being alone.

The Deceiver very much wanted to kill James, a slow torturous death, but his treatment of Amy would come in useful down the road. It would be The Deceiver who would leak the affair to Amy, and in doing so, she would become more pliable in the long run. She would be seasoned and brined by the pain, damaged just enough to facilitate his arrival.

So, he stalked Amy for four weeks before posting the card through her letterbox.

TO LET – two-bedroom apartment – available now.
Low rent – Ornate and historic – Spacious and private.
Parquet flooring throughout – new fixtures and fittings. Safety of tenants is paramount.

To avoid suspicion, he had canvased her entire apartment block, leaving a card for each of the other twenty-two residents. As such, forced to field calls and questions from other perspective renters, he simply screened their calls until Amy called with questions.

It was the reference to safety that led her to him. He would be first to admit it had been applied a little thick, but with the assault at the hands of Joe Briggs, and while he knew he was pushing it, he figured it would be too much for her to resist. With Amy hating her apartment and her noisy gamer neighbour, when she called, he spoke with a soft voice with a heavy emphasis on words like *quiet, safe, private*. In truth, he knew he had won her over even before she viewed the apartment. When she did, Amy not only accepted it but took to it with grateful surprise, energy, and appreciation for the new space.

And so, he watched her.

Daily.

However, watching quickly turned to chest-aching-need. He considered if anyone had ever loved a woman more than how he did Amy? Attractive, intelligent, sure, but it was her vulnerability that unsettled him so. Not just beautiful but a beautiful person, and to watch her hurt him deeply. Because of this and the inability to fight it, that, and the fact she had grown cautious with the letters, his presence, he decided to accelerate his plans.

So, his attention turned to the unwanted cellar. The interlinking collection of rooms and hallways, dust-filled, home to stacked boxes of junk, became his main base of operations.

He found the old chest freezer among Christmas decorations, a vintage dining table and chairs, an old Amour, and discarded electrical items. While it was huge, dated, and non-functional, it wasn't of concern. In fact, finding it had been the icing on the cake, like fate, as if placed there for him, to house and transport, fitting his endgame perfectly.

He spent twenty-six hours working on the item and used only hand tools when preparing it. He removed the shelves and inner linings before moving on to drilling holes and fitting the required tubes, vents and other accommodations needed. The soundproofing took considerably longer. When done, looking down at the appliance, appraising his work, admiring his craftsmanship, a smile pulled at his lips, one of achievement, of completion.

It had come as a surprise, the effort it took, the reserve used to achieve his goal. Though he was a highly encapsulated person, prudent and transitory, he had become all too aware of his age and the dedication required and recognised the need to condition himself.

After moving the freezer to the backroom, he secured the room with a new door, double-strength hinges, a heavy-duty padlock, and clasp: Oak but padded on the inside, rubber seals at its edge.

And there it would wait.

For the right time.

While keeping himself occupied with the local cats and dogs, strays, and pets alike, he would continue with the letters. They would, of course, soften Amy, indoctrinate, and seduce her. Then, and only then, would he finally declare himself.

PART FOUR

REVELATIONS, RESOLUTIONS, REDEMPTIONS

40

11 minutes, 9 seconds later...

Laying still, he listens and waits, unable to attend to the blood leaking from his wound. Controlling his breathing, holding it when he can, shallow at other times, he listens as the soft patter of his attacker's footfalls fade down the hallway.

After dragging Thomas from the living area, his attacker had dumped him in the bathroom.

Just how it was when viewed through the hole from the past.

And here Thomas waits.

Get up, move, goddamn it.

Hearing the door's guard chain rattle along with its runner, the door pulling open, Thomas waits in silence until the door again closes behind his attacker's exit.

Silence.

Heavy and dark, it drops over him.

Pulling his head up off the floor, he surveys the bathroom, the dark doorway. He sees nothing, no movement, nor the shifting of shadow.

Dragging himself up, his joints stiff from laying in the same position for so long, but strangely, no pain. On his knees, he fingers his wounded stomach and winces. Pulling up his shirt, inspecting the damage, Thomas finds no new wound, and incredibly so, his old wound has instead been reopened, almost entirely. Instead of burying in deep, the bowie knife had instead sliced into his gauze across the abdomen. Like a meteor would when bouncing off the Earth's atmosphere, the blade skimmed along the semi-healed scar, opening the wound anew, almost perfectly. The bandage and its padding must have acted like fresh tissue, mimicking the sensation of the knife pushing in deep.

Pushing himself up off the floor to his feet, the wound tearing slightly, he grunts a moan of discomfort into a fist. Shuffling to the doorway, staying inside, peering, he checks both ways before moving out into the hallway. Leaving the bathroom along the hallway, he moves to the front door. Securing it with the set of locks and bolts, and the guard chain, he stops.

It was locked before, so how the fuck did you get in here?

Now crying, utterly dumbfounded, he is left standing, like a child, unable to process such a contradiction.

Forcing himself away from the door, back along the hallway, around the corner, he heads to the kitchen. Sliding open a drawer, the second from the top, Thomas removes a roll of duct tape. Lifting his shirt, trapping the tail between his teeth, he stretches out the strip. Sticking it to his skin with one hand, flattening it down with the other, he pushes the gaping slit together. Pulling the tape, making it taught, he drags it across the wound, locking it shut beneath. Pain sears through him, through his eyes, watering them. Wrapping the tape around his waist, switching hands as he runs it around his back, he makes three tight loops before tearing it off with his teeth.

Tossing the roll aside, Thomas returns to the taping. Padding it down, he drops his shirt over it and breathes. Big gulps that shake on the intake, then wheeze on the exhale.

Removing a knife from the knife block, Thomas turns and returns to the hallway. Stopping, his eyes move to the paintings, to the hole.

How could Peter not have seen this? He had watched on after I left the wall.

Thomas considers this, and it hits him.

Maybe he did. Perhaps he saw precisely this.

Like Amy, with Thomas unable to change her fate, Thomas considers if Peter had decided that no action may be the best course of action to take.

That's why Peter was upset, not because of me dying, but because he saw me survive?

Turning, Thomas peers into the hallway, into the dim light, the knife shaking in his hands. He scans the shadows, and though still, they appear as if lurking with the intent to deceive him. His attacker would be back, back to finish what he started, to dispose of what should be a dead Thomas William.

Move now or die. It's that simple.

Surprising himself, Thomas is moving again. Turning, looking for his phone at the desk, finding it missing, he checks the kitchen counter but cannot locate it.

He's taken it.

Turning, upon moving down the hallway into the darkness, Thomas needs the wall for support. At the end, he peeps around the corner and again inspects the front door.

It was locked, as it was with Amy. I heard him unlock it when he left.

A cold wave rushes through him, stealing his breath. Both times, Amy and his own assault, the intruder came from the hallway, not from the front door, but from either the bedroom or the bathroom. He recalls the sounds the night he watched Amy's abduction, the ones that had unsettled him so, creeping into the living area from the hallway. Where he had associated the sounds with fear and the surreal situation, Thomas now knows for a certainty he hadn't been alone.

Moving to the bedroom, peering inside, from the locked window to the bed. All four corners.

Nothing.

Slowly, his eyes are drawn back to the bathroom. A sneer drops through his features, contorting them, turning to an expression of utter, gut-churning anger.

Entering the bathroom, closing, and locking the door behind him, he turns on the light, his fingers shaking around the light cord.

His head snapping, his eyes scan the room, attempting to take in every detail, all corners. Expecting to find something, anything, an explanation to the bottomless pit of a nightmare- but he finds nothing.

Sighing deeply, feeling the life seep down through him, out through his feet, Thomas moves to the sink. Placing the knife down, resting it behind the hot water tap, he opens the mounted cabinet and searches the contents. Finding a carton of painkillers, dumping five tablets into his shaking hand, he loses one through the gap between his thumb and forefinger. Bouncing off the sink's rim, the lone tablet drops to the tiled floor, skittles and disappears through a narrow gap between the tiles where there appears to be little or no grout.

Ignoring it, dumping the remaining four tablets into his mouth, he washes them down with water directly from the cold-water tap. Looking at himself in the mirror, his face wrung with pain and worry, adrenaline and fatigue, his expression drops, and his eyes glaze over as if they know something he doesn't.

Finally, it hits him.

'I'll be God-damned,' he moans.

The truth.

Turning, looking down at the floor, the gap where the dancing tablet had escaped, a line of missing grout runs around the end of four tiles. Bending down to inspect it further, he traces the line of missing grout, all but invisible, forming a perfect 2 x 2-foot square. Pushing down on the floor, it doesn't budge but knocking his knuckles against it, a dull, shallow echo succeeds it, hinting at an open space below.

Reaching up, retrieving the knife from behind the tap, Thomas rams the blade into the gap between the tiles. Hammering down the handle with a closed fist, once, twice, he levers the panel upward.

With a gap of an inch, he reaches in with his fingers, squeezing them into the pressed space. Gripping the lip of what is now clearly a false floor, pulling out the knife, Thomas places it down on the floor beside him. With both hands, he lifts the panel to reveal an open space below.

With anger flowing up inside of him, a wave of new, guttural anger, one born from the depth of his despair, throwing the board aside, Thomas spits, 'motherfucker.'

From beyond the bathroom door, along the hallway, activity at the front door alerts Thomas with a rattle, a thud.

The doors locked, asshole.

Considering the intruder's next move, turning back to the tunnel, recognising it soon to be his attacker's next move, Thomas readies him.

Down the rabbit hole I go.

Knife in hand, lowering himself into the hole, down onto his hands and knees, Thomas dips his head inside. Darkness meets him, as does the pressed, dusty air.

Sweeping his legs across the floor, dropping his feet inside, Thomas lowers himself through bared, gritted teeth. Straightening himself out, laying flat on his stomach, Thomas shuffles forward, an inch at a time, into the darkness.

Tracks for wet rooms or space carved out for air-conditioning ducts, either way, the hole drops into a tunnel, a box of sorts, and darkness. It runs away from Thomas in one direction – towards Amy's apartment. Dark, humid and for the claustrophobic, a place beyond nightmare. With barely enough room to move, Thomas detects the first signs of panic itching at his skin, clamping his heart, throbbing his vision.

Shuffling forward, the tunnel squeezes in at his sides. The air recedes all about him, deserting him, his lungs. Ahead of him, he spots a junction in the tunnel. Moving to it, sliding his legs along behind him, Thomas peers around the corner into an adjoining tunnel. The new passage travels a short distance where its end is cast in dim strips of lights.

Presented with two options: straight ahead and up into Amy's apartment, or down to the lower level, into the depths, into what could possibly be the bowels of hell itself.

Thomas decides upon the second option.

Shuffling around the corner, his jeans catching on something, tearing it clear, Thomas pushes into the new tunnel. A meter or so, and he comes to a knotted rope fashioned to a hook-like fitting at the vented escape port in the ceiling, dropping bars of light down into the vertical tunnel. Looking down, the rope with the tunnel descends into what looks like a black pit.

Placing the knife blade between his teeth, he scoots forward. Taking hold of the rope with both hands, he pulls, once, twice. Two further sharp tugs, but the rope hold firm.

Still holding it, pulling himself forward and up, Thomas transfers his weight to his hands. Managing to drag his legs along behind him, dropping them down into the dark space below, he grips the rope between his thighs. Starting down, shimmying, sliding, taking each thick knot one at a time.

Along with the fiery pain across his stomach, now returning to impede him, in seconds, a searing warmth cuts through his palms and fingers. Pausing, breathing heavily through his knife-pressed lips, he clamps his legs around the rope. Releasing his hands, removing the knife from his lips, he takes to blowing on his blighted palms. However, the warm air from his lips seems to aggravate the wounds, leaving them hot and itchy.

Returning his grip to the rope, taking hold of it tentatively, he peers down past his legs. Below his feet, he spots a second horizontal passage, presumably running below the first-floor apartments.

Shuffling again, lower, lower, Thomas peers into the shaft. Dim and narrow, like the one above, the short tunnel runs away from him before splintering left and right. Deciding to continue down to the lower level, the sound of muffled movement rattles up from below, reverberating up through the shaft, stopping him in his tracks. Looking down, the darkness at his feet begins to glow.

Shit!

Thomas instead angles himself to face the horizontal shaft, starting back up, quickly realising the effort required to climb is beyond him. Placing a foot flat against the opposite wall, he uses it to push himself inside. Thomas scoots forward three-quarters of the way inside, shuffling on his belly.

Stopping, listening, a popping noise, the sound of shifting through the tunnel below him, echoes with weight as it draws closer. Again moving, slithering forward, grunting against the blade still clamped between his teeth, he reaches the junction. Removing the knife from his mouth and looking over his shoulder, the glow from below has now intensified, leaving the vertical shaft showered in warm orange light.

Ok, left or right?

Dave or Ms Harmony?

Apartment 2a or Apartment 2b?

Choices, choices.

Drawing a blank, unsure which way to go, with the rope behind him vibrating, Thomas makes a snap decision, turning to the left. Shuffling forward, the sounds of his attacker climbing the rope chasing him into the dark.

Fumbling, looking up through the darkness, spotting a thin square-shaped line of light, he pants in relief. Presumably another false floor, Thomas aims for it with his head.

Unsure whether he is now alone in the tunnel or not, the sound behind him masked by the scraps and scuffles from himself, Thomas pushes up with the back of his head, neck and shoulders. Lifting the square an inch, searching with his fingers, he curls them around the panel's edge. Sliding the board to one side, while only scant light from above spills into the shaft, it does offer him a way out, so eagerly, Thomas reaches up through the new opening.

Dumping the knife onto the tiled floor above, gripping the lip of the opening with both hands, Thomas pushes up, dragging his shattered body up through the space. Twisting at the waist, pulling his wound, the action pulls a whimper of pain from his lips.

Dragging his heavy legs out from the shaft into another bathroom, turning again, Thomas is quick to snap back to the floor panel. Sliding it across, clicking it into place. Crouched, kneeling atop it, Thomas waits, listening, preparing himself for another assault. Breathing in heavy, ragged gulps, straining to listen, he hears nothing but his own laboured panting.

Pushing down with his hands, attempting to centre his entire weight down onto the panel, he waits.

Nothing.

Checking the room, the bathroom a copy of his own, and though dark and hard to know for sure, it appears bare and lacks any real character of personalisation.

With his breathing now regulating itself, from beyond the walls, he can now make the soft patter of rain against glass, the distant roll of thunder, but nothing else.

Time to move, you can't stay here.

Standing up, his bones creaking with the sudden burst of movement, Thomas steps to the door and pulls it open. Peering out, squinting into the darkness of the hallway, he finds a gathering of shadows, the rain and thunder now far more prominent but no signs of life.

Must be asleep?

Yet, a new uneasiness takes hold, filling him with caution and worry.

Edging out, he checks the bedroom across from him. Dark, quiet, empty; the bed, neatly made, is unslept in. Moving along the hallway to the living area, like the bedroom, the room is void of the life Thomas saw upon his previous visit. He recognises it as Dave's apartment but stands confused. Furnished but vacant – all personal items, the movie collection, including Charles and Diana, are now all gone.

41

4 minutes, 19 seconds later...

Thomas stands inside Apartment 2b. Like her neighbour Dave, Ms Harmony is absent, and her apartment, like Dave's, sits clean and empty, shadowed with worrying questions. Fearing for her safety, Thomas rushes to her bedroom. The bare bed, while made, appears stale, the room around it a cold vacant space.

Back in the living area, in the dark, it too now lacks all personality and life. It reminds Thomas of a theatre stage, obvious and cheap, one in need of an actor to bring it to life.

Stunned, and before he can move on, from above comes a series of concussions, the booming of stomping feet.

He's gone back to finish me off, to get rid of my body.

Having locked the door, forcing his attacker to use the tunnels, the thought now of him creeping, scurrying through them, leaves Thomas with a wave of sickness.

How long has he been coming and going?

How long has he been watching me?

Anger rushes up to meet nausea, swallowing it, darkening Thomas's eyes. For a moment, it is enough to mask the gooseflesh, his upside-down stomach, the world around him as it comes crashing in. Having limited time, he recognises the need to get moving, but the weight of it all pins him to the spot.

Thankfully, a flash of lightning jolts him into action. That and continued thuds and bumps from above. If not for them, he might stay this way. Leaving the room, and while a far less physical escape is possible via the front door, the potential exposure it offers leads Thomas instead back to the bathroom, the tunnels.

Thomas drops back inside the shaft, collapsing his knees, sliding the false floor back to its original position above his head. Shuffling forward, turning left at the junction, he presses forward, closing in on the rope waiting at the tunnel's end.

Taking the rope in his hands, looking to shift the knife back to his teeth, he hisses, 'shit,' remembering he had left it in the apartment above.

'Forget it,' he tells himself, taking the rope.

Pulling himself through, and like before, looping his legs around the rope, he starts down, shimmying through the knots. Each one racks at his thighs and calves while the rope returns to burn at his palms.

Reaching the bottom, Thomas is presented with two further options: a horizontal shaft running below the ground floor apartment and a grated cover at the bottom of the shaft, where below, through the slits in the metal plate, a subterranean area sits cloaked in darkness.

No more basements.

Gingerly, placing his feet down, toes first on the grated cover, Thomas shuffles into the horizontal shaft, where the sides quickly close in on him. Like the tunnels above, but far narrower, the sides press in at his hips, his shoulders, pinching him with spiteful pressure.

He manages to reach the square panel in the ceiling, but his heavy breathing has turned to wild, painful hyperventilating gasps. Crouched below it, with the tips of his fingers, he pushes the board upwards, an inch, two, three, enough to allow him to peer out through the growing opening. Scanning the dimly lit room across the tiled floor, Thomas spots the toilet's base, the bath panel, and the hallway beyond the open bathroom door.

Moving again, sliding the panel aside, Thomas drags himself up into the bathroom.

Mr Chen's bathroom.

Moving to the doorway, hugging the doorframe. The hallway beyond, long and murky, is lined with doors on both sides. It is a far larger apartment than the ones above, yet it follows a similar layout. As such, at the end of the hallway, an archway promotes the living area, be it one mooted in a thick layer of gloom.

The apartment, like the ones above, is deathly quiet.

Too quiet.

An all-too-common theme, one with no rational explanation.

Where the hell is everyone?

Stepping out into the hallway, sticking to the wall, he moves to the archway, his eyes fixed forward, § and wild, searching for his landlord.

'HOLY FUCK!' seeps from his lips.

A person, mere meters away, stands staring back at Thomas.

Like the hallway, the living area is heavily shadowed, leaving his eyes frantic as they scrutinize the still shape. Off to one side, the tall figure stands in ominous silence. Spotting a second silent figure, other profanities leave his lips, this time through harsh, ragged breaths. Seeing a third over at the kitchen, a fourth sat on the floor at the far wall, hands-on-hips, their back straight, Thomas lets out an almighty, weary sigh.

Mannequins.

A family of them.

Looking around, Thomas attempts to look beyond the mute strangers. Unlike the two apartments above, this feels lived in. Where dirty dishes sit piled up on the kitchen counter, on the floor, a collection of bin bags, stuffy with a rotten scent, wait to be taken out.

A noise, nondescript, faint, creeps in from the darkness, drawing his eyes back to the mannequins. Scanning them, one to the next, as the noise repeats, now louder, this time from behind him, it rattles along the hallway at his rear. Turning, looking into the pitted black with another crack, he recognises the sound belongs to a door, the front door, opening slowly.

Darting forward, the front door opening ahead of him, Thomas shifts to his left, through a doorway into a dark, almost pitch-black room. Closing the door, hearing the front door clattering shut from beyond, he can only hope the noise is enough to mask his own passage.

Standing still, his ear to the cold wood, he listens but struggles to trace the sound of movement.

Nothing.

No, not nothing; from the left, muted footfalls approach him but stop.

In the bathroom?

Mouthing a silent, 'shit,' Thomas now fully expects to be discovered along with the open hatch in the floor. New sounds, that of heavy feet stomping along the hallway, appear to validate this. The feet, thundering past Thomas, stop in the living area. Pausing there but for a moment, as if retracing his steps, the heavy feet pound the wooden floor, returning to the front door. Fading, they are chased from the hallway with the slamming of the front door, leaving a silence, as loud as the shattering of glass, to sweep through the apartment.

Releasing a chest full of air, one held since entering the darkroom, the exhale only adds to the moment, making the close call more dramatic. And to add to the excitement, Thomas is forcefully sick. Warm vomit splashes the floor at his feet, the effort bringing tears to his eyes and a zing of bile flooding his tonsils. Bent over, hands on his knees, spitting out what's left of the cud upon his tongue, he finally notices his surroundings.

At his neck, the air there comes alive, alert, pricking the hair. Turning, seeing them in the dark, their faint outlines bringing a loosening to his bowels, he hisses, a 'Jesus Christ,' a 'my God,' and one almighty, 'Holy fuck.'

Excellent, more mannequins.

With an outstretched hand, Thomas's fingers claw at the darkness, the wall. Finding the light switch and flicking it on, he sees four figures looming over him in the dim light.

Panting, Thomas checks the space between them. Not quite full mannequins, male torso busts, the type of dummy used by tailors and dressmakers, yet the shadows make demons of them all.

While the first bust is bare, the second supports a uniform of some kind. The overalls suggest manual labour or delivery driver. The third, a black tracksuit, three white lines on the sleeves, giving away the brand. The fourth, a blouse, cardigan, and...

Thomas stops, his mouth agape, eyes wide and fixed on the wig atop the bust.

Wig? Why, what...

The stark realisation hits him with the force of a 10lb sledgehammer.

The overalls.

The Adidas tracksuit

The cardigan and wig.

Recalling The Deceiver's words, his wild claims, Thomas shrieks inside. 'I can take many forms, I can be anywhere, I can be anyone. I have hidden in plain sight, the mundane and the generic, the man who passes you on the bus, he who tips his hat in greeting.'

The Great Deceiver.

Thomas needs to move, he knows this, but fear has him rooted to the spot. His mind, a mess of questions, races to answer them. With the dedication required, and the patience, Thomas finally realises what he's dealing with; a pure psychopath, one for the ages, who likes to hide, who can blend in with the world.

The devil.

As if sealed in cement, his legs are heavy, but finally, they start to obey. Moving to the door, placing his ear to it and hearing nothing, he douses the light and pulls it open, inch by inch. The hallway beyond clings to shadow, having lengthened with the recent revelation, appear now staunched, darker.

He's all of them, Mr Chen, Dave, Mrs Harmony.

Again listening, with total concentration, to the sounds of the apartment, the rat-a-tat of rain, the roll of thunder, now far closer, it splits the sky above his head.

Moving into the hallway, his legs, now ironclad and laboured, compete with his brain. Airy and muddled, a headache, fresh and growing, brings searing white flashes across his eyes. Above his head, thunder closes in, its tail, a long winding cackle sets his teeth clattering together, blinding him with fresh jolts of pain.

In its wake, just beyond the dying thunder, a new sound, all but hidden, brings Thomas to a stop. A dry squawk, faint and raspy, rushed out from the shadows of the open living area.

With hands rolled into fists, feet shuffling, Thomas moves to the archway and scans the room. As it was, counting them, the five mannequins from before, as if frozen in time, remain unmoved.

Turning to leave, Thomas stops. A cold chill runs over, through him, leaving his blood icy, his skin on edge and prickled.

Four mannequins, not five, wasn't there?

Turning to again face the room, his eyes work the pockets of black, counting the mannequins. One, two, three, four... and five.

I must be losing my mind.

Shaking his head, gulping air, Thomas tries to steady himself.

A second squawk, though far dryer, curls into a low cackle. It reaches out from the living area, from the fifth mannequin. Slender and athletic, a silhouette of black stands front and centre, staring back at Thomas.

I was right; there were only four before.

With a shriek, a bloodcurdling wail, one of a demon, the mannequin comes to life. Springing forward from the shadows. A shimmer of silver flashes in the passing light, forcing Thomas back on his heels. Turning, darting for the hallway, he makes for the front door. Finding four heavy bolts running horizontally across the door, he slides to a stop. With feet pounding behind him, a stampede of fury, Thomas turns and leaps for the bathroom, slamming the door behind him, locking it just in time.

Pounding erupts from the door, shaking it to its hinges. Even with Thomas throwing his weight against it, the door shudders with such force, a thunder of pain hits his shoulder in waves,

The door, rocking wildly, thunders with a new intensity, the wall spits dry plaster all about it. His face pressed to the door, screaming, Thomas is answered by the door falling still and a sudden, cold, jarring silence from beyond it.

With the pounding, its echo disappearing, Thomas's heavy, laboured breaths are left in its wake, fogging the hardwood. Shaking, his insides squirming, all he can do is wait. In the darkness, waiting, the fear builds, intensifies, and is such, Thomas dares not respond to it.

Silence... until fingers, light, rap on the door, and a voice, snakelike, whispers from the other side, 'the property has a garden, small, which is to be expected.'

The voice, creeping in through the door, while cruel in its teasing, is easily placed.

Mrs Turner, the realtor.

'In case I decide to steal the priceless antiques?' Thomas recalls saying when viewing the apartment and her response. 'In case you spill your wine and stain the floor.'

Thomas recognises, to his horror, The Deceiver knew him even then. Remembering back to her heavily used perfume, her thickly applied makeup, like the heavy accent of Mr Chen, the face mask used when playing Ms Harmony, and the exaggerated aliments of Dave, is another more than characters, a performance, one big charade.

'You see a gal like Amy, you'd don't forget her,' The voice now changed to Dave, before flicking to Mrs Harmony, 'I am sorry, you caught mid-wash, I like to take cold baths, does wonders for my ankles.'

Thomas stays silent.

'The key is discipline, discipline and planning, and the small details. Such as a face mask for my Ms Harmony and saturating each outfit with strong odours, forcing your subject to keep their distance. Strong perfume and an ugly appearance go a long way. You recognised my Ms Harmony, deep down anyway, so I'll give you that, but you lack the conviction needed. It's nothing personal; I simply needed someone to dump this on. Though not particularly bright, you took the role with all the gusto of the spineless man I thought, no, hoped you would be. You and your catalogue of failings were more than I could have hoped for, though I will admit, you do have ambition and, dare I say it, a smear of resolve. That friend of yours, StarKiller, a grown man stuck in the body of a fat teenager, I won't give you credit for him and how far he got. Grace and Marlene Edwards, he made it to the basement, stood mere inches from the oil drums I dissolved them in. Smart and curious, I'll allow him that, but a do-gooder and far too trusting. One look at Mr Chen and well, he was easy to kill, though I must say I took no pleasure in it.'

'Fuck you!' Thomas shouts, his voice wavering.

A short, snotty, nasally laugh is followed by, 'run Thomas, runaway, like you've always done. From your responsibilities, the beautiful Mary, and that little girl of yours, little Robin, hmmmmm.'

Backing away from the door, dropping his head, exhausted, done.

'I'm coming in there, you hear me, you not even a man, cannot stop me. And when I do, the devil comes with me,' The Deceiver continues, his words icy and calm, confident and final.

Stepping back, opening his mouth to scream a 'fuck you,' the floor disappears beneath his feet.

The open floor panel is quick to swallow him whole. Dropping through, his knees buckling, his back scrapes the rim as he drops inside. Landing on his butt, a shudder of pain races up from his coccyx to the base of his skull.

The bathroom door above him, now rattling on its hinges, has Thomas moving. Shuffling, twisting in the tight space, he starts away from the open panel, pain chasing him into the dark area.

Arriving back at the rope, taking it in his hands, Thomas stops before proceeding as a heavy thud against the door above races through the opening, along the tunnel. Pulling himself through, using the rope to joist himself up, Thomas drags his tired feet along behind his wilting form.

Placing his feet down on the crated vent panel, eyeing the dark basement below, it creaking beneath his weight, with no time to be conservative, Thomas pulls himself through. Standing, with all his weight pressing down on the panel, it pops and moans, but being confident it will hold his weight, he adjusts his hands on the rope.

A scream of metal, a whine, followed by a crack of concrete.

The panel disappears below his feet.

The dark space is quick to rip the words from his lips, replacing them with a short, surprised exhale of air. Dropping down through the hole, his arms flinging above him, Thomas plummets down and down into the bowels of the building.

Landing hard, his feet hammer the concrete floor. A snap and the twist of his ankle drag a hissed scream from his lips. The pain, a searing white slash, rifles before his eyes. Dropping further, the concrete quickly meets his rump with a hard kiss.

Somehow, he manages to hold on to his bladder. Gulping and muttering a 'fuck me,' he attempts to pull himself off the floor but fails.

The explosion of wood, the bathroom door burst open, has Thomas's head snapping back. His eyes peer up through the busted vent cover, straining with the tight space- he searches for him.

The darkness, pitted in the tight space, swells, but no face appears. Thomas expects to see a shadowed face, his dark eyes leering down at him, but instead, he sees a black, ominous square of uncertainty.

A laugh greets Thomas from the open panel, distant but close enough to pull him to his knees. Dry and horse, the laughter cuts the stillness of the basement like a knife. It echoes for a moment through the tunnel, fading like a ghoulish wail as it travels lower.

A horrible silence falls over Thomas.

'Shit!' He cries.

He's coming.

Using his hands, Thomas pushes himself up off the floor. Stumbling, he veers to one side, crashing side-on into a stack of boxes. Grunting, the box's sharp contents jabs at his side. Peeling himself free, with a vicious throb at his right ankle, placing his entire weight on the left, Thomas tries again. Uneasy feet, he manages to stand but sways as if drunk.

Breathing hard, Thomas scans the room around him. Brick walled, dank and utterly dire. A dwelling for the insidious, the grotesque.

A network of copper and plastic piping criss-cross the water-stained ceiling, where a pair of bare bulbs afford the place a dim, musky glow. With the faded brickwork, loose mortar, leaky pipes, it is clear mould, and melancholy took up residence long ago, clotting the air with dust, spores, and the haunts of evil men.

'Another goddamn basement,' Thomas spits.

Most floor space is taken up by stacks of musty old boxes. Sodden, their contents spilling out. Thomas notes worn books, magazines, coat hangers, damp clothes, and odd shoes. There are chrome taps, faucets, copper pipe-bits, bolts, fittings, stopcocks, clips, and conduits, hoarded in others.

Against the far wall, Thomas spots a stack of wood bits- splintered planks, shredded shards of skirting boards and architrave. His heart lurches as his eyes fix on the two large oil drums positioned in the far corner.

'Grace and Marlene Edwards, he made it to the basement, stood mere inches from the oil drums I dissolved them in.'

Recalling the Deceiver's words bring a gag of bile to his throat. Covering his mouth, holding back the vomit, Thomas pushes himself away from the boxes. His damaged ankle creaks as it trails behind him, and the throbbing pain rushes up through him in a wave of white, blinding light. Broken, fractured, sprained, either way, he's fucked. He knows this. A sitting duck, easy prey, a foolish man who's run his course.

I can't walk.

Fear is quick to immobilise him further.

Beaten, done, finished.

Yet still, he recognises the beating at his chest.

'Run Thomas, run away. Like you've always done. From your responsibilities, the beautiful Mary, and that little girl of yours.'

As The Deceiver's voice returns to taunt him, he remembers Peter's words and tone when quoting Thomas's work.

'There comes a time in every man's life when he needs to step outside and face the wolves at his door.'

And now he sees her.

Robin.

Like an angel in his mind, his daughter stands crying, her arms outstretched, needing her dad. A beacon of light, his greatest contribution to the world, only now does he recognise it. Tears fill his eyes, not from fear but in release. There'll be no more running, no more hiding away. The man he is, the things he's done, those he's neglected, deserve this place, this basement and pending death, but not the man he wants to be, the man he's becoming.

'There comes a time in every man's life when he needs to step outside and face the wolves at his door....' Thomas says. 'Yeah, that's Goddamn right.'

42

The Great Deceiver readies himself...

I think I'll gut him, yes, remove his innards, feed him his own.

Yes, nice and slow.

Before leaving the apartment, The Deceiver stops only to collect his mask. Sliding it on over his head, like always, the leather is quick to soothe in against his skin, licking it, energising him. As he laces it shut at the back of his head, pulling it taut against his face, the confusion, the maze of his mind, the schemes and plans, the thoughts of his mother, those who once pushed and shoved him, all fade to the back of his cranium. The ghosts, silent again, bow to him, basking in his magnificence.

Leaving the apartment, crossing the ground floor, The Deceiver unlocks the door beneath the stairs. Pulling the door open, almost giddy with excitement, he moves inside before turning and locking the door after him.

One way in, one way out.

He returns the key to his pocket, pats it for good measure, and dances down the lit but narrow stairwell to the basement. The wooden steps creak beneath his feet; there is no need for quiet now. The sound of his approach is needed, and he, Thomas William, will hear this and fear his arrival.

Calm and clean, he tells himself.

Smiling, he removes his bowie knife from its sheath. The blade, vast and cold in his hand, as always brings warmth to his groin.

Calm and clean.

Smiling beneath the mask, The Great Deceiver pushes through the door into a brick-walled passage. Slowly, up ending the blade, flicking it into a dagger, he skulks forward to the first door on his right. Pushing it open, he smiles as the door scrapes across the concrete like nails on a blackboard, the sound enough to terrify the silly man hiding somewhere ahead of him.

His eyes work the room, first finding the battered vent cover, noting the stillness in the air. Moving inside, he scans the stacked boxes before stopping at the centre of the room. Checking all four corners, confident Thomas has moved on, The Great Deceiver hurries back to the passageway.

Moving to the next door, pushing it open with his boot, surprising himself, The Deceiver stands in the doorway before entering the waiting room. His gloved hand, now sweaty, twitches as his fingers wrap around the blade's hilt.

Stepping into the room, the same vintage dining table and chairs, the old Amour, and broken electrical items appear as they did the last time he saw them. Knowing Thomas could be hiding behind any of them, The Deceiver creeps forward, stalking. First checking behind the tall Armour, he moves to the dining table. Ducking down, his knife at the ready, he reviews the dark space beneath.

Satisfied the room is clear, he moves to the door.

That leaves the back two rooms.

But those are locked, so there's no way he could...

The Great Deceiver returns to the passageway. Looking at the door at its end, a throbbing rises in him, leaving him sweating beneath the mask. The door, only slightly, sits open. Moving to it, he notices the wood around the lock and handle to be splintered and frayed, and darkness falls over his eyes.

My space, how fucking dare he!

Kicking the door open, standing in the doorway, his blood boiling, he booms into the quiet, dimly lit space beyond, 'You don't know what evil is, nor torture or pain, not like me.'

Stepping into the room, the knife twitching in his grip, he scans the collection of mannequins. Though he can see they have been disturbed, from his viewpoint, he is unsure how.

'I was all of them, Mr Chen, Mrs Harmony, Dave Rowe, the realtor Mrs Turner, even the hunchback watching you across the street as you met with your friend for coffee, did you know that? Of course not. I am suffering, obsession, the shadow on the wall, the voice on the breeze, the darkness closing in on you... I am now your god.'

The mannequins – prototypes for future projects, sit beneath white sheets in two neat rows of four.

Exactly how he left them.

His eyes narrow.

No, not exactly.

Thomas's deception is blatant and foolhardy. Of the eight sheet covered mannequins, one sits outed. Placed among the group of disregarded dummies piled high in the corner of the room, he identifies it by its outfit. Jeans and a peacoat, a character he fully intends to explore in the coming months, while muted in colour, are nonetheless visible through the stack of broken limps, heads and battered plastic torsos.

Sneaky little bastard.

He can't help but smile.

Stepping forward, his eyes checking the door at the back wall, seeing the padlock still in place, happy, he returns his gaze to the eight sheeted figures. Knowing now for sure one does not belong, he fixes his eyes on the mannequin's proper location and the imposter hiding beneath the sheet.

Readying the knife, it jubilant in his hand, he starts towards the mannequins. Moving between the two rows, with eyes trained on the last one on the left, his smile grows upon noting a smear of blood inside the sheet.

There you are.

The little imposter.

Silly, silly boy.

Moving forward, almost gliding on exhilaration, he offers glances at the sheeted figures when passing them. Giddy, almost unable to contain his excitement, he is forced to stifle a laugh at his lips. He wants to call out, mock him, but that can wait.

When I have him laid out on the slab, dismantled and finished, I will rejoice in his failure, and before I grant him death, he will know of what awaits all those he holds dear. Mary, Lilly, even little Robin- all will be mine.

Readying the knife, his gloved hand slippery with heated perspiration, he continues forward leisurely. Passing the imposter, merely throwing a casual glance his way, he smiles beneath his mask, a wide grin of jubilation and triumph.

Turning, moving back to the imposter, slowing his breathing, with a sudden burst of action, of rage, The Great Deceiver turns and leaps forward. Bringing the blade down, stabbing in long but deliberate slashes, tearing at the sheet, exposing what waits beneath.

A mannequin, but how?

Confused, his mouth springing open, he takes a step back. Looking at the outfit, the long summer dress, the cardigan, the wig, his mind stutters.

This shouldn't be here, or should it?

The question will linger in his mind, hanging there as if to mock him. A jab at his rear streaks a dagger of searing pain through him, sending a bright white light across his eyes before turning pink and spotted. A second blow to his lower back removes all feeling from the neck down. Dropping to the floor as if in slow motion, the light flickers and fades from his eyes.

He, he switched them...

With his last breath, his mind settles with one final thought:

He deceived me...

43

Looking down at the dead man, contemplating whether to remove the mask, Thomas considers what good would it do. Knowing that anything but the devil himself would be an insult, he decides to leave the mask in place. Knowing the creep's propensity to dupe and cheat, Thomas kicks his ankle hard.

Nothing.

Dead?

Only one way to be sure.

Dropping to his knees, with his left hand pressing the man down against the ground, with his right, Thomas takes hold of the piece of wooden skirting protruding from his back and pulls. The stake slips out with ease, with a slurry of blood quick to follow it out of the hole. The wound, wide and oozing, fails to close. Having twisted it after puncturing his spine, he had created far greater damage, yet Thomas left unsatisfied. Not from morbid enjoyment or revenge, but in need of completion, he brings the sharp stake high, and with a quick jab, he pushes it into his right ear.

The Great Deceiver jerks, his eyes growing wide, his lips pulling tight.

I knew it.

Another act.

One last performance.

Driving the stake in deep, like stabbing hard butter, crunching it through bone, Thomas watches as death shades the man's eyes black.

In watching him die, tears first tug before erupting from Thomas's eyes. Sobbing uncontrollably on his knees, he buries his face in his hands. Light fades as he feels all energy abandons him. Draining and dragging him down, down, until his eyes flicker. As sleep attempts to take him, Thomas lets his weight shift. Closing his eyes, dropping to the floor, he welcomes the darkness as it rushes up to meet me.

It's over, my god, help me, please...

A noise, something distant, a scream, drags him back from the brink, snapping his eyes open. Sitting up, his back muscles creaking with a new intrusive, weary coldness.

He listens.

Silence.

I'm losing my mind.

His eyes move between the covered mannequins, the doorway, and the locked padlocked door at the back wall.

Still nothing.

Wiping his cheeks, Thomas pulls himself up off the ground, his swollen ankle impeding him. Standing, straining, aching and sore, he heads for the exit. At the door, he is stopped by a second noise. Suppressed, obscure, distant, he looks over his shoulder, eyes scanning, finding only the mannequins.

And again, nothing.

Silence, but somehow, the absence of noise, is deafening.

Looking up at the ceiling, noting the network of old copper piping, labelling the sounds as the movement of water, pressure, whatever, he shakes his head in frustration, in exhaustion.

Again, a deadened moan, low and pained, passes through the room.

Turning, his eyes fixed on the far wall, on the door sealed with a padlock. The sound, breeze-like, a distant wind, comes again and is enough to drag him limping back through the room, past what remains of The Deceiver, moving between the dummies. Finally, he stops at the door. Wooden and thick, strengthened by heavy-duty hinges and a Yale padlock and clasp far too big for the door.

Taking hold of the lock, fat, cold and chubby, he tugs on it, but the door remains resolute.

You'll need a mitre saw to get through... unless.

Turning back to the dead body, limping, Thomas returns to The Deceiver's body. Dropping to his knees, Thomas searches the man's pockets, which isn't easy given his position. Wearing tight black spandex bottoms and a matching top, he yanks the trouser leg down, stretching the material.

A further noise comes from the door behind him, this time louder.

A scream?

Muffled and again distant, Thomas is now positive someone is behind the door.

With his fingers meeting steel, curling around a set of keys, he drags them, kicking and screaming, tearing at the fabric due to it riding up, but manages to free them from the pocket.

Returning to the door, looking down at the keys, finding the two marked *Yale,* he inserts the first into the barrel, turns it, but gets no movement. Trying the second key, with an underwhelming ping, the lock springs open. Dumping the padlock, it meets the floor with a thud. Flicking open the clasp, pushing the door inward, it opens into a small, darkened, fetid room.

A heavy smell hits him. Stepping forward, one stale, full of dust, faeces, and sweat. Looking for a light switch, he fumbles along the wall on his left, his fingers searching the rough brickwork. Finding it, flipping it up, a single bare bulb blinks on and off before finally casting the room in a dull yellow glow. Surveying the room from left to right, he notes the old mahogany desk against the wall to the left, the stack of books sitting neatly at its side, two plastic storage containers and the chest freezer running along the back wall, and the single, metal frame bed at the right wall. Finally, he sees the silk bedding and handcuffs fixed to the metal frame.

Confused and disappointed, he listens for the source of the scream.

Nothing.

Was it really a scream?

Moving to the desk, he views the scattering of papers atop it, the sketches and hand-drawn maps, lists and notes, careful not to touch them. The books beside the desk offer insight into the man's interests: hand-to-hand combat, different forms of Martial Arts (Karate, jujitsu, Aikido, Judo, Krav maga), knife use, sewing and dressmaking, makeup and theatre design, dissection, torture, morphology, and languages, including phonology and syntax.

Again, a hushed whisper finds him.

Swinging around, his eyes snap from wall to wall, from the freezer to the bed to the door, finally fixing on the pipes and vents at the ceiling. His gaze returns to the chest freezer. Large and long, a small section, white to match the appliance, mechanical, but out of place, as if tacked on.

It's an old freezer. Get a grip.

Shaking his head, turning back to the desk, he again reviews the drawing. Well-crafted illustrations of mannequins, all dressed in different attire, are accompanied by schematics and designs, detailed and numerous. Structural plans of Pinegrove, the tunnel network, and intricate outlines of what looks like an altered coffin of sorts, all boxy and modified with wiring and attachments.

Finding himself leaning against the desk, recognising it is time to leave, Thomas starts away, hobbling on one leg.

Flicking off the light, passing through the door, he turns wearily, his head low. Closing the door, another faint whisper is carried through the doorway, stopping him.

Only the wind, the storm through the pipes.

Limping, Thomas heads back to the hallway.

44

Passing the dead body, the row of mannequins, Thomas finds he is now crying. As adrenaline seeps away down through his feet, his body begins to crash. His limping has turned to him now, dragging his ruined ankle.

Stopping, turning again, a low whine at the door reaches me, stopping me, spinning him on his heels. He watches the mannequins, The Deceiver's still corpse, the door to the backroom, and something else.

The freezer.

The modified freezer.

Almost looks like a coff...

Suddenly he's moving again, the pain in his ankle gone. Bursting back into the room, hopping, all but falling, he reaches out for the freezer. Dropping against it, almost collapsing, he searches for the handle with now wild, electrically surged eyes.

Single and chrome, he grips it with an unsteady hand. Pulling it, the sound of the door latch pings, but he gets no movement from the lid.

A muffled grunt comes from inside, followed by a low whine, leaving Thomas's mind racing, throbbing. Examining the door further, where below the handle, he finds a heavy clasp. Tracing it along the line of the lid, with fumbling fingers, he locates a second padlock marked with the word *Yale.*

Returning to the keys, finding the two labelled and branded, he selects one and slides it into the barrel. Turning it, with a click, the padlock pops open. Tossing the lock aside, unclipping the clasp, panting, exhausted, he takes hold of the handle and pulls. Staining the lid's weight and lifting it an inch, he slides his left hand inside, cupping the top. Pushing his right hand in to meet it, with everything he has left, which isn't a lot, he pulls the lid up, up, up. Pushing it back, letting it drop backwards, the lid slamming the back wall, Thomas stands mute, looking down as tears return, warping his vision.

Looking up at him, eyes red and wild, tightly packed inside the soundproof and padded freezer, is Amy Porter. Bound with handcuffs fixed to steel hoops at both her wrists and feet. A PVC oxygen mask covers most of her face, the medical kind, transparent with a hit of green. Tubes run up from the mask into the modified section at the end of the freezer.

Bending down, fighting against the smell of urine and faeces collected within the makeshift holding cell, Thomas, with shaking hands, gently removes the mask. Resisting him at first, he smiles as warmly as possible. With his eyes on hers, he tells her, 'You're safe now.'

Gingerly, lifting her face, Thomas loops the mask's rubber strap up over her head.

Panting, eyes darting, clawing at the free space above her, Amy asks, 'where, where is he?'

'Dead,' Thomas tells her.

'What, I, um,' now crying, she closes her eyes tightly and asks, 'are you real?'

'I'm afraid so,' Thomas says and waits for her to open her eyes before smiling. 'Let me help you, please.'

Returning to the keys, he identifies the one required, a dainty thing like in the movies, and works on her binds. Left hand first before moving on to her right. Releasing her arms from the fitted cuffs, leaving red-raw rings looping her wrists. Frightfully thin, her face ghostly and hollow, obviously starved, her rosy, tanned skin from before is now gone, leaving her skin anaemic white and translucent.

Helping her up to a sitting position, crying, he moves to and frees her ankles. Bending over, reaching inside, looping his hands beneath her armpits, he heaves her stiff frame upward. Slowly, she rises. Placing her hands on the freezer's lip, she, too, pushes. Hooking her left leg over, they pull and push together, straining and crying. Thomas sees it happening, but before he can stop it, he falls backwards onto his hurt ankle.

Collapsing, he moans in pain, his rump thuds on the concrete floor, her on top of him. First landing on his chest, knocking the wind from his gut, he gently rolls her off and to his left.

With her arms and legs fraying, her trying but struggling to get up, Thomas places a hand upon her shoulder. Looking down at her, he smiles and waits for her to go still.

'It's alright now. He can't hurt you anymore,' Thomas tells her.

She takes a moment, her eyes drinking in the light, her surroundings. Confused and disbelieving, and still terrified, they finally glaze and find his.

'Thomas William?' She asks, eyes wide and hopeful.

'Yes,' he nods.

'I knew you'd come, I, I dreamed you would, over and over, night after night, for so, so many nights....'

Closing her eyes, shuddering, she cries a pitiful howl. And so, he holds her. Lifting her gently, he wraps his arms around her, cradling her. As he kisses her head, he hears her whisper, 'you found me, you found me in the dark like I knew you would. You saved me, you saved me....'

Pulling back, looking down at her, he is heart full, his eyes wide with gratitude, he cries, 'it was you, Amy, you who saved me. You saved my soul.'

Hugging him, crying into his chest, she thanks him.

'Plus, I had help. A friend called Peter, Timothy... Lilly,' Thomas tells her.

'Lilly, you've met my sister?' She asks.

Looking up at his, her eyes flicker with emotion.

'Yes,' he says, smiling, as a warmth grows through him. 'She's quite the woman, like her sister.

Slowly, if only slight, colour returns to her cheeks, her eyes.

'Is it, it over now?' She asks.

'Yes, you made it. We both did. It's over but our lives,' warm tears well, blurring his vision, and a shudder, a kickstart, passes through his core. 'But our lives, they start now, we can't let your abductor, nor James, Erika, our past, we can't let them destroy our future.'

'You act like you can see the future,' she says as a smile, be it slight, pulls at her cheeks.

'Well, as a matter of fact...' he stops himself. 'That can wait. Now, what do you say we get out of here?'

Nodding, dropping her head, she cries, and Thomas joins her. Two lost souls, strangers, brought together by a higher power, and then, against the odds, found each other again. Through the darkness, through time itself, they find themselves at the circle's end, huddled together in the basement; through their tears, the healing process begins.

CLOSURE

The doorbell sounds, the chime spritely, but Mary fails to notice. While the sound is clearly audible above the amalgamation of party music and the chorus of young voices, Mary's attention is stolen by the birthday cake awaiting cutting. Not just any birthday cake, but a bespoke, one-of-a-kind Rosalind Miller birthday cake. White chocolate and raspberry, plain, with a fondant violin topping the towering marvel.

Stepping away, slipping a knife clear of the wooden block, she returns to the cake, her mind calculating. Mapping out her cuts before committing the blade.

Twenty-four children and ten adults, meaning thirty-four cuts, is that right?

She readies herself for the task, the knife unsteady in hand, hovering above the cake with an uneasy sway.

Hearing the words, 'welcome,' followed by the sounds of people talking, Mary's eyes are drawn to the hallway, offering the cake a reprieve. Stunned, Mary watches Lewis enthusiastically leads her ex-husband and a pretty lady with fiery red hair through the foyer to the back garden.

Still holding the knife, it now shaking a wild Charleston in her hand, the blade reflects beams of golden light around the room. Intermittently it blinds her, burning into her retinas, but Mary fails to notice.

I'll kill him.

Hell, I'll kill them both.

Moving to the open bi-folding doors, Mary watches in amazement as Lewis directs the limping Thomas and the woman to the lawn and the erected stage at the rear of the garden. Wooden chairs set out in four lines of ten encircle the stage in a crescent formation. She had been pleased with her earlier work, but now, seeing Thomas and the woman take a seat in a front row, a stir of anger rattles her bones.

He shouldn't be here.

He can't be here.

With a fresh haircut and shave, and though smiling, his darting, dark eyes cannot hide their haunted stares. A pink elephant lamp, spotted with what looks like holes, sits upon his lap. He grips it tightly as if in fear it might be stolen. As if noticing this herself, the red-haired woman whispers something into his ear, soft words that warm her pretty face. Placing a gentle hand down upon his lap, the woman kisses Thomas on the cheek.

She doesn't want to, but Mary studies the woman, unable to look away. She's never seen Thomas with anyone else, nor has he ever spoken of anyone else but her. A man with remarkably few past lovers had stayed loyal even when her love for him had gone.

The woman is in love, of that Mary is convinced. Not just by her expression but how her eyes watch him. They beam and burn with longing and gratitude, and seeing it brings a lump to Mary's throat. Shaking with anger, shock, and something else, Mary is thankfully intercepted by Lewis at the door before she can leave the house.

'Where are you going with that knife?' He asks, a half-grin slapped across his handsome, tanned face.

'To kill you. What is he doing here? You know he's not allowed to just turn up; the court says he can't, you should know better,' she cries, furious, frustrated, utterly flummoxed.

'He didn't just turn up. I called him,' Lewis says.

'You, why?' She blurts out.

Her face turns a dark shade of ruby. The darkest shade. Frustration makes way for anger, blistering her eyes with tiny red veins.

Stepping in from the garden, Lewis reaches out and gently takes the knife from her. Reaching over, he places it down on the kitchen island and takes her hand.

'What are you....' She starts in protest.

'Please, you need to see this,' Lewis tells her.

Leading her, almost dragging her, Lewis pulls his wife through the kitchen, across the foyer, into the lounge area.

'Lewis, I don't have the patience for this, ok,' she moans, yanking her hand free of his.

Picking up the TV remote and turning it on, he tells her, 'I recorded this earlier.'

Flustered, hands on her hips, she waits as the television boots up from a black screen to being filled with colour and life. Finally, after selecting BBC News24, stepping back, Lewis simply stands in silence. Mary, unsure of what she is looking at and about ready to head back to the kitchen, is stopped by the news anchor's words.

And the photograph of Thomas.

Sat against the backdropping of a breaking news story.

'The woman rescued last week from a basement in Beckley Green has been named as Amy Porter, a healthcare professional who has been missing for over a month and presumed dead. Currently hospitalised and receiving treatment, it is said Miss Porter is in a stable condition though severely dehydrated, malnourished, and suffering from shock. Thomas William, a local author and former journalist, tracked Miss Porter to the basement of the apartment building they both share, rescuing her at great danger to his own life. It is believed the dead body of a man at the scene, whose identity is yet to be confirmed by Police, is solely responsible for the kidnapping, and possibly, a series of unsolved murders of other young, professional women.'

'My god,' Mary says, a whisper.

Her heart, no longer pounding in her chest, dissolves into a dull ache. A bitterness at herself, reflection, and a little shame rise in her, leaving her throat tight and tears in her eyes well and blur her vision.

With Lewis returning to her side, him taking her hand in his, she wipes away her tears before looking up at him. And patiently, he waits there, at her side, silent but somehow supportive. Turning, she looks up at her husband and meets his soft smile.

'Ok,' she says, nodding her head. Looking at him, now overwhelmed with feeling, she adds, 'I love you, and... thank you.'

Returning to the kitchen from the doorway, Mary looks out onto the garden. Thomas's slumped shoulders hang low, as does his head. The red-haired woman with him, her face warm with an infectious beauty, holds his hand in hers.

Looking over his shoulder, seeing Mary, Thomas and her lock eyes. Though smiling, he cannot hide the haunting glare, the darkness loitering there. They call out to her, not pleading but begging, hoping, needing.

To her surprise, she nods a yes, smiles, and for once, it remains. As does his, the worry in his eyes is eased, glazing them with gratitude.

When Lewis appears with Robin, leading her and her trusted violin to the stage, Thomas's smile warms, and the shadows and pain lurking there, though slight, begin to fade.

Breathing in deeply, welcoming the challenge and change now ahead of them, Mary strokes down her dress. Cupping a hand around her overdue bump, circling her child with a content sigh, she steps outside. Crossing the garden, with the warm afternoon sun finding her, warming her, cocooning her, Mary is eager to join her family for the first time in the longest time.

ABOUT THE AUTHOR

A writer of genre-blending adult mysteries, Steven enjoys exploring imperfect characters and the venal, spiteful side of human nature. When he's not writing, Steven spends his time reading books, listening to books, watching films, cooking, eating, all the while trying to solve the latest murder/disappearance themed podcast. An admitted 80's fanatic, Steven feeds his addiction by watching slasher movies on Sunday afternoons.

If you enjoyed reading this, please leave a review on Amazon. Steven Blackmore reads every review, and they help new readers discover his books.

Follow Steven at the following:

www.stevenblackmorebooks.com

@stevenblackmorebooks

Printed in Great Britain
by Amazon

80522881R00226